PROMISES
TO THE
FALLEN

A VIETNAM WAR NOVEL

GLYN HAYNIE

Promises to the Fallen: A Vietnam War Novel.
Copyright © 2019 by Glyn Haynie.
All Rights Reserved.

For information about this title or to order other books and/or electronic media, contact the publisher:

Glyn Haynie
www.glynhaynie.net
glyn@glynhaynie.com

ISBNs:
Hardback: 978-1-7340260-0-9
Paperback: 978-0-9982095-9-3
Ebook: 978-1-7340260-1-6

Printed in the United States of America.

Final Proof Editor and Typesetting: ebooklaunch.com

Copy Editor: MJV Literary Author Services

Editor: Dr. Melissa Caudle

Cover Photograph: John Baxter

Author Photograph: Shannon Prothro Photography

BOOKS BY GLYN HAYNIE

PROMISES TO THE FALLEN,
A Vietnam War Novel

WHEN I TURNED NINETEEN,
A Vietnam War Memoir

SOLDIERING AFTER THE VIETNAM WAR,
Changed Soldiers in a Changed Country

FINDING MY PLATOON BROTHERS,
Vietnam Then and Now

CONTENTS

PROMISES
TO THE
FALLEN

PREFACE

After writing memoirs, *When I Turned Nineteen, Soldiering After the Vietnam War* and *Finding My Platoon Brothers*, I wanted to write about the Vietnam War with more freedom than being restricted by my memory of fifty years ago, or from the old documents I had found. So I returned to Vietnam on June 14, 2018, and started my journey.

I revisited the locations where my platoon brothers lived, worked, played and died. Walking in the platoon's footsteps—up hills, through hedgerows and across rice paddy dikes, which I trekked upon five decades ago—I refreshed my memory of the physical sensations and landscape I traversed at the age of nineteen, during the Vietnam War.

As I authored this story, I drew on my own firsthand experiences of my year in Vietnam, in my assigned army unit: Alpha Company, of the 3rd Battalion, 1st Infantry Regiment, 11th Light Infantry Brigade, Americal Infantry Division. I also revisited the experiences of some of the firebases and locations we patrolled.

I didn't write in the "real" context regarding the places or incidents from when I served; I wrote them from my experience, and from those of other veterans' time in the war, to completely reveal what an infantry soldier went through and the things he thought, as he survived his three hundred and sixty-five days.

With that in mind, I offer this book not as a true story of the Vietnam War, but as a lens through which I hope you will be able to observe, with compassion and understanding, one infantry platoon's day-to-day struggle with survival, conflict, and death.

CHAPTER 1

SOMETHING ISN'T RIGHT

For the American soldiers huddled in the dark, bug-infected Vietnam jungle, the nightmarish fear lived within each tortured soul as they hid deep within the battle-torn overgrowth. The constant terror seeped even into their dreams, providing no escape from the bloody, no-win war.

Eddie Henderson, a feisty, skinny nineteen-year-old weighing no more than one hundred and thirty pounds, found himself desperate to prove his worth to his platoon. But his fear made him feel as though all his strength was draining away, and that his muscles lacked the power to move his body as he tossed and turned inside his poncho liner.

He slapped a mosquito dining on his ear as the butt of his M-16 rifle nudged against his shoulder as if it were his best friend. In the confines of Henderson's dream, mortar shells exploded, sending shrapnel and dirt through the platoon perimeter; with each explosion, his body rocked rhythmically.

Seconds later, AK-47 rifle rounds thudded into the berm which protected the rattled ten-member squad.

The fear of the slanted-eye enemy which encroached the platoon's position settled into each soldier differently. For some, the isolating feeling engulfed them as if trapped in a cocoon, isolating them from the rest of the world. For Henderson, the fear took over his entire body as his breathing shortened through whimpers he attempted to keep hidden from the others. *This isn't anything like the suburbs of North Carolina.*

They were outnumbered, as twenty enemy soldiers ran toward them, shooting and throwing grenades.

Beneath the enemy fire, Henderson heard his name being called. "Eddie, help me!"

His head jerked toward the plea's source. Despite the powerless feeling in his limbs, Henderson knew that he had to help. He needed to prove that he could—to himself and his squad. Young and small of stature, Henderson carried a huge imaginary weight on his shoulder—he must prove himself as skilled, as capable as the bigger, older, more experienced men who fought alongside him.

Weak men died quickly out in this jungle. Letting weakness win, for even a moment, admitted to the universe that he didn't deserve to survive. Deep within himself, he needed his friends to survive, or he had failed everyone—especially himself.

His terrified eyes darted toward his injured squad member, who had taken a bullet to the chest. "Hold on. I'm coming."

Henderson's blood bubbled in his veins as his heart thumped against his ribcage. "Don't you die! I'm coming."

"Eddie, I'm not going to make—"

"Don't talk like that." Eddie fought to be free of the sweat-soaked poncho liner, desperate to get to his friend and escape the advancing enemy. The struggle to untangle himself couldn't come quickly enough, but soon his feet hit the ground, and he was churning through the air as he ran through a grenade blast. "I'm coming. Stay alive!" *And keep your head down!*

He rolled against a tree, hitting it hard. There he sat, shaking, with his heart pounding against his chest, still dazed from his recurring dream—and his fear.

There was no attack. Henderson realized he was dreaming.

"Son of a bitch!" Henderson choked on the sweat which was pouring from his forehead. "Why in the hell did I join this shit!"

"Shh! Be quiet!"

Mitch Drexler, the Alpha Team leader, placed his dirty finger across his busted lip as he glared protectively toward Henderson. "I don't want you killed under my watch, so listen to me…" He tilted his helmet higher on his forehead and instructed, "Keep your head down, you idiot."

Henderson hunched lower in the brush, replying, "You may have been a jock in high school, but you're only a year older than me."

"That doesn't mean I'm not responsible for you." At a muscular five foot ten, Drexler felt a sort of big brother protectiveness toward Henderson. "You okay?" he asked.

"Shit! These dreams, you know?" Henderson wiped his hand sheepishly through his shaggy, caramel-colored hair. "I'll take over guard duty. I doubt I can sleep."

Drexler paused as he assessed Henderson's condition. "You look like shit!"

But he didn't want to question a stroke of luck. As a yawn spread across Drexler's lips, he added, "Okay, you win. I'm dozing off, and that won't be good for any of us. You get guard duty."

With that, Drexler rolled into his poncho liner, covering his ears with his arms, and fell asleep.

Henderson wiped at the sweat dripping into his eyes and running down his cheeks. *I need a smoke in the worst kind of way.* Out of habit, he searched through his pockets. "Damn it! No cigarettes."

He leaned against the tree, fully alert, as the men of Alpha Team slept behind him, under his watch. He stared into the dark jungle, waiting for the sun to rise over the horizon, until it spilled light through the trees and brush.

A rustle in the heavy vegetation caught Henderson's attention. He quickly bolted upright, pointing his weapon toward the noise.

A pair of glowing eyes glared through the jungle growth.

Before he could locate the enemy, a low growl resonated from the brush, then the light from the animal's eyes disappeared. Henderson took a deep breath. "Fucking tigers."

He slowly sank back to the ground and assumed his position, watching and listening for the Viet Cong.

•

As the sun peeked over the tree line, Henderson moved to each team member, kicking his boot against their feet. "Get up! It's another day in 'Nam."

"A simple wake-up call would do." Drexler yawned as he glared toward Henderson.

Henderson approached Lieutenant James Brighton, the first platoon leader, who was already awake.

"Thanks for taking guard duty last night," Brighton said. "Drexler needed to rest." He immediately began packing his gear.

"No problem, sir. I'm just carrying my weight."

Henderson approached Professor. He paused, noticing that the soldier's arm was wrapped around the M-79 grenade launcher, as if it were a child's stuffed animal. He was mumbling in his sleep. "Gooks are everywhere."

Henderson's foot connected with Professor's leg. "Professor, wake up. Morning has arrived."

Professor snapped awake, instinctively fumbling for his weapon.

"It was only a nightmare," Henderson reassured him. "Wakey, wakey."

After wiping the crust from his eyes, Professor shivered. "I'll be glad when we're called home."

"You don't have to worry about that. One way or another, we're all going home. Personally, I don't want to be in a body bag. So you keep that grenade launcher of yours operational."

"That's the least of our worries. In case you haven't noticed, there is an entire jungle of Viet Cong waiting to take us out."

"No reminder needed there."

Henderson made his way to the next platoon member.

"Good morning, mountain man." He looked down at Rocky. "Time to get up."

Rocky moved his M-60 machine gun closer to his rucksack. "Mornin', Henderson."

Henderson turned and strolled toward the second squad leader, Sergeant Terry Stahl. Before his foot made contact with the experienced combat leader, Stahl grabbed Henderson's boot. "I'd think twice before that boot touched me."

"Okay, Sarge, you don't have to tell me twice." Henderson backed away, moving toward the next platoon member, who was already stirring.

Stahl's eyes widened. "That *was* twice. Don't make it a habit."

"Got it, Sarge," Henderson said, over his shoulder.

Stahl rose and straightened his uniform, then started brushing his teeth with his finger. "Chow down, boys. You're going to need the nourishment. We move out soon."

"I'm already eating," Ronnie Porter gloated as he took another bite of C-ration ham and eggs.

Henderson looked at him. "That looks disgusting."

"Ever heard of protein?"

"That's more like dog food, if you ask me."

"Who asked?"

"Don't mind me."

Henderson grabbed his last pack of cigarettes, buried underneath his poncho. He lit one and slowly took a long drag.

Stahl shook his head at Henderson. "You won't have to worry about dying at the hands of the enemy. As much as you smoke, cigarettes will kill you first."

"Very funny, Sarge."

Stahl glared toward Henderson, "Now, eat."

"You've got to be joking." Henderson took another long drag.

Stahl opened a can of fruit, followed by a cake. "I don't make jokes. Eat! Everyone, eat!"

His cigarette dangling between his lips, Henderson abruptly opened his morning meal. As Drexler heated a cup of coffee, holding his canteen cup over burning C-4, he winked toward Henderson. "I think the sergeant means business. He got up on the wrong side of the jungle today. I don't think I'd mess with him."

"You got that right."

Drexler gulped his coffee and quickly spewed it onto the ground. "Damn, it's too hot."

Henderson smiled as he packed his rucksack, "What did you expect, after bringing it to a boil?"

Brighton suddenly stood and faced the platoon. "Saddle up. We move out in five mikes."

As if urgency suddenly prevailed, one by one the platoon packed up their gear and shouldered their rucksacks, waiting on Brighton's next order. He raised his M-16 and pointed north. "Henderson, take point. Move out!"

Henderson led the way as the platoon moved toward the outskirts of the ville.

•

The lieutenant's radio-telephone operator, RTO, Specialist Les Ledger, caught up with Brighton. "Lieutenant, the CO wants you."

Brighton raised his hand for the platoon to stop. He took the handset. "This is Tango one-six. Over."

The Company Commander, Captain Don Lyons replied, "Tango one-six, be advised NVA patrol went through the ville during the early morning, heading north. Need you to check it out. Over."

"Tango six, Wilco. Out," Brighton transmitted.

Brighton gave the handset back to Ledger and pointed with his M-16. "Henderson, follow that trail to search for an enemy patrol."

They traveled in silence, each man isolated inside his world. There was nothing new to Brighton about the dense jungle—he had been through worse places. Two years earlier, in 1967, he did a tour with the 1st Cavalry Division. When the branch of a tree poked into his arm, he didn't notice.

As he ran behind, following the Second Squad, he spoke into his handset. "Tango six, this is Tango one-six. Over."

He squeezed past a tall overgrowth of thick bushes covering the trail as he waited for a reply. Sweat glistened on his black skin, but he didn't allow himself to acknowledge the heat. It wasn't important. He had a mission to accomplish and orders to follow, and as always, he was keenly aware of his precarious position as a black man in a position of power. He couldn't merely survive and keep his men alive—he had to do better. He had to do *everything* better.

"Tango one-six, this is Tango six. What's your status? Over," Lyons said as his eyes darted wildly about him.

"Tango six, following enemy patrol, one klick west of ville. Over." As he spoke, Brighton took a long, deep breath and instinctively ducked beneath a large tree branch sagging across the trail.

"Tango one-six, let me know if you need support. Over." There were deepening furrows in Lyons's brow.

"Roger, Tango six. Wilco. Out."

•

Henderson took long, cautious strides as he attempted to catch the enemy patrol which was now running from the platoon. Because he was the point man, he was in front, while his team leader, Drexler, trailed not far behind.

As Henderson followed the new, two-foot-wide trail through thick brush, trees, and bamboo, he caught a glimpse of a man crouched next to the path, fifty meters in front of him. Henderson immediately fell to the ground and motioned for Drexler to move forward.

Drexler crawled up beside him on the opposite side of the trail. Both soldiers took a prone firing position. Looking at Drexler, Henderson pointed at the enemy soldier.

From their position, they observed three more North Vietnamese Army soldiers approaching their comrade squatting alongside the trail.

Henderson stared at the four soldiers, but when one of the NVA turned to look down the path toward them, Henderson averted his stare, afraid to make eye contact in case the enemy soldier could feel his gaze. As a fly walked along Henderson's nose, he didn't move a muscle. He waited for the soldier to turn his gaze back toward his comrades before sliding the selector switch of his M-16 rifle from safe to automatic. He aimed at the enemy patrol.

Drexler held up three fingers to denote countdown. Henderson watched as Drexler's fingers closed, one at a time. Then, on Drexler's signal, both men fired into the NVA patrol.

As he squeezed the trigger, Henderson fired three rounds at a time, each time hearing the metallic sound of the bullet slamming into the chamber and the clink of the hot shell casing ejecting from the right side of his rifle as the spent brass flew through the air, creating a small pile on the ground. Each loading and firing of another round took milliseconds as he fired at the NVA.

One bullet thudded into an enemy soldier, who collapsed; the other three ran into the jungle. Henderson and Drexler stopped shooting.

With his right thumb, Henderson slid the selector switch to semi-automatic, waiting for any sign that the enemy remained.

Within seconds, rounds started zinging overhead, thudding into trees and snapping off small branches as the cracking sound of AK-47 rifles echoed in the jungle.

Henderson and Drexler dug deeper into the earth as the rounds zinged around them.

•

After the enemy fired the last shot, Professor ran forward, panting, and fell to the ground between Henderson and Drexler in the center of the trail. With a scowl crossing his brow, he quickly lowered himself next to them and laid his M-79 grenade launcher on the dirt beside him.

"I have a rucksack full of ammo." His eyes darted about as if he were calculating odds. "Which way?"

Henderson rolled to his side. "Charlie is down the trail about fifty meters." He pointed to the last known enemy location. "I think we got one. Not sure where the other three are."

"Got it. I'll flush Charles out."

Professor started firing his M-79 grenade launcher at what remained of the NVA patrol. Each time he pulled the trigger, it created a thumping sound as the grenade left the launcher—then, a second later, *bam!* The grenades hit their target with a loud thump, throwing dirt and shrapnel into the air.

Every shot was revenge. With each shot, Professor thought about his younger brother—this war, these people, had killed him. If not for his brother's death, Calvin Cox would never have joined the military, where he earned his nickname "Professor" for being the only college-educated man in the unit. He'd never approved of the war—hell, he had protested the war—but there was only one thing he loathed more than the war; that his brother had died alone here in this Godforsaken jungle.

Henderson's ears rang from the blast. Lying quiet, he took short, hard breaths as he wiped at the sweat stinging his eyes with a trembling hand.

Movement behind him caught his attention, so he turned to look. Stahl was crawling along the trail toward his position. As Stahl reached Henderson, he lay low, close to the ground. "Any more movement?"

Henderson adjusted his position to mirror Stahl's. "Nope. At least, I haven't seen any."

"Okay, let's wait five mikes. Then the four of us will go check it out."

Stahl turned toward Rocky, a big man, who carried an M-60 machine gun. Because of his size and strength, he made carrying the weapon look effortless. In truth, Rocky's shoulders ached, but he wouldn't say anything about it. In fact, he quite liked the pain; it distracted him from all the rest.

"Pass it on to the lieutenant. We are sending a patrol in five minutes to check the enemy location," Stahl told him.

"Yes, Sarge, will do." Rocky turned, passing the message to Ronnie Porter, and along it went, down the line of the platoon members.

Henderson waited, while the hot, humid air in the jungle sucked the breath from his lungs. The air tasted stale as it clung to his palate. Sweat soaked his skin and his olive drab-colored jungle fatigues. After he removed his helmet, his long hair lay plastered against his forehead. He removed the towel he wore around his shoulders to keep the rucksack from cutting into him, and used the dirty cloth to wipe the sweat from his face. Then, pushing back his wet hair, he slid on the heavy helmet and adjusted its fit.

As he scanned the forest for hidden enemy soldiers, Henderson questioned what he was doing in Vietnam. It hadn't taken him long to realize that reading or watching movies about war was very different to being in combat. He sensed that the fear he faced each day had robbed him of his youth, and he resented the fact that no one had warned him of this. All the propaganda he had heard in high school made Vietnam seem like a grand adventure of comradery and honor.

"Henderson, time to move out." Stahl's orders jolted Henderson from his deep thoughts.

Sliding out of his rucksack, Henderson lifted his slender, five-foot-eight frame from the ground as slowly as possible. He took short steps along the trail, staying low to the ground, as he led the three squad members to the location where he and Drexler had shot the enemy soldiers.

Once they arrived at the site, Henderson told them, "Over here, look. I found blood on the brush, along with drag marks." He searched, but could find no trace of any bodies or equipment.

Stahl's eyes darted toward him. "Stay alert."

Henderson nodded and followed the blood trail ten meters to the north. He surveyed the surrounding area. "They must have carried off their dead and injured. How in the hell do they remove the bodies so fast?"

Stahl stopped and stared at him. "You didn't find any weapons? Gear? Bodies?"

Henderson shook his head no without saying a word. Then, after a moment of silence, he pointed. "The blood trail continues north."

Stahl suddenly flashed a wicked grin. "Stay here. I'll check it out."

Henderson knelt next to Drexler and Professor in the overgrowth as they watched Stahl disappear into the jungle. Minutes later, the crack of an M-16 firing one round resonated through the trees.

The men hit the ground, watching the direction their squad leader had walked in. They waited.

"Coming in." Stahl ducked below a branch as he closed in on the team.

Henderson popped his jaw. "What the hell happened?"

"Found a gook." Stahl smiled wryly. "Let's head back to the platoon."

Henderson noticed that the grin on Stahl's face appeared broader. "You sure that's all, Sarge? Where's his weapon and ammo?"

Stahl seemed perturbed by Henderson's questions. "Let's go, Henderson—the lieutenant is waiting."

Taking the lead, Henderson took quick strides along the trail to get back to the platoon. Drexler followed up at the rear to make sure that the enemy didn't sneak up on the patrol. As they returned, Stahl walked over to where the lieutenant sat and removed his rucksack.

"What happened on the trail?" Brighton pursed his lips. He didn't seem to be commanding an answer—he rarely did.

The men referred to Brighton as LT, and he didn't mind. He was one of two black officers in the battalion, and at six foot one of strong muscle, he seemed built for war. Despite this, Brighton intentionally took a softer style of leadership, preferring that his men trust him, rather than fear his command.

Deep down, though he would never have admitted it, he still felt awkward giving orders to a bunch of white boys—having been raised in South Carolina, that hadn't been the attitude bred into him. However, he had sure as hell earned the position, and that was something he often admitted to himself.

Stahl dropped his helmet next to Brighton and sat upon it like a chair. As they sat in silence, the rest of the platoon waited to hear the report from the sergeant. Stahl had concealed his smile from earlier, though the adrenaline which caused it still coursed through his veins. It was better to keep certain truths hidden; others might not see it as he did. He blew air from his nose. "Alpha Team found an enemy patrol. One dead NVA—we didn't find any weapons. None of our guys got hurt."

"Was that what the gunshot was about?"

"Sure was, LT."

Henderson shot Drexler a quizzical look, because he wasn't sure what the gunshot was about either. He did know that if Stahl had killed an enemy soldier, he would have undoubtedly returned with his weapon and ammunition.

Drexler didn't meet his gaze. He couldn't see why Henderson insisted on focusing on questions which may only become more uncomfortable when answered.

Brighton wiped the sweat from his brow. "We'll assume they moved away from us unless something indicates otherwise—no real choice. We'll continue operating as a platoon, conducting search and destroy missions around the local villages. Rendezvous with the company is in three days." He stood, taking a deep breath. "Okay, let's head to the ville."

"Henderson, take point. And remember what I taught you." Stahl was gazing upon Henderson as if giving him caution.

"You got it, Sarge."

With Drexler's help, Henderson slid into his rucksack and moved to the front of the platoon. Walking bent over from the weight of the pack, he traveled along the trail the way they had come, his eyes peeled for booby-traps or an NVA ambush.

CHAPTER 2

ANOTHER DAY IN QUANG NGAI PROVINCE

The small village, not far from Dien Truong, in the Quang Ngai Province, Republic of Vietnam, sat in the coastal plains area of the central highlands, twenty-five klicks south of the brigade headquarters at Duc Pho.

It was early June 1969, and resupply had been unreliable for the past three weeks. Attempting to stay hydrated, the soldiers drank four to six quarts of water each day to fight the relentless heat combined with the humidity, which drained their energy. It wasn't only the heat, but also the endless walking—which the infantry soldiers called "humping" when in the bush.

They humped along hills, through elephant grass taller than the average man, and brush, dense with bamboo thickets. They sweated every last ounce of fluid they had stored, replenishing lost liquid with the drinking water they carried.

As the platoon closed in on the exposed huts, the odd smells of the village greeted the men first. Stahl hardly noticed, so focused was he on mentally ticking off the task he needed to accomplish, while for Brighton, the smells were simply a part of the backdrop. For Henderson, however, those smells demanded attention. He couldn't adequately explain what they were—maybe rotting vegetables, mold, exotic food, and animals, all rolled into one odor.

The Viet Cong and NVA smelled like the aroma which was coming from the ville. Otherwise, the village appeared as any other he had searched or walked through.

Henderson stopped, letting the lieutenant move to the front of the platoon.

"We'll stay here to eat chow." Overseeing the First Platoon, Brighton moved as he talked, but he didn't look at his men. His dark eyes continuously scanned the village. He had seen threats pop up out of nowhere before. Not until he had finished his scan did he complete his statement. "You can refill your canteens. Squad leaders, make sure you have security in place. Get some rest."

Following the lieutenant's instructions, Stahl had his squad move to the west side of the ville, making sure they were close to a well, with shade.

•

Henderson and Drexler sat at the ancient stone well on the outskirts of the village, surrounded by waist-high elephant grass. To retrieve the water, Drexler dropped his helmet, attached to fifteen feet of thin rope, into the well. Once he heard the splash of the steel pot hitting the water, he waited for five seconds—then he hoisted the headgear to fill the empty canteens strewn around the base of the well.

After they volunteered to get water for the squad, the two friends enjoyed a relaxing afternoon. Knowing the detail had a minimal risk, they took their time.

Usually, Henderson flung himself into risky endeavors. He thought that to carry out hazardous tasks, like walking point or dropping into a tunnel, distracted from his skinny stature. On occasion, however, a relaxing task was simply what was needed and, after his nightmares of late, he needed a moment to breathe, even if the air did smell awful. He winced at the foulness of it.

Henderson missed the fresh smells of the mountains of his youth. Even though he had managed to kill the accent, he'd grown up outside Asheville, North Carolina. He thought he had known what the outdoors and small towns were like everywhere, but Vietnam seemed dead set on proving him wrong.

Drexler gave Henderson a knowing smile and breathed deeply. He didn't mind the smell. And, in moments like these—calm moments—he could even enjoy the quiet jungle sounds which came with that smell.

He'd gone through infantry training with Henderson at Fort Benning, Georgia. After all that time, in forced proximity and friendship, Drexler knew Henderson like the back of his hand. He could always tell when Henderson was thinking of home.

"No matter how hard you imagine it, you can't make this Carolina," Drexler said, slapping at a fly buzzing near his ear. "Forget about home for now."

Henderson shrugged. "If only it were that easy."

"It is. I could spend all day thinking about Sandra, but it would end up getting me killed. Focus on now."

"You write to her often enough."

"And I think about her—when it's the right time to." Drexler turned his attention back to filling the canteens. Now was not the time to think about Sandra; she was a part of home, not here in the jungle. She was something which brought out a softer side of Mitch, which was not a side he could let settle out here.

Drexler had married his childhood sweetheart right after high school. She was the only woman with whom he had ever been intimate, and someday he would go home to her. But not today.

Staring at the village while his friend filled the green, plastic canteens, Henderson looked in amazement at how primitive the Vietnamese in rural areas lived. No roads led into the community. They didn't have electricity, telephones, or indoor plumbing. Children ran around half-dressed, while the women wore black or white silk-like pajamas; most wore a sizeable conical palm-leaf hat to protect them from the sun. Their huts—or "hooches" as the soldiers sometimes called the dwellings—were made of straw, bamboo, hardened mud, and, on occasion, C-ration cardboard; they built the floor surface with wood or packed dirt.

The villagers penned the livestock, but Henderson often saw pigs and chickens roaming free. The animal pens were located behind the family hooch. Now, observing two women carrying buckets as they left an animal pen, he presumed they held animal shit. Once the women reached the rice field, they dumped the waste, using it for fertilizer. Animals and villagers alike fertilized the fields, the villagers using them as a public bathroom.

As he gazed westward, Henderson looked at the tall, steep mountains thick with jungle growth, giving the impression that they ran forever, parallel to the horizon. He looked across the lush, green, water-laden rice fields, observing workers laboring as they harvested their rice. Rice was their life; they were not able to do anything else. He wondered if they ever thought about different type of work. He watched the black-clad villagers bobbing up and down as they moved along the water-filled paddies, cutting the rice crop with a sickle or a handheld knife. After cutting the rice, the villagers used bamboo screens or a wooden platform to separate the grain from the rice straw. Behind the farmers, a water buffalo pulled a cart as the workers threw rice straw onto its bed. Sweating as he watched them toil, he didn't understand how they withstood the backbreaking labor and withering heat, along with the humidity, day after day.

Do these people even care that we are fighting a war? Henderson shuddered at the thought.

"I need some help; five left to fill," Drexler said, staring at Henderson as he stood. He had noticed Henderson's growing agitation, and knew that focusing on the task in hand was the only way to distract him from it.

"Sure thing," Henderson replied, looking away from the village, the rice fields and the mountains. He lifted a one-quart canteen while Drexler poured water from the helmet. His eyes were tearful for a moment from the dust which moved in the wind. "How many days left?"

"Two hundred and seventy-eight." Drexler always knew the exact number of days that they had left in Vietnam. That was how long it would be until he could see home again, and think about whatever—whomever—he wanted, whenever he wanted.

"No, we've been here longer. You sure it's right?"

"Yeah, I'm sure. We got *boo-coo* days to go. And for you non-French speaking soldiers, *boo-coo* means 'many.'"

"I know what *boo-coo* means." Henderson frowned. "Last one?"

"Done. Time to head to the squad."

Without any further talk, the two men loaded the canteens into a basket, and Drexler grabbed the handle on the opposite side to Henderson.

Moving to the squad position one hundred feet away, the two young infantry soldiers laughed as they approached their buddies, still arguing about how many days they had left in 'Nam.

The members of Alpha Team—which included Jason "Rocky" Garrison, Calvin "Professor" Cox, Ronnie Porter, and the Second Squad leader, Sergeant Terry Stahl—sat under a poncho liner, which they had stretched and tied between four trees for shade. Soldiers also used poncho liners as a field-expedient, lightweight sleeping bag. The liners were a constructed quilted nylon, layered with polyester, and had a camouflage pattern. At night, they were great for keeping warm, and they provided some protection from the mosquitoes too. They were also light; an easy item to carry in the rucksack, because each member of the platoon strapped one to his back like a pack mule when operating off of the firebase.

Carrying the full canteens, Henderson and Drexler dropped the basket, letting them spill onto the ground. The team gathered around, picking theirs from the pile.

Stahl faced the group of soldiers. "Put an iodine tab into your canteens before you put them away."

Porter stared into Stahl's eyes. "Who are you, my mother?"

The talking stopped.

Porter stood shirtless, exposing his round belly, holding a canteen with his jaw set. His goofy smile grew larger as he waited for a response—he always had a smile. His curly, blond hair hung over his ears, making him look younger than his twenty-one years. Raised in San Diego, California, he lived on the beach and thought it was fun to confront authority. Porter respected Stahl; he just liked to mess with him. Everyone knew Porter as a joker, but wondered if the squad leader thought that Porter had gone too far this time.

Then, both soldiers burst into laughter, and Stahl pursed his lips. "Yeah, you little shit. I'm your mom. Do what I tell you."

"Will do, Mom—I mean, Sarge." Porter chuckled as the other squad members, still laughing at the exchange between the two soldiers, went back to what they were doing.

Despite his earlier suspicions, Henderson respected and admired his squad leader. He looked at Stahl as he gave instructions, noticing his thinning, brown hair, which receded several inches on both sides of his forehead, leaving a strand in the middle which touched above the eyes. The corners of those deep-set, brown eyes had many wrinkles, and his thin lips were in a permanent downturn.

Stahl watched the men drop a tablet into their canteens. "Don't forget to take your malaria pills. Today is Monday, so take the big orange one too."

"Yes, Mom—I mean, Sarge." Porter quickly chugged the two pills, as did most of the men, downing them with the foul-tasting well water.

Henderson swallowed the daily white pill, but faked taking the weekly big orange pill because it upset his stomach and gave him diarrhea. He thought it was worth the risk of catching malaria, if it meant not having the shits. *Hell, if I get malaria, I could go home.*

The five infantry soldiers of Alpha Team had been together for three months, and they had learned to work together cohesively; they had complete trust in each other. Each member of the team knew his role within the squad and was efficient with his weapon. Fire Team Bravo had the same strength, but were riflemen, carrying an M-16, with no machine gun or grenade launcher.

Brighton rose and cleared his throat. "Move out in five minutes!"

"Saddle up, Second Squad." Stahl quickly stood. "Henderson on point."

After attaching his canteens onto his rucksack straps, Henderson stuffed the poncho liner into it. He slid into the straps of his rucksack, which held three days of rations, and weighed eleven pounds; six quarts of water, weighing twelve pounds; two hundred rounds of M-60 ammunition, weighing thirteen pounds; and twenty loaded M-16 magazines, weighing in at fourteen pounds for a total of fifty-two pounds—not counting his M-16 rifle, LAW, claymore mines, flares, grenades, and other gear he carried. He couldn't stand, the weight of the pack keeping him anchored to the ground.

He looked over at Rocky and Professor, each of whom carried extra weight—for Professor, the grenade launcher ammunition, and for Rocky, his machine gun. Yet, they never seemed any more tired than the rest. Henderson didn't get it, and decided to blame the entire thing on the fact that he was smaller than both of them.

He asked Rocky, "How do you make it look so easy, carrying all that weight?"

Rocky shifted the M-60 to his other shoulder. "I've lived in the outdoors all my life; carrying weight on my back is natural for me. Hell, I grew up in the Rocky Mountains. Long before 'Nam I was hunting elk and mule deer. Even had to lug the kill back to my cabin."

"No shit?" Henderson stared at Rocky, his eyes wide.

Drexler grinned toward Henderson as he extended his hand. "Come on; I'll help you up." Drexler grabbed Henderson's hand and pulled him to a standing position.

Henderson flashed a grateful smile. "Thanks. There's a lot of weight on my back."

"What's the matter, little guy? Can't handle the weight?" Porter pursed his lips as he moved toward Rocky. The two made an odd pair. Rocky was huge and ruggedly handsome, while Porter was pudgy, and always managed to look a little bit goofy.

As he struggled to his feet, Henderson glared at Porter. "Hey, chubby, I told you not to call me *little*."

Rocky laughed, narrowing his brows. "Well, you are."

Professor shook his head. "Come on, guys, leave the little fella alone."

"Let's go, Henderson." Stahl winked at Henderson to save him from more ribbing, and protect him from his short fuse.

As a squad leader, Stahl had the responsibility for ten to twelve men, one M-60 machine gun, and one M-79 grenade launcher—the rest carried M-16 rifles. That meant, at times, keeping the men under control and not allowing arguments to escalate. Stahl made a point of smiling at the good-natured teasing as he fell in line behind the men of Alpha Team, with Bravo Team following.

Stahl looked impatiently at Henderson. "Let's go! Move out."

Henderson stepped onto the trail which ran through the village, and the platoon followed the route Henderson chose to reach their position before nightfall.

Ledger handed Brighton the handset to the radio. Brighton pressed the button. "Tango six, this is Tango one-six. Over." He released the talk button and waited for the reply from Lyons.

"Tango one-six, this is Tango six. What's your status? Over." Lyons took a deep breath as he waited.

"Tango six, moving to the night logger. Over."

"Roger, Tango one-six. Out."

As he returned the handset to Ledger, Brighton nodded in affirmation. "Let's go. Move out!"

•

The First Platoon had twenty-five infantry soldiers, composed of two squads and the command group, comprising the platoon leader, a medic, the platoon sergeant and two RTOs. Henderson led the platoon through the village, with First Squad following him. Brighton and Ledger fell in line behind the Second Squad.

Walking point, Henderson had the responsibility to guard the safety of the soldiers behind him. During daytime or night, often in inclement weather, he led the platoon through the jungle, along trails, across streams, and through open fields, looking around him for any signs of the enemy, such as ambushes or booby trap, so he could alert the platoon to impending danger. Henderson had developed an awareness of this danger—a quality vital in the point man—and, being good at his job, he had earned the trust of the platoon.

As the men moved out through the far end of the village, elderly women and men smiled at them, showing black-stained teeth from chewing on "betel nut"—a stimulant drug masquerading as a nut. Half-dressed, barefoot children followed, yelling for "chop-chop"—food—as they ran playfully around the line of soldiers. Giving them friendly pats on the head, the soldiers handed the village kids chocolate bars. Henderson smiled at the children. *Kids are the same everywhere.*

Approaching the last hut, Henderson spotted a young mother with her son sitting next to her. At roughly eight years old, the boy wore black shorts. He had his right leg amputated below the knee, and his right hand severed at the wrist. He smiled at Henderson.

As Henderson walked toward the boy, a pit formed in his stomach, which seemed to weigh him down. He wondered if the boy had lost his limbs from a VC booby trap or, worse still, an American explosive device. His smile had turned to a frown as sadness overcame him; he knew that, because of the war, the boy would have a hard life.

The boy's mother wore a white, silk-like blouse which buttoned up at the front and black pants made of the same material. She put her arm around her son, pulling him tight against her bosom. With long, straight, black hair falling over her shoulders, she brushed a thick strand from her face as she glared at Henderson with dark, untrusting eyes. Making eye contact, she forced a smile.

Henderson stopped and smiled at her. "Hey, kid, you want candy?"

The boy quickly snatched the candy and giggled. "GI number one."

Henderson ruffled the boy's shaggy black hair. "Glad you like it. Take care of yourself and your mother."

The mother clutched her son closer to her bosom protectively. Turning away, Henderson continued toward the hill.

On the fringes of the village stretched a large clearing, then Highway 1, running north to south. On the opposite side of the highway, another open field stretched for roughly one hundred meters before reaching the hill. Overgrown with bamboo thickets, elephant grass, brush, and dense growth of thin trees, the slopes running to the hilltop looked impossible to climb.

As Henderson entered the field, he motioned for the soldiers behind him to spread out. The platoon members switched from a column of twos to the left or right of the person in front of them; the columns became staggered. No soldier walked behind another, keeping at least fifteen feet between them. Humping in this formation made it harder for the VC, or a booby trap, to kill more than one soldier at a time.

The platoon moved across the hard-packed field, barren of vegetation, and onto the two-lane, dirt Highway 1, referred to as the "Red Ball."

As Henderson walked across the highway, he passed three "Coke girls." Two of the girls each wore a white, button-up shirt with black, silk-like pants, while the third wore a black pullover shirt with black pants—like a VC would. They had an old, scuffed, sizeable ice chest, which was filled with dirty ice and buried Cokes. Coke girls could be found nearly anywhere selling their wares.

Each girl also held a basket, which contained different trinkets, necklaces, and bracelets made from spent ammunition brass. The average asking price was two dollars in military payment certificates. The three girls giggled as Henderson walked by them.

The eldest, dressed in a white shirt, held out a Coke. "Cold Coke—fifty cents."

The girl dressed in black held up several necklaces. "Two dollar."

"GI, boom-boom," the third girl said as she ran her hands across her breasts and down to her side.

Henderson flushed and smiled. *No sex today.* He continued to walk across the highway.

The soldiers merged into a single file to climb the four-hundred-foot hill in front. Henderson led the way, taking slow, purposeful steps while looking for booby traps and enemy soldiers who could appear from anywhere, at any moment.

The rest of the Alpha Team followed Henderson, and then the lieutenant with his RTO. Behind Brighton, the Bravo Team followed, with Staff Sergeant Willie Swift and his RTO, Specialist

Sam Brown, behind them. Rucksacks rattled as the platoon took guarded steps along the non-existent trail.

Cutting brush and elephant grass with a machete to clear a trail, Henderson continued the steep climb, following a ridge that ran to the top of the hill. At times, he found the green, razor-sharp blades of the elephant grass as tall as him; with their height, he couldn't see to his front.

The sweltering heat of the blazing afternoon sun slowed the pace of the line of soldiers as they ascended what appeared to be a mountain. To rest his arms, Henderson switched the machete from one hand to the other as he pushed forward, the tall grass and the weight of the rucksack slowing his progress even further.

Realizing Henderson was tired, Drexler moved closer. "Eddie, you want me to take over?"

"I got it," Henderson said, whacking at the tall grass with the machete.

"Don't be so stubborn."

Henderson ignored the comment. He knew Drexler wouldn't let him forget it if he quit now. "No way am I stopping."

"Okay, okay, keep going then. But let me know if you want me to take over."

"Wilco." Henderson whacked away at the tall grass, easing forward one step at a time. Henderson released a loud grunt with each step as he scrambled along the ridge cutting a path, as if this would help him to reach the hilltop. Listening to the sounds escaping involuntarily from his lips made him smile, and reminded him why infantry soldiers were called "grunts"; grunts do all the humping and fighting.

After another fifteen minutes of climbing and fighting the overgrowth, Henderson crested the top of the hill. When he stopped, he surveyed the area with his trained eye, looking for the enemy or booby traps.

Stahl walked past the waiting line of tired men as they leaned forward to balance the weight of their rucksack, the butt of each soldier's M-16 on the ground with their hand over the muzzle to support them. He stopped alongside Henderson. "We good? All clear?"

"I think so, Sarge." Henderson nodded and took a deep breath.

Stahl raised his right hand, motioning for the platoon to move into the clearing.

Brighton and Ledger stepped ahead of the stalled platoon, the lieutenant's radio squawking as he walked past Henderson. "Tango one-six, this is Tango six. Over."

"This is Tango one-six. Over," Brighton answered, continuing to walk as he waited for the response, with Ledger following. They moved past the platoon, beyond hearing distance.

Henderson watched the look on the lieutenant's face as he started talking in earnest into the handset.

Not a good sign.

ONE AT A TIME

After receiving his orders, Brighton called the platoon sergeant, Swift, and the two squad leaders, Stahl and Nash, to his location. Brighton spread his map as he gazed up at them.

"The company commander wants us to go on an ambush tonight, in the area between the village and Highway 1, on the main path leading into the village." He traced the route to the ambush site with his finger. "Intel has it—they expect the VC to move into the village sometime tonight, or early morning."

He paused and glanced at his NCOs to make sure the sergeants understood before continuing. "We'll use an *L*-shape ambush, with the First Squad at the bottom portion of the *L*, facing away from the village. The Second Squad is on the long portion of the *L*, facing north, running parallel to the trail. This is the only area with tall grass, which we can use for concealment; we can use the berm for cover. If the VC are going to the ville, they'll have to go through us."

Swift nodded. "I'll go with the First Squad."

"I'll be with the Second Squad." Brighton pointed down at the map. "Set up a perimeter here, but don't place flares or claymores. Have your men eat, then get some rest—we move at twenty-one-hundred hours. We need to be in position no later than twenty-three-thirty hours. Second Squad, you're on point."

The men acknowledged that they understood.

"Go get ready."

The two squad leaders took long strides to their squad positions.

Henderson watched Stahl approach. "What's going on, Sarge?"

"Ambush."

Henderson had a tight feeling in his stomach. "Shit. I hate ambushes."

"Yeah, me too; not my favorite thing to do." Stahl glanced around the group. "Everyone, listen up. We're going on an ambush tonight, so get some rest. Don't forget to get some chow, and make sure you tighten your gear. Remember, noise and light discipline. We'll leave at twenty-one-hundred hours, taking the trail along the south side of the hill. The ambush site is near the ville."

The men all acknowledged and agreed, but no one seemed thrilled about the announcement.

Stahl looked over at Henderson. "You got point tonight."

"Sure, Sarge."

"Any questions?" Stahl looked over the men.

The squad remained quiet.

Then, Porter raised his hand. His usual goofy smile was tugging at the corners of his mouth, and his blue eyes twinkled in his boyish face. The feeling in the group was getting too heavy, and Porter felt it was his duty to remedy that.

Stahl stared at him. "What, Porter?"

"Do we have to go?"

The team burst into laughter.

"Any *serious* questions?" Stahl said, laughing along with the others. "Okay, no questions. Have chow, then some sleep."

Alpha Team leaned against their rucksacks as they ate their supper meal of C-rations. While they laughed and swapped stories, the men devoured their food as if they hadn't eaten in days, washing it down with warm water or Kool-Aid.

Chewing on his beans and franks, Professor leaned toward Henderson. "Where are you going when you get home?"

Drexler stopped eating. He shot Henderson a look, because he didn't think his friend would want to answer that question.

Professor lifted his brows. "I mean, are you staying with your parents, going to school, or what?"

Henderson took a bite of his chicken and noodles as he stared past Professor into the jungle. "My parents died in a car crash last year. I don't have siblings, or any family left. Hell, I don't have a home." Henderson took another bite of his chicken noodles.

"I apologize. I didn't—"

"It's okay, Professor, you didn't know. I can always stay with Drexler's mom and dad—they're nice people. They let me stay with them while we were on our thirty-day leave, before coming here. Hell, Mitch's mom likes me more than she likes Mitch."

"I think Dad likes you best, too, Eddie. You can stay anytime." Drexler smiled.

Rocky's awkward attempt at a cough put an end to the discussion. "Does anyone really know what our mission is each day?"

Professor chugged his water. "I believe that's the hardest part for a new guy to wrap his head around. It seems so random, going from one place to another. There are no lines or front to join; we move forward, looking for the enemy. It's how we fight. We get up every morning and start humping. The platoon walks from one village to another, one paddy to another, through hedgerows, jungle, over mountains… Then we turn around and do it all over again. There doesn't appear to be any rhyme or reason to what we do each day."

"So, you're saying it's random, going from one place to another each day?" Rocky's brow creased.

"That's exactly what I'm saying."

To Henderson, it had always felt that way, but deep down, he assumed that someone, somewhere, must have a master plan—although, the longer he was here, the harder it was to believe. "It seems to me we try to get the VC to attack us, so we can call in artillery or air strikes on them." Henderson swallowed hard, almost choking on his words.

No longer wanting to discuss their purpose in Vietnam, silence fell over the men as they finished eating.

The team gave the appearance that they were a bunch of older teenagers sitting around bullshitting before going to their favorite spot for the evening, but concealing their fear had become second nature to them. Going on an ambush at night wasn't anyone's idea of a fun time.

Drexler wiped the sweat from his brow. "I hate ambushes; we can't move, smoke, talk, eat, or even take a piss. Surviving the night should be automatic, but … Christ … even if we don't encounter the enemy most of the time, all it takes is once, when one of us isn't following these simple instructions."

"Fighting the VC in darkness gives them the advantage," Professor said, holding up his spoon. "Charlie wants to fight after the sun sets."

The men fell silent again as they began getting their gear organized and checking their weapons.

Drexler leaned against his rucksack and began writing a letter to his wife.

"You writing Sandra?" Henderson smiled with curiosity.

"Yeah. Then my mom."

"Tell both I said hi."

"Wilco."

Drexler continued his letter—it was his fourth to Sandra that week. Once he had finished, he carefully folded the pages and inserted them into an envelope with her address already written on it. Reaching into his rucksack, he placed it with the three other letters. What if she never saw them? His words didn't do any good stuck in his rucksack.

Seeing the look on his friend's face, Henderson wanted to offer support. "A resupply chopper should be coming any day; you can send the letters then."

Drexler smiled and started the second letter.

While Drexler wrote, Henderson walked around the perimeter. As he approached a First Squad position, he noticed Diego Garcia resting there. Garcia was short and muscular, with straight, black hair worn in a military cut. His size ensured that they were fast friends. The little guys had to stick together. The scant mustache that Garcia proudly wore was the butt of many of his squad members' jokes. Garcia waved at Henderson.

"Henderson, want to trade for a can of chicken noodles?"

"What you want for it?"

"What you got?"

"How about a packet of orange Kool-Aid?"

"It's a deal."

"I'll get with you in the morning."

Overhearing the trade, one of Garcia's squad members, Alvin Smothers, pursed his lips. "Sounds like you're getting the better end of the deal, Henderson."

"Come on, you know Garcia is getting the better deal," Henderson said, walking away.

Each team posted a guard while the remaining team members rested, until it became time to leave for the mission. The chatter, laughter, and rattling of gear faded as the men of Alpha Team fell asleep under the Professor's guarded watch.

•

Around 2030 hours, Professor woke his team to prepare for the mission.

The soldiers stretched and drank warm water. Most lit a cigarette—the last of the night. Each man had a ritual to burn off the nervous energy which consumed him. They stuffed their gear into their rucksacks in a systematic way and made sure the straps were tight to prevent the equipment from rattling.

Walking over to the Alpha Team position, Brighton approached Henderson. "Henderson, are you ready?"

"Yes, sir, I'm ready." Henderson rolled over onto his knees so he could use his legs and arms to lift the weight of the rucksack as he stood.

"Be careful. It's going to be dark tonight, with the heavy cloud cover."

"Okay, LT."

"Let's move out!" Brighton said as he adjusted his gear.

•

Struggling along the rocky, brush-covered slope, Henderson descended to the valley, while following the invisible path down the opposite side of the hill they had climbed earlier. He took deliberate, short steps as the moonless night hid their progress. As they continued along the trail, Henderson heard the occasional crackle of a twig, or a branch swishing through the air. He became fearful that the VC could hear the sounds too.

Darkness became his friend as the sun faded into blackness. Henderson welcomed it as his protector against the enemy seeing his approach; tonight would be one of the few times that Henderson embraced the darkness. Although the sun had set hours ago, he saturated his jungle fatigues with sweat, making the color of the uniform appear darker. Not wearing underclothes, he felt the material chafing against his thighs with each step.

Henderson knew that Drexler walked five feet behind him, making sure he could see the outline of his body; he hoped that Drexler was close enough to render aid if he needed it. The rest of the platoon followed in single file, staying close enough to the man in front that he remained visible. The grunts followed the rucksack, struggling to step into the footprint left by the soldier before him. As they walked, they attempted to make the least amount of noise possible.

Once in the valley, Henderson followed the well-used trail which led to the village. Stopping one hundred meters short of the ville, he stood where the two paths met and signaled that they were at the designated ambush site. Brighton approached Henderson and studied the terrain around the joining trails. After confirming the site, he motioned for the two squads to occupy their positions.

Second Squad's location ran parallel to the path, providing concealment, with the machine gun positioned at the base of one of the trails. The First Squad lay behind the path, facing the way they had come to the ambush site.

When he removed his rucksack, Henderson felt the immediate relief from the heavy burden he carried. Lowering the backpack, he placed it on the ground without making a sound.

•

Lying side-by-side behind a small berm covered in knee-high grass and brush, Henderson looked at Drexler. "This waiting sucks."

As he looked toward the darkness to his front, Henderson couldn't determine any distinctive landmarks. Observing the village, he didn't see any movement outside the huts. Pigs and chickens which had run loose earlier were now locked in the pens. Everything remained quiet; even the dogs weren't barking. The lack of any noise felt strange; he couldn't fight off the sense of impending doom. It was too damn quiet—almost as if the villagers were waiting too.

Do they know the VC are coming?

While the platoon waited for the enemy, a light, steady rain fell, soaking the men as they lay, motionless. It didn't take long for the ground to become soaked. Henderson heard a squad member fidgeting to find a better body position or a dry spot. At one point, he listened to a low, nasal snore coming from the First Squad area. Otherwise, silence fell over the ambush site like a blanket, muffling any sound. Dense precipitation fog clung close to the ground, covering the field to their front and making visibility worse.

As the minute hand moved painfully slowly to the hour of 0200, Ledger squeezed the handset talk button twice to send a situation report that the platoon remained safe; he did this each hour on the hour. The radio volume was turned low, so he had to keep the handset against his ear.

Waking each other when they felt their eyes close, Henderson and Drexler took turns nodding off, as did the rest of the platoon.

At around 0320 hours, Henderson heard a rattling sound—like a metal ball rolling in a tin can—roughly one-hundred feet to his front. He strained to see if anyone was walking along the path toward his position, but only saw blackness.

He heard the sound again, and this time he observed a figure; what appeared to be a man who took slow, short steps, hunched over, as if looking at the trail or carrying a heavy load on his back. Henderson tapped Drexler twice on the shoulder to alert his friend that they could be in danger.

In turn, Drexler tapped Professor twice.

The signal followed the line of soldiers until all platoon members were alert.

Henderson lay in the dark, waiting, straining his eyes to see. Then, there they were…

Eight or more NVA combatants were walking in a single file along the trail leading toward the village.

Henderson waited patiently for the last man to enter the kill zone. Then, he opened fire.

Using his M-16, Henderson squeezed off three-round bursts into the line of approaching NVA, immediately noticing one soldier stepping backward, falling to the ground. He continued firing.

The rest of the platoon opened fire. Soon, the sounds of M-16s, AK-47s, and two M-60 machine guns were thundering across the valley. Henderson could see the M-60's tracer rounds—each fifth round—speeding toward the enemy, lighting the valley floor, then ricocheting skyward for the stars. Flashes from the enemy weapons, as they returned fire, became the targets for the platoon. Zinging sounds passed over Henderson's head as he returned fire.

Within seconds, Drexler had pulled the pin, released the handle, and lobbed a grenade into the enemy force.

Bam!

The explosion shook the ground, the light from the blast illuminating the ambush site for a brief second.

Hearing screams coming from the kill zone, Henderson caught a glimpse of the NVA fleeing the area.

Then, it became quiet. Henderson didn't hear another sound.

•

Brighton passed the order along the line of grunts to remain in place until dawn. Shivering, Henderson knew that lying here would make the night longer.

Is it the rain or the fear making me shake? Damn, I have to piss!

•

As the sun climbed above the horizon, Brighton called Sergeant Bob Nash over to his position.

Nash was the First Squad leader. Standing at six feet tall, with short, blond hair and a slender, muscular build, Nash presented a military appearance. His deep-set, blue eyes never wavered. Somehow, he managed to shave daily.

Brighton stared at Nash. "Take a team to the ambush kill area to get a body count. Retrieve any weapons they left behind. I'll tell the rest of the platoon you're there."

"Okay, LT."

Once Nash returned to the First Squad position, he called for Bravo Team to gather round. "We're going to get a body count. Look for weapons too. If you see any bodies, assume they're alive—no taking chances. Got it?"

After they had nodded that they understood, Nash walked with steady, watchful steps toward the kill zone, with Bravo Team following.

Nash was perfectly aware that many of them still questioned his ability to lead. In his head, proving himself to them had become a rite of passage. If he could do that, it made up for his having done a quick eight-week non-commissioned officer training course in place of the combat experience the other NCOs had.

As the six-man patrol reached the ambush site, they searched the overgrown grass.

Standing in the waist-high elephant grass, Garcia saw blood trails. "Sergeant Nash, get over here. It looks like they took the dead and wounded with them."

Nash approached Garcia with caution. "Anything else?"

Garcia picked up two bloody helmets. "A couple of helmets. Nothing else."

"Any weapons?"

"No, Sarge."

"They got their dead during the early morning hours," Nash huffed. *Damn it!* "That makes it impossible to do a body count."

Nash searched the area one last time. "Let's go!"

The crack of an AK-47 pierced the morning air. Garcia fell to the ground like a rag doll. Blood oozed from a hole in his forehead, below the rim of his helmet.

Nash's heart thrummed against his ribcage. "Hit the ground!"

The team took cover.

•

"Don't fire!" Stahl's tone was authoritative enough that no one would question him.

Watching the patrol react to the NVA soldier hiding in the elephant grass made Henderson want to open fire. But, knowing that he couldn't without endangering his fellow platoon members, he sat there. Feeling helpless, he looked at Drexler and saw the same look of frustration. He turned back to watch the action unfolding in front of him.

Moving his sizeable frame with ease, James McKinney crawled closer to the NVA soldier. He maneuvered into a prone position, firing two three-round bursts into the enemy combatant with his M-16. The NVA slumped to the ground. As the men in the patrol shot into the grass where the soldier was hiding, Nash rushed toward the NVA in seconds.

A cry echoed above the din. "Medic! Medic! Medic!"

Doc Randy Wheeler knelt over Garcia, then closed his eyes with his fingers. "He's dead."

•

Henderson listened to the radio transmission.

Brighton spoke into the handset. "Tango six, this is Tango one-six. Over."

"Roger, Tango one-six. Over." An unnerved feeling took over Lyons.

"Need medevac, ASAP. One KIA. Over."

"Say again, Tango one-six. You said one KIA? Over."

"Affirmative. One EKIA too. Over."

"This is Tango six. Wilco. Out."

Minutes after the transmission, Henderson heard the whirl of the dustoff as it approached, *Whop, Whop, Whop!*

Stahl popped green smoke for the pilot to see where to land, and the skids settled softly on the ground, the helicopter's blades rotating as it landed.

Henderson watched McKinney, Doc, and Nash carry Garcia to the rescue helicopter. When they reached the open door, they gently slid him onto a stretcher. The helicopter crew started to check him over the moment his body slid onto the deck.

Signaling ready for takeoff, the pilot used the controls to lift the Huey fifty feet upward, banked, then streaked toward Fire Support Base Bronco.

As the First Squad was loading Garcia onto the dustoff, Professor walked over to the dead NVA. He stood over the body, ignoring the many bullet holes in his chest, which had soaked the combatant's shirt with blood. He stared at the face of the soldier, looking for any sign that this was the enemy who had killed his brother, Bobby. After a minute, he grunted and walked away, making his way toward the Second Squad.

Henderson took a deep breath, as Professor approached. "Is he the one?"

"I don't believe that he is."

"How are you going to know?"

Professor removed his helmet, wiped the sweat off of his face, and stared across the field. "A buddy of Bobby's who was with him the day he died wrote to me. He told me that the gook who killed Bobby had a large, red birthmark or burn on the right side of his face. I don't know how he knew, but it's something to go on."

After returning to their positions, with McKinney carrying a pack and two helmets, the team sat and waited for instructions.

Nash carried an AK-47, along with his M-16, as he walked past his squad, not stopping until he reached Brighton. "Only blood trails. Found a couple of helmets with a pack. One dead NVA with this AK-47, sir."

Brighton bit his lower lip. "I'm sorry Garcia got killed; I found him to be a good man."

"Yesterday he told me the platoon was his family." After a minute of awkward quiet, Nash shook his head. "It don't mean nothin'." He quickly walked away.

•

Stahl looked over his shoulder. "Henderson you're with me." He walked toward the dead NVA soldier.

Henderson bolted to catch up with Stahl, who stood over the body.

Stahl kicked the ribs of the dead NVA. "Blow this bastard's head off," he said, sliding the selector switch of his M-16 to semi-automatic.

"I can't do it, Sarge."

Stahl's face contorted with anger. "Do it! He's not dead until he's dead."

"Sarge, I can't—"

Stahl pulled the trigger of his M-16, discharging a 5.56 round directly into the enemy soldier's head.

Henderson jumped backward. "What the fuck are you doing, Sarge?"

"If you weren't going to, I sure as hell was. I hate the little sons of bitches! Someone needs to make sure he never comes back to kill us. You'll do the same someday, and soon."

"Sarge, I'll never do it."

"We'll see."

Henderson walked with his head hung low, shocked by Stahl's actions, as they returned to the squad.

Drexler stepped in front of him. "What was that about?"

"You don't want to know." Henderson clenched his jaw.

Brighton glared toward Stahl. "Let's go to the hill."

Stahl nodded in affirmation. "Saddle up, Henderson. Take us to the hill."

Henderson took one last, long drag from his cigarette and exhaled, letting the smoke drift through the morning air. He tossed it to the ground and smashed it into the hard dirt with his foot.

After Henderson slid his rucksack onto his back, he struggled to his feet. Taking point, he moved along the trail leading to the hilltop they had descended the night before.

Soaking wet, with the early morning air seeping through his uniform, the hike to the top was cold, and Henderson's only thought was of being dry, wrapped in a poncho liner and getting some sleep. He was thankful for the light the rising sun provided.

CHAPTER 4

AND THEN THE DARKNESS CAME

After they reached the top of the hill, Brighton stood in the center of the clearing to assign positions to the squad leaders. "First Squad splits into four positions, covering the south side, running west. Me, Ledger, and Doc are with First Squad." Brighton pointed out the positions to Nash, the First Squad leader, as he spoke.

"You got it, LT." Nash nodded.

Brighton's finger traced the points on the map. "Second Squad has four positions too, covering north, running east. Staff Sergeant Swift and Brown, you're with Second Squad."

Stahl took a drag from his cigarette. "Will do, LT."

Securing the hill was achieved by assigning defensive fighting positions. Three-man-teams manned positions at strategic locations around the perimeter of the hill. After they divided the squads into three-man teams, the two squad leaders assigned each group to a position. The Alpha Team comprised Drexler, Henderson, and Professor in one team with Rocky, Porter, and Stahl in another.

•

"Put claymores and flares to the front of your position."

Stahl felt uneasy as his team fortified their position. He'd been in enough battles to trust his gut, and his gut was telling him this wasn't a moment to be lax. He paused, waiting for his stomach to settle.

"Make sure you choose an approach the VC may take. We don't want any surprises."

•

After grabbing two pouches, each containing a claymore mine and two trip flares, Henderson and Drexler walked fifty feet to the tree line, while Professor stayed behind to keep a watchful eye over his two fellow team members.

Henderson reminded Professor of his brother, and that they were going into a potential battle. Professor sometimes needed that reminder to overcome his naturally peaceful nature. His mind wandered back to his days of protesting the war, but his heart invariably led him forward.

Drexler stopped, close to a trail. "Here's a good spot for a claymore. We can put a trip flare across the path."

"Go ahead, set the flare. I've got the claymore."

Henderson flashed a fake grin as he pulled the claymore from his bag, untangled the one-hundred feet of wire, and extended the short legs. He positioned the mine, making sure that the printed instruction—"Front Toward Enemy"—faced the expected direction of the enemy's approach, then pushed the claymore's legs into the soft ground. He inserted the blasting cap, attached to the wire, into the top of the claymore. The blasting cap would detonate the C-4 and send steel balls hurtling toward the enemy. Putting these safeguards in place was a nightly ritual for the men of the First Platoon.

Drexler scratched his chin. "Eddie, give me a hand with the wire."

"You're getting weak."

"Yeah, right. Hold the safety pin while I tie off the wire."

Henderson knelt alongside Drexler's trip flare. He set the safety lever and made sure the device held firmly in place. "Go ahead, tie it off."

"Roger." Drexler wrapped the wire tightly around a tree, nearly three inches from the ground, across the trail from the trip flare.

Henderson let go and the pin held in place, the wire remaining tight. "Glad I could help," he said, a playful smirk crossing his lips.

Drexler smiled in return. "Early warning system in place."

With the system they had put in place, the VC couldn't get through without warning them—at least, in theory. Once an enemy hits the wire, the pin would slide from the trigger and *puff*—a flash of light. Henderson wished it was as foolproof as that. He tried to believe that it was.

Drexler stood, ready to set up the next flare. After they placed the second claymore, along with the trip flare, the two soldiers worked their way to their spot, pulling the claymore mines' cable behind them as they climbed. Once at the position, they connected the trigger to each mine. With the safety on, Henderson set the clickers to the front of where they were pulling guard.

During breakfast, they agreed to a two-hour guard shift. Watching the jungle to his front, Henderson had the first shift. He enjoyed his cigarette, blowing smoke rings into the morning air. With his stomach full, Drexler pulled his poncho liner around him and was asleep within the first hour of returning to the hill. Professor lay awake for a while, staring up at the green canopy.

•

The day passed like any other. The team had been awake since noon, talking, resting, cleaning weapons, and organizing their rucksacks.

The rucksacks had magnesium support and the pack attached, with one large main pocket and several smaller ones. The frame and canvas were olive drab. While Henderson carried his rucksack, he found that the frame pressed against his waist, causing bruises, due to his skinny frame.

Being the only personal space he owned, a soldier's rucksack became his home. Inside, or hanging on the outside straps, it held the items he needed to survive the war and the jungles of Vietnam. A soldier didn't worry if another platoon member took an article from his rucksack; they thought it as safe as their belongings were in their home with a family member.

It got closer to the dreaded darkness, now falling over the hills, paddies, and forest, where the men trudged and fought. The enemy used the night to conceal their attacks. Henderson took a deep breath.

"Let's eat; I'm starving."

Drexler gave his friend a knowing look. "Let me guess—you're having chicken and noodles, peanut butter with crackers, and pears. Kool-Aid is the drink of the day."

"No shit! I have that every night."

"My momma always said that variety is the spice of life." Professor grinned.

Ignoring the remarks of his friends, Henderson prepared dinner.

He reached into his rucksack, retrieving an olive drab-colored C-ration can without a lid. It had holes punched into the bottom, every half an inch around the rim. Tearing off a chunk of C-4 the size of a half-dollar, he placed it into what he referred to as his "stove." The plastic explosive remained safe until it had a detonator in it and, when ventilated, it burned with a concentrated white-blue flame—ideal for cooking canned rations or heating water. He attached the P-38 can opener to his dog-tag chain. After he took it off, he used the P-38 to open the tin of chicken and noodles. Leaving the lid attached, he peeled it back to use as a handle. Once he opened the chicken, Henderson struck a match, lighting the C-4. As the hot flame shot upward, he placed his main course onto the makeshift stove.

While the food simmered, Henderson cut the lid off of a can of peanut butter and jam and mixed the two. After opening the crackers, he crushed them in his hand, letting the crumbs fall into the mixture, using a plastic spoon to stir the contents together.

Within minutes, his meal boiled. To enhance the taste of his chicken dinner, he added a couple of drops of hot Tabasco sauce. Most platoon members had a family member mail them a bottle of hot sauce—Henderson always had Drexler's mom send him an extra one, along with Kool-Aid, in Drexler's care packages.

Henderson broke the silence while they ate. "What do you think happened to the young guys from the village? Are they VC, or not?"

"It's a possibility." Professor's eyes widened. "They could have enlisted in the ARVN or the NVA, or joined the VC, none of which is a good choice. Hell, they could've gone to the city for paying jobs."

Drexler shook his head. "I think most of them are."

"Hell, I don't care." Henderson knew the statement wasn't true as he said it; he was quite sure he cared more than he let on. "Just hope we don't see any tonight."

Tearing off another piece of C-4, Henderson dropped it into his stove and struck a match, lighting it. He poured water into a metal canteen cup, setting it on the can and allowing the flame from the explosive to heat the water. Once the water boiled, he poured a packet of cocoa into the cup and stirred the contents until they mixed into a dark-chocolate color. To appease his sweet tooth, he dumped in three sugar packets.

Drexler flopped next to Henderson as he took a drink of his hot chocolate. Drexler had his meal in hand and was busy consuming it.

Henderson frowned at Drexler. "Do you find it strange that the two fire teams in our squad don't mingle too much?"

"Alpha and Bravo know each other, but not as well as we know our team members—probably because we operate as teams most of the time, and not so much around the other guys." Drexler shifted his weight. "The truth is we don't need any more attachments out here. People die; better to limit exposure."

"Do you think Nash is as good as Stahl?" Henderson sipped his drink. "I have trouble believing that anyone who got a leadership position before combat experience could be a good leader. Trust me. I'm not the only one that thinks this."

Drexler shrugged. "I don't know. Maybe ask McKinney that question."

He suggested McKinney simply because he was the closest friend Henderson had in Nash's squad. Drexler thought that was because, at least in part, McKinney was the only person in the platoon younger than Henderson.

Henderson nodded. "I think I'll do that."

Henderson then took his sweet hot chocolate drink to McKinney's position to get the scoop on Nash. When he reached McKinney, he stood beside him. "Hey, big guy. How's it going?"

"Couldn't be any better, for being in 'Nam." McKinney was over six feet tall, and only in this position—with him sitting and Henderson standing—did McKinney get to be the one looking up.

"Sorry about Garcia."

"Yeah, a good guy." McKinney stood, redeeming the height differential back to its usual; Henderson strained his neck to gaze upward. "It don't mean nothin'."

Henderson took a long sip of hot chocolate from his cup. "How's Sergeant Nash?"

McKinney's eyebrows cocked upward. "What do you mean?"

With his face flushing, Henderson swallowed. "What kind of leader is he? Is he as good as Stahl?"

"He lacks experience, but he's good. He did fine this morning. I'll follow him."

"Why is he so gung-ho?"

"You don't know?"

"Know what?"

"His dad is a lieutenant colonel in the army and was in 'Nam two years ago—a World War II vet too."

"No shit?"

"Yeah, a real hard-ass, I hear." McKinney nodded. "He spent a lot of time at Fort Campbell with the One-Hundred-and-First Airborne. Nash was born in the army hospital at Campbell. He's an army brat."

"That explains a lot." Henderson looked away for a moment.

Henderson changed the subject. "Do you know if Williamson is still alive?"

"Man, I haven't heard that name since basic training. Who knows? He's probably dead by now."

"Why do you say that?"

"He had a death wish. All he thought about was dying a hero in this damn war."

"I hope *everyone* is still alive. It's hard out here in this forsaken jungle. Nice chat—we'll have to do it again."

Henderson rose and headed back to Drexler, who lifted his eyes. "What did he say?"

"Nash will do fine."

"Good news. I thought he would."

"Did you know his dad is a Lieutenant Colonel?"

"Nope, I didn't."

•

As the sun dropped behind the mountains to the west, Henderson, Drexler, and Professor spread their poncho liners on the soggy ground and arranged their gear for the long night.

Henderson lathered DEET mosquito repellent onto his exposed skin. "I can't believe how big these bastards are!"

Professor swatted at a swarm of mosquitos flying around his face. "Did you know the female mosquito is the one biting you? The males don't bite."

"Send the males to me." Drexler laughed as he slapped another mosquito.

Darkness fell over the hilltop as the three friends readied for sleep. Each of them would pull two-and-a-half hours of guard duty, in two shifts of one hour and fifteen minutes. Henderson took the first guard, then Professor, with Drexler last.

Moving to the small berm where the claymore triggers were laying, Henderson sat with his M-16 resting over his legs. As he watched the front of his position, he used his left hand to flip open the Zippo lighter and turn the wheel with his thumb to light his last cigarette of the evening. Keeping the cigarette cupped between his hands, he took a deep drag and blew a smoke ring when he exhaled. A sound of satisfaction escaped with the smoke.

•

The rest of the positions quietened, while the guards watched for the enemy. Before long, the men of the First Platoon fell asleep. Wrapped in a poncho liner, while using their rucksack for a pillow, with a hand resting on their weapon, the sleeping soldiers trusted the men on guard with their lives.

Drexler relieved Professor of guard duty and took the same spot to watch for the enemy.

Within thirty minutes of his watch—*Bam!*

The ground beneath him vibrated from the grenade exploding behind him. Falling forward, he took cover from the fragments of metal flying throughout the platoon area.

A cry went out. "Medic! Medic!"

Henderson rolled over, clutching his rifle, and spotted Professor facing in the direction of the explosion, ready for the enemy.

Another blast rang out, followed by the cracking sound of AK-47s firing. Rounds ripped through the platoon perimeter, the hot lead whizzing over Henderson's head into the tree line behind him. VC fired from the front of his position, with rounds striking the ground around the three team members.

Drexler took cover, shouting, "Grenade!"

Henderson forced his body lower into the ground.

Bam!

His body shuddered from the explosion. As the earth shook, a flame shot upward—the flying shrapnel barely missed the men of the Second Squad. Seconds later, their position became engulfed by the overpowering smell of gunpowder.

Henderson scanned the area in a daze. His ears rang and everything sounded as if he were in a tunnel.

Rocky provided covering fire as he squeezed off six-round bursts, nonstop, into the trees. Porter linked belts as they fed into the tray.

Stahl took the initiative. "Blow claymores!"

Grabbing both clickers, Drexler slid off the safeties and squeezed the triggers, creating an electrical charge which ran along the wires to the blasting caps.

A flash of bright light illuminated the trees where Henderson had earlier placed the two claymore mines. *Bam! Bam!* The explosions thundered along the hill, and screams of pain echoed through the trees from where the mines had detonated. A trip flare went off, lighting a twenty-foot area in the cluster of trees. As the flame burnt out, the area dimmed to darkness.

"More ammo!" Porter yelled, scrambling to take cover until the ammo arrived.

Stahl stopped firing at the VC and crawled to his rucksack, removing three-hundred rounds. Staying as low as possible, he crept along the hard ground and delivered the ammo to Porter.

"Gook in the perimeter!" The audible was barely heard from the soldiers covering the perimeter.

Drexler pointed in the direction of the suspected gook. "Professor, watch the center!"

Professor rolled to his left to watch for the VC behind his position. He pointed the M-79—loaded with a buckshot round, packed with twenty metal pellets—in the direction from where the enemy might attack.

Henderson caught a glimpse of a shadow, then the outline of a man appeared.

"NVA!"

Professor leveled his M-79 and fired, the round hitting the enemy soldier in the chest, no more than thirty feet away. As the buckshot ripped into the gook's body, he screamed, falling to the ground and writhing in pain.

Henderson crawled to within fifteen feet of the moaning soldier, who was attempting to take a grenade from his belt. Without hesitation, he fired two rounds into the NVA soldier's chest. "He's dead!"

More incoming rounds thudded into the earth around their position. They returned fire to their front at any muzzle flashes they detected through the trees.

Brighton grabbed the handset to call the company commander. "Tango six, this is Tango one-six. Need fire support. Over."

"Tango one-six, Spooky in five mikes. Over." Lyons clenched his jaw, knowing the platoon was in trouble.

"Need flares too. Over."

"Roger on the flares, Tango one-six. Out."

Within a few minutes, Brighton heard the roar of AC-47 engines overhead.

Suddenly, the trees and earth exploded as Spooky unloaded the airplane's three miniguns. A downpour of red rain dropped from the night sky toward the enemy as it fired fifty rounds per second on the NVA, delivering 7.62mm rounds at two-meter intervals around the perimeter. Flares fell from the aircraft, illuminating the hilltop and surrounding area; each hung on a small parachute, which floated for three minutes before extinguishing. The floating flares created an eerie mixture of light and shadows which danced along the hill.

Lying on the ground, the men of the First Platoon silently cheered Spooky and the end of the darkness.

Brighton grasped the handset. "Tango six, need medevac, one KIA. Over."

"Roger, Tango one-six. Dustoff in the air, it will be there in three mikes. Out."

When the battle finally subsided and the enemy was no longer in sight, the dustoff descended to the center of the hill, where Nash guided it to land.

Once it was on the ground, several First Squad members carried Smothers to the Huey and slid his lifeless body onto the floor. The pilot looked through the cockpit window and signaled ready for take-off. Then he climbed straight off of the landing zone, banking hard right, and the dustoff flew off into the darkness, heading to firebase Bronco.

Circling the hilltop, Spooky, also known as "Puff the Magic Dragon," continued to drop flares. The aircraft stayed with the platoon for several more hours, until getting low on fuel was the only reason the pilot finally left the infantry unit.

The platoon had appreciated the firepower and flares for the whole duration that Spooky stood guard over them. Now, as the aircraft flew off into the night, they watched the darkness creep over the hill, covering them like a blanket.

The squad finally returned to guard rotation, trying to get another two hours of sleep.

Bright sunlight slowly spilled over the hilltop as the sun rose to begin another day. It had been a long night. With the darkness gone, the men of the First Platoon felt safer.

•

Rolling out of his poncho liner, Henderson shook it, folded it, and stuffed it into his rucksack. While he was in the pack, he removed his breakfast of pound cake, hot chocolate, and peaches.

Drexler, the last on guard duty, had already stowed his gear away and was silently eating breakfast.

"Wake up." Henderson nudged Professor's arm with his foot.

"Not yet. It's not time."

"Yes, it is. Come on, Professor."

"Hell of a night!" Professor stood, stretching.

"It was." Drexler cocked his head to the side, tapping on his ear as if to stop the ringing in it.

Remaining silent, Henderson scrutinized the dead NVA soldier, thirty feet away, in a bizarre position of death. He looked toward Professor and watched him slurp his can of fruit cocktail, all the while staring at the NVA. *Does Professor think this gook was the one?*

The three friends ate without talking, each deep in their thoughts, until Stahl came over, clearing his throat.

"I need a volunteer to search the dead gook and get his weapon."

"I'll do it," Professor said quickly, standing before Stahl had a chance to assign any other squad member to the task. Professor threw his half-full fruit can to the ground and walked over to the NVA soldier. As he bent over the dead body, he rifled through his pockets. Not finding anything, he flipped the body over like a sack of potatoes, glaring at the dead man's face to see if he recognized him. Then he checked the front pockets, finding each one empty.

After taking the AK-47, with two magazines of ammo, Professor looked at him one more time. He moved in a daze back to his rucksack, where he sat staring into the jungle.

Henderson rubbed his lips together, hesitant to ask what was on his mind. "He the one?"

"No, not him."

A sudden sound drifted from the tree line to the front, and both soldiers immediately crouched, their weapons aimed and ready to kill the enemy. After a minute, they lowered their rifles and looked at each other, amazed by how paranoid they had become in such a fleeting period. The noise could have been anything moving through the jungle. Still, they knew that their quick reaction to any extraordinary sound could save lives.

Henderson took a deep breath. "Damn! Any noise makes me jump. Does it bother you, Professor?"

"I wish it didn't make so much sense. We have no front lines; any young village girl or farmer could be a VC in disguise; the rice fields conceal bomb craters; and the dikes are booby trapped—not to mention the trails we walk along in the mountains. Our only job is to kill them before they kill us, then count the dead bodies. The paranoia is simply a symptom of that."

Henderson noticed that Professor's face had turned red with anger. He remained quiet.

·

Brighton stood and grabbed his weapon. "Staff Sergeant Swift, Sergeant Stahl, and Sergeant Nash, on me."

Walking over to the lieutenant's position, Stahl and Nash talked as they walked. Stahl's brow creased as his jaw clenched. "What happened to Smothers?"

"Grenade went off in his position. He didn't stand a chance."

"Shit! That sucks!"

Nash looked at the ground. "Smothers only had two months left in-country. He had a wife, Linda, and a son, Mark."

"It's hard to lose a man. You'll get past this."

"Yeah, it don't mean nothin'."

Stahl put his arm around Nash's shoulder to comfort him as they walked toward the lieutenant. He knew there wasn't a word he could say to ease the loss of a squad member.

Once the three NCOs arrived at the lieutenant's position, the four of them sat.

Brighton said, "We have a new mission."

DROWN, SWIM OR RUN
LIKE HELL

After the briefing, Brighton stood over his rucksack, fumbling inside it for several minutes. He retrieved a pen, paper, and two envelopes, then looked around at the platoon, remembering the two soldiers killed in the last two days.

They fought well. They were good men.

He flopped to the ground and rested his back against the rucksack to write.

> *"Dear Mr. and Mrs. Garcia,*
>
> *I'm Diego's platoon leader, James Brighton. I know the army has informed you of his death, but I wanted to let you know what kind of man and soldier he became.*
>
> *On the day Diego died, he served our country. He died a hero, who served others and treated all with respect.*
>
> *You should be proud of your son."*

After signing the letter, he put it in an envelope.

Brighton then wrote his second letter.

"Dear Mr. and Mrs. Smothers,

I'm Alvin's platoon leader, James Brighton. I know the army has informed you of his death, but I wanted to let you know what kind of man and soldier he became.

On the day Alvin died, he was a hero. He saved many lives and served our country, to allow all the freedom we have grown to know.

You should be proud of your son."

He placed the letter into the second envelope, and then put both into his rucksack. Then, Brighton sat for a moment, blinking away tears. Writing to parents was never easy.

Damn this war. Damn the gooks.

•

Once Stahl had returned to the squad position, he stood before the men. "Gather around and make it fast. We have a new mission."

The squad quickly obeyed the command.

"We're going to patrol the area along the river, four klicks from the coast, for a couple of days. A resupply chopper should land in an hour with rations, ammunition, and water. We'll continue to operate as a platoon, and we will have artillery and air support if needed." He paused for a moment, looking over the squad, adding, "Any questions?"

Porter raised his hand. "Do I—"

"Yes, you do!" Stahl cut Porter off before he could be funny; Stahl wasn't in the mood for funny.

Drexler wrinkled his forehead. "What are we looking for?"

"Patrolling along the river, looking for NVA or VC. What else would we be looking for?"

"I hope we don't find any." Rocky looked at the ground. He rubbed his thick mustache, which helped with his mountain-man looks.

"They're using us for bait, to draw out Charlie," Professor said, scratching his neck.

Stahl's eyes darted about him. "I believe you're right, Professor. However, it is what it is. Any questions?" He scanned the squad members, who sat stone-faced. "Good, no more questions.

"Henderson, Rocky and Porter, meet the helicopter; get the rations and ammo for the squad. Professor, put the AK-47 and its ammo on the chopper, then help carry the supplies."

Drexler could almost feel his letters growing heavier. "Is the mail coming?"

"Good point, Drexler." Stahl flashed a thin-lipped grin. "Henderson, collect the outgoing mail and put it in the mail pouch on the helicopter. Porter, make sure you get the incoming mail for the squad. Any more questions?"

For a moment, the squad remained quiet.

Henderson stood and put on his crusty shirt. "Are we getting clean uniforms? It's been three weeks."

"Not this time. Okay, get your gear squared away. We'll leave around eleven-hundred hours, if it goes as planned."

After Stahl walked away, the Second Squad organized their gear. They packed what they could into their rucksacks before being resupplied.

Henderson walked around, asking each platoon member if they had outgoing mail, and collected the envelopes, placing them into his pants' cargo pocket for safekeeping—each letter was important. Stopping by the command group, Henderson saw Staff Sergeant Swift. "Sarge, do you have any mail?"

"No, I don't. Who has time to write?"

"Sarge, can I ask you a question?" Henderson blinked, slapping at a fly in the air.

"Sure, go ahead."

"Why does Sergeant Stahl say a gook's not dead until he's dead?"

"Why don't you ask him?"

"I'm afraid to."

Swift looked around the perimeter, then at the ground. "It happened before I got to the platoon. A soldier who was there told me, so all I have is gossip."

"Come on, Sarge, help me out."

"Okay, Henderson. Stahl was with the platoon for about a month when his squad set an ambush along a trail. When the VC entered the kill zone, the squad opened fire on the enemy, killing five soldiers."

"Sounds like a good ambush."

"It was, but the squad became reckless and grouped near one of the dead. He pulled the pin on a grenade, killing three squad members and wounding two. Stahl was one of the wounded; his best friend, Reynolds, was killed." He took a drink from his canteen cup. Henderson thought he could smell bourbon.

"Stahl and Reynolds were tight—kinda like you and Drexler. After that, Stahl believes you have to kill VC twice."

"Explains a lot." Henderson nodded.

Swift rubbed his jaw. "Let's not share that with everyone."

"I won't. Thanks, Sarge."

Henderson walked back to his position, thinking of what he had learned about Stahl.

Drexler came over to Henderson, extending his hand—it held four letters. "Make sure these get in the pouch. Sandra needs to know how much I love her."

"No problem, she'll get them."

Henderson strolled to the next position, where he found Gonzalez and Lanier sitting by their rucks, eating. He didn't have a lot of contact with Alex Gonzalez, although he knew he had grown up in Laredo, Texas, and didn't have a great childhood. Henderson heard that his mom had left him with a neighbor one morning when he was five years old, and never came back. He had grown up in foster care, and he didn't talk about it. Standing almost six feet tall, with an athletic build, Alex had to be the toughest guy in the platoon. He had one month left in 'Nam, but said that he planned on re-enlisting.

Henderson stopped about two feet from Gonzalez. "I'm picking up mail. You have any?"

"Nothing from me." Gonzalez rolled his eyes.

Lanier held up a finger. "I have two letters."

Bob Lanier had a different take on being in Vietnam. He acted like it didn't bother him in the least. What a talker! Hell, those guys from New York, talk, talk and talk! Henderson recalled how one night Lanier had said that he'd had to enlist in the army or go to jail. No one knew if that was true or not. In any case, Bob was a good guy.

"I'll see they get mailed." Henderson placed the letters into his pocket.

Hearing the whirl of the chopper blades growing close, he headed back to his position.

Right at 0900 hours, Swift popped purple smoke to alert the supply helicopter pilot to the landing-zone site. Raising the M-16 over his head, he guided the Huey to a safe landing, where the helicopter crew kicked cases of C-rations, five-gallon water containers, and full ammunition cans from the deck to the ground.

Drexler exhaled. "Porter, Henderson, Rocky and Professor, go get the supplies."

The helicopter created a powerful rotor wash, its blades turning fast. The force blew freshly cut elephant grass and dirt at the approaching soldiers, and they ran low and bent near to the ground while shielding their eyes.

As the four soldiers reached the helicopter, Henderson stuffed the envelopes he had collected into the mail pouch, while Porter grabbed the incoming mail pouch and slung it over his shoulder. Professor handed the crew chief the AK-47 with the two magazines.

The four then moved to the pile of supplies as the helicopter lifted and headed toward Bronco. Carrying as much as possible, it took them three trips to get it all to the squad.

Strolling to a case of C-rations, Henderson placed the barrel of his M-16 under the thin wire which held the carton together. With a twist of the rifle, he broke the wire, opening the cardboard box. As he pulled the flaps open, Henderson grabbed twelve meals, trying for the chicken noodle, but not too concerned. He wasn't intending on sticking with the twelve; he'd get what he wanted. The rest of the squad also picked out what they wanted.

Each soldier had twelve meals—four days' worth. They walked around, exchanging meals they didn't like for their favorites. Henderson knew who to ask. As if holding a bargaining chip, he approached several of the squad members.

"Professor, I'll trade you ham slices for your chicken noodle." They swapped without a word. "Thanks. Enjoy your ham."

Out of the corner of his eye, he saw Brighton, so he strode over to him next. "LT, I'll trade you turkey loaf for your chicken noodle."

"Fine. It all tastes like dog food anyway." They made the swap effortlessly.

Henderson smiled at McKinney. "I'll trade a beefsteak for your chicken noodle."

"You must really like that chicken noodle crap."

"It's the best meal we got out here, in my opinion."

It didn't take long for Henderson to trade for seven chicken meals. Henderson thought that wasn't a bad haul from twenty-eight cases of C-rations. He knew some of the platoon members only swapped to be generous, but it didn't make a substantial difference to him. It wasn't a point of pride. Those meals were merely a small joy in this hellhole of a jungle, infested with gooks.

What Henderson never told anyone was that eating the chicken and noodle meal every night meant that he would live another day; it was his good-luck ritual. Everyone had their superstitious routine to escape death or being wounded. Drexler kept a picture of Sandra inside the webbing of his helmet liner, tilting the headgear to the right, when humping. Professor wore a peace sign and love beads, which he rubbed during breakfast. Porter stared at a picture of himself riding a surfboard, while rotating his love beads around his neck three times during every meal. Rocky carried a small portion of an elk pelt, which he used as a pillow.

After they got the supplies packed, the supply chopper returned to retrieve those items that were not needed.

Relaxing against their rucksacks, the men started reading their letters from home. Several platoon members yelled in excitement, because their envelope contained more than a message from a loved one. Mostly, they held packets of Kool-Aid—adding Kool-Aid made the drinking water tolerable.

Henderson saw Drexler staring straight ahead, holding a one-page letter in his limp hand.

He walked over to his friend with concern. "What's wrong?"

Drexler wiped his tears as he looked up.

"Is Sandra okay?"

Without a word, Drexler handed Henderson the letter.

"You want me to read your letter?"

"Yes."

Holding the letter, Henderson read it.

> *"Dear Mitch,*
>
> *I don't know how to say this, but I'm going to try.*
>
> *Do you remember Billy Matheson? You played base-ball with him in high school. Well, we started talking not long after you left… friends at first. I became so lonely with you gone…*
>
> *I want a divorce…"*

Henderson stopped reading and gazed into Drexler's eyes. He dropped the letter near his friend, sat next to him, and put an arm over his shoulders. The two friends sat there, not saying a word.

Henderson thought about the first time he had met Sandra at their Basic Training graduation. She drove from their hometown, Indianapolis, to attend Mitch's graduation ceremony. Impressed by her intelligence, witty nature, and good looks, he had thought Mitch lucky to find a woman like her. Henderson could see how much they loved one another as he watched the way they touched and looked at each other. *How could she do this to him?*

"Henderson, come over here!" Stahl stood firm in his stance.

As he stood, Henderson squeezed Mitch's shoulder. He strolled over to Stahl.

"I'm going to make sure the NVA soldier is dead. Come with me."

"I told you I couldn't do it, Sarge. I'm not going."

"You will, sooner or later. I'll catch up with the squad in a minute."

Stahl turned to face his men. "Saddle up, move out!"

•

Struggling to stand from the load of their rucksacks, the men of the First Platoon moved with weighted steps to the east side of the hilltop, with Henderson in the lead. No more than three minutes after they set out, Henderson heard the burst of automatic rifle fire, echoing from the top of the hill.

He led the platoon along the rugged trail to the base of what appeared to be a mountain. Once he reached the bottom of the hill, he veered north, heading across the wet rice paddies toward the Song Lai Giang River. Walking on the dikes could be dangerous because of booby traps, and made an easier shot for an enemy sniper.

As they trudged through knee-deep rice fields, the men spread out in a long column. While they slogged along, they watched workers planting their rice—a long, arduous process, using age-old methods. Rice was their life, and Henderson noticed the smiles on their faces. Trekking across the field, the platoon members kept a watchful eye on the farmers, hoping that none of them were VC, ready to shoot at them as they passed.

Each soldier knew it was their responsibility to keep an eye on the man to their front. A buddy could step into a hidden bomb crater, causing him to sink underwater, unable to surface because of the heavy load he carried.

Henderson shivered at the thought. *Drowning in this war isn't an option.* He turned, looking to his rear. "Look out for craters!"

"I'm not drowning today." Drexler nodded in affirmation. "I need to get home and kill Billy Matheson."

Rain fell sideways, with the wind from the east blowing hard. Already wet, nobody bothered to put on a poncho. At first, the shower was refreshing, but soon they were being pelted hard by the raindrops, with visibility decreasing. Henderson kept wading through the rice fields.

After two hours of sloshing through the countryside in the rain, Henderson saw the ville along the riverbank. To leave the paddies, he stepped onto the well-used trail, following it into the hamlet. With each step on the solid ground, his boots made a loud squishing sound as water and mud squirted from the vent holes in the canvas upper part of his jungle boots.

When he approached the entrance to the village, Henderson noticed that it looked like any other ville, except the huts were on stilts, nearly three feet above the ground. As communities go, this appeared to be one of the smallest villes Henderson had been to, with fifteen hooches and a small community building. There were roughly forty-five villagers.

Brighton hadn't even noticed the size of the ville when the radio squawked. "Tango one-six, this is Tango six. Over."

"Go ahead, Tango six. Over." Brighton held his position.

"Tango one-six, be advised typhoon Tess heading your way in two hours. It'll be bad. Over." Lyons was shaking his head.

"Tango six, wait one minute for a new position. Over."

Retrieving his map, Brighton looked for a safe place to protect the platoon. The rice fields were treacherous; he certainly wanted his men out of them before anything else happened. He chose a small hill, one hundred and twenty-five meters to the southeast. He figured getting the platoon to the west side of the hill, into the thick stand of trees, would help protect them from the storm, and they would be high enough that they wouldn't drown.

"Roger, Tango six. Moving to grid Bravo Sierra four-five-one-seven-eight-two for night logger. Over." Brighton transmitted the platoon's position with confidence.

"Bravo Sierra four-five-one-seven-eight-two. Stay safe and check back with me when you get there. Out."

A downpour started, with the wind from the east gathering speed and bringing more moisture from the South China Sea.

Running to the front of the platoon, Brighton grabbed his three NCOs and pointed toward the hill. "Typhoon is coming. We need to get the hell away from here. Warn the villagers too. Henderson, head to the hill to your southeast. We'll place our positions on this side of the hill. The hill should give us some protection from the wind and rain."

While Brighton gave his orders, the villagers—which included older men and women, and young women with children—ran from their huts. The old men opened the animal pens, letting the chickens, pigs, and water buffalo free. Animals ran everywhere, clucking, oinking and mooing as if to warn anyone within hearing distance of unseen danger. The howling wind blew across the village, destroying anything in its path.

"What do we do with the villagers?" Swift said, covering his eyes to shield the piercing rain.

Brighton motioned for the villagers to follow. "Oh, hell, take them with us. Move, Henderson!" he yelled over the howling wind.

Henderson turned to head toward the hill, running through the line of waiting soldiers with the Second Squad following. Along the way, Stahl told his squad to take the villagers with them as the platoon moved to the hill. The residents were already on their way there.

Water rushed downstream toward the hamlet with a roar like a freight train, and it spilled over the banks and raced through the rice fields, slowly heading to the ville. The wind blew the huts off of their stilts, and the roofs and walls flew about, barely missing the villagers and soldiers. The water would do much worse if it caught them.

Platoon members scooped children up into their arms as they ran for the hill. Henderson saw McKinney carrying a child in one arm and an old woman in another. Looking to his right, he saw two water buffalo running alongside him, gaining speed as they ran ahead to the hill.

Wind speed must be sixty miles an hour, Henderson calculated as he fought his way to the rise. The water quickly rose to his shins, causing him more effort to move forward. For the first time, he was thankful for the weight of the rucksack; if it wasn't for the heavy pack on his back, he thought the wind would suck him into the dark sky. As he climbed the hill, the fear of drowning took no time to take over his body.

The platoon helped the villagers as they ascended the steep slope, slipping and sliding on the wet, muddy trail leading to the top. Nobody looked for the VC or even thought about them; survival was the only thing on their minds.

Nash, the last man in the formation, helped those in front of him. "Hurry, the village is getting flooded. You have to move faster. Go! Run to safety!"

While being pelted by the heavy rain and wind, Henderson saw a hut floating by in the swollen river, bobbing downstream as the rushing water crept toward the hill. Debris flew all over and, at one point, he thought he saw a pig flying over a hedgerow outside the village. A young boy and a woman were running alongside him, and he scooped the boy into his arms as he struggled to run uphill. The mother nodded at Henderson and smiled, as if to say thank you.

Once at the top of the hill, Brighton pointed to an area which seemed the safest place to take refuge. "Set up a perimeter in that stand of trees for protection against the storm. Take the villagers with you."

The squad leaders made sure the locals stayed in the center of the platoon perimeter. This was in part a protective measure, but the soldiers all knew that it was as much about protecting them as it was the villagers—to keep an eye on them to make sure there were no VC amongst them.

The men huddled in threes, forming a position to watch to the front, but keeping an eye on the group behind them as gale-force winds and sheets of rain pushed through the trees, attempting to get at the group of survivors. The platoon members gave their ponchos to the women and children for warmth and protection against the storm.

The chaos of the typhoon deadened their senses as they huddled to wait out its fury.

•

By late evening, the storm subsided.

The soldiers dug through their wet rucksacks to fix a cold meal, the villagers staring at the men as they opened cans of fruit, meat, crackers, and cake.

Henderson saw the woman and the young boy he had carried watching him intently as he ate. He looked at the young woman with her long, wet, black hair plastered against her attractive face. Henderson didn't think she was any older than him. Seeing him staring, she offered a pleasant smile. He returned it.

Henderson pointed at himself and tapped his chest. "Eddie."

The young woman nodded and pointed at her son. "Vinh." Then, she pointed at herself. "Mai."

"Hello, Vinh." Henderson smiled. "Hello, Mai."

Mai smiled.

Henderson retrieved two cans of fruit cocktail, opened them, and handed one each to the woman and the boy. They hungrily gulped the fruit, finishing within minutes. Feeling guilty, he then opened two cans of his prized chicken and noodles and gave it to them, knowing that by giving his rations to the two villagers, he wouldn't have enough meals to last until the next resupply. The rest of the platoon shared their C-rations with the villagers too.

Mai grinned. "*Cảm ơn bạn.*"

Henderson smiled. "You're welcome."

As Vinh ate his chicken and noodles, he started laughing, pointing at Henderson. Looking around him and not seeing anything, Henderson assumed that the boy was laughing at his appearance—wet and muddy.

Then, exaggerating a pointing motion, the boy aimed his extended finger over Henderson's head.

Looking skyward, Henderson turned to look into the large eyes of a water buffalo. Startled, he jumped to his feet, releasing a high-pitched "Help!" as he bolted away from the animal. Mai and Vinh pointed at Henderson, bursting into laughter.

Most of the squad and villagers saw Henderson's reaction and joined in the laughter. Henderson's comical response to the water buffalo had broken the ice between the soldiers and villagers; now, everyone relaxed.

•

Before nightfall, Brighton called the squad leaders over to his position.

"It's not safe. Make sure each position watches their front, but keep an eye on the villagers too. The locals can stay with us until morning. Then in the morning they can go home—or to what's left of it."

The three said, "Yes, sir."

"I'll call the CO tomorrow morning and ask for the supply chopper to drop off food and water for the ville. That's it; that's all I can do for them."

Nodding that they understood, the three NCOs returned to their positions.

•

Rain and wind continued throughout the night. The trees provided some protection, but not enough to stay dry. The villagers huddled together and were soon asleep.

Henderson tried to sleep amid the sounds of an occasional crying child and a mother's soothing voice, comforting them. It gave him hope that they were safe.

Waking for guard duty, Henderson found the young woman with her son curled next to him, asleep under his wet poncho liner. He stood slowly, careful not to wake them, and his eyes lingered on the mother. For a moment, he felt a sense of normalcy.

During his guard shift, Henderson thought that the sun would never rise. But eventually, light and warmth crept over the wet, cold soldiers and villagers.

•

Once they had enough daylight, Swift herded the villagers through the platoon perimeter, allowing them to return to what the typhoon had left of their village.

They moved downhill in a single line, along the slick trail toward their home. As the mother reached Henderson, she smiled and touched his hand. Surprised by the softness of her hand as it rested on his, he grinned as he gazed into her mahogany-brown eyes.

Mai met his gaze. "Eddie." Then she continued to follow the others down the trail.

The men of the Second Squad ate, the chatter and laughter increasing amongst them. Then, after breakfast, they laid out their poncho liners, shirts, and pants to dry in the welcoming sun.

Henderson approached Drexler. "You doing okay?"

"Yeah."

"You sure?" Drexler wasn't always a talker, but Henderson knew he was usually more than a one-word kind of guy.

"I can't talk to her from here. Can't do anything. I need to survive another eight months. And when I get home, I'm going to kill the bastard who took my wife."

Sitting next to his friend, Henderson remained silent, knowing there wasn't a word he could say to take the hurt away. He didn't believe that Mitch would kill Matheson. Well, he hoped not.

HOW CAN THEY DO THAT?

The platoon sergeant and his two squad leaders walked over to Brighton. Swift was shaking his head. "So, what now?"

"You guys look terrible." Brighton laughed at the sight of his NCOs.

"Look in the mirror, Lieutenant," Swift said, licking his sore lip.

"I'm sure I look as bad."

Brighton sighed and rubbed a hand over his chin as he gazed out at the wreckage created by the storm. No point worrying over it—the only sane thing to do now was to make a plan. That was the only way Brighton knew how to make solid ground on which to stand in life.

"We're going to stay here for the rest of the week until the water recedes, letting the lowlands dry out. Meanwhile, we'll run patrols around this hill and check the valley below to make sure no VC tries to take advantage of the situation. For today, get dry. Get some rest too. Today, the villagers should receive clothing, food and water, okay—nothing else. In a couple of days, we'll check on the villagers again. Tell your squads."

"Yes, sir."

The two left as Nash and Stahl stared at each other. Nash waited until they were out of Brighton's earshot, before saying, "Hell of a night."

"Yeah, sure was." Stahl cleared his throat. "At least we made it to the hill in time. That was lucky."

"I'll check with you later." Nash headed to his squad position; he was eager to get back to his men.

The men of the Second Squad looked on with anticipation as Stahl approached them. Stopping near Professor, he sat, looked around, and burst into laughter—a deep, belly laugh which the men of the Second Squad hadn't heard before today.

"What the hell?" Drexler's face contorted in puzzlement. "Did you get into Swift's flask?"

"No. You guys look like wet puppies covered in mud."

The men laughed. Stahl removed his helmet and sat on it on the ground. "Okay, let's get cleaned up. Dry out the best you can. We'll sit on this hill for the rest of the week, running patrols."

The men reacted to the news with smiles.

They cheerfully talked while cleaning their equipment. Within an hour, a Huey flew overhead in the direction of the village.

Henderson looked toward the sky when he heard the rotors slowing and the sound of the pitch change in the helicopter's blades; he recognized that it was lowering to land. The thought of the child and his mother getting needed supplies pleased him, and he smiled. His grin grew as he thought about the young woman with the straight black hair that hung over her shoulders, dark eyes, and soft hands.

He spent the rest of the day cleaning his rifle and drying out his gear before being assigned to guard duty that night, but Henderson felt a little extra lift in his step doing it.

•

When he woke on the third morning, Henderson noticed it appeared like the rest of them. Using C-4, Henderson heated water for the cocoa mix—then he opened the can of fruitcake and peaches for breakfast. The familiarity felt right to Henderson, and made him believe that he was safe.

Then he noticed Drexler reading a letter. "Not the same letter, is it?"

"Yeah. Maybe I missed something, or didn't understand it."

"You didn't. Quit reading the damn letter. It's not going to change. A 'Dear John' letter is usually official. It's over."

Drexler put the letter away and dug through his rucksack. After several minutes, he produced a couple of C-ration cans for his breakfast meal. Taking his time, he opened each one and ate, all the while deep in thought. Again, Drexler retrieved the letter from his rucksack.

Henderson sipped his hot chocolate, letting his friend absorb the terrible news from his Dear John. Seeing his friend like this made him thankful that he didn't have a girlfriend at home awaiting his return. *Bitch! I hate Sandra!*

The day passed, and the sun dropped below the horizon.

Having downtime to reflect, relax, write home, and be at ease for a couple of days helped the mental attitude of the men. With their stress levels lowered, they thought about what they would do after they returned home. Most of the time, they kept their thoughts hidden, knowing it was entirely possible they wouldn't return, or would return in a body bag, covered by an American flag. Usually, saying their plans out loud made it harder to accept that they might not come true.

In a spot of fading sunlight, Henderson leaned back against his rucksack as his friends conversed around him.

Rocky was wiping the sweat from his brow. "What are you going to do when you get home?"

Professor smiled as he pondered his answer, not sure if he should speak of it. "I'll probably take some time to relax and ruminate—and go to the beach to drink a lot." A warm smile filled his face.

"Come on." Rocky diverted his gaze. "What are you really gonna do?"

"Truthfully, I know I'm going back to school to complete my education. And, while on campus, I intend to protest this unjust war. It's got to stop." Professor felt his pulse running through his veins and his heartbeat increase.

Henderson noticed Professor's agitation and decided, for the sake of peace, that it couldn't go any further. "Way to go, Rocky. Get Professor all worked up."

"Sorry, guys," Rocky shrugged his hefty shoulders. "Didn't mean to. I forgot that Professor is always so serious."

The men became quiet, wrapping poncho liners around their tired bodies for a night of sleep on the hard ground. Lighting his last cigarette of the night, Henderson sat on first guard duty.

He watched the shadows move across the hill, framing it into darkness.

No more than forty-five minutes had passed when an AK-47 was fired in the distance. Henderson heard the faint murmuring of Vietnamese voices. His body stiffened. He knew there wasn't a thing he could do but hope that none of the villagers had been killed. He couldn't help seeing the pretty face of Vinh's mother in his mind.

The rest of the night, he slept fitfully.

•

In the morning, Stahl woke the squad with authority. "On your feet. Vacation time is over. We're moving soon."

After he woke, Henderson gulped Kool-Aid while eating a pecan roll with pears for his breakfast meal. The grunts remained quiet, anticipating an active day going into the village. After he finished eating, he packed away his gear into his rucksack. A sense of eagerness surged through Henderson's body as he thought about seeing the young woman again—and, of course, her son.

"Henderson, you're on point. We're going to the ville first." Stahl tilted his head to the left, indicating for Henderson to move to the front.

"Roger. Looking forward to it." Henderson took a deep breath.

Within minutes, Brighton walked over to Henderson. "You ready?"

"Yes, LT."

"Saddle up. Move out!" Stahl's order sounded as if the squad needed to hurry.

The men of the First Platoon stood to adjust their rucksacks. Then they followed Henderson as he struggled along the partially dry trail, heading toward the village.

Slipping in several spots, Henderson eventually led the platoon to the valley floor. With a sense of dread, he discarded his usual sense of caution and quickened his pace.

As Henderson walked into the village, he saw the young boy who had made fun of him standing over a woman and sobbing. He ran to the child and grabbed him by the shoulder. Looking into his eyes, he saw deep sadness.

He turned over the body, steeling himself for what he knew he would find, and there was the face of the young woman, Mai.

"Medic!" Tears burnt his eyes as they fell. "I need a medic over here."

Doc Wheeler ran to Henderson and looked him over, checking for wounds.

Henderson shoved him away. "Not me!" He pointed at the woman on the ground. "Her."

Wheeler dropped to his knees to check the woman. The wounds in her stomach immediately reflected her fate. "She's dead." He looked up at Henderson, concerned over whether Henderson was about to have a mental breakdown.

Henderson held the boy close to him as if to protect him from the truth, saying, "No, fix her."

"Henderson, she's dead. It's too late. There's nothing I can do for her."

In a daze, Henderson stared at the platoon medic, who stood nearly six feet tall, with a slender build. With his long, black hair and acne pockmarks, he looked more like a storybook villain than a soldier. But his willingness to risk his life to save others was what defined him as an extraordinary hero in his own right. If Doc said there was nothing to be done, then logically, Henderson knew it was true.

The villagers walked from the fields surrounding the village and peered through the doorways of the remaining huts. Several of the older women approached Henderson, touching his arm. They lifted the dead woman and carried her to a hut. The young boy followed. The wailing of women echoed throughout the village.

Henderson looked around. It seemed that everywhere he gazed, there were more dead villagers. "Damn it! This isn't right!"

He searched the village, and the more he searched, the angrier he became. The VC had stolen most of the clothes, food, and water Brighton had delivered.

Furious, Brighton waved his arm in a circle, pointing around the village as he approached one of the elders. "What happened?"

The elder pointed to the west. "VC, number ten."

Brighton put his fingers to his lips and whistled to get the platoon's attention. "We're going to head west and look for the VC who did this."

Stahl was surprised. He doubted the wisdom of moving out this soon after the storm. But knowing that the lieutenant was pissed, he didn't say anything.

"Have the platoon move, with the Second Squad on point," Brighton said, clenching his jaw.

Stahl nodded and smiled at Brighton. "Move out. Henderson on point."

While walking, Henderson's shock broke, and he felt his hatred for the enemy consume him. He understood that hatred brings the reaction to kill or be killed. His hate convinced him that others would harm those he cared for, and the only course of action was to kill them first.

When Henderson saw the dead villagers, they reminded him of the parents he had lost, and his desire for a family, peace, and ordinary life. The VC terrorized these friendly people. This act had not only threatened them—and, by extension, him—but also the peaceful future he wanted. He couldn't let that happen. He had to stop them.

•

After he had walked for two hours, Henderson slowed the pace. Anticipating danger at any moment, he watched the ground and the surrounding area with each short step. He saw the tall elephant grass to his right move, as if a gentle breeze flowed through the field, but he didn't feel a breeze.

Sniffing the air—as the scent of rotting vegetables, mold, strange foods, and animals reached his sensitive nostrils—he realized he could smell Charlie. His eyes widened. "Shit! Keep your eyes open!"

Their world exploded as rounds zinged everywhere. Henderson was so close to the enemy—he could hear the metallic sound of the bullets being loaded and ejected from their AK-47s. He took cover, as close to the ground as possible.

"Ambush!"

While lying low in the grass, the VC had allowed Henderson and several other Second Squad members to walk through the kill zone. Once they passed, the enemy attacked the center of the formation, where the command group and Bravo Team were located. The VC were firing hundreds of rounds at the patrol through the elephant grass.

Henderson turned to look at the platoon as soon as, to his dismay, a bullet ripped through Gonzalez's left leg. As he fell, another round hit him in the head, sending him tumbling backward. Then, he lay motionless, covered by the thick elephant grass. At the same time, Lanier, of Bravo Team, took two rounds to the chest and crumpled to the ground without a sound. Another soldier fell hard as the VC shot him in each leg. Over the sound of weapons firing, Henderson could hear the fallen soldier screaming, "Mommy! Mommy!"

Rounds flew overhead, zipping everywhere with a snapping sound, keeping the platoon lying as flat as possible.

Within seconds, Brighton ran through two scenarios; they could either run like hell from the ambush, or attack the enemy. He understood that making an effort to get away looked impossible with the platoon in the open; the enemy would slaughter them as they ran. He needed to decide, and now. He knew they had only one way to escape.

"Return fire! Move forward by teams! Machine guns covering fire!"

Rocky shot a massive stream of 7.62 rounds from his M-60, as did a counterpart soldier from the First Squad. Elephant grass flew into the air as the two machine gunners unloaded where they thought the NVA were hiding.

"First Squad, move forward by teams!" Nash shouted, moving forward in hot pursuit of the enemy. Alpha Team moved forward roughly fifteen meters, staying low in the elephant grass, while Bravo Team provided covering fire. Then, the men of Bravo Team jumped to their feet and ran until they reached Alpha Team. Enemy rifle fire increased, bullets zinging around the soldiers as the squad attempted to advance, forcing them to remain on the ground; they couldn't advance any further.

Brighton grabbed the handset from Ledger. "Tango six, this is Tango one-six. Need Sharks at grid Bravo Sierra four-seven-eight-seven-eight-five. Over."

"Wilco, Tango one-six. Sharks at Bravo Sierra four-seven-eight-seven-eight-five. Be there in ten mikes. Over." Lyons slammed the handset down.

"Roger, Tango six. Hurry! Need help now. Out."

The cracking of AK-47s, and the zinging of the rounds cutting through the tall grass, kept the men close to the ground as they returned fire at the invisible enemy.

Stahl took control of the squad. "Alpha Team, on me!"

Crawling next to his squad leader, Drexler gazed at Stahl. "What now?"

"Follow me—we're going to flank them. Rocky and Porter, stay here."

As they slithered through the elephant grass, the men of Alpha Team crawled to Charlie's right flank. Once the four squad members were in position, Stahl issued the command, "Open fire!"

Because of the proximity of the enemy, Professor fired buckshot rounds toward Charlie, hiding in the grass, while Stahl, Henderson, and Drexler unloaded three-round burst after three-round burst from their M-16s.

As Henderson hid in the grass, sweat dripped into his eyes, causing a stinging sensation. His mouth became so dry he couldn't breathe, and his hands shook as he fired at the enemy. Recognizing the symptoms, he knew he had to concentrate on killing the enemy to conquer the fear which was gripping him.

"Mommy!" the cry echoed in the battle zone. "Mommy!"

Across the field, crawling as close to the ground as possible, Doc reached the crying soldier and immediately began treating his wounds to stop the bleeding. "It's okay. You'll be fine, Ellis."

"It hurts!"

"You'll be in a hospital in no time."

"Mommy!"

"Be quiet!" Grass flew about them as the enemy pinpointed their position.

Enemy mortar fire echoed across the field, and the grunts burrowed deeper into the hard-packed dirt; they didn't leave any part of their body exposed.

Twenty meters ahead of the platoon, three mortar rounds exploded, one after another, throwing dirt and grass high into the air and sending shrapnel flying over their hidden bodies.

"Pull back! Pull back!" Brighton inched backward. "Pull back now!"

Doc and Swift grabbed Ellis's arms and dragged him as they crawled toward the other side of the field. Ellis still screamed in pain, "Mommy!"

M-60s firing, the platoon moved away from the enemy toward the tree line, approximately two hundred meters away.

Seeing the American unit withdrawing, the NVA opened fire with another barrage of small-arms fire and renewed confidence. Two more mortar rounds exploded, sending shrapnel over the platoon as they crawled away from the advancing enemy, and more incoming mortar rounds. As the platoon withdrew, Rocky jumped to his feet and sprayed 7.62 rounds toward the enemy. Porter stood alongside him, feeding belt after belt into the M-60.

As Stahl passed his gunner, he slapped him on the back. "Get going!"

Rocky and Porter dropped to the ground and crawled toward the tree line with the rest of the platoon.

Henderson crept alongside Drexler, staying as close to the earth as possible as he slithered through the elephant grass, using his legs to push and arms to pull himself along the ground. His heart pounded so hard that he could feel his temples throbbing. As he moved the thick grass out of his way to clear a path, the sharp blades cut his hands and arms. It looked as if the tree line was a hundred miles away, with no chance to reach its safety.

Crack! Crack! AK-47 rounds dug into the earth next to Henderson.

Then he heard the *Thump! Thump!* of enemy mortar and, within seconds, the ground shook, hot shrapnel flying overhead.

Henderson crawled faster for the tree line. On his elbows and knees, he inched forward as fast as he could move, knowing that he was going to die today. His rucksack rocked from side to side on his back, slowing him down as he crawled. The hard ground pushed back into his knees and elbows, drawing blood. He attempted to crawl faster. Reaching the safety of the jungle became his only purpose.

Then, from out of nowhere, the Shark helicopter gunship fired on the mortar position, four hundred meters away from the platoon. As the pilot flew closer to the enemy location, the Shark's miniguns, with their 2.75 rockets, took on the mortar. They destroyed it, killing the crew in minutes. The pilot then turned his attention to finding the advancing NVA. He flew pass after pass, firing into the field in front of the platoon.

After crawling for fifteen minutes, the grunts reached the edge of the jungle, which provided cover and concealment. Now they were in the forest. The enemy slowed its pursuit of the First Platoon as the Shark continued to search for them, its miniguns mowing down the elephant grass, as if cutting the lawn on a Saturday morning.

When they regrouped, Brighton assigned positions, telling his men to prepare to engage the enemy with all that they had.

As the sun dropped behind the mountains to the west, another gunship appeared, firing their miniguns and forty-millimeter grenades into the suspected enemy positions. While they made one run after another, the two gunships tore the earth apart in front of the platoon.

The NVA were no longer firing at the men concealed in the jungle's growth. As the sunlight faded, the VC vanished into the night.

•

"Lieutenant, are you leaving Lanier and Gonzalez?"

"We'll get them in the morning." Brighton nodded with certainty.

Swift clenched his jaw. "We can't leave them there."

"We have no choice—"

"The hell with that!" But Swift understood the decision; going to find them would cause more casualties. "Sorry, LT; you're right."

"Don't worry about it." Brighton thought only of the men he had lost in the last couple of days.

At nightfall, Brighton called off the two gunships as the enemy quit attacking the platoon. It appeared that they had withdrawn from the area.

Moving along the line of men, Brighton made eye contact with each soldier. "Stay alert for a counterattack. You can rest, but alternate with the man next to you to sleep or stay awake. Your goal is to stay alive and live another day in this hellhole."

Henderson heard Brighton make two radio transmissions during the night. The first was to arrange for two armored personnel carriers to meet at their position, after daybreak—the second was to have a dustoff on standby, waiting for him to give the go-ahead. Henderson figured that the lieutenant's priorities were to get Ellis to the hospital, then find the bodies of Gonzalez and Lanier.

At times, a soft moan and a call echoed in the quiet night, *"Mommy..."*

•

At dawn, the platoon woke to the sounds of armored personnel carriers approaching from the rear of their position. Within several minutes, two tracks pulled in behind the platoon. Brighton waved a greeting as he walked toward the lead APC to talk to the track commander.

APCs ran on tank-like tracks, and were armored with light-weight aluminum which protected the occupants from small-arms rounds, but not armor-piercing rounds or RPGs. They came equipped with a heavy, fifty-caliber Browning machine gun and two M-60 machine guns—enough firepower to support the infantry soldiers on the ground.

As well as its driver, track commander, and two M-60 gunners, the M113 APC could carry eleven infantry troops. Powered by a V-6 two-stroke diesel engine and driving on open, flat terrain, an APC could reach a speed of forty miles per hour, and could float on water at four. It could break through hedgerows with dense small trees, brush, and elephant grass.

Getting the platoon ready, Swift moved around the perimeter, telling the men to prepare to head out.

Then he hiked into the clearing, to the front of their positions, and threw a yellow smoke grenade.

Whop! Whop! Whop! The blades of the helicopter slapped the air as it approached.

Guiding the Huey to a safe landing area, Swift signaled the pilot when he landed. Doc and several platoon members carried Ellis to the dustoff and slid him onto a litter.

Ellis grabbed Doc's hand. "Doc, thank you."

"We'll visit you at the hospital."

Once loaded, the pilot took off for Chu Lai.

When Brighton returned, he called over his NCOs.

"Put both squads in a line formation to the front of the APCs. We'll sweep through the field to locate Gonzalez and Lanier. Shoot anything moving."

"Yes, sir."

They returned to their squad positions to get ready to move out.

Stahl addressed the squad. "Saddle up. Get in a line formation. Bravo Team on the right, with Alpha Team on the left."

The Second Squad stood at the edge of the tall grass, anxious to return to the field to find their brothers. The platoon moved forward with uncertain steps, knowing that the enemy could open fire at any time. Approaching the area where the VC killed the two men of the Second Squad, Henderson scanned everywhere.

"They're not here."

Brighton ran over to Henderson. "Damn."

Henderson could only shake his head.

Brighton's orders were clear. "Keep sweeping forward!"

Henderson walked another two hundred meters.

"I found them!"

Then, he turned his head away, a sob rising in his throat, and anger in his heart. "What the fuck?"

The sight of the bodies of his two brothers made him sick to the stomach; the fallen men lay naked and mutilated.

The rest of the platoon bolted over to Henderson, then stopped when they saw Gonzalez and Lanier. Doc knelt to offer medical assistance, but couldn't control himself. He turned his head and heaved until his stomach emptied.

Brighton stood over the bodies, unable to hold the anger while he cried. He wiped the tears away. "Ledger!"

Running to the lieutenant, Ledger handed him the handset.

"Tango six, this is Tango one-six. Over."

"Roger, Tango one-six. Over." Lyons's voice seemed to tremble.

"Need medevac. Two KIAs. Over."

"Roger. You need anything else? Over."

"Tango six, check out the two KIAs when they get there. Over."

"Wilco, Tango one-six. Out."

Brighton dropped the handset, letting it dangle from the curled cord attached to the radio.

Henderson and Drexler covered the two dead team members with ponchos. Without speaking, the platoon guarded their brothers while they waited for the dustoff.

Dazed, Henderson stood off to the side. *I hope one of those bastards comes back. I'll kill them where they stand.*

After Stahl popped red smoke, he raised his M-16 over his head and guided the dustoff to the landing zone. Then the squad members carried Gonzalez and Lanier to the waiting Huey. They gently slid the two lifeless bodies onto litters and gathered around the open door. Silently, they said their last goodbye to their brothers. The helicopter lifted and flew back to Bronco.

No one in the platoon ever talked about what they saw when they found Gonzalez and Lanier. It was a memory Henderson wanted to hide forever, but he knew that it would haunt him for the rest of his life. He thought it was probably best that they were dead before the NVA got to them, but he would never know for sure.

•

"Tango one-six, this is Tango six. Over." Lyons was tapping his foot as he waited for the return transmission.

Brighton quickly grabbed the handset. "Go ahead, Tango six. Over."

Watching the lieutenant talk on the radio, Henderson narrowed his brow and pursed his lips. *I wonder what he's discussing with the company commander.* He nodded toward Drexler. "I really hope he's calling in a B-fifty-two airstrike on the bastards!"

"That sounds good to me." Drexler crossed his arms over his chest. The rest of the squad nodded their approval.

"Sergeants Stahl and Nash, on me." Brighton waited for them to respond.

Only twenty feet away, the two squad leaders stood and walked to where the lieutenant sat with Swift. "Yes, Lieutenant?" Stahl made fierce eye contact with Brighton to let him know he was ready for action.

Brighton's gaze matched Stahl's. "Move your squads to the tree line—we'll have chow there. After we eat, we're going to the ville. Supplies are being flown in for the villagers again, but this time we'll make sure they get them. Then, after we unload the supply choppers, we'll use them to fly us east, to the beach. The company commander said there had been enemy movement in the area. Intelligence has it that the VC has been unloading junks with supplies. He wants us to check." He paused to let the information sink in. "Any questions?"

"No, sir!" the two NCOs responded in unison.

"Sergeant Swift, tell the track commander they are released; they can return to their unit."

"Wilco!" Swift hurried over to the two idling APCs.

CHAPTER 7

BEACH ON THE
SOUTH CHINA SEA

Once the platoon moved into the tree line, Henderson dropped his rucksack and sat. He wasn't hungry, but he understood that he needed to eat. The whole platoon sat in silence, eating. After Henderson ate, he lit a cigarette and leaned back against his rucksack, gazing at the sky while enjoying his smoke. He took a drag and watched the smoke filter upward.

The sky is beautiful in this hellhole.

"Saddle up! Move out!" Stahl's orders seemed to reverberate through the perimeter.

Second Squad readied for the hike to the village.

Henderson squashed the cigarette into the dirt. *I can't even finish a smoke around here!* After sliding into the straps of the rucksack, Henderson shifted the weight on his back. He then strolled to the front of the platoon and stepped from the jungle growth toward the ville. The two squads followed.

As he took short, hesitant steps, Henderson's breathing became heavy. That poor woman and her son.

Why did she have to die? She was nice. She had the softest hands.

His pulse rate increased with each step as he recalled the last memory of Mai, lying on the ground in a pool of blood.

I hope the old woman takes good care of Vinh.

He increased the pace.

In less than two hours, Henderson approached the edge of the ville. The first thing he saw was new huts. Chickens ran throughout the trails as if their heads had been chopped off, and the villagers were carrying out their daily tasks as if nothing had ever happened. A frown creased Henderson's forehead. *How can this be?*

Drexler stopped alongside Henderson, as he was shaking his head. "Everything looks normal."

"I don't get it. A typhoon swept their village away, the VC killed some of them and took what little food and supplies they had, and here they are, working away. Shit! Working, like a normal day."

"They're strong people."

"They haven't even had time to mourn the deaths of the other villagers." Henderson waved his hand, pointing at the people around him.

"There's no time for grieving during war."

"I guess you're right. It still doesn't seem fair."

"There is nothing fair in this Godforsaken place. Just keep doing your job and stay alive." Drexler lowered his eyes.

After entering the ville, Brighton found an elder, with hopes of communicating the plan to the villagers. The old man was roughly seventy-five years old, with a long, thin, gray beard, which accentuated the deep wrinkles on his dark face. He wore black pajamas and a conical hat that covered his bald head.

Brighton used a stick to draw on the ground while speaking in broken Vietnamese. He explained that the village would receive supplies.

As he finished talking, as if on cue, the supply helicopters approached the ville. Turning to face the villagers, the elder barked orders to them.

The squad looked to the skies at the approaching helicopters. The three Hueys flew overhead, then maintained their position. Without being told, the squad covered the area to protect the landing zone, while Stahl stood in the center of the small field, releasing yellow smoke into the sky to guide the helicopters to a safe landing.

Once landed, the crew of each Huey unloaded water, food, and bundles of clothing onto the ground. The platoon members gathered what they could carry and strolled to the village, dropping the supplies next to what remained of a community building. The villagers ran over to the helicopter to help carry the much-needed supplies.

As he dropped off several bags of rice, Henderson kept glancing around at what the storm had left of the village, hoping to get a glimpse of the young boy.

Then he felt a hand touch his arm, and turned to see an old woman staring at him. He squinted in puzzlement. "What's wrong?"

Tears filled her eyes. "VC *lấy con trai.*"

Henderson knew what that meant; the VC had taken Vinh.

Henderson felt a rush of sadness for the boy, and the world at large. His heart weighed heavy, and he knew he couldn't help Vinh. He grabbed the woman's gnarled, rough hand and squeezed it. She bowed. Stooped over, she shuffled with short steps into the village. He stared at her as she left, shaking his head.

I hope I don't have to fight that boy one day.

Swift kept a watchful eye on the unloading effort. When he noticed that the helicopters had been cleared out, he did a few checks, then signaled to the platoon with a raised hand. "Time to go. Board the Hueys!"

The platoon loaded onto the three waiting helicopters. Once boarded, the choppers lifted, flying over the same hill which had kept them safe from the typhoon.

A weary mix of relief and fear spread amongst the soldiers, each with a different outcome scenario playing out in their minds. They recognized that the situation they were entering wasn't likely to be much better, and not one of them deluded themselves otherwise as they headed east toward the sea.

Henderson closed his eyes. *Goodbye, Mia and Vinh. You both deserve better than this.* A single tear rolled down his left cheek.

Damn this war!

Once they reached the sea, the helicopters banked right to the south and followed the coastline.

From the open door, Henderson admired the white-sand landscape and clear, blue-green water. It reminded him of Ocean Isle Beach, where he went on family trips during the summer—those days were long ago. He found it odd that the world was as visually stunning now as it had been when he was an innocent child who believed that the world held only lovely things.

The Hueys swung to the right and landed in an area concealed by palm trees and vegetation, one hundred meters from the beach. The men of the First Platoon leapt from the helicopters and moved quickly into the overgrowth for concealment, each instinctively seeking to get out of sight without the need for direction. Once the platoon had safely dismounted, the three helicopters lifted and flew to Bronco.

After the noise of the retreating aircraft faded, silence fell over the men.

Brighton strode over to Stahl. "Move the platoon two hundred meters south where there's a small clearing. We'll set up our positions there until night."

"Okay, LT." Stahl nodded, then looked over at the men in his charge. "Henderson, take point; we're moving south."

"Moving, Sarge?"

Stahl flashed an impatient glance toward Henderson. "Move out!"

Henderson's boots sunk over his ankle into the superfine sand as he took slow strides toward the clearing. With the hot sun reflecting off of the white beach, his uniform quickly soaked through with sweat. "This heat feels like an oven." No one in the platoon responded as they trudged forward.

The platoon arrived at the clearing twenty minutes later.

Brighton quickly scanned the area. "We'll stay here, but stay alert. Everything might look calm and nonthreatening, but you never know when a gook will sneak in and kill you. Your assignments will be forthcoming."

Dropping his rucksack, Henderson prepared his spot in the perimeter next to Drexler. "The ocean looks beautiful, doesn't it?" Henderson said, pointing to the ocean. "Things could be worse."

Unamused, Drexler dropped his helmet and sat on it, facing the water. He pulled out the first C-ration he touched and began eating. "Eddie, you better get something to eat. You know how Stahl feels about that."

Henderson flopped down next to his rucksack and dug for his chicken and noodle C-ration.

As they faced the ocean, Henderson and Drexler ate their meal. The small, white-capped waves ran toward the beach, and the cool breeze blew across their faces. Drexler wiped the sweat from his brow. "This breeze feels fantastic."

"I agree." Henderson smiled as he took a deep breath. "In the baking sun, the water looks more than inviting, don't you think?"

"I agree with you on that, for sure."

Henderson looked over his shoulder. "Sergeant Stahl, can we go swimming? It's hot as hell out here."

"I don't know." Stahl eyed the water and the surrounding area. It had been a tough few days, and he knew his men could benefit from some relaxation, but not if it got them killed. "I don't see any immediate threat; go ahead. Have Alpha Team go into the water, while Bravo Team pulls security. Switch after twenty minutes. Return in forty."

The squad members smiled, stripping off their sweat-soaked, stinking uniforms, and Alpha Team bolted toward the beach with weapons and bandoliers in their hands. Bravo Team secured the swimming area, while Alpha Team swam and played like a bunch of teenagers. Professor even brought a bar of soap, which he shared. After twenty minutes, as agreed, Bravo Team dashed into the water while Alpha Team guarded them.

Stahl sat smoking a cigarette, using the quiet time with his men elsewhere. It was the one indulgence he would allow himself before getting down to the task at hand. Once he had finished with his cigarette, he retrieved the writing material from his rucksack and penned a letter.

"Dear Mr. and Mrs. Lanier,
I'm Bob's squad leader, Terry Stahl.
I know the army has informed you of his death, but I wanted to let you know what kind of man and soldier he became.
On the day Bob died, he was a hero…"

When finished, he folded the letter and stuffed it into an envelope.

Now Gonzalez.

He paused, realizing that the deceased soldier didn't have any family members or loved ones to write to about his death.

Stahl watched his squad walk along the beach toward the vegetation which concealed the platoon. They continued to laugh and horseplay with one another, none wanting to return to being a soldier and having to witness so much horror and death. A huge smile crossed his face as he waited for the teams to return.

Before the squad got to the position, he stuffed his paper and pen back into his rucksack.

"Get dressed. I'll brief you on the mission."

As they dressed, the chatter and laughter slowly faded.

After the last man finished dressing, they sat. Stahl, still with a smile on his face, directed his full attention at his squad. He couldn't hide the happiness he had felt as he watched his men escape from the war for forty minutes. But now it was back to business.

"Listen up! After dark, we're going to establish an ambush in a cove five hundred meters from here. S-two reported that the VC are bringing in weapons and supplies by boat, and the cove is where they meet. Our job is to stop the VC from being resupplied."

Drexler raised his hand. "So, how are we going to do that?"

"The platoon forms on the north side of the cove. The VC with the boats will dock against the bank of the inlet. The enemy receiving the supplies will come from the south."

"Sarge, how do you know those specifics?" Professor pursed his lips.

"I'm telling you what the lieutenant reported from S-two; they have the intel to support the mission. Any more questions?"

Porter raised his hand. His goofy smile returned.

The squad broke into laughter. Stahl shook his head, ignoring Porter. "Henderson, you're on point."

After yet another meal of chicken and Kool-Aid, in the shade of the thick palms, Henderson got his head straight for the mission. It was another nighttime mission—an undertaking he didn't enjoy.

The squad packed their rucksacks. They made sure that the straps were tight and their tools of war didn't rattle. Henderson checked his weapon by testing the selector switch, and a round was seated in the chamber. He ensured that the magazine had a tight fit in the housing. The rest of the platoon prepared their gear and weapon too.

As darkness swept across the beach, Brighton stood up. "Move out!"

Henderson headed south, taking slow steps and gauging his next, the light of the moon hitting the white sand, illuminating a path to their destination. The rest of the platoon followed Henderson in a single file, each keeping the silhouette to their front in full view. Occasionally, the gear rattled, or the sharp crack of a breaking twig echoed through the vegetation as they walked.

Professor jumped at every sound. Something about watching his friends die in the past few days had brought his brother to the surface of his mind. *Are these the same sounds my brother heard before he died?* He would never know the answer, but that didn't dismiss the question.

Henderson navigated around palm trees and scrub brush no higher than his knees. It was effortless for him to walk this trail, compared to the times he had humped through hedgerows, over hills, and around rice paddies. The waves hitting the shoreline brought back his memories of summer vacations as a young boy.

Once the squad arrived at the cove, with lush, green vegetation covering the three sides, they halted their advancement. The tall trees bent toward the center of the body of water, concealing the channel from the sky. The cove measured roughly thirty meters in width, with three hundred meters from the shoreline to the open sea—large enough for a junk to enter.

Henderson smiled. "Well, this seems refreshing."

He paused for a moment as he soaked in the scents from the seawater and the blooming flowers on the banks. Gentle waves splashed against the shore, creating a relaxing sound, and the air beneath the canopy of trees seemed as if an air conditioner controlled the temperature. He took in a deep breath, admiring the scenery illuminated by the moonlight. It felt as if he had walked into the Garden of Eden.

Brighton broke Henderson's hypnotic state by barking orders. "Listen up! Set up a perimeter along the bank. Rocky, take your gun and cover the two trails entering the cove's location from the south. First Squad covers the entrance of the inlet. Any questions? Good. Get in your positions, now."

The team members responded quickly and covered the territory of their ambush positions; everyone relied on each other for safety.

As Henderson removed his rucksack, he lowered it slowly to the ground. He took up a firing position behind the pack, then settled in for the long night.

As he lay there, Henderson listened to the night, soaking in each sound: the gentle breeze rustling the tree limbs; the waves breaking on the beach; the tide, pulling and pushing the water against the cove; and the mosquitoes buzzing around his head. He became accustomed to natural sounds. Henderson knew that if he heard any other kind, it could be the enemy approaching.

Henderson glanced at the illuminated dial on his watch, 0100 hours.

The men became restless as they waited to ambush the enemy's supply run.

Splash. Splash.

The enemy's paddles hit the water, sending Henderson into full alert mode. Chattering in Vietnamese alerted the platoon members; the grunts tensed and postured themselves in a firing position. No one made a sound as they placed their fingers on the triggers, waiting for the boat to dock in the cove.

Henderson used his right thumb to slide his weapon's selector switch from safe to the semi-automatic position. The sound of metal on metal and twigs snapping drifted toward him from the southern trail.

A line of eight VC emerged from the darkness as the bow of a junk docked against the inlet bank, out of his view.

Henderson touched Drexler's shoulder.

Drexler slid the selector switch of his M-16 to semi-automatic and maintained his position. One wrong move—a sneeze, a cough—would alert the enemy. No one moved.

Unaware that the Americans lay in ambush, four enemy soldiers stood on the bow of the junk, huddled together, smoking, laughing, and talking as the boat slowly glided into the cove. The VC on the trail called out to the soldiers on the boat as they spoke to each other in low voices. As the enemy on the path approached the junk, their conversation grew louder; their laughter agitated the waiting American soldiers.

Drexler's finger twitched on the trigger. Since receiving that letter, he had wanted nothing more than to kill something—an urge he hadn't wished to acknowledge. Now that time was closing in, his stomach tightened.

As the two enemy forces met to hand over the weapons and food, Henderson became anxious to start shooting at them, but he knew he had to wait for the order to fire. The more the enemy conversed, the more unbearable it became for Henderson not to pull the trigger.

Which one of you gutted Gonzales and Lanier? Now it's payback time!

But orders were orders.

Still, his patience weakened, and he raised his rifle, aiming at the first enemy soldier walking along the trail toward the boat.

Brighton gave the order in a low whisper, but everyone in the squad heard it. "Fire!"

Rocky opened fire on the VC on the trail, and another soldier fired at the soldiers on the boat. At the same time, the platoon members fired at all the VC on the trail and the boat. The enemy soldiers on the path fell, one after another, as rounds blasted from the platoon, hitting each gook many times. Bodies flew off of the junk, hitting the water with a loud splash.

Shooting the first man on the trail, Henderson moved his aiming point to the next in line, but was unable to shoot him. Rocky had already mown down the line of VC as if they were bowling pins.

As one enemy soldier ran for cover, Drexler aimed and squeezed the trigger three times. The soldier jerked, flying forward, and hit the ground face first, sliding for six feet before coming to a stop.

As they fired, the squad members exacted their revenge, chanting. "For Gonzalez! For Lanier!" The chant came each time a soldier pulled the trigger of his weapon.

Finally, after ten minutes, stillness drifted across the cove. There were no more VC to kill, so the men stopped firing. They lay in their firing positions for a while to make sure.

They were breathing hard, as if having run a five-mile race, as each watched the front, with their eyes wide and their hearts full of revenge. The enemy hadn't gotten off a shot.

Brighton broke the silence. "Sergeant Stahl, take a team to check the trail. Sergeant Nash, take a team to check the boat."

Stahl and Nash stood. "Okay, LT."

Stahl straightened his helmet. "Alpha Team, with me. Move out!" He headed toward the trail as Alpha Team fell into line behind him.

"Bravo Team, on me." Nash belched as he rubbed his stomach. Nausea had momentarily overtaken him because of the bloody battle, but he did his best not to let it show.

Henderson walked along the trail and stopped to check out a dead VC, quickly retrieving the gook's weapon and ammunition. Following his lead, the rest of the team did the same with the seven other dead enemy soldiers.

As he moved from one dead VC to another, Professor looked into their eyes, searching for his brother's killer; each time, he shook his head and moved on to the next dead soldier. "I'll find the bastard."

As Drexler surveyed the dead, he tripped on a rock, watching as a small snake slithered away. "Looks like we got 'em."

"Bastards never got off a shot." Henderson nodded confidently.

After they boarded the boat, Nash and his men gathered the enemy's weapons and ammunition. Nash waved at Brighton. "LT, we need help unloading."

"Form a line to unload the boat." Brighton pointed to a location. "Stack it over there." The platoon quickly stored the captured supplies.

Brighton scanned the area for Ledger. "Ledger, get over here."

"Yes, LT." With a quick stride, Ledger walked over to the lieutenant's location and handed him the handset.

"Tango six, this is Tango one-six. Over." Brighton gawked at the dead soldiers as he waited for Lyon's response.

"Roger, Tango one-six. Over."

As the lieutenant made arrangements to have the supplies transported, Henderson and Drexler sat next to their rucksacks, enjoying a can of pound cake and drinking water. Stahl approached.

"Henderson, I'm going back to the trail. Do you want to come?"

"Why are you going back, Sarge? We got all the weapons."

"He's not dead until he's dead."

"Sarge, I told you—"

"You will someday."

Stahl turned away from Henderson and walked south along the trail. After five minutes, the crack of a rifle firing echoed from the trail. Henderson rolled his eyes. "I guess he's dead now."

That night, Henderson fell asleep staring into the night sky. Professor stayed awake to pull guard as the squads hunkered down for the night.

•

As the sun climbed above the horizon over the South China Sea, the soldiers on guard woke the rest of the platoon. They ate breakfast and heated coffee or hot chocolate.

Watching the sun rising over the South China Sea, Henderson stared in amazement at the beauty, and admired the colors the sun created as its light glimmered across the water.

Sitting next to Drexler, he lit his first cigarette and inhaled deeply. He released the smoke, still hypnotized by the scene the rising sun created. With his thoughts returning to his family summer vacations, Henderson sighed. "How many days left?"

"Two hundred and forty-eight."

"Damn, a lifetime."

"Yep. *Boo-coo* days to go."

Brighton called his NCOs over. "At zero-eight-hundred, a Navy boat is pulling into the cove. We'll transfer the captured supplies and weapons to their boat. Have one team from each squad help them load it. When you finish, destroy the junk in the cove."

The three NCOs nodded. "Yes, sir."

"Great work last night." Brighton flashed a congratulatory smile. "We captured two rocket-propelled grenades, twenty-five AK-forty-sevens, and one fifty-one caliber machine gun, with a lot of ammunition; many bags of rice too. Hell, we killed eight VC on the trail, with another four on the boat. A good night's work. Share this with your squads." Brighton paused, then reflected. "Gonzalez and Lanier would be proud of you guys." The NCOs remained silent, not wanting to let go of the moment.

Interrupting the quiet, Swift exhaled. "Anything else, Lieutenant?" His hand moved to the flask at his belt, though he knew he wouldn't get in a drink anytime soon. The thoughts of those poor, lost boys made him want some contact with his numbing agent.

"Yes, I received word that we're going to the same ville by the river. Sergeant Stahl, when we're ready your squad takes point— move us to the clearing where we landed yesterday. There will be three choppers, so we'll load the same as usual. Second Squad takes first chopper."

Stahl returned to the squad to address them and give the order to move out. "We're going to the ville. It looks like Intel is reporting more VC activity."

"Great, I'd like to check on them." Henderson smiled, hoping all were safe. Still his heart ached, knowing that the enemy had kidnapped the boy.

"You'll get the chance. The Hueys should be here in two hours, and we're on the first one. Henderson takes point. Head to the LZ we used to get here. We're moving right after the Navy arrives."

Soon, the sound of diesel engines purred to Henderson's ears as two river patrol boats sped toward the cove.

Henderson stood. "LT, boat coming!"

The platoon gathered around the inlet and observed the boat entering the cove as the pilot throttled down the engine. The second boat remained in the sea, protecting the entrance. Steering the first boat, the pilot expertly drifted into the channel and inched the boat alongside the junk.

Two sailors moved to the bow of the vessel. One tossed a rope as it touched the bank, while the other slid a gangplank off of the bow to the ground. Grabbing the line, Rocky and Porter held the boat steady against the bank.

Henderson watched as a tall, slender man stepped off of the boat, carrying himself with authority and confidence. Once he was on the ground, Brighton greeted him with a smile. "Welcome to our beach."

"Good morning, Lieutenant. I'm the skipper, First Class Petty Officer Hazleton. I hear you got some cargo for me."

Brighton pointed to the supply area. "Yes, we do—it's behind those trees. We'll help you load. Henderson, lead the way."

"Thanks. Let's get her done." Hazleton strode quickly to where Brighton had pointed, not wanting to waste a minute.

With the men of the First Platoon and the four sailors loading the weapons, ammunition, and rice, it took no time to get the captured goods on board. Two sailors secured the cargo, and when finished they stood on deck, waiting for their skipper.

Hazleton waved at Brighton. "Thanks for the excellent work, Lieutenant. We'll get this stuff inventoried and turned in when we get to firebase Charlie Brown."

"Thanks. Have a safe trip."

After the sailors slid the gangplank onto the deck, the boat slowly backed into the sea. Once in open water, Hazelton gunned the dual diesel engines, driving the river patrol boat south, with the second boat following along the coastline. Diesel smoke and fumes trailed behind them.

Brighton gazed at Rocky. "Rocky and Michaels, bring your guns."

Both soldiers strolled over to the platoon leader, each carrying an M-60 with a one-hundred-round belt of ammo twisted around its barrel. They stopped next to the lieutenant.

"Sink the junk."

Each gunner lowered his M-60 at the junk, allowing the ammo belt to dangle from the top of the gun. With Porter feeding the belt for Rocky, and Reeves for Michaels, they fired in three-round bursts. They raked the boat from bow to stern, below the waterline. The junk listed to the right, then slipped into the deep water of the cove.

Brighton watched the junk sink, claiming the small victory. "Ceasefire."

Both gunners released the triggers of their machine guns.

As the boat sank to the bottom of the cove, the gurgling of water resonated across the inlet. The First Platoon stood mesmerized as they watched the boat slide under the water until no longer in sight, then a great celebratory roar of excitement came from the men.

Brighton clenched his jaw, knowing that the morale of the platoon had lifted a little.

"Henderson, take us to the LZ."

GOING BACK TO THE VILLE

As the three Hueys' skids settled on the field, the men of the First Platoon jumped to the ground and ran to a hedgerow at the front of the village to provide cover for the helicopters. After the grunts unloaded, the choppers were in the air.

Henderson stood to adjust his rucksack, then started, with long strides, along the well-worn trail to the village.

Several dogs barked as they reached the entrance to the village, which caught Henderson's attention. He knew these dogs weren't always trained, and getting bitten by a villager's dog seemed like a disgraceful way to end up with the medics. He would never live it down; the "little guy" getting taken out by a dog! Still, after he passed the first couple of hooches, the mongrels vanished.

Smiling, he observed that the reconstruction of huts and animal pens had continued. Villagers had used C-ration cardboard for walls on several of the dwellings. A pig stopped in front of him, snorted, then sped off to the other end of the ville. Hearing Vietnamese voices, he motioned for the platoon to move on through after making sure that they were friendlies.

When Brighton walked by, Henderson heard the radio transmission. "Tango one-six, this is Tango six. Over."

"Go ahead, Tango six. Over." Brighton walked toward the community building as two small, light-brown dogs emerged from the shadows, yapping at his heels. Brighton barely registered the dogs. They seemed to him more like gnats buzzing in the background.

As Henderson watched the lieutenant, he removed a Marlboro from his C-ration four-pack, lit it, and sucked in the smoke. Then he took another long drag, savoring the taste.

A small hand tugged on his shirt, and he looked down. A huge smile crossed his lips as he gazed at the face of Vinh—the young boy from the typhoon. He dropped his cigarette and swooped Vinh into his arms, giving the boy a bear hug.

Finally, he squatted and set Vinh back on the ground. As he looked at the boy, tears welled in his eyes. Vinh grinned and wiped Henderson's tear away with his finger. A feeling of relief surged over Henderson as he drew a deep breath.

The boy picked up the lit cigarette, took a drag and exhaled, then handed it back to Henderson. With the cigarette back dangling from his smiling lips, Henderson playfully ruffled the boy's dark hair.

The old woman who had told Henderson about the VC abducting Vinh flashed a toothless smile and nodded her approval at Henderson. Her lips were stained black.

He touched her shoulder. "*Cảm ơn bạn.*" Somehow, saying thank you in her native language didn't seem like enough for the boy's safety.

Drexler strode toward Henderson. "Hey, is he the same boy?"

"He is; he must have escaped."

"That's fortunate for him." Drexler was reasonably confident that Henderson knew how these things went, but his friend still seemed to be getting very attached to this boy. "They'll come back for him, you know?"

"I know." Henderson watched as the little boy and the old woman shuffled away. He knew Drexler was right, but he could still hope for a better life for the kid. "Shit, I wish things were different for this kid."

"Glad to see your head's still in the game. Getting attached isn't the wisest thing you can do; you must distance yourself."

"Who are you to preach?"

"I'm someone who has been there and done that. Come on, let's go over to Sergeant Stahl and see what's happening."

"After you, soldier," Henderson said, extending his hand in the direction of Stahl.

As they strolled toward their squad leader, Drexler put his arm around his friend's shoulder. "I'm glad that Vinh is back to his village, despite what I said."

"At least I know he's safe, for now."

Stahl briskly strode into the community building. "Second Squad, over here." His head pounded from lack of sleep, but already the worries rolling around inside told him that he wouldn't sleep well that night. "We're staying in the village tonight. Intel expects the VC are en route to raid the village again. After we eat chow, I'll post the guard positions running along the north side of the ville. Any questions?"

Porter raised his hand.

"Not now, Porter."

Porter lowered his hand as a frown of rejection creased his forehead.

No one had any questions, for which Stahl was thankful. He retreated to the side of the room to eat and to try to calm his growing headache.

Henderson and Drexler went to the old woman's hooch and sat on the front porch. They watched the villagers go on with their daily routine as they repaired their damaged huts, farmed the field, separated the rice from the straw, took care of animals, and tended to one another.

After an hour, the old woman peeked through the doorway and motioned for the two soldiers to come inside. In the center of the large room, a pot was set over an open firepit as a strange aroma drifted from its boiling contents. She gestured for them to sit on the floor, then the old woman poured soup from the pot into wooden bowls, handing one to Henderson and another to Drexler. After serving her guests, she poured a serving for the boy, then for herself.

Henderson stuck his nose close to the floating objects, but couldn't detect what the smells were. With his index finger, he poked at the grayish-colored meat. *Definitely not chicken noodle.* He looked at her with a quizzical expression.

The old woman smiled. "*Chó.*" She motioned for the men to eat. "*Chó.*"

Henderson shrugged his shoulders. "I don't know what that means."

Vinh acted like a dog. "*Woof, woof!*"

Henderson's eyes widened as he gagged. The boy laughed at his reaction.

"*Chó.*" The woman motioned for them to eat.

"*Woof, woof!*" The boy slurped his soup.

Drexler made a choking sound. The soldiers stared at each other in disbelief and attempted to smile as they nodded a thank you, acting as if they'd had the dish before. As Henderson slurped the last of the soup, the old woman offered to refill his bowl.

"No, thank you. I've had enough." One bowl of dog soup was plenty for him.

Drexler swallowed a mouthful of soup. "Henderson, it's not so bad if you don't think about what you're eating. It beats eating C-rations daily." He swallowed another mouthful as he glanced around the hut. "These poor people. Losing my wife seems like nothing to this." Henderson remained silent.

After Henderson and Drexler finished their soup, they stood and bowed to the old woman. Henderson smiled and nodded. "Thank you for sharing."

The woman nodded back.

Drexler and Henderson returned to the porch, where the young boy followed them and sat between the two soldiers. Henderson lit a cigarette, took a drag, and offered the smoke to the boy, who happily accepted it. Removing a second cigarette, Henderson lit it, then they sat together, enjoying the smoke.

Drexler suddenly cleared his throat, as if he were gagging. "What did you think of the soup?"

Henderson took a drag from his cigarette. "Thought it was okay, but I tried not to think about where the meat came from."

"*Woof, woof!*"

Both men's eyes darted toward the young boy. Henderson scruffed the boy's hair.

"What did you think of it?"

"I thought it tasted like chicken." Drexler paused. "I haven't had a home-cooked meal in a long time. I guess with Sandra divorcing me—I won't again for a long time."

Stahl strode over toward Henderson and Drexler.

Henderson quickly stood and threw his cigarette to the ground. "What's going on, Sarge?"

"You two stay at this hooch tonight. Keep inside. The rest of the squad members are at the huts to your right. Rocky is with Porter, guarding the trail. The First Squad is on the other side of the village. Hopefully, we'll have a quiet night."

"Sure, you got it, Sarge." Drexler belched.

Stahl walked away as he rubbed his temples. Henderson sat back down next to the young boy.

As Henderson lit a cigarette, the old woman came out to the porch. He gazed at her. "Ma'am, can we sleep here tonight? Would that be too much to ask?"

The woman frowned, not understanding the questions.

Henderson pointed to her hooch and held his hands against his head, as if in a sleeping position; he pretended to snore. "Can we sleep here?"

She nodded her head in affirmation. "*Vâng.*"

The boy displayed a broad smile. "GI sleep here; keep safe."

Henderson tapped Drexler's arm. "See? We're communicating and getting along fine."

"Let's hope we don't have dog for breakfast."

Henderson smiled at the boy. "We have to check the perimeter. We'll be back." The boy shook his head as if he understood.

As the soldiers walked away, Drexler put his arm around Henderson. "I'm warning you. You're getting too close to that boy.

There's going to be nothing but heartbreak for you if you're not careful."

"I know what I'm doing."

"If you say so."

"If I wanted your opinion, I would've asked for it."

"You got it anyway."

"Let's focus on surveying the perimeter."

After Henderson and Drexler spent the late afternoon checking the perimeter of the village, fatigue and exhaustion hit them. As the sun sank behind the forested mountains, having a place to sleep lined up pleased them as much as it did the old woman and the boy.

As they approached the hooch, Henderson gazed toward Drexler. "Do we knock, or do we walk in and make ourselves at home?"

"I say we use our manners and knock."

Before Henderson could lift his hand, the boy scampered out of the door and hugged him, not wanting to let go. He scruffed the boy's hair. "I'm glad to see you too."

"Come. Come." The boy tugged Henderson's hand, pulling him inside.

The old woman flashed a smile, pointing to the left corner. She placed her hands against her face and pretended to sleep and snore.

Henderson released a belly laugh as he approached the corner and dropped his rucksack. "Thank you. This is perfect."

Drexler nodded. "Yes, thank you."

The night quickly fell, and the hooch became silent. As darkness crept through the village, Henderson couldn't hear any laughter or talking. Even the animals were quiet.

The two grunts rested, lying on the floor with their heads against their rucksacks—one slept while the other kept guard. Through the open door, they had a clear view of the center of the village. The old woman and the boy slept in the smaller room. On his watch, Henderson heard her occasional soft snoring.

Minutes after midnight, Henderson heard an unidentifiable sound, and he crawled through the open doorway, onto the porch.

Two dogs barked, and he listened to a man whispering commands to the animals—the instruction wasn't in English. Whatever he said made the dogs stop yapping.

The profiles of several men came walking into the clearing, near the community building. He could tell by the silhouettes that each man carried a weapon; they were not American.

Within seconds of his seeing the silhouettes, the firefight commenced.

Henderson heard the M-60 firing from Rocky's position and grabbed his weapon. "Drexler, grab your rifle!"

The center of the ville was suddenly lit up by muzzle flashes.

Gripping his M-16, Drexler crawled next to Henderson, and both shot at the silhouettes running toward their hooch. In an instant, the shapes became VC, armed with AK-47s. As Henderson and Drexler fired, the approaching VC flew backward as rounds hit them.

Near the community building, Henderson observed a VC carrying a rocket-propelled grenade launcher as he ran for cover. He knew that it would only be moments before the enemy soldier was aiming the RPG at him and Drexler. "RPG! I'll grab the boy; you get the woman."

Both soldiers ran inside. They didn't have long. Drexler felt time ticking away as he moved. Henderson scooped up the boy.

After he got the woman and his rucksack, Drexler punched a hole through the rear wall with his foot. "Jump!"

Henderson and Drexler tossed their rucksacks first, then, with the boy in his arms, Henderson jumped, landing in a pile of water buffalo dung. He let go of the boy, pushing him flat on the ground, and raised his M-16, ready to protect Drexler and the old woman as he motioned for Drexler to jump.

Drexler lifted the woman and jumped, falling hard on the ground inside the animal pen.

Whoosh!! The RPG round fired.

Drexler pushed the old woman to the ground. "Stay down! Everyone stay down."

Bam!

As they lay flat, the explosion rocked the ground. The hut blew apart, its walls and ceiling flying in different directions. Only half of the structure remained standing, and flames climbed the wall on the south side.

Drexler pointed to the hedgerow. "Move out! Stay low."

Henderson nodded.

The two soldiers, the old woman, and the boy crawled toward the hedgerow behind the hooch, moving as fast as they could and looking for cover.

From his position, Stahl spotted the VC who had fired the RPG. "I'll be damned if I let you take out my men." He aimed his M-16 toward the enemy soldier and shot him in his forehead, dead center. The VC jerked to one side, dropped his weapon, and fell.

"Die, you son of a bitch!" Stahl fired another round into the dead body. "You're not dead until you're dead!"

As he watched the path, Henderson saw the outline of a man walking along the trail. He raised his M-16 and fired a three-round burst into the enemy soldier's chest, knocking him backward. The VC was dead before he fell into the overgrowth. Unlike his squad leader, Henderson didn't question that certainty.

Rounds zinged around the two soldiers, hitting the trees and thudding into the ground close to their hiding place. Henderson listened intently to distinguish the different types of weapons fired.

Drexler glared at Henderson, as if preemptively imploring him not to question what he was about to say, then began. "One of us has to take a risk. You stay here with the woman and boy. I'm going around to get to the center of the ville. I'll return to get you."

"Understood. Be careful."

They looked at each other as if it might be the last time, and Henderson knew there was a real chance that it could be. Then, Drexler jumped to his feet and ran toward the center of the village, hunched over.

The old woman and the boy snuggled in close to Henderson, trembling in fear against his body.

Shit. Can I protect these two people?

Henderson took a deep breath. His heartbeat, and the breathing of the two villagers, seemed to amplify as time slowly ticked away.

Footsteps loomed nearby, and Henderson pointed his rifle in their direction. "I've got this. I'm not going to let you two die."

"Eddie, Eddie, I'm coming in!" Drexler's voice accompanied the push through the vegetation, and Henderson sighed in relief.

"Over here."

"I think it's over. The VC ran away."

"I almost shot you."

Drexler smiled. "Let's get the woman and boy back into the ville."

Henderson and Drexler grabbed the two villagers and ran toward the community building. As they approached the structure, Stahl and the rest of the squad strode toward them, stepping over four dead enemy soldiers.

Henderson counted the dead. "One, two, three, four…" *We need to kill more!*

Brighton addressed his squad leaders. "Everybody okay?"

"First Squad's good." Nash nodded, clearly relieved.

"Same here; we're good." Stahl double-checked his squad members' headcount. "Everyone is accounted for."

"First Squad, drag the bodies over to the community building. Get their weapons; don't forget the ammo." Brighton looked as if anger were filling his soul.

Nash waved for his squad to follow him. "On it, LT."

"I'm going to the trail to get the weapon from the guy I shot." Henderson's tone seemed to exude pride that he had killed a VC.

Drexler bolted after him. "I'll go with you."

They ran to the rear of the smoldering hooch, where the two friends found the dead VC, taking his AK-47 and an ammunition belt.

Henderson shivered. "I'd say he's dead."

"For sure. I don't think he could be *any more* dead."

"Not according to Stahl," Henderson said, as they strode back to the center of the ville.

Drexler maintained a close distance to Henderson. "Forget about Stahl. Always do what is right in your heart."

"Trust me. I intend to."

When they returned, Stahl waved them over. "Return and stay at your positions until daylight."

"Understood, Sarge."

Henderson watched Professor studying all the dead VC, moving from body to body while checking each face.

Drexler cleared his throat. "There's no position to go back to. The hut is destroyed."

Henderson pointed to a small hooch, which remained intact. "Let's take the woman and Vinh to that hut."

"After you."

Drexler and Henderson found the old woman and Vinh and escorted them to the hut. Henderson put his hand on Vinh's shoulder. "You'll be safe here; we'll be right here on the porch all night." Then, Henderson bowed. "Goodnight." He extended his hand and motioned for the old woman and the boy to enter.

"GI boo-coo dinky dau." Vinh smiled, entering the hut with the old woman.

The two friends dropped their rucksacks onto the porch, then stretched out next to them to get a couple of hours sleep.

•

The morning sun rose above the rice paddies, shining its bright rays of sunlight over the village.

Henderson sniffed the air. "Damn, we stink!"

"I think you stink worse than me." Drexler laughed, knowing that the smell would only get more unpleasant.

After lighting a cigarette, Henderson looked around at the destruction created by last night's firefight. The VC had destroyed the old woman's hooch, yet it appeared that the rest had sustained only bullet holes, without any significant damage.

Drexler's stomach growled as he searched through his rucksack. "Let's fix breakfast."

"I am hungry." Henderson grabbed a can of peaches and a hot chocolate mix.

"Yeah, you usually are—for such a skinny guy."

While heating water for the hot chocolate mix, Henderson ate a can of peaches. As he watched the water boil, he poured the cocoa into the canteen cup, then added three sugar packets, stirring the mixture with his plastic spoon. Henderson enjoyed his drink as he watched the sun rise over the horizon.

He pointed to Brighton and the three NCOs huddled together across the ville. "Wonder what they're talking about."

"Figuring how they're going to walk us into death," Drexler said, taking a bite of his fruit cocktail.

When they finished eating, the old woman approached Henderson and Drexler, carrying two wooden buckets of water. She set the buckets on the porch and pointed at Henderson's shirt and pants. After a minute, the two soldiers understood that she wanted to wash their clothes.

"I guess we do stink."

Drexler shoved Henderson's chest playfully. "You stink, and she knows it."

"Let's do it." Henderson stripped off his uniform.

Both soldiers handed the old woman their uniforms, then stood naked, because they didn't wear underclothes. She flashed a grin, offering them several large palm leaves.

The Second Squad members walked over to them, with Porter in the lead. "Hello, boys! Are you missing anything?" Rocky gave a wolf whistle at the sight of his two friends.

"At least we're getting clean uniforms," Henderson said, pointing to the old woman, who busily scrubbed the uniforms.

After laying the uniforms in the sunlight on the front porch, the old woman dumped the dirty water from her buckets. Then, smiling, she left the men standing on the porch.

"You guys don't even look embarrassed." Stahl chuckled.

Drexler readjusted the palm leaf to cover up a little more. "Trust me, we are."

"Naked or not, while I have you assembled, we have a new mission."

The squad quietened, ready for the bad news.

Stahl grinned, unable to hold it back. "We're going to firebase Debbie to pull security for a week. Henderson, you have point. You'll take us to the clearing, where we landed yesterday."

Rocky shoved Porter on the shoulder. "Great news."

"Downtime!" Porter grinned.

"The Hueys should be here at thirteen-hundred hours. We're on the first one." Then, Stahl stared at Henderson and Drexler, pointing at the palm leaves. "Think you guys could get dressed before we leave?"

A DAY OFF AT LAST

Fire Support Base Debbie stood high above the valley below—which was known as the "Rice Bowl"—eight klicks south of the Brigade firebase. When the Brigade first built Debbie, the command referred to it as Landing Zone Debbie, but once artillery augmented an official landing zone, the designation changed from LZ Debbie to FSB Debbie. Most of the soldiers arriving didn't know this and didn't care—what the firebase meant to them was a place where their guard could be down, and where they could relax.

Twenty bunkers—to protect the infantry soldiers guarding the perimeter—surrounded the oval-shaped firebase, with approximately one hundred feet between each one; enough distance to have interlocking fields of fire between them. Each shelter housed five men.

The engineers had built a helicopter pad, located in the center of the firebase, big enough to accommodate three Hueys at a time. Twenty meters from the landing pad sat the mess hall, where the cooks prepared three hot meals a day. Given field conditions, the soldiers were happy enough with this number of meals—they didn't even mind the quality. The only other feature of the base that the soldiers found half as important as the mess hall were the four shitters—they sat in the open, side-by-side, close enough together for a man to sit on the wooden seat and carry on a conversation with the soldier sitting next to him.

Two days after the platoon's arrival at Debbie, the company clerk interrupted Brighton as he ate breakfast in the mess hall. "Sir, you've got some replacements."

Brighton laid his fork down on his tray and sighed. "When did they arrive?"

Introducing new men was never easy, but they needed the manpower. He hoped they would be good soldiers—and that he wouldn't have to watch them die. "How many replacements are there?"

"Sir, five of them. Got here an hour ago."

Brighton nodded curtly. "I'll be going to the command post shortly."

"Yes, sir." The clerk nodded.

Brighton finished his breakfast, then tilted his head toward Swift. "Sergeant Swift, come with me. We got replacements."

"Okay, LT." Swift stood, leaving his unfinished meal. He grabbed his coffee cup and joined Brighton.

As they walked along the well-worn path, Swift caught up to Brighton. "I hope the replacements are good soldiers."

"It will be hard to replace the five platoon members we lost in the last couple of weeks." Brighton's forehead creased. "They have big shoes to fill."

Receiving replacements had become a common occurrence. Soldiers spent three hundred and sixty-five days in-country before being rotated home. However, this wasn't the usual manner in which to receive new soldiers. Replacements typically reported to the platoon one at a time, and left the unit one at a time; getting five at once didn't occur, unless they were replacements for wounded or killed platoon members.

The two leaders arrived within minutes of being notified. They observed the five new soldiers sitting outside the command post, and Brighton eyed the men. They looked young, fresh and clean. He knew that soon they wouldn't be, and wondered how they would take to that. Brighton didn't correlate this situation to his arrival but, unbeknownst to himself, he saw a lot of his earlier incarnation in these men.

When the new arrivals saw Brighton, they jumped to attention and saluted.

"At ease. While in the field, no saluting or jumping to attention when approached by an officer—this is the first rule to remember."

"Yes, sir," the men said as they assumed the position of attention.

Brighton shook his head and looked over at his platoon sergeant. Swift stepped forward. "You men are assigned to the First Platoon?"

"Yes, Staff Sergeant," the new arrivals said in unison.

"I'm the platoon sergeant—Staff Sergeant Swift—and this is Lieutenant Brighton, the platoon leader."

The clerk came to the door and handed Swift a piece of paper, listing the replacements' names, ranks, and their hometowns. After he read the list, Swift handed the paper to the lieutenant.

Brighton read from the list of names. "Ransom, Hays and Clark"—he looked up—"you're going to the Second Squad. Sergeant Stahl is your squad leader." His eyes diverted to the paper. "Kelly and Flores, you're going to the First Squad. Sergeant Nash is your squad leader."

He scanned the new arrivals. "Welcome to the First Platoon. We have great NCOs in the platoon. You'll find the squad leaders to be the best anywhere. If you want to stay alive, you need to listen to your squad and team leaders. They know what they're doing. Now, get your gear and follow us."

The five soldiers grabbed their gear and ran after the two leaders, trailing them along the path to the bunkers housing the First Platoon. As Brighton and Swift walked ahead of the replacements, Brighton glanced toward Swift. "Damn, these replacements look younger and younger."

"LT, they look inexperienced and nervous as hell."

Once Brighton reached the First Squad bunker, he faced the new arrivals. "Sergeant Nash!" His call drifted toward the bunker.

Nash quickly exited the bunker, squinting his eyes as the bright morning sun glared. "Yes, LT?"

"Sergeant Nash, here are two replacements, Kelly and Flores. Get them squared away."

"Yes, sir, will do."

The replacements stood out. Kelly, a draftee from Kansas City, Missouri, stood at five foot eight, with broad shoulders and a muscular build. Flores stood a little over five foot, and appeared much smaller standing next to Kelly. They were best friends and, during training, workout buddies, having been to the gym whenever they could. This was the only consolation they had as they faced their rough-looking new leader—that they were assigned to a squad together.

Walking to the next bunker with the three replacements following them, Brighton approached Stahl as he talked to Henderson, Drexler, and Madison. "Sergeant Stahl, got three replacements for you: Ransom, Hays, and Clark. Get them squared away."

"Okay, LT"

Brighton and Swift walked away.

Henderson watched and listened to the introductions with interest.

"Welcome to the Second Squad," Stahl said, pausing as he assessed each new arrival. "The three of you will go to Bravo Team. Jerry Madison is the team leader."

Madison nodded at the replacements.

"Here's the deal. You guys are 'fucking new guys,' what we call 'FNGs.' We don't care what you did in the world, what a great athlete you were in school, or how much college you got. What you need to do is carry your weight, listen, and learn. Don't question shit; do what you're told. No drugs. You need to earn our trust. Once you earn our trust, you won't be called an FNG any more. One last thing to remember. Each member of the squad has your back—and, they expect you to have theirs. Any questions?"

The three FNGs stared at Stahl in awe, without uttering a word.

"Okay, Madison, you can introduce the FNGs to the team."

"Roger, Sarge. You guys come with me."

•

On the morning of the third day, Drexler walked into the bunker and approached Henderson and Porter. "Henderson, Porter—shit-burning detail."

Henderson frowned. "Really?"

"You guys gotta."

As Henderson and Porter followed the worn trail and drew closer to the shitters, their noses twitched from the distinctive smell of human waste and diesel fuel polluting the air from the fiery drum.

Henderson squinched his nose. "I hate burning shit."

"The VC don't stink this bad! Being in the bush is better than this."

"Yeah, it ain't complicated. You're looking for VC, or the VC are looking for you."

"Well, maybe shit burning isn't too bad." Porter laughed at the comparison.

Before starting the dreaded detail, they slid on engineer gloves. The two needed to work together as they pulled the full drum—a fifty-five-gallon drum, cut in half—away from the shitters.

Henderson grunted, as he wiped sweat from his brow. "You pour the diesel; I'll light it."

Porter poured the diesel fuel from the five-gallon can. "Do you think that's enough? I sure as hell ain't doing this again."

"You did it perfect."

"Okay, light it."

Henderson wrapped toilet paper around one end of a stick and lit it with his Zippo lighter. "Watch this." He touched the stinking mixture with the flame.

Flames shot from the drum, mixing the strong odor of diesel fuel and burning shit. The smell made the two soldiers move backward several steps. Dark, black smoke rose to the sky, curling across the firebase, along with the awful smell which followed it. Henderson grabbed his handkerchief from his pocket and covered his mouth and nose to catch his breath before tying it around his face.

"I can't believe you beat me to that." Porter quickly tied an olive drab-colored handkerchief around his face to help block the smells from entering his nostrils.

They grabbed the brown-stained sticks at their feet and stirred the burning mixture while waiting for the fire to extinguish.

Porter shuddered. "I think it's cool enough."

"Grab a handle and let's slide it back in."

Sliding the drum under the wooden seat, they moved on to the next.

After six hours of burning shit, they were relieved of their detail.

Before going to the mess hall for dinner, the two soldiers headed to the squad bunker. The smells of the work they had done clung to them. Henderson pinched his nose. "I don't know about you, but I'm heading straight for a shower."

"I'm with you; we can't go to the mess hall smelling like this."

To the right of the shitters were two showers, each with three walls. A fifty-five-gallon drum of lukewarm water was set on top, heated by the sun. When a soldier pulled the drawstring, it released enough water to get wet; another pull provided enough water to rinse off the soap. Nudity and the lack of privacy were accepted practices for the soldiers.

Drexler was sitting outside on a pile of sandbags when the two arrived. He looked toward them. "I could smell you coming."

"Not funny." Henderson flipped him the bird.

"We've been burning shit all day. What's your excuse?" Porter grinned, tapping Henderson on the shoulder to show solidarity. "Me and Henderson are going to the showers."

"Good idea." Drexler laughed at the two team members as they walked away.

•

In the late afternoon, Brighton called the platoon together to talk about an upcoming mission. He tapped his foot as the grunts gathered.

"We've received a report from S-two that the enemy could be about to attack the firebase. The battalion fears that the enemy will attack from the west side of the mountain in the next three days. The company commander is sending the First Platoon on an ambush tonight. S-two selected the ambush site, several hundred meters outside the wire. Your squad leaders have the details. Be ready to move by twenty-one-hundred hours. Nothing else."

After they left the lieutenant's position, the platoon members headed to their bunkers, talking about the upcoming mission. They speculated on how likely it would be for the enemy to cross their ambush. Mostly, the talk was to distract them from the memories of their fallen squad members resurfacing.

When they arrived there, Stahl was already waiting outside the bunker, looking around to see when the squad returned from the briefing.

"Henderson, you're point tonight. We're only going two hundred meters outside the wire."

"Okay, Sarge."

"Remember noise and light discipline—tighten your gear, no smoking or flashlights, no talking. Team leaders, make sure you get the FNGs up to speed."

He retrieved the map from his pants' cargo pocket, spread it on the ground, and looked inquisitively toward Henderson. "You see this trail leading from the wire to where these two other trails join?"

"I do, Sarge."

"Follow the trail and stop at this junction," Stahl said as he traced the route. "Then, I'll assign positions."

"No problem, Sarge."

•

As the moonlight filtered through the thick stand of trees, the platoon traveled in a single file, watching each step they took as they moved toward the ambush position. Guided by dim light provided by the clear, bright night sky, Henderson followed the path downhill until he reached the junction Stahl had shown him on the map. He stopped and looked over the terrain to ensure no enemy soldiers hid in the ambush site, then signaled all clear.

Stahl moved forward, positioning his two fire teams in a half-circle, facing west, with a view of the ridge. Without difficulty, the enemy could use the trail along the ridgeline to ascend the mountain. Hidden in the thick overgrowth, the infantry soldiers lay in a prone position, with weapons pointed toward the junction where the two trails met, ready to open fire at anyone approaching the firebase. The soldiers alternated watch, while one soldier slept, the guy next to him stayed alert.

Not long after the platoon was in position, Henderson heard the call of the Tokay gecko lizard, echoing to his front. *"Fuckyou."*

Smiling, he recalled his first time hearing the sound. He thought it might be the NVA, taunting him during the night. But, with experience, he learned that the grunts in Vietnam fondly referred to the lizard as the "Fuckyou lizard" because of the sound it made.

I hope the new guys have the same experience I did, Henderson thought, stifling a laugh.

Around 0300 hours, a rustling noise—a long distance from the squad's position—alerted Professor. He nudged Henderson awake. Startled, Henderson looked at Professor with a questioning stare.

Pointing toward the bottom of the ridgeline, Professor whispered, "Thought I heard movement."

The moonlight exposed a line of VC, Henderson catching a glimpse of the patrol as it walked along the trail, one hundred meters away. He pointed in the direction of the noise. His eyes never diverted from the location. "Think I saw a bunch of VC heading south along the base of the hill."

"They're too far away to engage."

"Should we alert the squad?"

Professor's eyes darted around the perimeter. "Hell, no, let them pass. There's too many."

As the enemy patrol disappeared, they sat without making a sound—almost as if not breathing. Eventually, Henderson fell asleep, leaving Professor to guard their position.

•

He was nudged awake by Drexler's foot tapping his arm. Henderson opened his eyes.

"Prepare to move to the firebase."

Stahl moved around the circle, giving the order to each team member, and the men of the Second Squad stood, walking as slowly as possible so they wouldn't make a sound.

With Henderson in the lead, they took careful, short steps on the same hard-packed, narrow path. As the early morning darkness faded, giving way to the sun, they headed toward the firebase. After walking for twenty minutes, the platoon finally moved inside the three strands of concertina wire, heading toward their bunkers.

As Henderson passed the helipad, he saw the Second Platoon entering the three Hueys, while three other helicopters circled above the firebase. Once loaded, the three choppers slowly climbed skyward, banked, and headed to the valley below. Dust blew into the eyes of the men of the First Platoon as they skirted around the helipad. As soon as they flew away, the three circling helicopters landed, Third Platoon loaded, then those helicopters lifted and followed the first flight.

Henderson gazed at the choppers. *Good luck.* Then, he continued toward the bunker.

•

As the twenty-five infantrymen of the First Platoon sat around a bunker, they talked and napped, enjoying a lazy day. The grunts considered the downtime a treat, having stayed awake through the night for the ambush.

As he gazed east, the South China Sea calmed Henderson. He took a deep breath and reflected on the cool ocean water, and how refreshing it would be to go for a swim.

As if reading his friend's mind, Drexler looked at Henderson, narrowing his eyes. "Eddie, you remember being on firebase Charlie Brown?"

"You bet! What a relaxing time. We even got to swim in the sea." Henderson grinned as he exhaled.

"I think being in the ocean cured my jungle rot."

"Me too, but it's returned. Sores cover my arms and legs."

"Because you're always in front, getting cut by the elephant grass and thorns."

"Let's go inside; it's way too hot out here. I thought July was hot in the world, but here it's a scorcher!"

The two friends entered the bunker.

The hot rays, which beamed down on the backs of the rest of the platoon members, were relentless. The soldiers sat under a poncho liner, or went inside the shelter, for protection against the heat.

A shadow blocked the sunlight as Clark entered the bunker. He flopped next to Henderson. "Man, it's hot out there."

Henderson fanned himself with a piece of cardboard. "It's not much better in here; it's stifling."

"No shit." Drexler gave the FNG a casual glance.

Henderson had heard that Clark was from Georgia, and went to Fort Benning for basic and infantry training. He had a slim build and didn't appear any older than eighteen or nineteen. Henderson often thought about Benning, and believed they might have something in common.

"How come you guys take orders from that *boy*?" Clark said, shifting his weight to his left.

Puzzled by the question, Henderson creased his brow. "What are you talking about—you mean the lieutenant?"

"Y'all know them boys ain't leaders."

Henderson stood up, grasping his rifle. "You need to shut the fuck up!"

"That ain't going to happen until I get a white lieutenant."

The butt of the rifle hit Clark square in the jaw, leaving a large, red welt as blood dripped from his mouth. Clark released a loud grunt, his eyes glazing, and he fell onto his side, holding his face as he cried.

With his eyes wide and his heart pounding, Henderson stood over Clark, ready to hit him again if needed. "His name is Lieutenant Brighton, and that's how you'll address him! Got it?"

Clark sobbed as he spat out blood. "Yeah, Henderson, I got it."

Drexler followed Henderson out of the bunker, leaving Clark to ponder his fate with the platoon. "Don't worry about it, Eddie. He deserved it. No one better than the LT."

Henderson later sat, staring into the valley, as he reflected on what Clark had said. Since leaving his hometown, this was the first time he had heard another person talking that way. Henderson knew he needed to let go of his anger.

His mind wandered back to the war, and he thought about the two other platoons, humping in the heat, looking for the NVA or VC. As he looked down into the Rice Bowl—a known North Vietnamese Army and Viet Cong stronghold—Henderson drew a deep breath.

I'm lucky to be sitting right here, and not down there in the valley with those guys.

CHAPTER 10

NAPALM, FIRE AND DEATH

Five hours after his confrontation with Clark, Henderson stormed to the lieutenant's bunker to talk with Doc.

Doc, smoking a cigarette in the shade next to the platoon leader, twisted his lips as he watched Henderson's approach.

Henderson fist connected lightly with Doc's shoulder. "I forgot to tell you thanks for helping with Mai at the ville."

"I didn't do anything." Doc flickered a frown in remorse. "Sorry she was killed."

A voice blared over the static on Brighton's radio. "Tango one-six, this is Tango six. Over." Within seconds, the voice came again. "Tango one-six, this is Tango six. Over."

Henderson wiped sweat from his face. "That's not a good sign. For Lyons to be calling out himself like this, something big must be happening." Henderson held his breath as he listened.

Jumping to his feet, Brighton ran over to where his RTO sat with the radio, not giving Ledger a chance to bring him the handset. After he passed the handset to the lieutenant, Ledger turned up the radio volume. Brighton pressed the talk button to transmit. "This is Tango one-six. Over."

"Tango one-six, I'm sending First Platoon to my location. Over." The static in the transmission almost cut off Lyon's message.

After hearing the order to go to the valley, Swift stood. "Everyone move to the LT's bunker for instructions of an upcoming mission."

At once, the platoon members proceeded to the destination, where they gathered closer to listen.

During the transmission, automatic weapons fire, followed by explosions, could be heard in the background. The soldiers looked toward the valley to see what was happening to the company.

A unit had made contact with the enemy. Henderson's head turned toward the faint echo of weapons firing, and explosions rolling along the valley floor, followed by small puffs of smoke.

"Roger, Tango six. Over." Brighton's heart thrummed hard against his rib cage.

Everyone went silent to hear the reply.

"Your transportation will be there in ten mikes," Lyons said. "It's a hot LZ. Over."

"Roger, Tango six. Heading to the pad in ten mikes. Over."

"Tango one-six, join on the east of Tango two-six. Over."

"Wilco, join on Tango two-six. Over."

"Tango one-six, hurry! Out."

Brighton turned to the platoon. "Travel light: weapons, ammunition, grenades, and water only. Second Squad, Swift, and his RTO are on the first Huey. The command group, with two members from each squad, is on the second chopper. First Squad goes on the third helicopter."

The platoon routinely flew with these general helicopter assignments. There was something comforting in this regularity, and the calm manner that Brighton delivered the instructions. He reassured the soldiers without them even realizing that the soothing effect came from him.

After a short pause, Brighton cleared his throat. "The Second Squad takes point when we hit the landing zone. You'll join Second Platoon."

As soon as he had given those instructions, a nearby artillery battery of six guns opened fire. Each 105-artillery piece had a crew of four to six artillerymen, firing roughly three rounds per minute.

"Incoming! Hit the ground!" Stahl took cover as he kept an eye on the soldiers under his command.

Henderson and the rest of the Second Squad hit the ground, covering their heads with their arms. Within seconds, they realized that the rounds were from artillery, headed toward the enemy's position in the Rice Bowl. They immediately jumped to their feet, laughing at each other to shake off the fear that the artillery firing had triggered.

An officer from S2 dashed over to Brighton, and they spoke for several minutes. As the artillery fired their cannons, Brighton then turned to the platoon, with grave concern creasing his brow. "A large enemy force ambushed our company and E Troop. There are casualties. Be alert—ready for anything—as we move from the LZ to join the Second Platoon. Expect the LZ to be hot!"

Drexler turned to Alpha Team, ready for combat. "Bring plenty of ammo and water. Let's go."

Alpha Team ran to the bunker, where the team members quickly gathered their gear. Not a person spoke as they prepared for battle. Henderson grabbed two bandoliers from his rucksack. He tied one around his waist and the other across his left shoulder; the fourteen loaded magazines of 5.56 rounds for his M-16 hung loosely on his slim torso. He slid two fragmentation grenades into his shirt's left cargo pocket, and clipped a one-quart canteen and a first-aid pouch to his pistol belt. He then put a second first-aid pouch into his right shirt pocket. *One for me, one for a buddy*. He stuffed a can of pound cake and peaches into his right leg cargo pocket. Drexler stared at him as he pocketed the food.

Henderson's face turned beet red. "A man has to eat."

Drexler gave his friend a broad smile of approval. Somehow, that little act of watching his friend stowing away food had lifted a small portion of the weight from his shoulders. But he had more serious matters to consider—making sure his team survived, whatever came next.

Drexler reached into the ammo can, picking up a hundred-round belt. "Each of you carries one hundred rounds of M-sixty, for Rocky."

One by one, the team members took a hundred-round belt of 7.62 from the ammo can to carry for the machine gunner. Henderson clipped his hundred-round belt across his right shoulder, over his bandolier holding seven M-16 magazines.

Loaded with weapons and ammunition, the squad raced to the helipad to join the platoon.

As they waited for the Hueys, one of the FNGs—Ransom— moved closer to Henderson. His blond hair still had a fresh military cut, and even an outsider could have told he was a newbie, from this and a certain softness around his farm-boy blue eyes.

Ransom rubbed his hands together as beads of sweat covered his upper lip. "What's a hot landing zone like?"

Henderson tilted his helmet back and stared into the valley. "Well, not all combat assaults are hot. Your adrenaline is pumping; you start sweating like never before; you're shaking like you have Parkinson's—nervous as hell! The chopper lands in a clearing, with the tree line thirty meters away, and you jump from the helicopter before it lands while wearing a sixty-pound rucksack, hoping you don't break an ankle. Hell, that's not even the bad part! You hit the ground running for the tree line, asking yourself if the enemy is hiding in the direction you're running to. Now, if you want, I can talk about how it feels if someone is shooting at you as you run. That's a hot LZ."

Ransom's face turned pale. "No, it's okay. I get the point. Thanks."

Henderson was polite enough to stifle his snicker. He didn't think that Ransom was managing to hide his fear in the least, but he had enough respect for the FNG to let him pretend.

They'd talked a little earlier about Ransom's history. From a small farming community in Ohio, Don Ransom worked his father's farm from an early age, learning the industry and the value of shutting the hell up. Henderson had already recognized the twenty-year-old soldier's work ethic and strength.

"I suppose…" Ransom said, "I'll find out soon enough… all on my own." When he talked, it sounded as if his words had a half-second interval between each one. Some of the squad members thought him a little slow, but Henderson discounted that rumor. The content of Ransom's words was never off.

Looking skyward, Henderson watched the three helicopters approaching the helipad as they circled high above the landing area. His eyes followed their flight path as they came in low. Then, both squads and the command group ran, bent over, holding their helmets with one hand. They climbed aboard through the door-less openings on each side of their assigned helicopter.

As they sat on the floor of the chopper, they placed the muzzle of their weapons facing downward. Even though they weren't supposed to, each chambered a round, ready to engage the enemy when landing, if needed. Only the FNGs didn't do this, and they would learn soon enough—survival meant more than rules.

Henderson sat across from Drexler, making eye contact. They both smiled, as if to say, "I'm ready." In truth, they were scared, but didn't want to show fear.

As they lifted into the hot, humid air, the Huey with Second Squad on its metal floor climbed fifty feet or more. Then the pilot pointed the nose downward and accelerated toward the Rice Bowl. The other two helicopters followed.

The members of Alpha Team sat shoulder to shoulder as they watched the firebase fade behind them. Looking from the right side of the Huey as they flew low across the fields, Henderson saw dry rice paddies with hedgerows. The squad acted as if they were ready for another day at work, but all were deep in thoughts of what could happen when they landed. The lack of any conversation was a dead giveaway.

As the first helicopter descended to the landing zone, Henderson hit the forward assist on the right side of his rifle. Using the palm of his hand, he struck it several times to ensure a round was seated in the chamber. As soon as it neared the ground, all were prepared to jump off of the Huey.

Immediately as the Huey descended, the enemy directed AK-47 rounds at the helicopter.

The door gunner yelled, "Take this, Charlie!" while firing the M-60 machine gun, shredding branches from the small trees in the hedgerows around the LZ. With the Huey two feet above the ground, Stahl yelled, "Get the hell off! Incoming!"

Jumping to the ground, the soldiers hit hard before the skids touched down. They drew small-arms enemy fire before their feet had even hit the ground. Then, the members of the Second Squad ran for cover in the overgrown hedgerow to secure the landing zone.

Henderson recognized the sounds of tearing metal as the helicopter he alighted took hits. *Fly away!!!* Looking over his shoulder as he ducked into place, he watched the pilot pulling skyward. He took a deep breath of relief, even though he and the others were still drawing enemy fire. He observed the other two Hueys approaching the landing zone, both door gunners firing their M-60s. The command group jumped off of the second helicopter with several other platoon members, while Second Squad provided covering fire.

When Henderson glanced at the door-gunner on the second Huey, two rounds from enemy fire thudded into the gunner's chest. He slumped over the machine gun as the Huey lifted and darted toward Debbie.

"Son of a bitch!" Henderson tightened his jaw. *At least it isn't one of mine!* He didn't even have time—at the moment—to feel bad for having that thought.

First Squad jumped from the third helicopter before it touched the ground, with Nash leading the way. Once in the field, both teams fired as they ran for cover. The hedgerows to their front consisted of bamboo thickets, clumps of brush, and were thick with trees. Brighton got the platoon to spread out and head toward the enemy.

A look of determination crossed Stahl's face and body stance. "Henderson, move to the front! Make sure Charlie isn't hiding in the hedgerows before we move through them."

"Okay, Sarge, moving now!" Henderson nodded as sweat rolled off the tip of his nose.

As the point man, Henderson stepped forward, with Drexler thirty feet behind him. He couldn't see an enemy, but fired his M-16 nonetheless, in case enemy soldiers were hidden in the hedgerow. He cleared one hedgerow after another as the platoon followed him. They received small-arms and machine gun fire as they advanced, but it didn't appear that the enemy knew their exact location, because the incoming rounds didn't hit anywhere close to the squad. Henderson's confidence increased; they seemed to have this part down.

Drexler suddenly yelled, "Charlie!"

Thinking he had seen movement off to Henderson's side, he raised his M-16 to his shoulder. Drexler fired two automatic bursts of three rounds each into a thick stand of bamboo in the hedgerow to the right of Henderson. As he watched his rounds rip through the bamboo trees, an NVA soldier suddenly stood and dropped his AK-47. He stumbled forward several steps, then fell hard into the dry rice field.

Henderson froze for several seconds before he approached the body, which was lying fifteen feet away. He saw three holes in the soldier's chest, blood seeping through the enemy's green shirt. The dead man stared at him with open eyes, then they rolled upward, until only the white of his eyeballs was visible.

Henderson turned to his rear and looked at his friend. "Thanks."

As he continued his advance toward the battle, he wondered, *When did I start saying thank you after someone is killed?*

Henderson burst through a hedgerow into a large field of rice paddies. To his left, he witnessed what appeared to be the right flank of his company, with the Second Platoon taking cover behind a dike; to his front, hundreds of meters away, a mountain range overlooked the rice fields. A haze of smoke floated in front of him. The gunfire, explosions, and sounds of men yelling were deafening.

Hiding behind the barrier, Henderson signaled for Stahl to move forward to his position, while the enemy continued to concentrate its firepower on the main force of Alpha Company and E Troop. Stahl jumped to his feet and ran to Henderson's position, hitting the ground next to him. Within a minute or two, Brighton and Ledger had made their way to Henderson and Stahl.

As he peered over the dike, Henderson pointed at the Second Platoon, dispersed along an embankment.

Brighton glared at Stahl. "Sergeant, move your squad to the Second Platoon position, by the dike. I'll have the rest of the platoon follow you."

As sweat dripped from his face, Stahl wiped it off. "Yes, sir."

Brighton called Lyons on the radio. "Tango six, this is Tango one-six. Over."

"Roger, Tango six. Over."

"Tango six, I need covering fire to move to Tango two-six. Over."

"Roger; you've got it. Move now. Out."

As soon as the company commander said the word "out," the infantry company opened fire on the mountains to their front, hurling thousands of rounds toward the enemy's positions. The sudden rattling of bullets sliding into their chambers, and the explosion of the round sent down the barrel when pulling the trigger, erupted so immensely loudly that the soldiers couldn't hear each other. Gunpowder hung in the humid air.

Turning to the Second Squad, Stahl screamed, "On me!" After he gave the command, he signaled to move forward.

Bent close to the ground as they ran through the paddies, with Henderson in front, Alpha Team advanced to the Second Platoon. Within seconds, the Bravo Team arrived. The rest of the command group followed Bravo Team, with Nash leading the First Squad. Once in position, the platoon blasted their firepower toward the mountains, along with the rest of the company. The company now extended across most of the Rice Bowl, below the hills to the front.

Henderson looked to his left, acknowledging a Second Platoon soldier fifteen meters away. His face covered in sweat and dirt, the soldier stared at him. His wide eyes went to Henderson, then darted toward the hills. Within seconds, the soldier glanced back at him again, his body trembling. The soldier reminded Henderson of a wild animal caught in a trap.

The artillery shells coming from Debbie flew over Henderson's head with a *whoosh!* The explosions on the hill, where the enemy hid, reflected in his eyes. One after another, the 105-mm rounds flew overhead, *Whoosh! Whoosh! Whoosh!* Each round hit its target.

No soldier could survive that barrage of incoming artillery, Henderson thought with a shudder as he continued firing toward the enemy.

•

The battalion commander flew overhead in the command and control Huey, positioning the APCs in a line behind the company. As a World War II veteran, he relished the idea of attacking the enemy in a frontal assault, applying the same tactics he had used in that war.

He directed the platoons to move in a line, from rice paddy to rice paddy, using the dikes for cover and concealment. E Troop provided cover fire with the .50 caliber and M-60 machine guns, while each platoon gave cover fire for the other platoons as they advanced.

As the APCs rolled ahead, the metal tracks of the vehicles clanked the hard earth behind the line of infantry soldiers.

Henderson looked to his rear to make sure the armored vehicles weren't closing in on his position, fearful that the tracks would crush him as the sounds appeared to draw closer. *What a way to die in Vietnam!*

"Move!" Stahl yelled as he motioned to move forward again toward the enemy.

Relieved to receive the command, Henderson jumped to his feet and ran toward the next dike. He sweated heavily, and his heart pounded from the physical exertion and fear. Each time he moved to another dike, he lay as flat as he could for protection against the incoming rounds. The dry paddy dirt mixed with the sweat which covered his face.

Drexler ran over and fell to the ground next to him. He flashed Henderson a reassuring smile. "It'll be fine."

"Yeah, sure." Henderson laughed nervously. "Hell, you're as scared as me!"

Drexler nodded. "Yeah."

"Thanks for protecting me back there."

"Anytime; that's what brothers do."

Enemy rounds thudded into the dike wall, spraying dirt as bullets zinged over their heads. The two soldiers raised their M-16s above the dike, exposing their heads as they returned fire.

Several meters from Henderson, Rocky sprayed a continuous stream of fire from his M-60, while Porter linked the hundred-round belts of ammo, feeding them into the tray. It appeared as if the barrel of the machine gun was glowing as Porter wore a shit-eating grin.

"Unbelievable!" Henderson shook his head.

Professor fired a high-explosive round, as quickly as he could open the breach of the grenade launcher, each time loading a new cartridge, as if he were enjoying using the ammunition. Professor's face was distorted, his eyes bulged. When he noticed Henderson looking at him, he stopped firing his weapon. Henderson knew that he was savoring the fight with the enemy, but he also knew that if he asked later, Professor would have denied it, claiming his standard line that all life was sacred.

Professor again turned to face the enemy, loading, firing, and unloading his M-79. The distinctive thump the grenade launcher made when it discharged echoed across the paddy.

As Henderson moved with the rest of the unit, he ran forward to the next dike, with Drexler at his side. They leapfrogged ahead by platoon, the soldiers shooting at the enemy as they received incoming rounds. They took mortar, machine gun, and small-arms fire, rounds filling the air and mortar shells exploding near them. The enemy remained far away, on a hill overlooking the paddies, but because of the distance, the company couldn't gauge the effect of their fire to maneuver.

As Henderson lay behind the dike, he watched Second Platoon rise as one. They ran across the paddy toward the next embankment, roughly twenty-five meters to their front. The enemy suddenly increased their volume of fire as the Second Platoon ran toward cover, AK-47 and .51 caliber rounds tearing into the earth. Explosions from the mortars threw dirt into the air, blocking Henderson's view for a few seconds.

As Henderson glanced upward again, he saw four members of the Second Platoon shot by incoming rounds. They fell to the ground in a heap, hitting hard, their weapons and helmets flying through the air. Two of the injured soldiers struggled to crawl forward, and Henderson felt helpless. Several of the Second Platoon members ran to the wounded men and dragged them to the dike as the enemy continued to fire at them.

From the Second Platoon soldiers, the team heard the loud cry, "Medic! Medic! Medic!"

Henderson waved toward Brighton. "Let Doc help!"

"I can't hear you."

"Let Doc help."

"Stay put!"

Doc felt as if someone was squeezing his heart out of his chest. Shouting over the weapons-fire, he yelled, "LT, let me go!"

"I can't; you won't make it."

"They need a medic." *I don't want to lose any men, but the wounded need help.*

After several seconds of hesitation, Brighton relented. "Damned if you do and damned if you don't! Go!"

Doc jumped to his feet and raced across the dry field. The incoming AK-47 rounds sprayed dirt at his heels, following him until he reached the dike.

Henderson's throat tightened, making it hard to breathe as his finger squeezed the trigger. *I hope this gunfire is reaching the enemy!*

Brighton's radio squawked, with Lyons transmitting. "Tango one-six, this is Tango six. Over."

"This is Tango one-six. Over," Brighton confirmed.

"Tango one-six, airstrikes heading to the hills to your front in five mikes. Over."

"Roger, Tango six, airstrikes. Over."

"Stay where you are, Tango one-six. Out."

The order to stay put filtered to the squad and the teams. Henderson took a deep, confident breath. *No problem.*

Then, one behind the other, jets raced over the line of infantry soldiers lying behind their dikes. Henderson glanced upward and flashed a smile of relief.

Once over the target, the F-4s dropped their armament of explosives on the enemy's location. Bomb after bomb fell from the sky, exploding on target and sending large chunks of shrapnel through the dense smoke, climbing high above the hill. The F-4s flew so low that Henderson swore the ground shook beneath him— he could read the aircraft markings.

As the last jet passed the enemy positions, dropping its load of two napalm bombs, the enemy firing stopped. Before the bombs hit, the jets banked, streaking off in the direction of their airfield.

The napalm bombs dropped end over end as they fell, and Henderson watched them tumble toward the earth. When the first bomb hit the ground, a ball of bright orange fire reached for the sky, followed by plumes of black smoke.

Right after that explosion, the second bomb hit the mountain-top with the same effect. Henderson knew that the soldiers beneath the two napalm bombs wouldn't survive, and that they would die a horrendous death, of burns and suffocation.

Better them than me.

Henderson gave a thumbs-up toward Drexler and, as he looked into Drexler's eyes, knew that he was thinking the same—guilt or not, he was glad it wasn't him.

•

After the airstrikes, with the NVA no longer firing on the advancing American forces, the company received orders to move toward the hill. Lyons assigned the Second and Third Platoon to take the weapons they found and load them on a helicopter when it arrived. The platoon leaders instructed their soldiers to search the bodies and packs for letters, maps, or documents—they were told to turn over anything they found to the S2 officer. Then, the company commander assigned the First Platoon as the lead unit, with a mission to secure the hilltop.

"Let's move." Brighton nodded at Henderson.

"Okay, LT. Moving."

With the platoon following, Henderson trekked along the trail toward the hill with calculated, vigilant steps. He climbed its steep slope toward the top, knowing he could die at any moment as he navigated the terrain, looking for an ambush site, or booby traps placed along the path. As the point man, he had the responsibility to protect the men behind him.

Although exhausted from the battle, Henderson created a trail as he made his way to the burnt-out hilltop. The squad struggled along the path, staying thirty feet behind him. He had a difficult time keeping his balance while climbing, as he stumbled over concealed rocks protruding below the vegetation. But he pushed forward, forcing his way through the massive overgrowth of tall elephant grass. As sweat flowed from Henderson's tired body, soaking his filthy uniform, he pushed even harder to scramble toward the top while he looked for the enemy.

Drexler, behind and downhill of him, dodged rocks which Henderson dislodged in his climb, ready to assist if needed.

It took more than an hour before the platoon crested the hilltop. When they did, they discovered thirty-five dead enemy soldiers and blood trails; there were no signs of resistance. Henderson saw NVA soldiers sprawled over the hilltop in unbelievable bodily contortions, covered by burns, and often without arms or legs. The smell of burnt flesh hung in the air. Still smoldering, one soldier's body remained curled in a fetal position, his hands over his head as he had tried to shield himself from the falling bombs.

As Henderson and Drexler observed the carnage, neither spoke. Henderson removed a cigarette from the small Marlboro C-ration four-pack he kept in his breast pocket, and lit it with his Zippo lighter. Inhaling deeply, he blew a steady stream of smoke into the air.

In a measured, steady gait, Professor strolled into the carnage to stare at the faces of the dead soldiers. If he couldn't see a face, he flipped the body over to examine the NVA With a determined expression, he moved from body to body until he had looked at each soldier.

Henderson nudged Drexler, breaking their trance. "He's obsessed with finding his brother's killer."

"I know. Maybe it's what keeps him sane." Drexler became fixated on Professor's actions.

"You think he believes he'll find the NVA who did it?"

"No, I don't."

Reaching for his canteen, Henderson licked his lips. Unscrewing the cap, he tilted the container to his lips and gulped the warm, foul-tasting water. Then he passed it to Drexler, who took a long swig. Handing the canteen back to his friend, Drexler nodded his thanks and walked away to survey the damage.

The hilltop appeared clear of any vegetation, as if a forest fire had scorched the top of the hill, devouring the landscape in its path. Smoke drifted upward, the smell of burnt wood and human flesh overpowering Henderson's senses. Over time, the terrain wouldn't be like this. He questioned how anything could grow from this destruction.

While he surveyed the aftermath of the battle, Henderson inhaled deep drags from the cigarette, which hung from his dry lips. He sensed a person stood next to him, and when he turned, he saw Porter. He was staring at the smoldering dead body of the soldier curled to protect his head; Porter's smile had disappeared. He blew air from his nostrils.

"What a mess."

"It is. You okay, Ronnie?"

"Sure."

"Did you see the guys in Second Platoon getting hit?"

"Yup. Bad shit! It don't mean nothin'."

Henderson looked at his friend, acknowledging that he understood. He knew what Porter meant. Seeing his wounded brothers wounded him; it affected him. It scared him.

It don't mean nothin'.

These young men felt that saying those four words excused them from having to show the emotions which were screaming to escape from the depths of their humanity. This irrational belief went beyond understanding. Infantry soldiers believed that if they said "it don't mean nothin'," the words would protect them from remembering the horrors of war they witnessed.

Most importantly, they chose this as the way to grieve for a comrade who had died on the battlefield. Being in the bush for three hundred and sixty-five days, a soldier couldn't allow himself to carry the death of his friends along with his rucksack; the extra weight was too much. It helped to shed the weight, saying, "It don't mean nothin'."

Like the song, by The Hollies, "He Ain't Heavy; He's My Brother." How many brothers can you carry, before you can't walk anymore?

A tear escaped Henderson. Taking one last drag from his cigarette, he flipped it toward the dead NVA soldier, who still fascinated Porter.

Standing shoulder to shoulder with Porter, he removed the can of peaches from his pants' cargo pocket, opening it with the P-38, then retrieved a white, plastic spoon from his breast pocket. He dug in hungrily, slurping the juice and chewing the warm peaches. Lifting the can, with the spoon in it, he offered it to Porter.

With a quick smile of thanks, Porter shook his head. "Eating and dead bodies don't do it for me."

"More for me, then," Henderson gulped another mouthful. He remained standing next to his friend, not wanting to leave him alone as they stared at the dead bodies.

Stahl yelled, "First Squad on the west side, for LZ security—choppers landing in five mikes."

Henderson and Porter looked at each other, acknowledging that they were both okay, and followed their squad leader to the west side of the hilltop, where the rest of the squad had moved into position, to secure the LZ for the company. They moved to a clearing away from the destruction and waited for the Hueys to transport them back to Debbie.

During the battle, Alpha Company and E Troop suffered six wounded in action and three killed in action. The medevacs flew them all to Chu Lai, to the 91st Evac. Hospital.

The First Platoon kept the landing zone secure for the company. Then, when the helicopters returned the third time, the First Platoon loaded up for their trip to Debbie.

Henderson sat quietly, watching the landscape zoom by as he thought of the brothers who were killed or wounded. When the choppers landed on the firebase helipad, they all jumped off and headed to their bunkers, without saying a word—tired, hungry, and thirsty.

•

Later that evening, at the mess hall, Lyons stood to address the soldiers. "Please, I need your attention for a minute."

The hum of chatter, and the banging of trays and flatware, went quiet.

"You know that the Second and Third Platoons had casualties this afternoon." He paused to compose himself. "Kilroy and McDuff, from the Second Platoon, died an hour ago from the firefight this afternoon." He waited several seconds for his words to sink in, then continued. "Third Platoon's Smith, Reedy, and Jameson were killed in the ambush earlier today." Again, he paused. "Let's say a prayer for the four wounded and five killed."

The men sitting in the mess hall all bowed their heads to speak to their God.

Lyons waited for the talking to subside before saying, "After the noon meal tomorrow, the chaplain will have a memorial service in the mess hall. I'm done. Finish eating." At that, he exhaled loudly enough that anyone sitting in the mess hall could hear, slumped into his chair with eyes lowered, and placed his head into his hands.

Lyons was an older officer—thirty years of age—with prior service. He had served with Special Forces before going to OCS, and was as hard as nails. But he was not hard enough for this.

After the announcement, the men of Alpha Company sat silently. As the minutes ticked by, the sounds of trays and flatware banging, and men quietly talking, resonated throughout the mess hall.

Henderson looked at Lyons. "A damn good officer." He felt humbled by the way the deaths of the men in Alpha Company troubled his company commander.

Drexler looked at Henderson. "This war sucks. But, losing brothers…" His voice trailed off as tears clouded his eyes.

Henderson tried to reassure his friend. "It don't mean nothin'."

HOW THEY LIVED

Two days later, Stahl stuck his head inside the squad bunker's entrance. "Everybody outside."

Half of the squad already waited in the open air for the remaining members to gather around Stahl. Henderson and Porter were among the group which waited outside, in the heat. Small beads of sweat covered Henderson's face. He did his best to wipe them away, but as soon as he rubbed his face with his dirty handkerchief, the sweat reappeared.

Standing next to Porter, Henderson said, "It's only zero-eight-hundred, and this goddamned heat is killing me."

"Yup, you're sweating like a pig … me too." Porter wiped the sweat from his brow. "Let's find some shade."

The two moved underneath a poncho liner, which stretched six feet above the ground next to the bunker. "There's no breeze, but the liner is better than nothin'," Henderson said, wiping at his forehead again.

"You don't need to tell me about it; I'm standing in this too. We've found a shady patch in hell." Porter wiped his face to remove the sweat dripping from his forehead into his eyes.

When Bravo Team arrived, Stahl raised his eyes. "Looks like the whole squad is here. We have a new mission today."

The soldiers grumbled. He waited for it to subside. "The platoon is going to a ville in the Rice Bowl to search for VC, weapons, food, and tunnels. You'll work in teams of two. The platoon starts on the south side of the ville, working north. E Troop will provide transportation. There'll be four tracks waiting by the mess hall. We'll meet in thirty minutes. Travel light, with weapons, ammo, and water. The tracks have rations for lunch, and we'll return before dinner. If we miss chow, the mess hall will stay open for us. Any questions?"

A soldier raised his hand. "Are we expecting contact?"

Stahl sighed, trying not to show his annoyance, but it clearly showed to every soldier. "We're going to the Rice Bowl, so yeah."

"I thought I would check." The soldier looked chastised, but not embarrassed. "Nothing else."

"Get ready." Stahl clenched his jaw. "See you at the mess hall in thirty mikes."

Silence hung in the air as the squad members readied their gear for the mission.

After he had secured his ammo and full canteen, Henderson reached into his rucksack to remove a can of fruit cocktail. Remembering that the tracks had rations, he reluctantly dropped it back into the ruck. When he was ready, he looked around at his friends as they prepared for the mission.

"Hey, guys, I heard we're going home."

"Come on, Eddie. You don't believe it, do you?" Drexler waved him off with a flick of his wrist. "Rumors like that are never true." Drexler didn't want to think about going home—not until he knew for sure. There was too much to sort out at home, which would seep in and distract him if he let it.

Henderson shrugged. He *wanted* to believe it, and sometimes that felt as real as genuinely believing something you may have heard. "I don't know. I heard it from one of the new guys. Take a minute and recall what Nixon said when he ran for president."

Professor shook his head. "Remember, he's been president for over six months—that is potentially enough time to get plans in motion. Does he have some mechanism in place to end this damn war? Have you seen it?"

"Not sure, Professor." Rocky's rough voice came out a bit too loud. Going home was personal, and it stirred things up inside him. Sometimes, when that happened, his words came out forcefully. "Nixon said he would withdraw US troops from this shithole, and the Army of the Republic of Vietnam would take over. It's a nice thought."

"Have you seen any ARVN units fighting, or heard of any American units leaving? Besides, those son-of-a-bitch politicians will lie to your face without compunction." Professor ground his teeth.

Porter rolled his eyes. "Maybe our unit will go home. You know, like a special favor, because we're such good soldiers."

The team laughed at Porter's comment and relaxed. They all wished the army would send them home, but believing it hurt too much for some, especially if the hopes proved false.

"I don't see any reason to believe a reprieve will happen during our time. Plan on spending your three-sixty-five in this hellhole called war." Professor furrowed his brow and fisted his hands.

The team remained quiet for a moment, digesting the conversation.

Stahl stuck his head in the open doorway. "Get moving."

The thought of the upcoming mission took precedence in the soldier's minds, the conversation already forgotten. Loaded with their essential gear, the men of the Second Squad joined the First Squad. They strode in the direction of the mess hall, most of the soldiers joking, laughing, and telling stories of their past life. As they reached the crest of the hill, Henderson spotted the four APCs idling as they spewed diesel fumes into the air, not far from the mess hall.

Stahl raised his hand. "Alpha Team on the first track and Bravo Team on the second track."

Swift nodded. "Brown and I will be on the second track, with Bravo Team."

The First Squad moved toward the third and fourth tracks, with Brighton and Ledger on the latter.

Once the platoon found places to sit on the top of their assigned APC, the drivers put the tracks into gear and lurched forward to begin their trip on the unpaved, rugged mountain road. The track commander stood behind the .50 caliber machine gun, while the two M-60 gunners swiveled their weapons to cover each side of the track.

Drexler glanced toward Henderson. "Ready for a Sunday drive?"

"You bet," Henderson yelled over the roar of the engine. "It beats walkin'!"

Porter and Rocky looked at their team members and smiled.

When they reached the valley floor, it was time to get serious. Perched on the top of the moving APC, the infantry soldiers kept a sharp lookout for ambushes and booby traps as the four tracks drove through dry rice paddies, over dikes, and through two hedgerows.

They reached the village three klicks from the firebase. They followed a trail that led to its entrance, and the APCs stopped one hundred and fifty meters from the village. After the driver placed the gear into neutral, the tracks idled, the noise of the engines drowning any sounds coming from the ville.

Brighton cleared his throat as he double-checked his weapon's readiness. "Off the tracks!"

The Alpha Team jumped to the hard, dry rice paddy, hitting the ground with their full weight. They ran with bandoliers of magazines pounding against their chests and helmets bouncing, until they reached the rest of the Second Squad. There, they fell to the hard, packed dirt behind a berm. The First Squad followed the Second Squad, running to the berm in front for cover.

Swift looked at Henderson. "You'll be taking point." Then, he turned toward the platoon. "Spread out until we get to the ville."

Henderson stepped forward with slow, careful steps as he approached the village from the main trail on the south side, which led into the center of the ville. The platoon followed.

Two APCs moved to the west side, while the remaining two tracks stayed on the east side of the community. They followed the platoon along the outskirts of the ville as the soldiers searched the huts and surrounding area. Older men and women kept working in the rice fields surrounding the community. They acted as though armed troops entering their village was a common occurrence.

While walking along the trail, Henderson felt sorry for the residents, knowing that the American forces were in the ville during the day, and that the VC came at night. These villagers were in the middle of this terrible war. However, he also suspected that some of the inhabitants were VC, too, so his feeling toward the villagers was conflicted.

The rice paddies surrounding the ville were a good source of food for the Viet Cong, which meant that the VC came there for support. To eliminate enemy support, they needed to search and destroy any of those resources, including weapons. Henderson understood they would need to enter the villagers' huts and search through their belongings. Searching a dwelling wasn't a task he or any of his brothers enjoyed, but they had to do it for their safety.

Dogs barked throughout the ville. As the first line of huts came into view, Henderson saw movement to his right. Branches moved in the thicket, causing him to swing his M-16 around and slide the selector switch from safe to semi-automatic, ready to shoot whoever came out of the brush. Seconds later, two large, snorting pigs sprang from the vegetation and ran into the ville. A smile crossed his lips as he slid the safety back on. But he left his thumb resting on the switch.

As he entered the ville, Henderson observed a pagoda—a sacred Buddhist building. The village was a copy of the dozens Henderson had seen during his time in 'Nam. There were thatched mud huts, constructed with the main room and a smaller one for sleeping. Animal pens were behind the structures. A community building stood under the shade of a huge tree. Henderson figured that there were over forty huts in the ville, and three times as many villagers.

When Henderson passed the first two huts, two old women, one young woman, and three boys peeked at the soldiers from their open doorways. One of the old women greeted Henderson with a toothless smile—the young woman stared at the ground as he passed.

He stopped, allowing the rest of the platoon to move past him.

Brighton pointed at the community building. "*Di chuyển đến đó!*" He paused, then yelled again, "*Di Chuyển Ngay!*" He kept repeating the two phrases until the villagers complied with his instructions.

Henderson looked at Drexler. "What's the lieutenant saying?"

"I think he's saying 'Move there; move now.'"

Brighton wanted all of the inhabitants accounted for, and moved them to the community building. Anyone who remained outside the building would be suspected Viet Cong.

Then, working as a team, the two friends searched the village, going from one hut to another. Each time Henderson entered a hut, Drexler covered him. Inside, he lifted mats on the floor to look for tunnels, and searched through baskets, blankets and any other location where the enemy could hide weapons or ammunition. Once they cleared a hut, they moved on to the next one. When Drexler searched the animal pens and food storage bins, Henderson covered him.

Madison waved his rifle in the air. "Found a tunnel!"

The Second Squad gathered around Madison and looked to where he pointed.

"Found a tunnel." Madison nodded proudly.

Stahl glanced toward several men before selecting the man for the job. "Henderson, check it."

"Why me, Sarge?" Henderson gawked at the hole with trepidation.

"You're the smallest."

"You're not supposed to say that, Sarge."

"Okay, we *need* you to go in the tunnel. Are you happy now?"

"Fine." Henderson stripped off his gear and helmet. No one was going to accuse him of being a coward. "Rocky, your gun."

Rocky handed him his pistol. "Need a flashlight?"

"Yeah."

Rocky nodded as he handed Henderson his flashlight. "Be careful."

"I will." Henderson didn't seem able to get more than two words out at a time, his throat was constricted and dry.

He used his arms to lower his body through the tight tunnel opening, and dropped to the tunnel floor. His breath quickened, and his heart pounded against his chest. He realized that he had the option to remain still—to be quiet enough to choose how to fight, should he need to. Everything was silent as he stared down the darkness.

Henderson turned on the flashlight, with the red lens inserted. With the cocked .45 caliber pistol facing into the blackness of the tunnel passageway, he remained frozen in the same crouched position, waiting several minutes for his eyes to adjust. He hoped no enemy soldiers were there to greet him. The same smells he detected in the village lingered in the dark, cramped space.

He sensed danger, and sweat ran into his eyes, which surprised him, because the tunnel felt cooler than above ground. As he wiped the sweat from his face, he continued to stare along the length of the dank, dark passageway, studying the tunnel. Finally, Henderson settled on the best way to move along the corridor, doing his best to identify any locations which might be booby-trapped.

Within seconds, fear took hold of him, but he knew he had to shake it off to continue the search. He stepped into the darkness, moving along the tunnel floor without touching the ceiling or dirt walls, and with only enough room to walk bent over. With each step, Henderson checked for enemy soldiers and watched the ground for tripwires, which could set off a booby trap.

As he walked around a bend, he stepped into a small room six feet long, four wide, and six high. He leaned against the far wall as he observed the cache. There were at least a couple of dozen AK-47s, along with an RPG and ammunition, which the VC had stored in the chamber.

Shining the light past the room toward the long, narrow tunnel, Henderson could see nothing but blackness.

He moved back to the tunnel opening as quickly as possible, standing where the light shimmered into the darkness.

"Get me out!"

He lifted his arms overhead as Rocky and Professor grabbed him by the wrists, pulling him to the surface.

He squinted in the sunlight and looked at Stahl. "Found a weapons cache."

"How many?"

"Nearly twenty-five weapons, with ammo."

Brighton strode over to Stahl and Henderson. "What's going on?"

Stahl confirmed Henderson's find with confidence. "Found a cache of weapons."

Brighton smiled—an honest, open smile, which seemed to congratulate the soldiers without words. "Send in two men to remove the weapons and the ammo. Then we'll blow the tunnel."

After members of the Second Squad had removed the weapons from the tunnel, Brighton ordered them to load the arsenal into the fourth track to transport to Debbie once the platoon had completed the mission.

As the platoon prepared to finish the search, they heard the command, "Fire in the hole!" Within seconds, there were muffled explosions as the concussion grenades exploded. The ground shook, and a spray of dirt erupted from the tunnel's entrance.

Nash tapped his foot. "Those two grenades should have collapsed the tunnel." He said it as if to reassure himself; all the soldiers there already knew the drill. If they hadn't been in the field with him, some of the men might have commented on his stating the obvious.

As they reached the last huts on both sides of the ville, the platoon completed their search. Then Henderson and the rest of the platoon walked toward the north end of the village to meet the four tracks at the designated location.

Suddenly, they were slammed by an earth-shattering *wham!*

The grunts hit the ground as the explosion created a ball of fire. Parts of the third track hurled through the air, and smoke filled the sky.

Henderson heard a loud thud and saw a blackened steel wheel embedded in the ground, twenty feet from him.

While taking cover, the platoon waited for the barrage of incoming AK-47 rounds which often followed an explosion. They never came.

After several minutes, the platoon stood up to see what had happened.

Outside the village, the third APC in the column burned, the smoke billowing skyward. Henderson noticed that one of the huts near the explosion had caught fire too.

As the three surviving APCs circled the destroyed track, Brighton took the lead. "Everyone stay in place."

Henderson leaned close to Drexler. "What the hell happened?"

"I don't know. No VC that I can see. They'll tell us once they know. Just stay alert."

After several minutes had passed, Brighton moved toward the platoon with a quick stride. "Doc, Drexler, and Madison, remove the bodies from the track. Let me know if there are any survivors. While you remove them, I'll call for a medevac. Move out."

He got on the radio. "Tango six, this is Tango one-six. Over." Brighton waited on Lyons's response.

"Go ahead, Tango one-six. Over."

"Need a medevac at our location, four KIA. Over."

"Roger, Tango one-six. Wilco. Be there in thirty mikes. Out."

Drexler, Madison, and Doc discovered that there were no survivors. In the track they found three of the four bodies burnt beyond recognition. The explosion had ejected the track commander from the APC, leaving his legs and one of his arms in place behind the .50 caliber machine gun. Doc found the rest of him thirty feet from the track, and knelt next to the gunner.

From where he stood, Henderson saw Drexler lean out of the APC and heave his breakfast.

Flames climbed the far side of the hut as the villagers used buckets of water to attempt dousing the fire. Old women were at the two wells, filling bucket after bucket. When they were full, the women handed them to an older child to carry to the burning hut.

Henderson pointed to the hooch. "Porter, Rocky, let's help."

"Let's do it." Porter bolted toward the hut.

"Count me in." Rocky quickly followed.

The three rushed to the hut and took positions to the front of it, compelling the villagers to pass the water-filled buckets to them. As each bucket reached the soldiers, they threw the water onto the flames. A strong odor of burning straw filled the air, and flames licked at Henderson's uniform as he emptied bucket after bucket.

It took five minutes to douse the fire, but by then half of the hut had been destroyed, leaving the large living area exposed. An old woman wailed as she searched through her scorched belongings.

As they waited for the dustoff, Henderson's brow was furrowed. He stared at Drexler, dumbfounded. "What happened?"

"The lieutenant said the APC ran over a two hundred and fifty-pound mine. I can't believe it was so close to the ville."

"That's bad shit." Henderson's cheeks turned crimson.

After thirty minutes, the three platoon members had the four bodies wrapped in ponchos, ready for the medevac. Stahl popped smoke for the dustoff to guide the pilot.

Once the dustoff landed, Drexler, Doc, Madison, and Stahl loaded the four bodies into the waiting helicopter. Then Stahl signaled the all-clear sign, and the pilot lifted the Huey skyward, accelerating toward firebase Bronco. Without saying a word, the men of the First Platoon watched the helicopter fly away.

After the dustoff took flight, Brighton addressed Nash. "Have your squad remove weapons, ammunition, communications equipment, and any personal property from the blown APC; store them in one of the other APCs. Once you've recovered the equipment, destroy the track."

"Will do, LT."

"McKinney and Livingston, get some C-four from another track and rig this APC. Blow it in place." Nash's voice, although authoritative, sounded agitated.

"Roger." McKinney grabbed Livingston by the arm.

After they inserted blasting caps into several pounds of the plastic explosive, they strung the wire. McKinney covered his ears, shouting, "Fire in the hole! Fire in the hole!"

The platoon took cover.

McKinney looked at Livingston. "You ready?"

"Yep, let's blow it."

"On the count of three. One, two, three—"

Both soldiers pressed the triggers, sending an electrical current through the wire.

Wham!

The APC exploded, and the ground shook.

McKinney gave Livingston a look of satisfaction. "Nothin' left for the VC to take."

"Nothing." Livingston grinned. "Just the way I like it."

After the track blew, Henderson sat next to Rocky and Porter in silence as they waited to leave the ville.

Rocky cleared his throat. "You believe they're putting a man on the moon?"

Porter scratched his ear. "I read it in the *Stars and Stripes.*"

"Some guy named Armstrong—a Navy pilot—will walk on the moon. Unbelievable." Rocky rubbed his mustache.

Henderson licked his lips. "That's cool. You'd think if they can put a man on the moon, they could end the war."

Both soldiers looked at Henderson and nodded.

Swift yelled, "Get on the tracks."

As they climbed onto a track, the platoon members addressed the crew. "Sorry for your loss."

Henderson clenched his jaw and took a seat, preparing for the drive to Debbie.

As they rode to the firebase, Henderson reflected on the track exploding, and of Drexler's reaction removing the lifeless, charred bodies. He glanced over at him and saw the moisture in his friend's eyes.

The narrow mountain road led to the entrance into Debbie. As they entered, Henderson's stomach growled, and he realized that he hadn't had lunch. After the tracks stopped, the soldiers jumped to the ground, heading to their bunkers.

Henderson tapped Drexler on the shoulder to get his attention. "Let's clean up then get something to eat—I'm starving."

"Not sure I'm hungry." Drexler shivered as he wiped his hands on his pants.

"You gotta eat. Come on."

"Okay, I guess I'll go."

The two friends strode along the worn path toward the bunker like two older men, carrying the burden of war. They put their gear away and cleaned up before heading to the mess hall.

Henderson swallowed as he wiped the sweat from his brow.

Hell of a day. I hope tomorrow is better.

ANOTHER BEAUTIFUL
SUNRISE IN 'NAM

At 0100 hours, Drexler shook Henderson's shoulder. "Let's go. It's your turn for guard duty."

"Ten more minutes, please." Henderson covered his eyes with his poncho liner and rolled over.

"Nope." Drexler gave Henderson a less-than-friendly shove.

Drexler's limbs felt laden with fatigue. He would never have admitted it, but another hour and he might have passed out. "On your feet."

"Christ, okay! I'm awake!" Henderson flashed a smile at his friend as he hopped off the ground, grabbing his M-16, helmet, a bandolier of ammo, canteen, and a can of fruitcake from his rucksack. He stifled a yawn as he strode past Drexler toward the doorway.

Drexler climbed into the spot where Henderson had slept, falling asleep before Henderson left the bunker.

Henderson stepped into the darkness and stood for a minute to let his eyes adjust to the blackness of the night. Once his eyes had adjusted, he scrambled to the top of the bunker and sat behind a three-foot-high wall of old, multicolored sandbags. The crisp, night air felt refreshing compared to the heat of the day. A breeze of ocean air had found its way to the mountain, cooling him as it drifted against his exposed skin.

He picked up his two-quart canteen and took several long gulps of cherry Kool-Aid. While he checked the thick, overgrown terrain one hundred feet to his front, he retrieved his P-38 can opener from his chain and punctured the fruitcake's lid, severing around the top of the can. Once opened, he took small bites of the cake, savoring the taste. Taking several more gulps of Kool-Aid, he kept an eye open for any movement which signaled that the enemy was near.

Time for a smoke to end the meal.

He took out a cigarette and lit it, keeping the flame hidden as he inhaled his after-dinner nicotine delight.

As Henderson maintained a watch for the enemy, the buzzing of gigantic mosquitoes echoed around him. At first, he swatted the pesky insects, to no avail; then, he blew smoke in the direction of the sound they made. Finally, he surrendered. He retrieved the DEET from the band holding the camouflage cover over the steel pot and poured a generous portion into his hands, smearing the repellent onto his exposed skin. He hoped that the buzzing would stop. It was the third time in twenty-four hours he had applied the repellent. For the rest of his life, he would never again be able to smell DEET without feeling the heat of the Vietnam jungle, and the ghost of the taste of Kool-Aid.

The minutes on his watch slowly ticked away the time until, at last, it displayed 0200 hours. As Henderson climbed off of the bunker roof, he only had one thing on his mind, sleep.

He strode quickly into the bunker, headed straight for Professor, and nudged him. "It's your turn."

Without a word, Professor stood, stretched, grabbed his weapon, and hurried toward the entrance.

Henderson lay in the vacant spot for the next few hours, obtaining his much-needed sleep.

•

The platoon woke as the sun climbed over the South China Sea.

After taking a cold, early morning shower, Rocky and Porter returned to the bunker. The two soldiers wore nothing except jungle boots and the towels wrapped around their waists. Drexler blew a wolf-whistle at them, which drew laughter from the squad.

Rocky proudly stuck out his hairy chest. "At least I'm clean."

After a brief flash of embarrassment, Porter grinned broadly and stuck out his gut to exaggerate the slight pudge. "Me too ... clean and gorgeous."

A shower—cold or warm—was a gift the soldiers were thankful to receive after weeks of being dirty, and it was well worth a mild ribbing from the other guys.

After Rocky and Porter entered the bunker, they slipped into their soiled, foul-smelling uniforms.

The rest of the squad bathed at the shelter, using their helmets, which they filled with water from a five-gallon can. They scrubbed with bars of soaps they carried.

While Henderson washed up, he looked east toward the sea. "Sunrises here in 'Nam are beautiful."

Drexler stared at Henderson in disbelief that his friend would say anything good about 'Nam; the place was a nightmare which they couldn't escape.

Henderson recognized the irritation in his friend. "Come on, you know it's true."

"Sure. If you say so."

Henderson knew that Drexler didn't find any beauty in Vietnam, so he changed the subject. "Let's go to the mess hall before the rest of the guys get there. I'm hungry."

"You're always hungry. Let's go."

They slung their M-16s over their shoulders, put on their helmets, and the two friends strolled to breakfast along the worn path which led to the mess hall.

After breakfast, Stahl called the squad over to the back of the bunker. Once they had gathered at his position, he addressed the soldiers. "I want you guys to clean your weapons. If you've already cleaned it, check it again. No one can afford for their weapon to misfire or jam—our lives depend on it. Most of you have fired a lot of ammunition in the last couple of days. Let me know if you need more. I'll get it for you."

Soldiers scrambled to retrieve the necessary cleaning supplies. Some chose to remain in the bunker, while others worked outside in the heat. Henderson and Drexler chose outside, even though the sun beamed down on their backs.

"My weapon stays clean," Henderson proudly noted as he wiped the barrel with a rag.

"Like mine's not?"

"Drexler, I don't see you cleaning your rifle every day. Don't you think you should? Like Stahl said, our lives could depend on it. What would you do if you fired at the enemy and your rifle jammed?"

"Not likely; it's clean enough."

Professor oiled his gun and inspected it. "Mine is ready."

Henderson darted his eyes at Drexler. "Hand it over; I'll inspect it."

"Not on your life! I never hand my weapon over. Concentrate on your own and don't worry about mine."

Henderson ran a cleaning rod down the barrel of his M-16. "I don't know about you, but I'll be glad when the politicians back home call this war off."

"I thought we agreed not to talk about politics." Drexler laid his M-16 on a towel. "You know how angry I get."

"Fair enough. It's a fine, hot day in hell. Is that better?"

Professor glanced up at Henderson. "I'll talk about politics. My dad wrote to me the other day. He said we should drop an atomic bomb on North Vietnam." The chatter stopped, and the area where they were sitting grew quiet. "And I agreed with him."

"Calvin, you're kidding." Henderson drew a deep breath. Seldom did Henderson address Professor by his first name.

"Do you know one GI who would trade a barrel of US soil for this entire country?" Professor clenched his jaw.

Henderson recoiled; unintentionally, he pictured Mai and her son. "Of course not. I hate it here as much as you, Professor, but dropping an atomic bomb? Come on, man."

Drexler entered the debate. "Professor, you have a point, but I agree with Eddie on this one. Using an atomic weapon isn't the answer."

"I'll concede on the atomic bomb issue." Professor shrugged. But he didn't, really—he wouldn't mind seeing the whole country as a smoking pit. "But it's my opinion we should pack up and get out of this hellhole. The propaganda argument that we're fighting against communism is the biggest bunch of shit I've ever heard."

Stahl cut into the conversation; his stern face seemed to weaponize. He couldn't let this sort of talk continue, because it did nothing but create friction within the squad, and that got men killed. He glared at them. "We're fighting for each other—no other cause. Let's not forget it. Look to your left and right. The NVA and the VC are the reasons you fight."

The squad members muttered their agreement to Stahl's statement.

"Wow, Sarge, I didn't know you were a philosopher." Professor flashed his leader a smile, and the venom had now gone from his face. He couldn't argue that these were his brothers gathered around him, and he had lost more than enough brothers already.

The men laughed, but they knew Stahl spoke the truth; they fought the enemy for each other, and no other reason.

Drexler placed his weapon across his lap. "I do hate this hellhole. I'll be glad to get home."

Henderson nodded as he continued to oil his M-16. "When I get home, I won't tell anyone about being in Vietnam."

"I'm going to live in the mountains by myself." Rocky's stern gaze instantly became a dreamy smile which crept onto his face, though it was mostly hidden by his mustache.

Professor rolled his head, cracking his neck. "When I return home, I'm growing my hair long again and teaching kids not to fight wars. Not to start them, either. If we have an option at all, then peace is the way to go."

Henderson's stomach growled. "Anyone hungry?"

Stahl stood. "It's close to lunchtime. Put the cleaning equipment away."

After the soldiers cleaned the area and put things away, they strode in small groups toward the mess hall.

Henderson smiled, listening to the laughter of the men he thought of as brothers.

I don't want any one of them to die, but I know that at least one will.

•

A couple of hours after noon, Brighton approached his men. He felt a deep pride for them, but when he reached them, he got down to business. "First Platoon, gather round!"

Once the platoon assembled, Brighton took his time. As his eyes connected with every soldier, he commanded, "At sixteen-hundred hours, Hueys are going to airlift the platoon to firebase Bronco. At Bronco, you'll be resupplied, showered, issued clean uniforms, and get some much-needed rest."

Shouts of thanks and laughter erupted from the platoon.

"Quiet!" Brighton's stern tone reflected that there was something else he must address. The platoon fell silent.

"Later, you'll get a briefing on our new mission."

The men remained quiet as they digested the news. The unknown troubled them, made clear by the looks on their faces.

Stahl rubbed his earlobe. "What's the mission, sir?"

"We'll get a full briefing tomorrow by Battalion Operations, S-three, so hold your questions until tomorrow. I don't know any more at this time."

"Okay, LT."

Swift rolled his shoulders. "Squad leaders, have your men get their gear. Report to the helipad at fifteen-forty-five hours."

Sergeants Nash and Stahl replied, "Yes, Sergeant."

After leaving the briefing, Henderson walked toward the bunker with Drexler at his side. "Why the secrecy?"

"I don't think anyone has that answer but LT."

"I overheard one of the guys saying we're going to Cambodia."

"Really?"

"I heard we're going to Laos." Rocky increased his pace to catch Henderson and Drexler.

"Maybe we're going home!" Porter jumped in front of Henderson, walking a couple of steps backward before turning around. His statement drew laughter from the platoon.

Henderson rolled his eyes as he increased his stride toward the bunker. *The rumors have started.* Rumors and war are like gasoline and a lit match.

Once inside, Henderson found the squad quiet while they gathered equipment and packed their rucksacks. He stuffed his poncho, with the liner, into his backpack. Remembering that he had a pair of socks hanging on the bunker window, he put them on top of the poncho.

After pulling two hundred rounds of M-60 from the ammunition can, he strapped the ammo over the top of his rucksack, beneath the flap. He tightened the straps to hold his gear in place.

While sitting, he slid into the harness of his pack, letting it rest against his small frame, then stood. *Damn, this is heavy!*

With weighted steps, Henderson walked out of the bunker and up the hill toward a landing Huey. He watched the men of the Second Squad scramble aboard the Huey, finding a seat on the deck of the helicopter. He and Drexler were the last to board. They sat together, facing the open doorway, with their feet dangling over the skid, allowing the weight of their rucksack to keep them from sliding forward.

The helicopter rose quickly into the air. The pilot pushed the nose downward, banked, left and accelerated toward Bronco, while the door gunner swiveled his M-60, looking for the VC.

A BRIEFING THAT CHANGED EVERYTHING

Alpha Company flew by UH-1D Iroquois Huey—transportation provided by the 174th Assault Helicopter Company—to the 11th Brigade firebase, located at Fire Support Base Bronco. The firebase sat outside the village of Duc Pho, in the southern portion of South Vietnam's I Corps.

Two hours before dusk, the helicopters headed for the helipad in a single file. Once the fleet of Hueys landed, the men of Alpha Company jumped off and ran to the right side of the helipad, gathered by platoons, where they waited for instructions.

The company leader, First Sergeant Raymond Hall, puffed on a large pipe, with the stem clenched between his teeth. A career soldier in his mid-thirties, he had an air of authority, with short, dark hair and a medium build. He sounded gruff, but the men believed that under the layer of hardness he displayed, he had a fondness for the soldiers of Alpha Company. If asked, not one soldier could have said where this assumption came from, but they didn't question it. Luckily for them, it was true.

The enlisted men and officers fondly referred to Hall as "Top." Being the top enlisted man in the company, he earned the nickname.

Hall stood in front of the soldiers. "Welcome home!"

At the sound of those words, Henderson erupted into a cheer. The men didn't consider Bronco home, but to the soldiers who had been there for six months or more, it had started to look more and more like it to them. Six months in a combat zone was a lifetime for many of the soldiers of Alpha Company.

As the cheers subsided, Hall clenched his jaw. "Platoon sergeants, have your platoons get clean clothes from supply, take a shower, then go to the mess hall for a steak dinner. Don't forget to have your platoons drop off the dirty uniforms at supply after they shower."

Henderson had been in the field for a month, operating on and off at Debbie, so going to firebase Bronco felt like arriving at a vacation resort. Most importantly, there were no extra details either, like shit burning. He recognized this as a haven from the mountains, jungles, rice paddies and, especially, the enemy.

Seldom did the NVA or VC attempt to probe the firebase, much less attack it in force—the occasional mortar or rocket attack provided their only fears. Henderson sensed all the men in the squad relax.

The helicopter's turbine engines whined as Swift addressed the soldiers. "First Platoon, follow me to supply in a single file. Meet at the front of the company headquarters at eighteen-hundred hours for your building assignments."

As the platoon walked toward the supply room, Henderson felt a sense of excitement in anticipation of clean clothes, a shower, and a steak meal. *Oh, the little things in life.*

As Alpha Team strolled toward the supply room, Henderson looked over to Drexler. "Tonight, we get the three most important things in life."

Drexler took the bait. "Yeah? What's that?"

"Come on, you know. Safety, sleep, and chow." Henderson laughed.

"You bet that's the three."

The men of the First Platoon formed a line outside the supply room and entered in fours to receive clean uniforms. Henderson stepped into the room through the open doorway, with Drexler following. The clerk waited at the counter between him and the men he served.

Henderson flashed the clerk a wide-toothed grin. "I need an extra-small uniform."

The clerk glanced up toward Henderson and chuckled. "I bet you do."

"I don't need shit from you! Give me the uniform."

The clerk grabbed a set of extra-small from beneath the wooden counter and slid the clean uniform across to Henderson. "Here… Here you go." Appearing anxious to escape Henderson's cold stare, he diverted his eyes to Drexler. "Next!"

With uniforms in hand, the two friends laughed about the clerk's reaction. Then, they headed to the shower to wash away weeks of built-up filth.

After showering, they returned to supply. As the two soldiers entered the building, Henderson approached the counter and handed his dirty, foul uniform to the same clerk, with a smile. "Thank you."

The clerk's nose tilted away from the odor of Henderson's stinky uniform, and his face twisted. He almost gagged from the odor as Drexler tossed his dirty uniform onto the counter too.

Henderson's stomach growled as he turned to Drexler. "Now for the best part. Let's eat."

"You're speaking my language."

Without another word, they quickly strode to the mess hall for the promised steak dinner. Outside the mess hall, cooks grilled fifty steaks at a time over the red-hot charcoal. When ready, they placed the steaks in a large, metal container, which they took into the mess hall for the waiting soldiers.

Henderson's mouth watered. "Damn, those steaks smell good! I think I could eat the whole cow; I'm so hungry."

"A side of beef would do me fine." Drexler sniffed the aroma of the charred steaks and savored it.

As they entered the mess hall, the Second Squad were sitting together. Porter motioned for Drexler and Henderson to sit with them.

Henderson waved. "Porter, save us a seat."

Porter nodded in acknowledgment as he stuffed a huge chunk of steak into his mouth.

As the two soldiers strolled toward the long counter containing the meal of the day, they slung their M-16s across their shoulders.

As they stood in line, about twelve deep, waiting to fill their tray, Henderson smiled. "Looks like they have all the fixings to go with the steak. I can't wait to chomp on a piece of it and chow down on a hot baked potato—eat me some corn and some homemade yeast rolls. This is almost too good to be true."

They slowly inched their way up the serving line.

"I concur, but I'm really after that chocolate cake I see at the end."

They grabbed a tray from the stack and retrieved flatware from a serving container. Behind the counter, soldiers on KP duty slopped food onto their trays as they progressed down the line.

"Damn, Drexler, this looks good." He held his tray toward the servers, who heaped the food onto his tray.

Drexler followed him, doing the same. "Smells good too. Man, those steaks are making my mouth water."

After going through the chow line, Henderson grabbed a carton of cold chocolate milk—the drink of the day. They returned to the table with trays full, sitting with their squad brothers.

As Porter looked around at the squad, he said, "How do you know the difference between the villagers and the enemy?" He paused for effect. "The VC is the one shooting at you."

They laughed at what Porter presented as a joke, but each knew he spoke the truth.

To elaborate on Porter's statement, Professor decided to interject. "Hell, that is entirely intentional on the VC's part. It wasn't always that way. Over the years, the Viet Cong got smarter; he learned to dress like a farmer. When he sees US soldiers coming, he grabs a hidden rifle and shoots a couple of rounds, hides the gun. Then he disappears into the village. That precise thing happened to us right after we got to 'Nam."

Rocky almost choked on his food. "Once, when a VC fired on us, we entered the village and tore the place apart, looking for the guy. In the process, we pissed off the villagers. Hell, they all turned against us, making it harder to patrol the area."

Stahl plopped onto a chair next to Henderson, interrupting the conversation. "Formation at zero-eight-hundred hours tomorrow, at the company headquarters."

Henderson chewed fast and swallowed. "What's going on?"

Rocky nodded. "What's up, Sarge?"

"Wait until morning for the briefing."

Henderson darted his eyes toward his squad leader. "Come on, Sarge."

Stahl forced his nervousness not to show. His men weren't the only ones on edge waiting for the news. "I don't know anything else. We'll find out tomorrow."

When the squad finished eating, they headed for the enlisted club. The sound of upbeat music drifted along the walkway as they strolled at a slow pace toward it. Entering first, Henderson found a table large enough to seat the squad.

Drexler bellied up to the bar and waved down the bartender. "Give me ten beers." He slid five dollars across the bar.

Professor joined Drexler. "Carrying all those beers will be quite a task. I'll give you a hand." He carried six beers to the table for the thirsty soldiers.

Rocky reached for a cold brew. "Falstaff?"

"All they got." Drexler set the beers on the table.

Porter frowned. "Not even Pabst Blue Ribbon?"

"Nope, not even Pabst," Drexler said with a sigh.

"Least it's cold," Henderson said, pressing the can against his forehead.

Each platoon member grabbed a beer. As the squad members opened them, they raised the cans in their right hand. Professor stood. "To our brothers—Garcia, Smothers, Gonzalez, and Lanier."

"Garcia, Smothers, Gonzalez, and Lanier," the squad said, in unison.

"May they be remembered." Henderson lifted his eyes toward the ceiling.

The squad members touched the cans and, as one, they said, "May they be remembered."

Porter shook his head. "It don't mean nothin'."

"It don't mean nothin'," the squad said while they stood, touching cans again.

They drank the rest of their beer as the music thumped in the background. It appeared to the men of the Second Squad that the ritual of saying "it don't mean nothin'" was indeed continuing to keep them safe from their memories of war.

The jukebox arm moved to insert a new record to play and, after a moment, the lyrics to "Where Have All The Flowers Gone," by Peter, Paul and Mary, exploded from the speakers.

Stahl gulped the last of his beer and put his can on the table. "Shit, not the downer song! Let's get the hell out of here! Time to get some sleep. Don't forget the zero-eight-hundred formation."

The squad nodded in acknowledgment.

"No guard duty tonight. The Rear Echelon Mother Fuckers will protect us."

Porter grinned ear to ear. "You have to love the REMFs."

The squad laughed as they stood to leave. As they walked through the doorway, heading to the squad's assigned building, the song continued to play.

As Henderson looked for his bunk, he repeatedly hummed the lyrics, *"…soldiers gone? …to graveyards…"* He sat on the edge of his bed, unlaced his jungle boots, slid them off, and placed them near the head of his bed.

I can't even remember the last time I removed my boots before going to sleep.

Henderson flopped over onto the clean sheets before removing his uniform. He fell sound asleep in seconds. It didn't take long for the rest of the Second Squad to fall asleep too.

•

Henderson woke up to a strange combination of sizzling, whistling sounds.

He was reaching for his M-16 when the company executive officer, Lieutenant Roger Davis, flung the door open and yelled, "Incoming! Run for the bunkers!"

A siren blared a warning to the occupants of the firebase, adding to the confusion as a rocket exploded on impact outside the perimeter. Henderson shook as his bunk vibrated for several seconds.

Davis screamed, "Incoming! One hundred and twenty-two-millimeter rockets!"

"What the hell!?" Henderson sat upright and grabbed his weapon.

"Run to the bunker!" Clearly, the soldiers knew the drill; as Davis rousted men from their bunks, everyone quickly went into action.

Stahl took swift action too. "Lieutenant, have you ever seen what a rocket can do to a bunker?"

Davis yelled, ignoring Stahl's comment. "Go!"

Stahl relented. "Move, Second Squad! Now!"

With weapons at the ready, the grunts dashed to the bunker to the right of their building. Once inside, they packed together tightly, sitting on the wet, dirt floor. Another rocket sizzled overhead. They remained silent as the rocket continued over their shelter and exploded outside the wire.

Porter took a deep breath. "Nothin' to do, except pucker up and wait."

Again, the squad heard the whistling sound.

Wham!

The explosion was closer, and the ground rocked beneath them. The rocket had hit near the helipad, which wasn't far from the bunker protecting the Second Squad.

"It's in the hands of God." Rocky made a cross in the air as he prayed silently.

After the last explosion, the siren eventually signaled the all-clear.

Henderson slapped his thigh. "Another day in 'Nam."

The squad climbed from the bunker, returned to their bunks, and were asleep within minutes.

·

After a few hours of sleep, containing dreams of more rocket fire, Henderson lay on his bunk, rubbing his eyes. The sun peeked through the east side of the building, casting a little light.

Hearing a CH-47 Chinook helicopter land, his suspicions rose. *Strange, for a Hook to be landing so early.*

Henderson put his boots on and made sure the laces were tight. He stretched across the bunk, grabbed Drexler's arm, and shook it, hard. Drexler, looking confused, sprang from his bed.

"What the hell?!" Drexler rubbed the hard-crusted sand from his eyes.

"I'm hungry. Let's eat." Henderson's stomach growled.

"I've told you not to touch me when you wake me up."

"But, it's funny the way you jump."

"It's not funny to me."

At 0755 hours, Hall called to the sergeants to gather their platoons for company formation in front of the mess hall.

"First Platoon, fall in on me," Swift said, then turned to face Top. The other two platoon sergeants ordered their soldiers to fall in too.

The men of each platoon formed two lines to the left of their squad leader, with the platoon leaders standing centered in front.

Hall gave the first command. "Company … attention!"

The platoon leaders echoed the command.

The soldiers in the company executed the command, snapping to attention. He did an about-face and saluted Lyons. The captain returned the salute.

Henderson's body remained fixed. *I haven't seen anything this formal for a long time. This shit must be real.*

The first sergeant dropped his hand and stepped to the left side of the company commander, facing his soldiers. Lyons pursed his lips. "At ease." He raised his hands, signaling for the men to sit on the ground.

Once they were seated, he could see the anticipation on their faces. He knew that the words he used today would set the tone for the task he was about to ask of them. He stood tall, his feet shoulder-width apart, his left hand on his hip, and his right hand rested on the butt of his holstered pistol.

Lyons addressed the soldiers. "As most of you know, the division is responsible for a large region in I Corps. There is a portion of the South-Central Coast region known as a VC stronghold. The enemy has conducted numerous ambushes and attacks against ARVN and American troops. Quang Ngai Province became one of the first provinces in central Vietnam to organize self-defense units; it's considered a hotbed of enemy activity."

He stopped talking to observe the faces of his men as they digested the information.

"Alpha Company has a new mission."

The hum of men whispering increased to the point where Lyons had to address it. "Be quiet. Let me finish."

Once silence returned, he began again. "You, the men of Alpha Company, are tasked with building a new firebase, seven klicks west of Quang Ngai City. You'll have the assistance of the engineers, with the support of E Troop, the one-hundred-seventy-fourth, AHC, and the Sixth Battalion of the Eleventh Artillery, with one-hundred fives. The S-two reported that the company should expect to get hit daily while building the firebase. The expectations are mortar, rocket, seventy-five-millimeter recoil-less rifles, sappers with small units of NVA, and VC attempting to penetrate our defenses. Our assignment won't be easy."

The soldiers shifted about on the hard ground, uncomfortable with the information of the new mission so far. Lyons allowed the men to talk and move around briefly, before he commanded, "Quiet." The soldiers settled.

"We'll have sixty days to build the firebase. This means building roads, bunkers, helipads, gun positions, filling thousands of sandbags, and stringing concertina wire around the base." He stopped talking as he looked at the men sitting in front of him.

Henderson glanced toward Drexler. "What the hell!? That's a bunch of work."

"Yup, I agree, but it might be better than being in the bush."

Lyons continued. "Bravo, Charlie, and Delta Companies will patrol the area around the new firebase while Alpha Company builds it. There will be a battalion of ARVNs patrolling the area too."

Professor lifted his hand. "I feel much safer knowing that the ARVNs will be there protecting us." Porter and Rocky chuckled at his sarcastic remark.

Lyons remained focused. "Your platoon leaders will provide specific instructions to you after I've finished."

On cue, carrying a four-by-three-foot sign, Hall joined Lyons. Top leaned forward to read the sign, its blank side to the men. After a brief hesitation, with much laughter, Top flipped the sign over.

L.Z. Hill 100 F.S.B.
Owned & Operated By
A-3-1.

Lyons placed his hand on his hip. "The new firebase's name is 'Hill One Hundred.'"

The men sat there, uninspired by the name of the firebase. A soldier asked, "Why the name, sir?"

"Who cares about the name?" Stahl glared at the young soldier. "The name won't be what keeps you alive or gets you killed."

Lyons continued, ignoring Stahl's comment, "I know it's not original, but the name represents the height of the hill at one hundred feet. It's pretty straightforward."

The sound of their voices rose to a low hum. Lyons motioned for the soldiers to be quiet, and the men returned their attention to the company commander.

"First Platoon, you are the lead platoon—the first to land at our new home. That's it."

The members of Alpha Company stood as Lyons and Hall walked toward the company headquarters.

Swift wiped the sweat from his brow. "Gather over here."

The men moved over, surrounding their platoon sergeant and platoon leader.

Brighton nodded. "You heard the CO. I don't have much to add. We'll load on a Hook as a platoon, departing at thirteen-hundred hours. The other companies are already patrolling the area. We don't anticipate a hot LZ. However, we are expected to clear the area of mines and booby traps left by the VC on the new firebase. Take a maximum load of ammunition, with five days of rations. Your squad leaders can answer any questions you may have."

The lieutenant took long strides as he headed off in the direction of the company headquarters.

Swift moved to the middle of the platoon. "Make sure you have a good lunch. Meet at the helipad at twelve-thirty hours. Don't forget to get extra ammo and rations. Go pack."

As they milled around, the platoon talked about the upcoming mission. Then, one by one, the men strolled to the barracks to pack their rucksacks. While getting ready, the atmosphere in the room became somber, each platoon member deep into his thoughts.

In Vietnam, they didn't consider *any* kind of change a good thing. Infantry soldiers liked the sameness of each day. That's what kept their sanity intact. Sameness meant they were likely to live another day—change possibly meant that they wouldn't see another sunrise.

After Henderson was ready, he went outside the barracks and lit a cigarette. He took a deep drag and blew smoke rings skyward, as if painting.

I'd better enjoy this now. I might not be alive tomorrow.

Flashing through his mind's eye were images of his platoon brothers getting shot; finding Lanier and Gonzalez; Mai lying on the ground; and the smoldering NVA soldier.

A soldier approached him. "Henderson."

Looking to his right, Henderson saw the supply clerk he had encountered earlier while collecting a clean uniform—the one who had made fun of his size. *What in the hell does this guy want?*

The supply clerk stopped in front of him. "Here are some extra socks for you. They're brand new."

Henderson took the two pairs of socks, and guilt washed over his youthful face for thinking ill of the clerk. "Thanks, this means a lot." And it did. He couldn't control whether he lived or died—he couldn't even control where he went—but he could take this small comfort with him.

"You're welcome." The clerk turned and walked back to the supply room.

Henderson lit another cigarette while he waited for Drexler.

MOVING TO WHERE THE VC LIVED

With its twin-engines running and the tandem rotor spinning at a low speed, the CH-47 Chinook waited for its load.

Rucksacks slowed the soldiers as the platoon moved with short, quick strides toward the helipad. The crew considered carrying a platoon of infantry light work, the Hook being a heavy-lift helicopter. The helicopter crew chief stood at the end of the ramp, motioning for the platoon to begin boarding. In a column of twos, the First Platoon stepped onto the ramp and hurried to their seats.

Henderson lowered himself beside Drexler. He pointed at the two forward doors, where the crew mounted and manned an M-60 at each opening. "They're fired up and ready to take on hostile fire."

"Wouldn't you be, too, if that was your only job?"

"I guess, but it's good to know they have our backs."

After the crew chief sat between the two gunners, he laughed with them as they waited to take off.

Henderson leaned closer to Drexler. "Look, the crew chief is wearing a wedding ring."

Drexler shook his head. "Should I congratulate him, or what?"

"No. I'm just saying he has a lot more at stake than me. He might have children too."

"I try not to think about those things." Drexler shifted in his seat. "He knew what he signed up for."

Henderson leaned in closer to Drexler. "Maybe he had to, because of the draft."

"Henderson, shut up about it! You should be more concerned about your life, and not the crew chief's."

Henderson rolled his eyes as he took a deep breath.

The pilot slid the collective pitch control lever and moved the throttle forward, and the Chinook climbed above the firebase as the men of the First Platoon sat quietly.

Henderson's stomach churned as he sensed the helicopter turning. Then the rear of the Hook rose as the pilot forced the nose down to accelerate, flying north toward Quang Ngai, leaving Bronco behind them.

Many of the platoon members fell asleep as soon as the Hook took flight. Henderson and Drexler wanted to talk, but the roar of the engine and the rotors slapping the air drowned out their voices, which made it impossible to communicate. Drexler nodded off to sleep, resting his head on Henderson's shoulder. Henderson listened to the sounds of the Hook while watching the crew chief talk into his headset.

In a short time, the crew chief strode toward the rear of the helicopter. As he passed the sleeping soldiers, he tapped them on the knees to wake them.

Henderson's eyes popped open as the engine noise of the Hook changed—it slowed and lost altitude, alerting the platoon. Within a minute, the Hook thudded, its wheels, settling on the hard ground. The crew chief pushed the button, lowering the rear door.

Although the LZ wasn't supposed to be hot, the platoon ran from the rear door, with First Squad turning left, bolting to find protection. Just as they'd learned to fall asleep whenever there was an option, the soldiers had learned to wake up instantly, ready to fire on the enemy without warning. Not one of them moved sluggishly or appeared as though they'd been asleep only moments earlier. The Second Squad turned right as they ran through the open doorway.

As soon as the squads found cover, they fell to the ground with their weapons pointed toward the tree line.

After lifting skyward one hundred feet, Henderson watched the nose of the Hook rotate to face south, and it accelerated forward.

Swoosh!

Wham!

An explosion.

Henderson looked skyward and observed a gaping hole through the Chinook's rear door, flames shooting from the opening.

Henderson yelled, "Incoming! RPG!"

"Open fire!" Stahl ordered.

The helicopter twisted and turned like a harpooned whale as its metal splintered and ripped. The sounds echoed across the rice paddy field.

Suddenly, the crack of AK-47s firing echoed from the tree line. Rounds ripped across the left side of the Hook, punching holes from the burning rear door to the cockpit.

Second Squad fired into the thick line of trees to their front, one hundred and fifty meters away from where they lay. Hearing the firing from the other side of the LZ, Swift called out to the First Squad, "Move on me to Second Squad."

First Squad rose as one and followed Swift, hitting the ground behind a small berm to the right of the Second Squad. Nash screamed, "Open fire at the tree line!"

The two fire teams of First Squad unloaded round after round into the trees to their front.

Lying next to the RTO, Henderson heard the radio transmission. "I'm hit! I'm hit! I'm hit!"

The helicopter climbed higher, out of control, as it glided toward the trees where the enemy hid. The Hook shook hard, and the rear rotor spun off, hitting the dirt. Metal flew in every direction, like projectile missiles. The men of the First Platoon watched the blade spin over them.

The pilot transmitted, "We're going down! We're going—" Then, the radio broadcast static.

The helicopter shuddered. It flipped to one side and fell apart as it crashed into the forest. Seconds later, a fierce explosion rattled the ground, and a ball of flames shot high above the trees.

Brighton shouted into the handset, "Tango six. Receiving fire; Hook down; need support! Over."

"Tango one-six, Sharks on the way. Over," Lyons yelled.

"Roger. Don't come in, hot LZ. Over."

"Tango one-six, Wilco, we'll stay in the air. Out."

Once the Hook exploded, the NVA turned their firepower toward the platoon. Rounds whizzed overhead and thudded deep into the berm to Henderson's front as he returned fire.

Drexler yelled, "Rocky, fire to your left twenty meters and sweep right—I see NVA!"

Without saying a word, Rocky shifted his aim as instructed and sent a steady stream of M-60 rounds at the enemy. He continued to rattle off round after round as Porter fed the ammunition belts. Professor pumped the M-79 rounds, with their distinctive *Thump! Thump! Thump!*

The platoon fired its ammo toward the enemy, to kill them or drive them away, as both squad leaders shouted orders at their squad members. Directing his squad, Nash noticed that Jim Casey wasn't firing his M-16 and crawled over to him. "Use your weapon! Fire!" When he reached Casey, he saw the bullet hole in the side of his head as blood streamed down his neck.

"Medic! Medic!" Nash took cover behind Casey as bullets whizzed by.

Doc Wheeler quickly crawled toward Casey's body. "I'm coming!"

"Help Casey, Doc. He don't look so good! Stay with us, Casey." But even as he said it, Nash touched Casey's shoulder, as if to say goodbye.

After examining the wound, Doc took Casey's pulse. "He's dead."

"Shit!" Nash slammed his fist into the ground.

"I'm hit!" another soldier screamed as more bullets whizzed through the air.

Doc crawled over to reach the injured soldier. After examining the wound, Doc stopped the bleeding and wrapped a field dressing over the gaping hole in his leg, tying it tight to maintain pressure. "You'll be okay."

Doc felt a brief tinge of envy, despite himself. "It's a million-dollar wound."

"You think so?"

"You bet it is."

With a huge smile spreading across his face, the soldier drew a deep breath. "I'm going home."

Henderson recognized the sounds of gunships swiftly approaching.

Two Shark gunships fired their miniguns with deadly accuracy, causing death and destruction in the enemy positions. The pilots also opened fire from the 40-millimeter grenade launcher in the turret on the nose of the helicopter. The stream of grenades destroyed the earth, and the enemy, too. If that wasn't enough, rockets streaked to their targets from the 2.75 rocket pods on each side of the modified Huey.

"Ceasefire! Ceasefire!" Brighton ordered.

After ten minutes of destruction, as it waned to a halt, the quiet sounded strange. *Whop, Whop, Whop...* the faint sound of the two gunships' blades as they hovered above, like two vultures waiting for a meal.

Shortly, the CO gave the order to release both gunships. They turned, flying back toward Bronco.

The two Chinooks carrying the Second and Third Platoons landed nearly one hundred meters away. Both platoons ran from the rear door and found positions, creating a larger perimeter around the LZ.

Brighton held the handset against his ear. "Tango six. Need medevac. Need medevac. Over."

Lyons shook his head. "Roger, Tango one-six. How many down? Over."

Brighton transmitted, "One KIA and one WIA. Over."

"Roger, Tango one-six. Dustoff in fifteen mikes. Out."

Brighton stood over the poncho covering Casey. Sadness came over him.

Swift put a hand on his shoulder to comfort him. "Nothing you could do different, LT."

"Yeah, but it didn't need to happen. We didn't lose any others?"

"One wounded, but he might even return to the platoon." Swift smiled.

"Good to hear. Who was wounded?"

"Livingston, from the First Squad."

Henderson yelled, "Dustoff coming!"

As the red smoke drifted skyward, Stahl raised the M-16 over his head, guiding the medevac to a landing spot near the platoon. The company of infantry pointed their weapons toward the tree line, ready to protect the dustoff.

With the Huey blades rotating, Nash and Doc helped the injured soldier stand and assisted him onto the waiting helicopter. Once on a litter, a medic treated his wound. Four soldiers carried Casey—they slid his body onto a stretcher, remaining silent out of respect.

The wounded soldier, Livingston, reached across the litter and placed his hand over Casey's lifeless hand. "When does it end?"

As the rotors rotated faster, the dustoff lifted, banked, sped over the paddies, and gained altitude as it headed toward Chu Lai, to the 91st Evac. Hospital.

When Brighton and Ledger walked by Henderson, the radio squawked. "Tango, this is Tango six. Need a recovery team. Hook down. Over."

"Roger, Tango six," the battalion commander transmitted. "The team should be there in thirty mikes. Out." The radio then went silent, except for the occasional static of the handset.

Lyons decided to send a platoon to secure the crash site and look for survivors. He held the headset next to his ear. "Tango three-six, this is Tango six. Over."

"Roger, Tango six. Over," the Third Platoon leader said.

"Tango three-six, take your element and secure the crash site. Look for our people. Over."

"Wilco, Tango six. Out."

The Third Platoon leader, Lieutenant Smyth, gave the order for the platoon to move toward the forest, where the smoke drifted above the trees from the crash site.

As the men of Third Platoon walked through the First Platoon positions, the grunts of both platoons nodded at each other, exchanging words of encouragement.

"Get the son of bitches!" shouted Rocky.

A Third Platoon member said, "If VC are there, we'll get them."

"Hey man, stay safe," Porter said.

The grunt nodded and said, "Thanks."

The soldiers pushed forward, disappearing in the tree line, hoping to find the Hook crew alive.

MAKING A SAFE PLACE TO LIVE

From where Henderson stood, he observed a bulge in the earth above the fields, one hundred feet high and cleared of any vegetation. Rice paddy fields, thick hedgerows created by tall trees, brush, and bamboo surrounded the future firebase.

The city of Quang Ngai stood to the east. To the north flowed the Song Tra Khuc River, and to the west were the Truong Son Mountains.

While at Bronco, Henderson heard rumors that the French had had a base there in the 1950s. Then, the Marines arrived there in March of 1966. To the east of the small hill, there appeared to be the remains of a crumbling, concrete wall, standing nearly a foot off of the ground; farther away were overgrown remnants of a small airstrip.

•

Lyons held the handset. "Tango one-six, Tango two-six, Tango three-six, on my position. Over."

"Tango six, Tango one-six. Wilco. Out," Brighton said.

Rangel said, "Tango six, Tango two-six. Wilco. Out."

Smyth transmitted, "Tango six, Tango three-six. Wilco. Out."

The three platoon leaders moved with caution to the company commander's position at the base of the hill on the south side.

Brighton arrived first for the briefing. As he strode into the command group area, he discovered Lyons studying a map, which he had spread out on the ground.

Lyons noticed Brighton standing over him. "Have a seat, Brighton."

As Brighton sat next to his CO, Lieutenant Rangel, the Second Platoon leader, and Smyth, the Third Platoon leader, joined the two officers. When seated on their helmets, they nodded at Lyons, flashing a quick smile at Brighton.

"What the hell happened with the LZ being hot, sir? We lost two men today."

"Let it go, Brighton. I'll handle it."

"With all due respect, sir—"

"I said let it go."

Brighton glared at the captain and nodded in agreement. "Yes, sir."

Lyons looked at Smyth. "Good job on the recovery of the crew."

"Thanks, sir. Sorry none of them made it. I understand they didn't find the crew chief's body."

A soldier Brighton didn't recognize approached and stood beside the officers. There was a momentary lull in the conversation before Lyons continued. "We need to establish the company's position before nightfall. If you find any mines or booby traps, let me know. We have two teams of engineers to dispose of any explosive devices found. We suspect the VC left some, so be careful."

He paused for a moment to make eye contact with them. "The First Platoon will have two positions on the south side and five positions on the east side. The Second Platoon will join First, with two positions on the east, two on the north, and three on the west side. The Third Platoon continues around on the west side, joining the First with seven positions."

Lyons fixed his gaze on the officer, who was standing to one side of the group. "This is Major Albright, the engineer commander. He has a couple of things to say."

Albright handed each one a map. "On your maps are the bunker locations. My team, along with Captain Lyons, selected the best site for each bunker. Three bulldozers will arrive tomorrow morning. They'll dig the areas for the bunkers. After we dig the positions, we'll install the framing. A truck will come around and drop off enough sandbags for your men to fill and stack around the bunker. We'll create a landing pad, artillery one-hundred-and-five pits, mortar pits, and build a mess hall. The TOC is near the center of the hill, behind the last position of the First Platoon, on the east side."

He stopped and removed the canteen hanging from his pistol belt, taking a long drink. Wiping his left hand across his face, he rubbed off the dripping sweat and dried his hand on his pants. After taking another long swig, he placed the canteen into its cover. "Concertina wire, with steel pickets, will be dropped off at intervals around the firebase for a triple-concertina wire fence. Your men need to lay three rolls of wire—two for the base and one on top. My men will give instructions on the installation. I will provide any equipment you need: gloves, clamps, wire cutters, sledgehammers… It sounds like a lot, but you should be able to get it done in two days… three days, tops."

Lyons lifted his brow, as if to acknowledge the directions Albright had presented. Albright rolled up his map. "I'm finished."

Lyons glanced at the others. "Any questions?"

"No, sir," the three platoon leaders said as they stood.

"Great. Move your platoons to their positions to climb the hill in thirty minutes. One more thing—after you reach your assigned positions, prepare for the night. Hunker down deep and low."

Once at the platoon location, Brighton yelled, "NCOs, on me!" He sat on the ground behind the berm, spread his map on the ground, then gently smoothed it out.

Detecting the urgency in his voice, the three NCOs raced to the platoon leader's position, taking long strides to get there as quickly as possible.

Swift stood over the platoon leader. "What's going on, LT?"

Sweat dripped from Brighton's face as he stared at the map. Droplets ran off of his nose to hit the large sheet of paper, leaving a wet stain, which made it hard to read the terrain features. After each drop hit the map, he wiped at his face. Soon, he realized that the sweat wouldn't quit, so he stopped worrying about the map. He looked at his NCOs. "Take a seat."

They removed their helmets and sat next to Brighton. They stared at the map spread on the ground as Brighton ran his finger across it to indicate the platoon positions. He then recited the same instructions he had received from Captain Lyons.

•

When Stahl returned to the squad position, he told his men to gather around. Henderson sat next to him.

Stahl rubbed his chapped lips together. "We're moving to the hilltop in twenty minutes. If you see any booby traps, call out; the engineers will disarm them, or blow them in place. The Second Squad has three bunkers. Here are your assignments. In the first one, after the command group, is Ransom, Hays, Clark, and Madison; the next one is me, Ames, Rocky, and Porter; the last one has Henderson, Drexler, Professor, and Doc."

He took a quick breath and wiped the sweat from his brow. "Rocky, make sure you have a good field of fire to cover the platoon front—if not, let me know. As soon as you get to your bunker location, place claymores and trip flares, then it's time to eat. Don't forget to establish the guard rotation. Any questions?"

Porter raised his hand, but before he could ask his question, Stahl said, "No, Porter, you don't have to go."

The men of the Second Squad laughed, letting the humor between the two soldiers lighten the tense atmosphere.

•

Henderson slid into his rucksack and stood next to Drexler. "How many days left?"

"One hundred and ninety-five to go."

"I think we've been here longer. You sure it's right?"

"Yeah, I'm sure. We got *boo-coo* days to go."

Stahl rolled his shoulders and twisted at the waist to crack his back. "Henderson, take point. Second Squad, move to the base of the hill. Watch for booby traps."

Henderson moved to the front of the platoon and ascended the barren, rocky hill. He took short, calculated steps, looking for evidence of booby traps—small mounds of earth; a stack of rocks; new dirt; tripwires; or objects protruding above ground which didn't belong or looked suspicious. With his nerves near the breaking point, Henderson continued along the path. Halfway up the hill, he halted the platoon.

As he knelt and searched the ground in front of him, he spotted a small, circular object protruding a fraction above ground level. "No one move. We have a Bouncing Betty mine."

When a soldier stepped onto the circular trigger, then stepped off, the mine would explode several feet into the air. It could kill the soldier who stepped on it and wound others around him.

Henderson held up his hand. "Mine! Need engineers!" He stood, waving his arms, until an engineer approached.

The soldiers waited in place, afraid to take another step. An engineer ran to Henderson's position. "What do you have?"

"Right there, to my front." Henderson pointed at the object in the ground. He watched droplets of sweat splatter near the mine as it dripped from his face; it felt as though his heart would explode. One more step and he would have been standing on the pressure plate instead of the engineer removing the explosive device.

The engineer knelt next to the mine. He pulled a survival knife from its sheath and surgically dug around the device.

"What's the procedure for extracting that?" Henderson's heart raced.

"I insert the knife into the ground at a forty-five-degree angle and work my way around the device. Now, I have the circumference. Then, I dig it out to expose the top of the booby trap."

"Sure you don't want to concentrate while doing that?" Henderson suddenly felt uneasy at the sound of the engineer's voice being the only thing heard in the silence.

Unfazed, the engineer nodded. "Looks like a Bouncing Betty. Not a problem." He removed a grenade pin from his pocket. "All I have to do is put this pin in, and we're good to go." With a steady hand, he inserted the pin into the trigger location of the explosive device. Then, he dug further around the mine until half of it became exposed. After removing more dirt, he gently lifted it from the hole. "All clear. You can continue."

"All clear!" Henderson motioned the platoon forward and continued to make his way to the platoon bunker position, which took twenty minutes.

Several times, the company stopped when they heard the call from an engineer, "Fire in the hole!" The grunts fell to the ground, as low as possible—the explosion followed.

Shit, how many mines did they bury here? Henderson shivered in the blistering heat.

Finally, Henderson arrived at his assigned position, pulled the release on his rucksack strap, and allowed it to slide off of his right shoulder. It thudded to the ground. Drained of energy, Henderson stood quietly, waiting for Drexler to reach the bunker location. He gazed upon the rice fields and hedgerows below, and the hair on the back of his neck stood on end.

How in hell will we be able to defend this small piece of real estate?

Stahl supervised his squad members, making sure each had the correct location of their new home. Around thirty meters of rocky soil separated each bunker.

As Drexler approached his bunker location, he waved at Henderson. "What did you find?"

"A Bouncing Betty."

Drexler dropped his rucksack at Henderson's feet. "You have good eyes. It's why you walk point."

Drexler glanced over at Doc and Professor as they dropped their rucksacks. "After you get settled, you two need to put trip flares closer to the base of the hill—Henderson and I will pull guard for you. Once you return, we'll place four claymores to the front, and you watch over us."

Professor nodded to confirm the instructions. "Not a problem."

Once the soldiers placed the claymores and trip flares, the evening ritual began, like any other in Vietnam. The team members dug into their rucksacks and removed poncho liners, rations for dinner, and a canteen of water or Kool-Aid. The repetitive actions calmed the men in this stressful situation.

Henderson already had his chicken and noodles heating from the burning chunk of C-4 in his makeshift stove. While the main course cooked, he opened a can of pears, leaving the lid partly on for a handle. He did the same with a tin of fruitcake. Henderson removed the steaming chicken and noodles and poured a couple of drops of tabasco sauce onto the meal. Then he leaned against his rucksack, ready for dinner. After blowing on the chicken to cool it, he took a bite.

Drexler, Professor, and Doc ate too, as they remained silent. The only sounds to be heard were chewing, slurping, and the Kool-Aid gurgling as it drained from the canteens.

Once finished, Henderson released a long, loud burp, which made everybody laugh. He lit a cigarette and inhaled deeply, savoring the taste. Then he blew the smoke skyward, enjoying the instant jolt of nicotine to his system.

He glanced over to Drexler. "I'll take first watch, if it's okay."

"Sure, go ahead—you earned it today."

Professor nodded. "Indeed, you did a truly good job on the mines, Eddie."

"Thanks. The Bouncing Betty did scare the shit out of me."

"It'd scare any of us." Professor pursed his lips. "Bettys are nothing to mess around with. I'd worry more about you if it *didn't* have you perturbed."

They didn't say anything else—they welcomed the silence.

Drexler watched the sun sink behind the mountains to the west. "Let's get some sleep. The engineers should be here early with the wire."

Henderson moved to the edge of the position so he could see along the hillside as the rest of the team curled into their poncho liners, falling asleep within minutes. Every hour and thirty minutes, the men exchanged guard duty, until the sun rose over the rice fields and hedgerows to the front of their position. Last on guard— Professor woke the team members.

•

While drinking his hot chocolate, Henderson saw a cloud of dust. Then he heard the rumble of metal on metal—the tracked vehicles coming from the direction of Quang Ngai City. Within minutes, a convoy of three bulldozers, four APCs and five deuce-and-a-half trucks came into view, a sight the infantry soldiers hadn't witnessed before today. With blades lowered, the bulldozers created a road as they moved toward the hill.

As the convoy reached the base of the hill, the bulldozers drove along the bottom of the slope, clearing an area for the wire. The trucks followed the bulldozers, dropping off concertina wire and posts, with the hardware, at twenty-foot intervals. The APCs followed behind, stopping in different positions to guard the infantry soldiers when they strung the wire.

The whirl of the helicopter's blades became part of the daily background routine. One after another landed on a makeshift helipad, delivering framing for bunkers, sandbags, and other supplies to build the mess hall and TOC.

Engineers loaded thousands of bundled sandbags into trucks, drove to the positions, and dropped enough bundles to fortify the bunker after they erected the framing. Along with the sandbags, each location received two long-handle shovels to fill them.

•

Stahl cupped his hands around his mouth. "We're moving in ten minutes! Travel light, with weapons, ammo, and water. We'll meet at the bottom of the hill, in front of the lieutenant's position. I'll assign the tasks there. Let's go."

"Okay, Sarge." Henderson grabbed his gear and weapon.

Drexler raised his weapon. "Let's go, Alpha Team."

Both teams of the First and Second Squads moved as one, jumping over tripwires and dodging claymore mines, down the slope to the bottom of the hill.

Stahl caught up to his men. "We'll do bunkers four through seven. If you have any questions concerning the wire, ask an engineer. Any questions?"

The squad looked at Porter, waiting for him to raise his hand, but he sat silent.

As one, they jumped to their feet. The infantry soldiers removed their shirts and put on thick engineer gloves so they could safely handle the wire. They each had their assigned tasks. Henderson and Drexler stretched the wire to full length; Madison hammered in a post, while Ames held it; Professor and Porter clamped the concertina wire to the post; and Rocky walked along where the fence would be installed, leaving a post with clamps every ten feet.

Stahl observed his men with an eagle eye. "Remember, we are doing three rolls—two on the ground with one on top, laying centered."

The men worked throughout the hot and humid day stringing the wire, which proved hard work. Periodically, Henderson looked at the APC crew, staying vigilant over the grunts as they worked.

When it was close to dusk, Stahl called quitting time. "Return to your positions."

The men dispersed.

Henderson looked to his rear as he walked along the new road to his bunker, watching the APC following him. He saw the two rolls of concertina neatly stretched around the firebase, which gave him a sense of security. Professor, Doc, and Drexler strode next to him. He nudged Drexler. "Tomorrow, we install the top roll of wire; no more wire to string!"

"Yeah, but what about the bunker?" Drexler gave an exhausted smile.

"Point taken. Building a firebase is endless."

When the team arrived at the bunker location, the engineers had dug their position, with a massive mound of dirt pushed to the front, and stacked thick, wooden beams in the bunker area.

Henderson stood as confusion took hold of him. "What the hell is this?"

Professor took a quick breath. "It appears as though this is how they'll build the bunker."

Doc calculated a number in midair with his index finger. "There must be a thousand sandbags piled over here."

Drexler smiled. "At least we have shovels."

"It'll take forever." Shocked, Henderson narrowed his brows as his team members burst into laughter.

Drexler put his arm over Henderson's shoulder. "It's okay. We'll get it done in no time."

•

Not long after daylight the next day, the First Platoon strode along the new road to the base of the hill. They separated into their fire teams and installed the third row of concertina wire on top of the two rows on the ground. As they moved from section to section on the fence line, the soldiers talked, laughed, and smoked. In general, they made a good time of it while working. As the sun moved across the sky, the temperature and humidity increased. The heat made them work harder.

Shirtless, Henderson stood next to the last bunker, gazing toward the hedgerow to make sure the APC crew were staying alert. He noticed the gunner behind the .50-caliber machine gun, watching to his front, and the two M-60 gunners, who were bullshitting, but also alert.

Thankful that the APC watched over them, Henderson pulled at one end, while Rocky tugged at the other end to uncoil the last roll of wire. The team lifted the long strand of concertina wire, laying it on top of the two strands. As Henderson released his end, an AK-47 fired.

The platoon hit the ground and scrambled to retrieve their weapons.

Crack! Crack! Crack! The rounds echoed along the base of the hill.

Stahl jolted his head toward one direction. "Where are they firing from?"

Nobody replied. From concealed positions, they searched the hedgerow, one hundred meters to their front.

A loud, metallic rattling sound came from the APC as the gunner loaded .50-caliber rounds and shot into the hedgerow. The more bullets he sent toward the enemy, the louder the noise became when chambering and ejecting a round. As he fired, small trees fell to the ground and bamboo splintered, the earth exploding where the bullets hit. Both M-60 gunners raked the hedgerow with 7.62 rounds.

The NVA didn't return fire—they had fled the area.

The gunners on the APC quit firing, and it became quiet. The short firefight had happened so fast that the platoon hadn't had time to return fire.

"All clear!" Stahl drew in a deep breath.

Porter gazed toward Henderson. "They have some nerve, attacking us while we string wire."

"They thought we would be caught off guard."

Porter laughed. "What a bunch of dumbass VC—to shoot at us."

"Be thankful the APC had our back." Henderson shivered. *Thank God the VC didn't have better aim.*

Stahl rotated his finger in the air as if to indicate wrapping things up. "Okay, let's finish, then go home."

The squad moved as one to install the last coil of concertina wire. After they completed their work, the platoon strolled along the road to the bunker positions, with the APC following to protect them from any further attacks.

Once on the hill, Stahl gazed across the area. "Have a meal and get some rest. Tomorrow, we fill sandbags."

Porter raised his hand.

"Yes, Porter. You too."

The squad laughed as they walked to their positions.

They stopped in front of the bunker. Henderson gawked in amazement at the massive beams, now installed, which formed the eight-by-eight-foot shell. They needed to fill sandbags for the sides and the roof.

Professor swallowed. "They did an impressive job engineering the bunker."

"Sure looks like it." Drexler licked his lips.

Henderson assessed the area. "Damn, how many sandbags will it take?"

Drexler shoved Henderson. "Let's not worry tonight."

•

Morning dawned, and Henderson lit his first cigarette of the day. While smoking, he looked at the bundles of sandbags, which lay next to the mound of earth. He already dreaded filling them.

The other team members roused and began preparing for the work they needed to do to finish the bunker.

"We'll work in pairs," Drexler said as he took a bite of his fruit cocktail. "Me with Henderson and Doc with Professor."

"You'll get no complaints from me." Professor held up his thumb.

Once they had removed their shirts, the team members slid on the engineer gloves. Then, the four soldiers started the backbreaking task of filling and stacking the sandbags. Henderson would scoop a shovelful of loose dirt and empty the load into the sandbag, held by Drexler. When filled halfway, a fourteen-by-twenty-four-inch sandbag weighed roughly thirty pounds.

"Can't believe it takes three full shovels for a sandbag." Henderson wiped the sweat from his brow. Then he pretended to wipe Drexler's face.

"Yeah, it's surprising. At least we only fill them halfway. I'll switch with you when you get tired."

"Shit, that won't take long." Henderson smiled at his friend.

As the company of grunts worked, they saw Hook after Hook approach the firebase. The helicopters hovered over the helipad, while each carried 105 artillery cannons, with ammunition dangling from a sling under its belly. Artillerymen unhooked the sling and rolled the gun off of the helipad into a pit the engineers had dug earlier. They loaded the ammunition onto a truck and drove to the pits to unload and stack the crated shells.

The soldiers continued to work through the heat of the day, filling, lifting, and stacking one sandbag after another. They stopped only for a couple of short breaks and lunch. Henderson switched tasks with Drexler several times, as did Doc with Professor.

Late in the evening, Drexler looked at their progress. "One quarter finished. Time to quit."

Professor dropped the shovel. "I have to agree with that; it'll be dark soon."

"Man, I'm hungry." Henderson's stomach churned.

Drexler, for once, agreed with Henderson. "Chow time. Let's eat."

Across the hill, the soldiers working on their bunkers stopped at the same time. It became eerily quiet as the sounds of talking, laughter, shovels hitting the loose dirt, and equipment moving waned, then stopped. Henderson gazed around the valley. For a place in hell, it sure did look and sound peaceful.

Thump! Thump! Thump! The noise reverberated from the east side of the hill.

"Incoming!" Drexler yelled.

Mortar fired.

Henderson, Doc, Drexler, and Professor dove into the bunker, hiding behind a stack of sandbags.

Bam! Bam! Bam! The mortar rounds exploded in front of their position, sending shrapnel and dirt in every direction. While waiting for mortars to fire again, the men on the hill sunk lower into the earth.

Boom! Boom! Boom! Boom!

Each boom shattered the stillness after the enemy mortars exploded. The ground beneath them shook.

At first, Henderson had no idea what had happened, but soon realized that the artillery was answering the NVA mortar crew. After a long pause, explosions amplified in the distance. The artillery sent four more rounds to mute the enemy mortars.

After waiting several minutes, Stahl yelled, "All clear!"

Henderson bolted from the bunker. "I can't believe they're such poor shots."

"Guess we should be thankful." Drexler wiggled his finger in his ear, as if he heard a ringing sound.

Henderson eased to the front of the position to survey the damage. "Damn it! We have leaking sandbags! Looks like a sprinkler went off."

Running around to the front, Drexler stopped in his tracks when he saw Henderson. "You hurt?"

"Look at the sandbags. We'll have to replace half of what we did today!"

"It's okay. Better the sandbags than one of us."

"You got a point."

•

For the next seven days, the men of Alpha Company labored to build their bunkers, stopping work each evening to take shelter from the enemy's mortar attacks. After enemy mortars fired at the hill, artillery answered with three times the number of rounds they shot. It became a nightly duel between the NVA mortar crew and the artillerymen.

After sunrise one morning, Stahl stood in the shadows of the doorway, with the morning light filtering through the darkness.

Professor saw his silhouette. "Who's there?"

"It's me, and I'm bringing good news." Stahl stepped from the shadows.

Henderson rose. "What good news, Sarge?"

"The mess hall is open for business. So are the shitters."

"You got to be kidding! Can't believe it took four weeks, but it's great news."

Drexler rubbed his empty stomach. "Let's get to the mess hall before it gets full."

The soldiers laughed and grabbed their weapons as Stahl proceeded to the next bunker, to share the good news.

Doc stayed seated on a stack of sandbags. "Go ahead. I'll keep guard."

"I can smell the eggs and bacon from here." Drexler smiled as he strode quickly toward the mess hall. Professor, Henderson, and Rocky were following close behind.

Professor sniffed the air. "I smell fresh brewed coffee."

Henderson caught up to Drexler. "After breakfast, I'm going to sit on an actual shitter."

"Thanks for the shitter update." Drexler increased his pace. "You're not getting in front of me. I'm hungry."

The group increased their pace, almost to the point of jogging. They entered the wood-frame mess hall through the screen door, laughing hard from the excitement of eating hot food. Henderson looked around, observing the spacious room with fifteen homemade picnic tables sitting on hard-packed dirt—each table held six soldiers. Along the rear of the mess hall stood a long counter filled with containers of food, and at the end of the line of food, a cook prepared eggs to order.

Henderson smiled. *This is first class.* Sometimes, it was the little things that made this hellhole seem not so hellish.

Once seated, the group ate their first hot meal in weeks.

As Henderson chewed his last bit of bacon, he asked, "Who thinks we're winning this battle between the NVA mortar and the artillery?"

Drexler's brows lifted. "We are, and now that we have hot meals, the NVA don't stand a chance. No telling what they're eating for grub."

Rocky sipped his coffee. "You hear about some festival in Woodstock, New York?"

"I heard about it on *Armed Forces Radio* a couple of nights ago." Porter chewed his food.

"Isn't that where a half-million hippies, draft dodgers, and dopers got together?" Henderson looked around the table at his team members.

"I guess you could say that. But you can bet the music was great! I wish I were there." Professor lowered his gaze. "I wish all of the squad could have been there."

Henderson gulped his food. "Guess that'd be better than being here. *Anywhere* but here is better."

Silence fell on the group as they ate the rest of their morning meal in reflection.

Drexler shoved his tray away from him and readjusted his position on the uncomfortable bench. "I think we should add a three-foot sandbag wall on top for protection while pulling guard."

"Good idea." Henderson's eyes seemed to brighten. He glanced at Professor, who stared at the hill. "What's the problem, Professor?"

"No problem. I was thinking that we now have a full-fledged firebase with artillery, mess hall, and a black cloud of stinking smoke from the shitters."

The three soldiers agreed with his observation.

Drexler nodded. "Let's build the wall on top."

Each nodded.

Henderson, Drexler, Professor, and Doc then filled, tied off, lifted, and stacked the sandbags on top of the bunker.

Henderson observed Brighton and Stahl approaching their position. "Who's in trouble?"

The group went still as they watched the two leaders approach, but when they arrived, there was a lightness to them which settled the nerves cramping in Henderson's gut.

"How's it going?" Brighton stood almost at attention out of habit.

"Great, LT," the four men said in unison.

Stahl stiffened his shoulders. "Drexler, front and center."

Drexler climbed from the roof and stood in front of Brighton, ready to receive his order or message.

"Specialist Drexler, I promote you to Sergeant."

Stahl handed a new set of stripes toward Henderson. "Henderson, you want to help pin on the stripes?"

With a huge smile, Henderson climbed off of the bunker. He strode to Drexler and took the sergeant's pin from Stahl. While Stahl pinned one on the left collar, Henderson pinned the other on

Drexler's right collar. Drexler smiled and saluted Brighton, who returned the salute.

The Second Squad cheered.

Henderson beamed a proud smile. "Well deserved."

Doc shook Drexler's hand. "Yes, very well deserved."

Professor nodded. "It couldn't have happened to a better soldier. Congratulations."

Stahl stepped forward. "Quiet. We aren't done. Henderson, front and center."

Henderson faced the lieutenant, who nodded. "Private First-Class Henderson, you are promoted to Corporal."

Again, the Second Squad cheered.

Professor reached out to shake Henderson's hand. "Way to go."

Drexler and Stahl pinned the corporal stripes to Henderson's shirt collar. Henderson saluted Brighton, and he returned the salute. The four shook hands before Brighton left with Stahl.

Henderson went into the bunker and returned with a two-quart canteen. "To celebrate—I'm buying."

"What's in the canteen? You didn't get into Swift's bottle, did you?" Rocky smiled, rubbing his mustache.

"Black cherry Kool-Aid. My favorite." Henderson grinned from ear to ear.

The men of the Second Squad passed the canteen around—each member toasting the two soldiers while taking a long swig.

•

Sitting on the bunker roof, Henderson and Drexler observed the rice fields and hedgerows below their position. After lighting a cigarette, Henderson inhaled deeply, letting the smoke drift from his mouth and nostrils while he enjoyed the flavor.

The sounds of helicopter blades slapping the air resonated along the valley below. *Whop! Whop! Whop!*

"Wonder why the helicopter is coming in so late." Drexler's eyes darted toward the sky.

"Probably bringing in a general. Look, it's flying roughly a hundred feet off the valley floor. There's some kind of mist flowing from the bottom of the Huey."

The pilot circled the firebase, following close to the road the engineers had built, and sprayed the area. After each pass, the pilot sprayed farther away from the firebase, into the fields and hedgerows.

Professor climbed to the roof to join his two team members watching the chopper. Henderson nudged him. "What do you think the chopper's doing?"

"Spraying a chemical to deprive the VC of food and concealment. It'll kill all vegetation."

"I've heard of that." Drexler rubbed his chin. "I think it's called 'Operation Ranch Hand.'"

Professor nodded in agreement. "That sounds right to me."

"Good idea." Henderson sighed. "It'll make it harder for the VC to sneak up on us."

The three combat brothers watched in silence as the Huey completed its mission and then banked, headed toward Bronco. As it headed south, the helicopter flew over the firebase, with a light mist trailing it.

"I wonder how long it takes to kill everything." Henderson's lips twisted. "Soon, I hope."

Drexler shook his head. "Let's call it a night and see what tomorrow brings."

CHAPTER 16

CHARLIE DOESN'T WANT
US HERE

Henderson dropped stones through a hole in an empty soda can. Then he ran a short piece of wire through an opening and handed the contraption to Drexler, who attached it to a strand of concertina wire, carefully twisting the wire to secure it. He hit the can hard, several times, to make sure it didn't come undone, and the stones rattled inside.

Henderson briefly closed his eyes. "Makes plenty of noise, I think."

"You don't sound so sure."

"It's supposed to be a warning system. I prefer loud over soft any day in this damn jungle."

"It sounds louder at night when everything around us is still."

"Do you think we've strung enough?" Henderson looked down the line at the twenty cans they had already fixed to the wire.

"Yep, let's move to the bunker." Drexler headed out from his current position.

"Wait. How about three more?"

Drexler looked over his shoulder as he continued to walk away. "It's enough. Now, come on."

While scrambling along the rocky hillside, the two soldiers avoided the many trip flares—they walked around the claymore mines too.

Henderson stopped, staring at one of the claymores. "What the fuck?! Look at this."

"Holy shit!" Drexler stopped at Henderson's side and glared, wide-eyed, at the mine.

"The claymore is backward."

"Look! There are two more facing the wrong way."

For several seconds, they looked around, wondering who had set the mines to face the wrong way.

Drexler bit his lower lip. "Shit. The VC must have come through the wire and turned the claymores to face us. If we blew them like this, the blast would be at us, not them."

"We better tell Sergeant Stahl."

"Agreed, but let's turn them around first. We don't want any of our men killed."

Soon, the word spread that the enemy had turned the claymores to face the bunkers. The commanding officers sent soldiers downhill to check all the claymores. They found that most faced the wrong way, and not toward the enemy's avenues of approach.

•

Back with his team, Henderson tried to relax, cleaning his M-16, while Professor and Doc played cards. Drexler glared off into space. After Henderson finished cleaning his weapon, he pulled a cigarette from the Marlboro pack. He tapped the filter onto the package, lit it, and took a long drag, sucking the smoke deep into his lungs.

Professor tilted his nose in Henderson's direction. "What is that wondrous scent?"

"I lit a smoke." Henderson took another drag.

Professor's brow furrowed. "No, that's hardly a smell to note. It's something different."

"It smells like steaks grilling. It's coming from the mess hall." Drexler stood and headed for the exit.

Henderson smiled. "Chow time." He snuffed the cigarette and quickly put away his cleaning equipment.

Doc bolted for the exit. "I'll race you there."

The other men jumped to their feet and raced for the mess hall.

Out of breath, Henderson arrived first, followed by Doc, Drexler, and Professor last. They burst through the doorway to find that a line of hungry soldiers had already formed, twenty men deep.

As the line moved forward, Henderson made his way to the cook grilling steaks. "I'll have a large one. Medium rare, please."

With a sweat-drenched face, the cook poked one of the steaks with the grill fork. "You sure? You don't look big enough to eat a large steak."

"Not funny to say to a man who could eat the whole cow; I'm really hungry." Henderson ignored the soldiers behind him laughing.

Drexler nudged Henderson to inch forward. "You're not supposed to say anything about his size."

"No sense of humor." The cook tossed a sixteen-ounce steak onto the grill. "Just for you, Henderson."

While waiting for the steak, Henderson grabbed a baked potato, loaded it with butter and sour cream, snatched several rolls, and served himself a large spoonful of corn. "I'll be right back for my steak."

"It'll be ready in a few."

Henderson quickly strode to the ice chest and retrieved two cartons of milk. He returned to the grill and waited until the cook lifted the steak with a large fork, sliding it onto Henderson's tray.

"Cooked exactly like you requested. But I'll be surprised if you can eat the whole thing."

"I get that a lot. I eat like a horse." Henderson was embarrassed to have so much attention called to the challenge—he would rather not get teased. But it was better than having everyone looking at him. "Forget it."

Henderson isolated a table for him and his fellow soldiers, sat, and immediately cut into his steak. Before he could swallow the first bite, the rest of the team joined him. They devoured the meal, the only sound throughout the mess hall was the rattling of trays and flatware.

Once Henderson finished eating, he carried his tray to the far corner of the room, with the rest of the team doing the same. With full bellies, they casually strolled back to the bunker.

Drexler blew air from his lips. "Damn it."

"What's wrong?" Henderson's eyes darted toward his friend.

"I forgot to leave a team member at the bunker to stand guard."

Laughter followed Drexler's statement.

Professor tapped Drexler's shoulder from behind. "Sergeant, we'll keep this one between us."

"This will be the only rookie sergeant mistake I make."

After Henderson got to the bunker, he arranged his rucksack, while the rest of the team squared away their gear, knowing that the sun would set in an hour.

Henderson took off his boots and socks and tossed them at his feet. Then he retrieved his new pair of socks and placed them over his dirty feet, wiggling his toes. *Too bad they're not clean.*

Doc's nostrils flared. "Wow, your feet stink."

Henderson quickly put his sock-covered feet back into his combat boots and tightly laced them. "You know I can't help it."

Professor wrinkled his nose. "I hope the engineers install the showers soon. It's been over a month since we've been able to get clean."

"You know how it is—the showers are the last structure built." Drexler glanced at his filthy uniform.

The soldiers moved outside the bunker, climbed on the roof, and sat quietly. The four friends gazed at the lush, green rice fields and the thick hedgerows to the front of their position. After lighting a cigarette, Henderson passed it to Professor, then lit another one and gave it to Doc. Finally, he lit one for himself, inhaling the smoke. As they enjoyed the nicotine fix, they watched the sun drop behind the mountains.

Henderson drew in another deep puff. *It'll be another long night.*

Drexler slid off the roof of the bunker. "Guard duty is Doc, me, Eddie, and Professor. We'll each pull an hour shift, twice."

Professor and Henderson followed, leaving Doc to pull guard.

Henderson went inside to prepare for sleep. Without speaking, he retrieved his poncho liner, removed a couple of cans of C-rations, and placed them next to his canteen of Kool-Aid. He wanted them ready, knowing he would get hungry while on guard. Next, he bathed in DEET to fight off the attacking mosquitos. Within minutes, he was asleep, trusting Doc to watch over him and the others.

A couple of hours later, Drexler shook Henderson's arm. "Wake up. It's your turn."

"Shit, really? Five more minutes."

"Not happening. Let's go."

"Okay, okay, quit shaking me. I'm going." Henderson stretched and stood.

He grabbed his M-16, a bandolier of ammo, canteen, and his snack. Exiting through the open doorway, he threw his gear onto the roof before climbing the makeshift steps of sandbags.

As he sat behind the three-foot sandbag wall, he opened his peaches and cake. He dug in with a plastic spoon, devouring his snack in no time. As he watched to his front, he wanted a luxury he couldn't have—a cigarette. But he didn't dare light one, knowing that the VC might be watching.

Every five minutes, he glanced at his watch, which made the hour seem like two. On occasion, he flinched at what he thought was enemy movement, but determined that the shadows moving to his front weren't much of anything. As the minute hand on his watch dial ticked to the number twelve, Henderson watched the hand sweep past 2300 hours, and his shift ended.

But, because he was now wide awake, he knew that struggling to go to sleep would be useless, so he decided to sit with Professor for a while until he was drowsy. He left his gear, climbed off of the roof, and walked into the bunker to wake Professor. He gently shook his shoulder. "It's time for your shift, Professor."

"I'm awake." Professor rubbed his eyes. He grabbed his gear, stood up, slipped on his ammo vest, then walked through the doorway, with Henderson following. Confused, he stopped and turned to Henderson. "What are you doing?"

"I can't sleep. I'll sit with you for a while."

Professor turned about-face and continued to his position. He climbed the sandbag steps to the roof, with Henderson following him.

Both soldiers sat side by side, watching the front without saying a word, and enjoying having a brother next to him.

As he sat, Professor shifted his weight, removing his vest holding the M-79 grenade rounds. He leaned closer to Henderson. "This vest is heavy and hot. I shouldn't need it anyhow."

Henderson barely heard Professor. Something out in the night had caught his attention. Henderson pointed. "You see it?"

Professor darted his eyes in the direction Henderson was pointing. "I don't see anything."

Both soldiers strained to see through the darkness.

Thump! Thump! Thump! The noise echoed from behind the hedgerow.

"Incoming!" Henderson took cover.

Bam! Bam! Bam! The mortar rounds exploded inside the fence, to the front of their bunker.

The sound of numerous AK-47s joined in the chaos of the moment, firing at the First Platoon. The zinging of rounds sped overhead, along with the thud of bullets hitting the sandbags to Henderson's front. The noise level of weapons firing increased as most bunker positions opened fire.

"Eddie and Professor, stay where you are!" Drexler blasted the order through the small window cut into the front of the bunker,

Professor cupped his hands around his mouth. "Gooks coming up the hill!" As he leveled his M-79 at the VC approaching the position, he fired one round after another, reloading as fast as he could.

Henderson leveled his M-16 and squeezed off one round at a time, struggling to keep himself from panicking and expending his ammunition too soon. Drexler and Doc fired through the bunker window, but the enemy continued to advance through the hailstorm of bullets. Henderson could see the VC's AK-47 muzzle flashes closing in on their position.

He rolled to the end of the sandbag wall on the roof and peered around the corner of the bunker. He spotted a figure, clad in black shorts with no shirt, raising his right hand. The enemy held a grenade! Henderson fired three quick shots, and the VC tumbled backward. The grenade exploded, still clutched in the soldier's hand. Shrapnel slammed into the front of the bunker, the flash of light from the explosion momentarily blinding Henderson.

"Watch out!" Henderson yelled. "The bastards are getting close!"

He glanced to his right and noticed the bunker next to him also engaged with the enemy. The steady rhythm of Rocky's M-60 machine gun firing brought Henderson relief as it raked the front of the platoon positions, blasting the area with 7.62 rounds.

The NVA fired three mortar rounds. *Thump! Thump! Thump!*

Henderson and Professor dropped flat behind the wall of sandbags. Then the Second Platoon bunker to their left exploded, sending sandbags and soldiers flying through the air as all three rounds hit.

The six artillery guns fired back. The crews loaded and fired three high explosive rounds a minute, each one resounding across the firebase. Every time the 105-round exploded on its target, Henderson watched a fireball shoot into the sky.

•

"Tango six, this is Tango one-six. Over!" Brighton yelled into the handset.

"Roger, Tango one-six. Over," Lyons replied.

"Need support at my last bunker east side. Second Platoon bunker destroyed. Send APC. Over."

"Wilco, Tango one-six. Out."

After Lyons ordered an APC to the Second Platoon position, he knew the company needed air support. He called Battalion on the handset. "Tango, this is Tango six. Over."

"This is Tango. Over," the battalion commander said.

"Tango, we need Spooky. Start on the east side of the perimeter. Over."

"Roger, Tango six. Anything else? Over."

"Affirmative, Tango. We need four or five medevacs. Over."

"Wilco, Tango six. Out."

Within minutes, a track drove between Henderson's bunker and the smoldering Second Platoon bunker to cover the area. While firing the .50-caliber machine gun, the gunner sent a trail of tracer rounds pounding the hill slope. Both M-60 gunners on the track opened fire too.

Henderson witnessed more than fifteen enemy soldiers approaching the platoon positions. The VC crawled a short distance, springing to their feet as they fired AK-47s and lobbed grenades toward the bunkers, then continued to advance. They were closing in fast, showing no fear. Henderson continued to fire at any movement.

Bam!

A grenade went off in front of the bunker, forcing Professor and Henderson to lay flat. *Wham!* It felt like bunker's roof jumped several inches, then settled back into place. Dazed, Henderson looked around to see what had happened.

He spotted Stahl running in a zig-zag pattern.

Stahl raced across the thirty-five meters to the bunker to his left to see if the two explosions had caused any injuries to his soldiers.

Crack! Crack! Crack!

The impact of the three rounds sent Stahl tumbling backward, falling to the ground in a heap.

Henderson's heart raced as, fearing the worst for Stahl, he continued to fire on the enemy.

Through the loud noise of battle, Henderson heard a soldier in pain calling out, "Eddie, help me!"

Henderson's head jolted toward the bunker, realizing that whoever had called was inside. He slid off of the roof and hit the ground hard, outside the doorway. As he entered the shelter, Henderson was overcome by smoke. The smells of burnt flesh and gunpowder hung in the air, choking him. He rummaged through the collapsed sandbags and shredded rucksacks until he uncovered Doc, lying in a prone position. Blood spurted from his torso where his legs were once attached. The metallic smell of blood, mixed with the other odors, caused him to gag as he threw equipment from his path.

"Drexler! You okay? Drexler!"

"I'm here! Over here!"

Henderson crawled over to Drexler and sat next to him.

When he observed a figure coming through the doorway, Henderson raised his M-16. He immediately lowered it at the sight of Professor standing at the entrance.

"Check Doc. I'm sure he's dead." Henderson was shivering from panic.

Professor inched toward Doc. "He's dead."

As Henderson held Drexler, the inside of the bunker became eerily quiet, even though outside was chaos, as soldiers screamed at the enemy or called for a medic. As Professor stood guard, he listened to Drexler and Henderson talking.

Henderson grabbed Drexler's right hand, which was covered in blood. "Where are you hit?"

"The gut, I think." Drexler took a short breath, wincing in pain.

"You'll be okay. You'll be okay." Henderson applied pressure on the gaping wound with his left hand, while he attempted to find a bandage.

"I don't think so. I need you to listen to me."

"Don't talk. Let me help you." Henderson applied more pressure to stop the bleeding.

"Listen, Eddie, please."

"Sure, anything you want."

"Tell my parents what happened, and that I love them."

A tear escaped from Henderson's eye. "You'll tell them when you get home."

"I'm not going home. You have to tell them that I love them."

Henderson found a bandage and placed it over the wound, but then realized that he didn't have a dressing large enough.

"Remember, they'll treat you like a son, so don't worry about hanging around the house. Hell, I think my mom loves you more than me anyway." Mitch tried to laugh, but it sounded forced.

"I love her too, Mitch."

"Tell Sandra that I love her. Look in my rucksack—you'll find a letter I wrote. Give it to her."

"I'll tell her, and I'll give her the letter."

"One last thing."

"What is it?"

"Promise me, when you get home, you'll kill that son of a bitch Billy Matheson."

"Mitch … I don't know if I can do that."

"Promise me!"

Henderson swiped at the tears streaming down his cheek while looking through the haze in the bunker, searching for a sign—an answer.

"Okay, I'll kill the bastard."

"Professor?" Drexler looked around.

"Yes, Mitch? What do you need?"

"Help Eddie count the days left. He can't subtract."

"You got my word."

"Hang in there, Mitch." Henderson felt warm blood flowing over his hand as he applied pressure.

Drexler then closed his eyes as his head slumped to the right, against Henderson's chest.

Henderson felt the blood pounding in his ears. It was as if the world moved in slow motion for him—he no longer heard the noises of the battle. In a blur, he saw Professor speaking, but no sound reached him.

A sickly sweet odor—the smell of death—filled the inside of the bunker. Black dots danced in front of his eyes when he thought of the enemy who had killed his friend. Anger, sadness, and revenge ripped through his body, causing him to shudder uncontrollably. He embraced his brother one last time.

Drexler and Doc lay lifeless as morbidity took hold.

Henderson studied the wreckage with eyes barely more alive than those of his friend. He couldn't feel any life within himself. "Damn it! How come I'm still alive and Mitch is dead?"

Professor slid across the dirt floor as Henderson sobbed like a child.

"Look at me, Eddie!"

"What?" Henderson wiped his tears.

"Listen to my words. It don't mean nothin'."

"Shit! No, I'm not fucking saying it, Professor!"

"Eddie, you have to."

Henderson knew he could only move forward by repeating the words. He wiped his tears. "It don't mean nothin'."

Light filtered into the bunker as the sounds of the battle became louder. Professor and Henderson watched streams of red rain falling earthward from Spooky's three miniguns. The aircraft dropped flares too, shedding light on the firebase as they drifted to the ground.

Within minutes, all became fear-invoking quiet.

"Medic! Medic! Medic!" drifted around the perimeter of bunkers.

Henderson took one long look at Drexler and lowered him to the ground. Then, with Professor, he turned and strode outside.

The men of the Second Squad walked as one to where Stahl had fallen. Porter knelt and rolled Stahl over to see if the enemy had killed him. Then he stood and shook his head. "He's dead."

Henderson stood over Stahl, looking at his peaceful face one last time, his mind and body numb from the loss of Drexler. He couldn't cry or feel—he could only stare at his fallen leader.

Rocky placed his arm around Porter's shoulder. "It don't mean nothin'."

Henderson nodded. "It don't mean nothin'."

Brighton and Swift bolted to the group, gathering around Stahl.

"KIAs are Drexler, Sergeant Stahl, and Doc. No wounded." Henderson's cold stare told the rest of the story.

"Damn it!" Brighton's faced turned crimson.

For a moment, his head hung and he did nothing. Then, he sucked in a breath and reached for the handset from Ledger. He pressed the talk button. "Tango six, this is Tango one-six. Over."

"Go ahead, Tango one-six. Over," Lyons said.

"Three KIA. Need dustoff. We'll check to verify EKIA. Over."

"Roger, Tango one-six. Son of a bitch! Sorry to hear that. Dustoff in five mikes. Over."

"Roger, Tango six. Out."

While the lieutenant spoke on the radio, the APC approached along the road. Henderson flagged him to stop.

"What you need?" The track commander's eyes widened.

"Can you take the dead to the helipad?"

The rear hatch lowered and Bravo Team escorted Stahl inside, where they gently laid him on the floor. Rocky, Porter, Professor, and Henderson carried Drexler, wrapped in a poncho, and placed him next to Stahl.

Henderson sat next to Drexler. "I'm not leaving Mitch alone."

Without saying a word, his team members left. They returned in minutes with Doc, and laid him next to Drexler. The four soldiers remained in the track as the hatch closed. It started forward, rumbling along the rutted road to the helipad. Once at the pad, they saw three Hueys, with blades rotating, waiting to take the precious cargo to Duc Pho.

One hell of a night!

Henderson wiped another tear away. *Why Mitch? It should've been me.*

One by one, the soldiers slid each of the fallen soldiers onto a litter on the floor of the Huey. The crew made sure they were secure, and that the ponchos wouldn't fly off.

Henderson grabbed Drexler's exposed hand and held it to say goodbye one last time, as the tears flowed.

Professor put his arm around Henderson and led him away from the helicopter. "Let's go."

As they stood to the side of the pad, the blades gathered speed. The Huey lifted, rotated left, and accelerated toward Bronco. Henderson watched his brother fly away as he wiped at his tears.

Other platoons arrived, placing their dead with the wounded on the other two Hueys. Once loaded, the pilots lifted off of the pad, straight into the night sky, rotating south and speeding off into the darkness toward Bronco.

In unison, the four remaining members of Alpha Team turned and strode along the dark trail toward the bunkers.

Henderson pushed back his wet hair. "This ain't over. We have four more hours of darkness. The enemy wants to kill all of us." Henderson stumbled. "It don't mean nothin'."

Once Henderson and Professor returned to their bunker, Henderson hesitated before entering. "Go on up to the roof. I'll be there in a minute."

Henderson walked to the front and stood over the dead NVA. Staring at the man, about the same age as himself, he felt nothing but hate. He slid the selector switch of his M-16 to automatic.

"Sergeant Stahl, you're right. I am doing it someday."

He pulled the trigger. The M-16 muzzle flashed with the rapid firing of his 5.56 rounds, destroying the enemy soldier's head. He stared at the enemy with hatred in his heart.

"He's not dead until he's dead." He turned and climbed the sandbags to the roof, where Professor waited for him. Professor didn't say a word.

They sat together, watching into the darkness.

GROWING UP TOO FAST

Waking early, Henderson shook Professor's arm. "It's morning." "Okay, okay, I'm awake."

Once Professor stood, the two tired soldiers slipped off of the roof, dropping to the ground. Professor shivered when he viewed at least twelve dead VC, several of them three or four feet from his position. As Henderson stood in the doorway, he peered into the darkness of the shelter, surveying the destruction—the smells of death and gunpowder lingered. Stepping backward several steps, Henderson stumbled as he wiped at the tears clouding his eyes.

After he took a deep breath, Henderson paused, trying to find the right words. "Professor, go check the bodies. Look for weapons too. I'll have Rocky and Porter help."

"You got it."

Henderson spotted the machine gunner and his assistant sitting on the roof, bullshitting. "Rocky and Porter, before you eat, help Professor check the dead VC. Collect any weapons or ammo you find."

"Roger that!" Rocky yelled.

Porter raised his hand.

Henderson rolled his eyes. "Not now, Porter." He walked away.

While the three team members checked the dead, Henderson went into his bunker. He moved equipment around and threw destroyed gear outside. He worked alone at this task—his way of facing Drexler's death.

"Why you?" His eyes closed for a silent prayer before he began the task of cleaning the mess.

After an hour, he sat in the corner, next to Drexler's rucksack, and removed the many letters he had received from Sandra. Neatly arranging the letters, he saw one addressed to her that Drexler hadn't mailed. He slid the envelope into his pants' cargo pocket, knowing that he had the letter which Drexler had asked him to send.

Once he had pulled shrapnel from the rucksack's exterior, he attempted to wipe off the blood splatters, but to no avail. He gave up. Henderson tightened the straps and placed it in the corner, then sat staring at the dark bloodstains covering the dirt floor and the ceiling of sandbags.

Professor peered into the doorway. "We checked the dead. Got nine AK-forty-sevens, along with several grenades."

"Thanks for checking." Henderson's eyes remained in his stare. "Did you find him?"

"No, not there. Henderson, the lieutenant is here."

Henderson stepped out of the bunker into the bright sunlight, squinting. "Morning, LT." He noticed Ledger standing behind Brighton, and nodded in his direction.

"How are you doing, Henderson?" Brighton looked exhausted, but his voice had the same sharp clarity as ever.

"Okay, sir."

"You have a situation report?"

"Yes, LT. Professor found twelve dead gooks, nine AKs, and three grenades. Our bunker sustained some damage, but is fixable. The squad's other two bunkers had minor damage."

"Good job, Henderson. Thanks for taking charge. I'll call the CO to have the dead NVA removed."

"Thanks, sir."

As the lieutenant walked away, on the temporary road to his bunker, Henderson heard the platoon leader's radio. "Tango six, this is Tango one-six. Over." The transmission faded as Brighton strode away, Ledger following closely behind.

Henderson adjusted his weight to his back foot. "Rocky, can you watch our bunker until we return?"

"You got it."

"Let's go eat." Henderson's stomach churned.

Professor put an arm around Henderson's shoulder, and the two men strode along the trail toward the mess hall. With the smell of eggs and bacon floating on the breeze, Henderson realized that he needed to eat. For one moment, he forgot about the death and destruction he had witnessed last night.

After a meal which he barely touched, Henderson carried his tray to the counter, where the dirty ones were stacked. He plopped the mess tray onto the stack and walked outside, stopping to light a cigarette. He took a long drag, holding the smoke in, until he thought his lungs would burst. Then he exhaled, enjoying the taste of the Marlboro.

The screen door slammed, which made Henderson jump.

Professor stood in the doorway with a caring smile spreading across his face. He lit a cigarette. "Are you ready to head over to the bunker?"

"I reckon." Henderson took the first step, with Professor at his heels.

When they arrived at the bunker, the lieutenant and Swift stood outside the doorway. A frown crossed Henderson's face. "What's going on, LT?"

Swift's spine stiffened. "Professor, get the rest of the Second Squad over here."

Professor covered the thirty-five meters with long strides. When he reached the side of the bunker, he yelled, "Second Squad, LT wants you over at my bunker!"

Rocky and Porter jumped from the roof, landing hard. They strode toward Brighton, with Ransom following. Professor ran to the next position, yelling for the occupants to meet at his bunker. Madison and the other two team members trailed behind the Professor as he returned to the bunker.

"The squad is here, LT."

"Thanks, Professor. Thank you all for the great job you did last night. I know it's hard losing men—your brothers—but we have no choice but to continue. We can't change what happened." With a short pause, he looked around. "I'm promoting Henderson to Acting Sergeant and squad leader of the Second Squad. Henderson, front and center."

After facing the lieutenant, Swift pinned sergeant stripes on Henderson's right collar, while the lieutenant pinned one on the left.

"Thank you, sir." Henderson saluted.

"You deserve it." Brighton returned the salute.

The Second Squad members slapped Henderson on the back, congratulating him on his promotion. After the short promotion ceremony, the Second Squad headed to their assigned bunkers for another day in 'Nam.

Henderson turned to Professor. "What in the hell is an Acting Sergeant?"

Professor laughed. "You have the authority, responsibilities, and work of a sergeant without drawing the pay."

"It doesn't sound fair, if you ask me," Henderson said.

"No, it doesn't. Congrats!"

After climbing to the roof, the two friends lit cigarettes. They sat quietly as the morning sun beat down on them.

Henderson looked at the paddies outside the wire. "I think I'll go on R and R."

"Why so soon?"

"I need to get away from this hellhole—I need time to grieve for Mitch. If I stay here, it won't happen. Mitch needs me to mourn for him. If I don't leave, I could get one of us killed. Hell, I need to be alone."

Henderson slid off of the roof and, as he strode along the dirt road which ran behind bunkers and circled the firebase, his mind raced. *How do I tell Brighton I need a break? Do I tell him Mitch's death got to me more than I thought?* He drew in a long deep breath as he spotted Brighton sitting in the shade of the bunker, writing on a piece of paper.

Brighton lifted his pen and wiped the sweat from his brow. He placed the pen's tip against the paper and wrote:

> *"Dear Mr. and Mrs. Stahl,*
> *I'm Terry's platoon leader, James Brighton.*
> *I know the army informed you of his death, but I wanted to let you know what kind of man, leader, and soldier he became.*
> *On the day Terry died…"*

Henderson's shadow reached his platoon leader first, as he stood over him. "Sir."

Brighton continued writing.

Henderson cleared his throat. "LT, I need to talk to you."

The lieutenant stopped writing and glanced upward. "What, Sergeant Henderson?"

"I want to go on R and R."

"Okay, let Top know. He'll get you orders for your rest and recuperation next month."

"No. Today, sir."

"Why do you need to go today? You recently got promoted—you have responsibilities here."

"LT, trust me. I need it."

"Wait here." Brighton stood and walked into the bunker, where he found Ledger asleep. Henderson overheard the radio. "Tango six…" He heard no more of what was said.

After several minutes, Brighton returned. "Henderson, you leave at seventeen-hundred hours for Bronco. Top has your orders. Is Hawaii okay for your R and R?"

"Sounds great. Thanks, LT."

"Are you going to write Drexler's wife and parents?"

"No, sir. I'm going to call his parents while I'm on R and R. I have a letter Drexler gave me to mail to his wife."

"Do you want me to write to them?"

"Appreciate it if you would, sir."

"Have a good trip." Brighton sat and gazed at his paper, with pen in hand. "Go on, Sergeant Henderson."

"Yes, sir." Henderson slowly strolled toward the bunker's entrance.

> *"Dear Mr. and Mrs. Drexler,*
> *I'm Mitch's platoon leader…"*

Brighton's face contorted. It was never easy penning letters to parents or spouses concerning their loved ones, but he knew that critical duty fell upon his shoulders.

As he strode to his bunker, Henderson knew the lieutenant had to use personal favors to get him on R and R so quickly. *The lieutenant is a good officer.*

Once he reached his position, he spotted Professor. "I got it. I got my R and R!"

"Congrats! At least one of us is getting out of this hellhole."

"Don't tell the others. That's my responsibility now."

"You got it. It's all yours. I wish I were going with you."

"Maybe next time. We're a couple of men short, if you get my drift."

"Loud and clear, Sarge!" Professor mockingly saluted Henderson. "When you set to leave?"

"Today!" Henderson flashed a smile. His grin soon faded into deep-boned grief across his brow. *To say goodbye to my brother.*

After calling the squad together, Henderson broke the news. "I'm leaving for R and R today. Madison, look after the squad until I return. I'll be gone for a week. Don't you guys do anything stupid while I'm away."

His brothers stared at Henderson. They knew why he had decided to leave.

"Nothing else. Get to work."

Henderson felt a tinge of regret, wanting to take leave at this critical point, but he knew he must address his grief or he wouldn't be any use to anyone, much less fit for a battle. He smiled at his squad members as he entered the bunker to pack his rucksack. Once packed, he slid into the straps of his ruck, then extended his hand so Professor could pull him to his feet.

"How's that, little fella?" Professor grinned.

"You know you're not supposed to call me little." But his words were lackluster. Henderson didn't care. He needed this time off.

Professor reached for Henderson, pulling him into a bear hug. "Remember what you have to say."

As his smile disappeared, Henderson nodded. "It don't mean nothin'."

Henderson shuffled like an older man toward the waiting Huey for his ride to Bronco. He had begun his journey to fly away from Vietnam and the war. *I get to leave this hell!* For a week, at least.

As he climbed onto the helicopter, his mind drifted to his youth, high school, and his parents, who had died less than a year ago. Henderson knew that he had aged twenty years in such a fleeting period—his youth forever lost.

The helicopter lifted fifty feet and flew over the firebase at a slow speed. With feet dangling over the skids, Henderson gazed downward, spotting Professor, Rocky, Porter, Madison, Ransom, Hayes, Clark, and Ames, who all stood on the roof of the bunker, waving goodbye. Henderson raised his M-16, acknowledging the farewell as he fought the tears.

They're my family—my brothers.
Why am I leaving?

THE WAR ISN'T OVER

B righton took long strides to the Second Squad bunkers as a soldier ran behind him, struggling to keep up.

When they reached the position, Madison sat outside, leaning against the sandbag wall with his eyes closed. Madison was acting squad leader for Second Squad during Henderson's absence, which left him exhausted.

Brighton kicked his boot. "Madison, you have a replacement for the Second Squad. This is Private Ray Laurel. He's from Montgomery, Alabama."

Madison slowly opened his eyes. He noticed a skinny kid with short, bright-red hair and freckles, who looked no older than fourteen. When Laurel smiled, Madison noticed his missing front tooth.

"Thanks, sir." Madison sat upright.

Brighton wiped the sweat from his brow. "It's going to be a while before we get a medic. I want Porter to carry the first-aid bag—let Ames be the assistant gunner. I understand Porter had some medical training before coming into the army."

"Yes, sir, he did. Good choice." Madison nodded.

Porter looked up as Madison approached with a soldier he didn't recognize. Porter darted his eyes at the recruit. *Fresh out of training. Poor kid.* "What's up?"

"Lieutenant Brighton said you're the temporary medic. Get your stuff and go to Professor's bunker."

Wiping at the sweat dripping down his face, Madison turned to face Ames. "You're the assistant gunner for Rocky, so you're in Alpha Team. Have Porter brief you on your duties before he leaves."

"Sure, Madison," Porter and Ames said, then headed to the bunker.

Madison strolled back to the road with Laurel in tow. "That's Porter and Ames. They're in Alpha Team. Good men."

When he reached Professor's position, Madison yelled to Professor as he sat on the roof, "Got a replacement!"

"Let's check this guy out." Professor jumped off of the roof and assessed Laurel.

"First, a couple of changes. Porter is the platoon medic—I'm assigning him to your bunker. Ames is the assistant gunner for Rocky."

"Great. Ames is a good guy. So, who's the new guy?"

"This is Ray Laurel, an FNG, so take care of him."

Before Madison left, Professor gave Laurel the once over again. "How old are you?"

"Damn it! I'm eighteen! Why does everyone keep asking me that?"

"A little touchy about your age, are you?" Professor smiled. Despite not being all that much older, he felt suddenly paternal toward the kid. "Not to worry. People won't mention it after a day or two. Let's get you settled."

"Before you ask, Laurel lost his tooth during training." Madison smiled as he turned to head along the road toward his bunker.

Professor and Laurel strode into their humid, dark bunker. Professor pointed to Drexler's old space. "Store your gear over there. It's where you sleep, so make yourself at home."

Laurel dropped his rucksack, releasing a deep sigh with the weight of the pack no longer on his back. He unfastened the straps and pulled out his poncho liner, laying it on top of his ruck. Next, he retrieved his canteen and took a large gulp of warm water.

As Laurel looked around, he saw shrapnel embedded into the wooden beams, and spotted where new sandbags lay alongside them. The dark red stains on the beams and sandbags got his attention. "What happened?"

"I'll tell you someday. First, let me go over the stuff you need to know to survive Vietnam and this war. When Sergeant Henderson returns, I'm sure he'll have much more to add."

Professor spoke for thirty minutes, reviewing what he thought necessary for an FNG. Laurel didn't ask too many questions.

As Professor briefed the FNG, Porter arrived with his rucksack. He silently stowed his gear, listening when Professor told Laurel the realities of being in Vietnam. After his talk, the men chatted regarding the "world" as Laurel updated them on what had happened at home before he left.

As the room grew silent, Porter's stomach churned. "Time for chow."

The three soldiers stepped into the bright light and heat, then turned to walk along the worn trail toward the mess hall.

"We'll return shortly." Professor waved at Rocky. "Can you watch the position for us?"

"Sure." Rocky nodded in affirmation.

After the evening meal, Professor, Porter, and Laurel settled in for the evening, sitting on the roof of the bunker. Each lit a cigarette while staring at the rice paddies below, not saying a word—all lost in their thoughts as the sun faded behind them.

Professor interrupted the tranquility of the evening. "Hey, Laurel, we've all been together for a while now. Why don't you tell us about yourself?"

Laurel sat quietly for several moments, because he wasn't sure what to tell his new friends. "Born and raised in Montgomery, Alabama. I graduated from high school—a vo-tech high school. I'm an auto mechanic. My dad worked at a cotton mill. Mom worked at the drug store. Before working at the mill, my dad served in World War II, in the infantry. He went airborne too. He served at Bastogne, with the One Hundred and First Airborne Division. After I graduated from vo-tech, I enlisted in the infantry, like my dad. I took my basic at Fort Polk, with my infantry training at Tigerland—that's at Fort Polk too. So, here I am."

They nodded their approval and sat without speaking, lighting another cigarette. After blowing smoke rings, Professor followed them with his eyes until they dissipated.

"I think most of us serving in this shithole are sons of World War II veterans. My dad was a pilot. He flew bombers. He flew the B-seventeen Flying Fortress in Europe. I don't recall how many sorties he flew, though he told us at length when I was a kid."

"My dad enlisted in the Navy," Porter said, taking a long, deep breath. "He served on the USS Missouri as a gunner. I remember he told me how the Japs surrendered on his ship." He looked at his watch, then continued, in a darker tone. "Get in the bunker. It's time."

"What do you mean?" Laurel's brow contorted as his fright showed for a moment—the fear of the unknown unnerved him.

Professor tapped Laurel's shoulder. "We don't need to answer that question. You'll see."

Laurel jumped to the ground, following the two old-timers, and entered the bunker. He sat next to his rucksack, watching the two soldiers in the far corner, who seemed relaxed under uncertainty.

Porter looked at his watch again. "Nineteen-hundred hours."

Thump! Thump! Thump! Thump!

The sound of the VC firing four mortar rounds echoed across the firebase.

"Incoming!" Porter covered both ears. Professor and Porter sat staring at Laurel, watching his every movement.

Wham! Wham! Wham! Wham!

One after another, the explosions rocked the bunker. Loose sand fell on the men as the bunker vibrated from the blast. Two blasts landed close to their position, but didn't do any damage—the other two exploded outside the wire.

The artillery answered the NVA mortar crew. *Boom! Boom! Boom!*

Professor observed Laurel curling in a fetal position, striving to become as small as possible. As the mortar fire slowly tapered off, no longer able to hold it in, Professor and Porter laughed.

"Quit laughing!" Laurel quickly stood.

Professor licked his lips and wiped the dust from his eyes. "Relax. You'll get used to the mortar attacks. They happen every night like clockwork."

"You could've warned me. Not funny!"

"We get entertainment where we can." Professor shrugged. "If you are going to survive, you'll need to loosen up."

Porter readjusted his stance, aiming to defuse the situation. "What's the guard rotation?"

Professor huffed, "Pull one hour thirty minutes each, with two shifts. Porter, Laurel, then me." He stopped talking and made eye contact with Laurel. "You'll need to remain awake. This is *not* a joke. If you think you're going to fall asleep, wake me. Remember, there are four claymore triggers on the roof. If you think you see Charlie, open fire. Kill the son of a bitch with no hesitation. That is how you earn our trust. Got it?"

"Got it, sir." Laurel swallowed hard, knowing now that he had joined the hellhole ranks of the Nam' jungle—once nothing but bits of conversation he had heard during basic training.

I can't get killed here! Not here! Momma would kill me if I did.

•

Porter grabbed a snack and his M-16, with a bandolier of ammunition, then headed to the roof to pull the first shift of guard duty. Once settled behind the sandbag wall, he lit his last cigarette of the night while watching the shadows fall across the rice fields. The long night dragged on for the men guarding the perimeter while their buddies slept.

After his second shift ended, Porter went into the bunker to get Laurel. He tapped Laurel's foot. "Time for guard duty."

"I'm awake." Laurel bolted upright fand ran his hands across his crew cut. "What time is it?"

Porter looked at the illuminated dial on his watch. "Near zero-two-thirty."

Laurel grabbed his weapon and ammunition. He hurried through the doorway of the bunker and climbed to the roof. He sat behind the wall, watching to his front, while his eyes got used to the darkness.

After twenty minutes, Laurel heard tin cans rattling to the front, dead center of his position. While he was watching for any movement, a trip flare popped, the light illuminating the area for a minute.

Laurel strained to see into the darkness. His eyes watered and his breathing became ragged and harsh. With a trembling hand, he wiped at the sweat trickling down his neck. "What do I do?"

He clutched a claymore mine trigger, slid the safety off, and waited.

Pop! Another trip flare went off, illuminating the slope to his front.

Laurel spotted shadows, so he squeezed the trigger.

Bam!

A flash of light shone as the mine exploded, sending hundreds of steel balls hurtling toward the enemy.

When Professor and Porter heard the explosion, they threw off their poncho liners and scrambled onto the roof, crawling toward Laurel. Porter raised his M-16, sliding the selector switch to semi-automatic. He squeezed the trigger, sending round after round to the spot where the flares illuminated the area. When the flare finished burning, he stopped shooting.

Professor looked at Laurel. "What did you see?"

"Shadows moved, then the flares went off. I detonated one of the claymores." Sweat dripped off of Laurel's face, and his hands trembled as he positioned his M-16 to fire at the VC.

Professor attempted to calm him, by touching his shoulder. "Laurel, good job—way to watch our backs."

•

Madison spotted shadows moving toward their bunker. He ordered his men to open fire.

With Ames linking the ammunition belts, Rocky swept the front from the Second Squad position with the M-60 machine gun.

The rest of the team fired M-16s along the slope, hoping to kill the VC they couldn't see.

"Blow claymores!" Madison yelled. "They're getting closer!"

Ransom grabbed three claymore triggers and slid the safeties off, squeezing each one.

Three flashes of light followed. *Bam! Bam! Bam!*

Each blast reverberated along the hillside. After the explosions, screams from fifty meters away caught their attention.

Madison caught a glimpse of an enemy soldier crawling toward the bunker next to his. He raised his M-16 and fired an automatic burst of 5.56 rounds. The bullets thudded into the enemy's chest, not far from the bunker's entrance.

Wham! An explosion shook the ground. The men on the bunker roof felt the vibration from where they lay.

Porter looked to the south and observed flames at the area where Bravo Team had a bunker. Rocky sprayed the front of the positions with 7.62 rounds, while Ames continued to link the belts of ammunition.

Silence fell over the firebase as quickly as the VC had attacked.

"Medic! Medic!"

Porter hesitated for a moment, expecting to see Doc run out. Then the cold realization that Doc had died, and those calls were for him, hit home. He jumped from the roof and ran into the bunker. After grabbing the first-aid bag, Porter bolted toward the cries for help.

A soldier yelled, "Over here!"

When Porter ran toward the call, he saw a soldier lying on the ground, with a hole in his chest, as Madison worked on him. "He can't breathe."

Porter reached into the bag, removed a bandage, and opened it. He tore off the cellophane and pressed it against the wound. After pulling out the tape, he tore off several pieces, taping the cellophane to three sides over the hole in Clark's chest. Next, he applied the dressing. Porter knew that it was a sucking chest wound, and the soldier couldn't breathe. "Help me roll him over."

Porter slid his hands under Clark's shoulders, while Madison slid his hands under the soldier's hips; together, they rolled him onto his right side.

"Oh, shit!" Porter's mind echoed the expletive.

Madison frowned. "What is it? What's wrong?"

"It's the exit wound. There's a hole the size of my fist! I'll see if I can stop the bleeding." As he applied pressure with several bandages, Clark's warm blood flowed through the dressing, over his hands.

Porter felt him go limp, and he knew the soldier had stopped breathing. For the first time, he looked at Clark's face and realized that it was one of the new guys who lay lifeless on the ground. He never had a chance. Porter's throat went dry.

"He's dead." Porter shook his head. "I failed—the first time my platoon needed me."

The rest of the Bravo Team stood around Clark, staring at him in disbelief.

Whop! Whop! Whop! The approaching dustoff snapped the men from their trance.

Madison pointed. "Get a poncho. Carry him to the helipad."

After they rolled the lifeless body onto the poncho, four squad members grabbed each corner and lifted him. As they trotted in silence, they carried him to the waiting helicopter. Once they reached the dustoff, they slid the body onto a litter. Then, they stood at the open doorway, watching a crew member check the fallen soldier, covering him with a blanket. Without speaking, each soldier said goodbye.

Porter looked at Madison as they walked away from the helipad. "Did you know Clark well?"

Madison stopped and stared at the ground. "I didn't."

As Porter walked away, Madison called to him, "I killed a VC near the front of the bunker. Tell Professor to check him."

"Will do. Thanks."

Once at his position, Porter entered the bunker. He grabbed his canteen, taking several long swigs to wet his parched lips and dry mouth. It didn't help. He noticed his blood-covered hands and poured water over them, rubbing as hard as he could to remove the blood.

Watching him, Professor took a bar of soap and a handkerchief from his rucksack. He soaked the handkerchief in water and handed it, and the soap, to Porter.

As Porter cleaned his hands, he looked at his two team members. "I don't want to be the platoon medic."

Professor tightened his jaw. "What happened?"

"I have enough enemy deaths on my hands. I can't take fellow soldiers' deaths too."

Professor looked at Laurel. "Take a good, hard look around you. This is what this war is about. We kill each other, one at a time. One day, we kill one VC; the next day, the VC kills one of us. And we send it up the chain of command—one VC killed. The NVA sends it up *their* chain of command—one American killed. We announce the number to prove the NVA is losing the war; the NVA announces it to cause more demonstrations back home..." Professor paused, leaning his head into his hand.

Laurel waited for him to continue, still shaken at seeing his first real battle, as Porter sat silently off to the side.

Professor tried to keep his voice neutral as he spoke, aware that his brother was only one more in the tally for the VC. "It's a numbers game—one at a time. I'm tired of the killing, and this war."

Laurel wiped his palms on his pants. "The death toll comes on the news every night at home. From what I see, it's over two hundred Americans dead a week, to more than one thousand enemy soldiers killed. But you're right. Out here, it's one at a time; those other numbers don't mean shit."

Deep in his thoughts, Professor was no longer listening to his team members. He thought of his days at the University of California at Berkeley, and his involvement in the anti-war movement. He remembered protesting against this unjust war every day, and becoming a campus leader against the political regime sending their youth to war. Even with his younger brother, Bobby, fighting in Vietnam, he held his conviction for protesting against the war. Then, the day came when his mom called, telling him Bobby had died fighting the VC. Even then, the thought of joining up had been the furthest thing from his mind. Devastated, he went after politicians with a newfound zeal to end the war.

Yet, as the weeks went by, his anger developed into hatred toward the VC who had killed his brother. Before he knew what he was doing, he arrived at the Medical Entrance Processing Station, taking the oath of enlistment into the US Army. He only wanted to kill the VC. Nothing else.

Porter cut in, breaking his silence. "Professor, there's a dead Charlie by the bunker. You may want to check him before they move him."

Professor stood and shook his head. "I'll go make sure."

As he walked along the road in the darkness, Professor covered the hundred meters in a short time. Approaching the bunker, he saw Madison, who stood on the backside, smoking a cigarette. "You doing okay, Madison?"

"Yeah, I'm okay. You here to check the dead VC?"

Professor nodded as he walked to the front of the bunker.

He rolled the VC onto his back and knelt to take a long look at his face. Professor then shook his head, stood, and walked along the road toward his bunker.

When he reached the bunker, Porter looked at him.

"He the one?"

"Nope, not him."

"How are you gonna know, anyhow?"

"Everyone asks that question. I *understand* that I'll never know. I do it because I promised my mom that I would look for the VC who killed Bobby."

Laurel glanced up. "She knows you don't know who done it, right?"

"I believe so." Professor lit a cigarette. "She's sick with grief and isn't thinking right."

"It sounds like she wants revenge." Porter seemed very somber, still looking at his hands as if the blood still stained them.

"That says it about right. And so do I."

•

The next morning at the mess hall for breakfast, Porter said, while chewing a bite of an egg, "I wonder how Henderson is doing."

"Me, too." Rocky sipped his milk. "You were with him, Professor. I know Drexler and Henderson were best friends—like brothers— but there appeared to be more bothering him regarding the night he died. Do you know what got to him?"

Professor took his time to answer, eating a forkful of scrambled eggs. "I'm sure Mitch getting killed was plenty. If there is anything else, you should ask Eddie when he returns."

"Well, I hope he's having fun with the women." Porter smiled, as if jealousy took him over for a brief moment.

Professor swallowed as the three soldiers lifted their milk cartons, touching them together, and toasted Henderson. "To Eddie. May he find peace."

NEED TO BE ALONE

Henderson peered through the window, watching the clouds speed past the airliner.

Over the hum of the aircraft, men talked about meeting their wives or girlfriends in Hawaii; he detected the excitement in their voices. He wanted to be alone, so Henderson didn't mind that he didn't have a loved one waiting for him. He drank Jim Beam and Coke during the seventeen-hour flight, ignoring the surrounding soldiers.

He found one of the stewardesses eye-catching—long, blonde hair; a small waist with a full bust; and round, blue eyes, which sparkled each time she served him a drink. She was the first round-eyed woman he had seen in seven months, and he enjoyed staring at her. After lighting a cigarette, he watched her as she passed through the narrow aisle, taking care of the servicemen.

She served another drink while giving him a gorgeous smile. "You going to be in Hawaii for a week?"

He thought of being alone with her. "Sure am."

With her smile spreading across her face, she handed Henderson his drink. "My name is Mandy."

"Your name fits your face. Both are beautiful," Henderson stammered. His face turned bright red after he spoke.

They laughed, and their hands touched as Henderson accepted the drink. Both were smiling as she walked away to serve the other passengers.

The sleeping soldier seated next to Henderson jumped as a muffled cry escaped from his lips. "Gooks everywhere! Get down!" His head flopped onto Henderson's shoulder.

Instead of waking the soldier, Henderson allowed him to sleep. He understood that reaction to a dream; he had many terrifying nightmares too. Henderson patted the soldier's arm to comfort him. "It's okay. You're safe."

As he lit another cigarette and took a sip of Jim Beam and Coke, Henderson's thoughts turned to Mitch again. He recalled the sensation of holding Mitch in his arms as his friend talked, and how his head lay against his chest, with blood streaming from the open wound. After Mitch's last breath, Henderson had felt the warmth leave his friend's body.

Dread crept over him. Henderson felt the same way he did when walking in a minefield—afraid to move his feet. In this state, his mind offered only one thought—he couldn't avoid going to Indiana. He had given his word to Mitch that he would kill a man.

As the plane darted through clouds, Henderson devised his kill plan. Once he arrived in Hawaii, it would be easy to catch a flight to the mainland. After getting to Indianapolis, he could determine if Billy lived with Sandra, or if he lived alone. In either case, it would be simple enough to commit murder. He had killed many times in the war. How would this be different? An enemy is an enemy.

He ran through many scenarios. He needed to buy a hunting rifle with a scope to kill Billy when he left the house, early in the morning. Then he'd get rid of the gun and catch a returning flight to Hawaii. Nobody would be the wiser. Henderson smiled, because he knew he had a workable plan. He became excited about landing.

At last, the pilot announced, "Please buckle your seatbelts. We are on the final approach for landing."

The pilot's announcement woke the soldiers from their restless sleep, and they cheered at knowing that they would soon be landing. Flight attendants walked along the aisle, checking each passenger. Henderson felt the excitement building as each serviceman anticipated meeting a loved one after they stepped from the plane onto American soil. The clicking of belt buckles echoed throughout the cabin.

Mandy stopped in front of Henderson, reaching to check his belt with a soft tug on the buckle. "Stay safe. Enjoy your time in Hawaii."

Henderson nodded as a broad smile crossed his lips. "Mandy, thank you."

Once the wheels squealed onto the runway, the servicemen cheered as one, and thundering laughter boomed throughout the aircraft. After the pilot pulled into the terminal area, the passengers stood to retrieve their bags. When the doors opened, the soldiers rushed forward to get off of the aircraft and meet their wives and girlfriends.

Henderson sipped the last of his Jim Beam and Coke, not in any hurry to leave the plane. Mandy stood near his seat as the servicemen moved along the aisle to the exit, as if to let Henderson know that there were people who cared. As the last soldier walked past, Henderson stood and moved to the aisle.

He looked into Mandy's eyes. "Nice to meet you."

Mandy touched his arm. "Please get some sleep. And try to have some fun while you're here—you seem like you need it."

"I will."

Well, he would try. The thought of going to kill Billy wasn't exactly his idea of fun, or R and R time, but he had to do it for Mitch. How could he let his brother down?

He strode along the aisle and down the steps onto the tarmac. The heat hit him, but it wasn't like Vietnam's scorching jungle. He found the temperature comfortable, with less humidity and a gentle ocean breeze flowing across the airfield. Henderson looked around, studying the tropical beauty. Even the smells of the trees, flowers, and the ocean were a relief from the awful smells of the deathtrap called Vietnam.

Henderson followed the stragglers into the terminal, but he didn't head for the exit. Instead, he walked along the long corridor toward the ticket counters. The sights and sounds of people strolling through the airport—laughing, talking, and generally having a good time—looked so foreign to him.

Hell, where is the point man? What about noise discipline? For God's sake, spread out. He laughed as he realized his irrational thoughts.

As Henderson reached the ticket counters, he headed to the Trans World Airlines counter and approached a ticket agent—an older Hawaiian man wearing a colorful shirt and a lei around his neck. He seemed pleasant enough.

Henderson nodded. "Morning. I want to purchase a ticket to the Indianapolis International Airport for today. I want to fly standby, if necessary."

"You a soldier?"

"Yes, sir, I am."

"May I see your orders?"

Baffled at being asked for orders, Henderson handed the agent his R and R orders. "Why do you need my orders?"

After he read the orders, the agent leaned forward against the counter and whispered, "Son, these orders are for Hawaii only. You can't go to the mainland. I'm supposed to report you to the MPs, but I'm not going to. Go and enjoy yourself in Hawaii."

Henderson stood, confused, but didn't say a word.

The agent looked past Henderson. "Next!"

Still trying to figure out the situation, Henderson turned away from the counter and followed the exit signs to the front of the terminals. He knew he had missed the briefing and transportation to the hotel. When a yellow cab pulled up in front of him and stopped at the curb, Henderson opened the rear door, sliding into the hot, black vinyl seat.

The driver turned in his seat to face Henderson with a cigarette hanging from his lips. "Where to?"

"The Reef Hotel." Henderson slammed the door.

The driver pulled into the stream of traffic as he looked into the rearview mirror. "You comin' from 'Nam?"

"Yeah, I am."

The driver wanted to keep the conversation going. "I bet it's tough over there. What unit you with?"

Henderson looked intently out of the window as he lit a cigarette. When he didn't answer, the driver shrugged and returned his attention to the road.

As the cab traveled toward its intended destination, Henderson observed the buildings, people, and cars he passed.

Why didn't I try harder to get to Billy? I made a promise to Mitch—that has to count for something. The guilt he was feeling made him sick to his stomach. He hadn't made enough of an effort to get to Indiana. He felt alone, angry, and scared.

Once the driver pulled the car up alongside the curb, he jumped from his seat and opened the door for his passenger. Henderson wasn't even aware that they had arrived at their destination. He grabbed his bag, while fumbling for his wallet. He pulled a five-dollar bill from his wallet and handed the money to the driver. "Thanks for the lift."

"You're welcome. You get some rest now, son; you look like shit." The driver lit a cigarette as he walked back around the car to get into the driver seat.

Henderson stood on the curb as the driver pulled out onto the busy street. He faced the hotel and spotted the "Welcome" sign. As he walked along the sidewalk into the hotel entrance, Henderson felt sad and depressed, thinking about Mitch and how he had failed him.

Once inside the air-conditioned lobby, he approached the desk clerk—a good-looking Hawaiian woman, not much older than himself, wearing a colorful shirt and lei. She smiled at him. "How can I help you, sir?"

"I'm not a 'sir.'" His face became red hot. He had given an army response to a civilian question. In the military, "sir" addressed an officer. He waited a moment before speaking again. "Eddie Henderson. I have a reservation."

She smiled, showing white teeth against her tanned face; her dark, almond eyes looked as if they glowed. "Yes, Eddie, you do have a reservation—room one-hundred and twenty-one, facing the beach. I hope you find it relaxing."

"Thank you. I'm sure I will." He realized he had been saying "thank you" an awful lot—it felt like the only thing to say.

The clerk handed him the key and he grabbed his bag. "Thank you."

Henderson walked along the corridor toward his room, checking room numbers as he went. Within no time, he had located his room. Henderson entered the cold, dark space, throwing his bag onto the bed. He hadn't stayed in many hotels, but he knew this was a lot better than the Victory Drive Motel at Fort Benning—the same motel Mitch and Henderson had stayed at while on a weekend pass. The night Mitch died flashed before him.

The room had a large bed with two nightstands, a black-and-white television on a desk, and a large bathroom. Looking out of the sliding-glass double door, the view to the clear, blue-green water of the ocean took his breath away. Hundreds of people frolicked on the long stretch of beach in the sun's glory.

After a long, hot shower and a shave, Henderson changed into civilian clothes. He left the room and headed to the lobby. As he stood in the middle of the foyer, gazing at the interior, he heard a voice call his name. "Eddie."

The desk clerk called again. "Eddie."

As he strode to the front desk, nerves he couldn't explain churned inside him. "Is there a problem?"

"Oh, no. You looked a bit lost, so I wanted to help you."

"A 'bit' is an understatement." He smiled, letting some of his nerves show. "I'm not used to being able to move around so freely. Where is the bar?"

"We have one in the lobby, right off the hallway." She pointed in the direction of the bar. "We have another on the patio, not far from your room."

"Thank you." There it was again—that "thank you"—yet, he meant it every time. "Good to know. I'll go to the bar on the patio."

As Henderson sat at a table with a Jim Beam and Coke in front of him, he stared at the endless ocean. He enjoyed the fresh air, the smell of the sea, the beach and the laughter coming from the tables around him. Many tables were occupied by young couples, who held hands and stared into each other's eyes.

He felt alone. He knew he had no one to love him, except for Mitch's parents. *I don't have much to live for.* It wasn't far to go from that thought to the one buried beneath it—it should have been he who had died.

After he slugged his drink, Henderson shook his head to remove those thoughts. As a waiter walked by, Henderson ordered another bourbon.

He couldn't help but stare at one couple in particular—they reminded him of Mitch and Sandra. He tried not to stare, but was so busy doing so that he didn't see a woman approaching him. "Hello." The woman waited for several seconds.

"Hello?"

Eddie glanced up. She appeared to be twenty-one, with long, red hair, cute sun-kissed freckles, a smile which would win anyone's heart, and a killer body. He didn't say a word.

"I called you several times, but you ignored me."

"I didn't ignore you," Eddie stammered, taking a drink. "What can I do for you?"

"Can I sit with you?"

Surprised, he stood out of respect. "Sure, please sit."

"I'm Cheryl." She extended her hand.

He took her smooth hand into his. "My friends call me Eddie."

She looked into Eddie's eyes and slid her hand from his. "What are you drinking? Oh, it doesn't matter; I'll take whatever you're having."

Henderson signaled the waiter. "One more Jim Beam and Coke, please."

After they got their drinks, Cheryl gazed into his eyes. "Eddie, are you on R and R from Vietnam?"

"Does it look obvious?"

"I know the look. I'm here with my mom, visiting my father. He's here on R and R too."

Henderson barely kept himself from swearing. "Wait a minute! How old are you?"

After her laughter subsided, she inhaled gently. "I'm twenty; I'm in college."

"Scared me for a minute. Where do you go to college?"

"I attend the University of California at Berkeley. I'm a junior."

"Oh, shit!" He paused, the heat rising in his cheeks for the second time that day. He knew better than to swear in front of a lady, but running around with a bunch of soldiers, he'd gotten into the habit. "You're not going to lecture me about the war, are you?"

"Oh, no, not me." She smiled as she pushed back the hair which fell over her right eye.

"I have a buddy who attended Berkeley, before he enlisted."

"What's his name? I could know him, but perhaps not. It's a big campus."

"We call him Professor, but his name is Calvin Cox."

"*The* Calvin Cox!"

"He's the only one *I* know."

"I didn't know him well, but he became a big man on campus with the anti-war movement. Faculty and students looked up to him; they listened to what he had to say."

"Well, that sounds like Professor. Small world." Henderson smiled.

"I remember one rally I attended—please don't tell my parents any of this—"

"Mum's the word."

"Calvin, with a beard, stood in front of thousands, wearing torn jeans and a T-shirt; he had hair to his shoulders. I didn't think highly of him at first, but when he spoke—well, he gave a brilliant speech. He talked of his mistrust of politicians and the war."

"He still hates politicians. He does, for sure."

"I heard he disappeared one day, but I didn't know he'd joined the army."

Cheryl and Eddie talked for hours. They even shared an evening meal. Eddie had a hamburger and fries, with a chocolate milkshake, and Cheryl had a large salad.

After several more drinks, with the sun setting, Eddie thought it best to leave. With darkness came the fear. Although he knew he was in a safe place, his mind and body reacted differently. "Time for me to call it a night."

As he stood, he extended his hand to shake hers.

Cheryl stood, took his hand, and pulled him close to her. "Can I come with you?"

"Yes, of course," Eddie flashed a grin, surprised by her response.

The two walked to his room, holding hands and acting like they had known each other for years. He opened the door, allowing Cheryl to enter first. Once inside, he went straight to the telephone. "Should I order some drinks from room service?"

"I don't think so." She closed the door.

After a long hug, they kissed.

Cheryl batted her lashes. "I can't spend the night, because I don't want my parents to think badly of me."

"I understand."

•

An hour later, Henderson looked into Cheryl's green eyes, smiling—the first happy smile he had exposed in a long time. Within minutes, the smile faded.

Cheryl gazed into his eyes. "What's troubling you?"

"Please, hold me." He fell into her arms.

While Cheryl held him close, Eddie couldn't suppress the memories any longer. He told her of the death and the killing happening in Vietnam, and even about how Mitch had died—his best friend and brother. He didn't tell her of the promise he had made to Mitch. That was private—that was what he told himself. Hidden beneath that was a worry that she wouldn't understand, or that she would think less of him.

For reasons unknown to him, he wanted to share the guilt and shame of war that he kept hidden. He told Cheryl of the enemy soldiers he had killed, as well as the horrible events he had experienced. The words came out, driven by a torrent of emotion.

Without saying a word, she wiped the tears away from his face, and he wiped tears from hers. They lay intertwined while she comforted him. At last, he stopped talking.

He felt better, but it saddened him that he had burdened Cheryl with his time in Vietnam.

•

Late morning on the second day, Eddie and Cheryl sat in his room, talking while drinking Cokes.

He stood and stared out of the glass doors. "I need to call Mitch's parents, but I don't want to."

"You *need* to call them."

"I can't. I don't know what to say."

"Trust me, Mitch's mom wants to hear from you. She needs to know; so does his dad. I would want to know how my dad got hurt, and who cared for him."

"You sure?"

"Yes. I'll sit with you while you make the call, if you want."

"I would like for you to sit with me. Thanks."

He lifted the receiver and asked the front desk to dial the number.

Cheryl moved closer, taking his hand to comfort him during the call. It was the second hardest thing he had ever done. The first was watching Mitch die.

•

Eddie and Cheryl spent every spare minute together over the next few days. They swam in the ocean, played in the sun, took long walks along the beach, and shared quiet moments in the evening.

When his leave was over, Cheryl and Eddie kissed goodbye. They promised to write, and to get together when he returned home. As the driver opened the taxi's rear door, Henderson pulled away from Cheryl and slid into the back seat. She stared at him for a minute longer until he closed the door. As the cab sped off toward the airport, Henderson turned in his seat to look at her.

He smiled, thinking about the past seven days.

As the plane took to the air, the beautiful, caring woman—with flowing, red hair and the cutest freckles—flashed before his eyes as his last memory of Hawaii. He fell asleep smiling.

HELL IS WAITING

Henderson walked off of the airliner in Da Nang to the familiar smells, heat, and landscape hitting him in the face. As he followed the line of soldiers returning from R and R, he thought of his brothers in the First Platoon and wondered how they were. He wanted to return—not for the madness of war, but to be with them.

Henderson waited in the hangar for more than an hour for the plane to Duc Pho, until the Noncommissioned Officer in Charge finally called the flight for boarding. Henderson approached the C-130 along the tarmac with a group of soldiers and used the open rear door as a ramp. Once they were seated, the door closed. The aircraft held equipment, supplies, and five other soldiers returning from R and R.

The C-130 taxied onto the airstrip and lumbered along the runway until it gathered speed, lifting into the air. The flight was short—Duc Pho sat one hundred and twenty miles south of Da Nang. After a steep descent, the plane landed.

Henderson grabbed his bag and walked from the airstrip to the Alpha Company headquarters. He opened the screen door and entered.

Hall peeped over the rim of his glasses. "Welcome home, Sergeant Henderson."

"Thanks, Top. Glad to be back." Henderson dropped his bag.

"You have a good time?"

"I did. It was good to get away."

"Check in with supply; get your gear and change. Once you finish, see me. I'll get you on the supply chopper to the firebase." Hall grinned.

"Will do, Top."

Henderson left the office. The firebase was familiar to him, and he felt a sense of surprise at the thought that he had returned home. How could it be?

Once he entered the supply room, Henderson recognized Smitty—the same clerk who had given him new socks months ago—still working behind the counter. When the screen door creaked, Smitty looked up to see Henderson. "Welcome home, Sergeant."

"Thanks, Smitty. I'm here to get my gear."

"I'll get it."

Smitty left the front area, heading to a room in the rear of the building. He returned carrying Henderson's rucksack, helmet, and boots. After the clerk dropped it on the counter, Henderson inspected it.

"The gear looks the same as when I left it here. Thanks."

"I put in six chicken and noodle meals. I filled your canteens too."

"You didn't have to. Means a lot."

The clerk's face beamed as he reached under the counter to get a new uniform. He held the shirt so Henderson could see the front, with the Combat Infantry Badge sewn over the left pocket, above the US Army label. His name was above the right pocket, and subdued sergeant stripes were on each sleeve. The best part of the brand-new uniform was the label size, extra-small.

"Wow! Thanks, Smitty. I appreciate it."

"Welcome. You can use the back room to change. Leave your khaki uniform here. I'll store it with your other gear."

Henderson left the supply room after he had changed, heading toward the arms room to get his rifle. The armorer had him sign for his M-16, and he received three bandoliers of magazines, loaded with 5.56 rounds.

"I need grenades too."

"How many you want?"

"I'll take eight—four frags, two concussion, and two smoke."

"Here you go." The armorer slid the grenades across the counter as if Henderson had ordered milk and bread.

"Thanks." He put the two concussion and smoke grenades into his rucksack and hooked the four frags to the front straps of his ruck.

Now ready to join his platoon, Henderson slid the rucksack onto his back. The weight felt familiar, yet oddly more substantial than he recalled. He walked through the doorway and strolled to the company headquarters. "Top, ready to go."

"Look at you, Sergeant, looking pretty in your new uniform." Hall took a long draw from his pipe. "Supply chopper leaving in thirty minutes—you're on it."

"Thanks, Top."

Henderson adjusted the rucksack on his shoulders. He hoped he hadn't lost the edge—the sixth sense for survival in war—and he readied himself. Although only gone for seven days, he felt as if a year had passed. As he approached the helipad, he spotted the supply chopper, its blades slowly rotating.

Before he climbed aboard the Huey, Henderson greeted the crew chief with a wave. Then he sat on the deck in the open doorway, his feet dangling over the skids.

The sound of the engine's whine increased as the blades turned faster, lifting the helicopter off of the pad. Henderson held his M-16 tighter as he prepared to go home to his family. The Huey shot skyward fifty feet, rotated to the right, and the pilot accelerated, taking a flight path to Hill 100.

I hope I'm ready.

Henderson watched the countryside zoom by as he stared at the familiar ground—the villes, rice paddies, hedgerows, mountains, and jungles. He was lost in thought as the helicopter approached the firebase, but he did notice that the TOC, mess hall, artillery pits, and his bunker all looked the same.

Excitedly, Henderson jumped off of the supply chopper as soon as the skids touched the ground and strode along the familiar trail to his position. He smiled at the thought of seeing his squad members. As he approached his position, his heart pounded faster, and he quickened his pace.

Henderson saw Professor, sitting with his body leaning against the bunker, head tilted and sound asleep.

"Wake up, soldier!" Henderson kicked Professor's boot.

Startled, Professor jumped to his feet while fumbling with his M-79. He stared at Henderson. "Henderson?"

Henderson's smile grew ear to ear. "Nobody else."

Professor embraced Henderson with a bear hug. "How was your R and R? Tell me about it."

"Let me put my rucksack away—then we'll sit and talk. Where are the rest of the guys?" Henderson said over his shoulder as he entered the bunker.

"I thought I heard you!" Porter eased from the corner of the bunker. "Welcome home." He grabbed Henderson and hugged him before he could say anything.

"Thanks, Ronnie. What are you doing here?"

"I'm the platoon medic until we get a replacement. Ames is the assistant gunner."

"Sounds good to me. Ames is a good soldier."

As Henderson dropped his rucksack to the ground, he looked around him and saw the bloodstains. "Let's go outside. I'll tell you guys about my R and R."

The two soldiers stepped into the sunlight and walked to the rear of the bunker to join Professor. A soldier approached along the trail from the shitters.

Henderson frowned. "Who's the new guy?"

"The FNG? That's Laurel. He got here the day after you left. He's a good kid. Ask him his age." Professor laughed.

When Laurel reached the three soldiers, he stopped and looked at Henderson.

Henderson extended his right hand to the FNG. "Laurel, I'm Eddie Henderson, the squad leader. Welcome to the Second Squad."

"Thanks, Sarge." Laurel shook Henderson's hand. "The guys have been great to me."

Henderson smiled as he looked at his squad members. "Glad to hear it. They're good men."

"Yep, they are."

"Laurel"— Henderson suppressed a smile—"how old are you?"

"Gawd damn it! Why do you guys keep asking? I'm eighteen! Is it a problem, Sarge?"

Professor laughed as he slapped Henderson on the shoulder. "Good question, Eddie. He's a little sensitive about his age."

"Okay, let's get Rocky." Porter nodded toward the gunner. "Rocky, get over here!"

Rocky looked up, while cleaning his M-60. "Why?"

Porter pointed at the squad leader. "Henderson is here."

Within seconds, Rocky appeared. "Glad to see you." He shook Henderson's hand with such vigor that Henderson yanked it away.

"Damn, Rocky! Not so hard!"

While they readied for Henderson's story, Porter passed his Zippo around for each of the soldiers to light a cigarette.

Henderson sat on a stack of sandbags. "I didn't do anything special. I got a hotel room, near the Fort DeRussy R and R Center, on Honolulu's Waikiki Beach, where I drank and watched the girls. I swear, the bikinis are getting smaller, or the tits are getting bigger!"

After digging into his breast pocket, Henderson retrieved a Polaroid photograph of Cheryl. In the picture, she wore a green, one-piece bathing suit, and he stood next to her, with his arm around her. He took a glance at the picture before handing it to Professor.

"Her name is Cheryl. She's funny, pretty, and great at talking. She's twenty; she had the cutest freckles. And, she goes to UC at Berkeley."

Rocky stroked his mustache. "You didn't go with a commie, did you?"

Professor shook his head, but didn't look offended.

"She wasn't a commie." Henderson smiled at the comment. "She went to Hawaii with her mom to visit her dad—he was there on R and R too."

Rocky gave Henderson an elbow in the side. "I guess that's okay."

Henderson stared into Professor's eyes, excited to share the latest information he had got from Cheryl. "Hey, Professor, Cheryl said you were *the man* on campus. Is it true?"

Professor played with his lighter as he passed the photograph to Rocky. "Let's say I became involved."

"Forget Professor. Did she stay in your room?" Porter wiggled his eyebrows suggestively.

"Well, Porter…" Henderson leaned toward Porter. "A gentleman doesn't say."

"When were you ever a gentleman?" Porter laughed.

After the laughter died, Professor took a deep breath. "Did you call Mitch's parents?"

As he ran the phone call through his mind, Henderson formulated what he would share with his buddies. He chose not to share the part where Cheryl had convinced him to call, and held his hand during the conversation. "Yes, I called late morning on the second day, because I knew I would drink a lot—I wanted to call before I got drunk."

"Sounds smart." Rocky smiled while taking a drag from his cigarette.

"I have to admit it took everything I had in me to dial the number. The phone rang four times, and I was close to hanging up. But, then, I heard the receiver lifting off the cradle, and Mrs. Drexler answered. I called her Mom when I stayed there, so I said, 'Mom, it's Eddie.' She cried. I cried too. She asked me if I was in Vietnam. I told her no, I was in Hawaii for seven days. I couldn't believe it, but she wanted to know how *I* was doing. She asked about you guys by name, too. 'Professor,' 'Rocky,' 'Porter…'"

Porter smiled. "That's probably where Drexler got his kindness."

"She asked the question I didn't want to answer—if we were together on the night Mitch died. She asked what happened. I told her we were together. Then I went on to tell her that he didn't feel any pain, and he said that he loved her. Then we cried more. Mrs. Drexler said she would send care packages to us each month, and she wants me to write to her, so she won't worry about me. She also said I could stay with them when I go home."

"You should take comfort in that." Professor nodded, as if he were the first to have thought this.

"After she finished talking, she gave the phone to Mr. Drexler. He told me not to drink too much. I think he knew, because he served in World War II, and had an idea what I might be going through. He told me to keep my head down, and said for us to take care of each other. Before he hung up, he said he'd see me soon."

Henderson gulped his cherry Kool-Aid. "Then, I hung up."

Professor shook his head. "How are you taking the loss at this point, Eddie?"

"To be truthful, hard. Mitch and I were like brothers. I miss Sergeant Stahl, too—I hope I can do as good as him."

Henderson didn't want to talk about Drexler anymore. "I'm hungry. Let's eat. I hope the VC hasn't hit the mess hall."

The soldiers stood, laughing. Professor rubbed his belly. "Nope, it's still standing."

Rocky, the last to look at the photograph, returned it to Henderson. "Cheryl looks like a keeper."

Henderson grinned from ear to ear. "I think she might be."

As they talked during the meal, Henderson learned what had happened in the last week. When he heard that Clark had died, he didn't feel the anger or sadness he had when his other brothers died. *He was a racist.*

After he ate, he went through the line and loaded a plate for Laurel, who stayed behind, pulling guard. Then, Henderson walked past the table. "Let's go."

Within minutes, the soldiers were at the back of the bunker. Henderson handed Laurel his meal while the other soldiers lit cigarettes and bullshitted about the world and what they would do when they returned home.

Laurel wolfed his food as he sat at the rear of the bunker. After finishing, he drank several long swallows of water, and once done eating, he lit a cigarette to complement the meal.

Porter looked at his watch. "Getting close to nineteen-hundred hours."

"Some things don't change." Henderson sighed as he stood.

"I'm heading to my bunker." Rocky turned and took long strides to his bunker, wanting to get inside before nineteen-hundred.

In a single file, Henderson, Professor, Porter, and Laurel entered their bunker through the open doorway. There, each soldier found a comfortable spot to wait for the mortars.

Thump! Thump! Thump! The mortars traveled along the slope to their bunker.

Porter covered his ears. "Get ready."

Wham! Wham! Wham! Seconds later, the explosions rocked the structures on the hill after they hit near the Third Platoon's positions.

Henderson rubbed his ears after the last explosion. "Can't believe they keep doing this each night."

With a nervous laugh, Professor glanced toward the newbie. "Should've seen Laurel his first night."

"It wasn't funny." Laurel's cheeks flushed crimson.

"Laurel"—Henderson's tone shifted easily into a commanding voice—"with me to the roof. We need to make sure the VC doesn't decide to sneak in."

"I heard we're leaving the firebase any day now," Professor said as he got out his cleaning kit.

Porter ran his hand through his hair. "It's about time."

A CAGE IN THE HORSESHOE

Swift approached Henderson as he ate breakfast, straddling the bench to sit next to him. Staring at Henderson, he took a long drink from his canteen cup—the odor of bourbon drifted from its rim. Not saying a word, Henderson ate his breakfast.

Swift took a deep breath. "Sergeant Henderson, I need you at the lieutenant's bunker at zero-nine-hundred hours. New mission."

"No problem, Sergeant Swift." Henderson halfway saluted Swift with two fingers. "What's the mission?"

"Best wait to let the lieutenant tell you. I'll tell you one thing, though, we expected it."

Henderson arrived five minutes early, nodding at Brown and Ledger. When he looked over at the far corner of the bunker, he noticed Nash sitting on his helmet, smoking a cigarette. Henderson walked over, removed his helmet, and sat on it, next to Nash. He pulled his Zippo from his pocket, spun the wheel, and placed the flame at the end of a cigarette, taking several deep drags.

"How's it going, Henderson?" Nash puffed his cigarette.

"Going okay. How about you?"

"Doing as well as expected. Glad you're here."

Henderson felt a shadow falling on him. Looking up, he noticed Brighton standing over him. As he got to his feet, he extended his hand to the lieutenant, who grasped it with a firm grip, holding it a little longer than one would do with a handshake.

Slowly, Brighton released Henderson's hand. "Welcome back. How are you doing, Sergeant Henderson?"

"I'm rested. Ready to go, LT."

Brighton removed his helmet and sat next to the two squad leaders. Swift joined the group.

Brighton surveyed his NCOs while he appreciated a peaceful moment. "We've been here for sixty days. Now, Bravo Company replaces us. We're leaving tomorrow morning, at ten-hundred hours. Let's leave a good impression of our hard work for the last two months." He lifted the canteen cup to his mouth and blew on the hot coffee before taking a long sip. After licking his lips, the lieutenant took another sip. "We're going to the Horseshoe tomorrow. We need to be on the helipad at ten-hundred hours. Let's assume it's hot. The rest of the company flies in after we secure the LZ." Swift nodded.

"A truck is coming round to drop off four days of rations and ammunition. Make sure your men fill their canteens too." As he stood, Brighton put on his helmet. "Any questions?"

The three NCOs stood as one. Henderson stepped forward. "Which squad has point, once we're on the ground?"

"Second Squad has point." Brighton took another sip of coffee. "Who's going to walk point, Sergeant Henderson?"

"I would like to keep walking point, if it's okay with you, LT. I know my way around booby traps and the men trust me. No need changin' that around."

"Not a problem. Let's go get ready."

Before they could walk away, Brighton cleared his throat. "Oh, one more thing before you leave. I convinced the CO to let me stay as the platoon leader for the rest of my tour."

The NCOs looked at each other. That would double Brighton's time out in this hellhole! As a rule, officers rotated from a line unit after six months, leaving the soldiers to adjust to a whole new person in command. It was suitable for the officers, but could be rough on the men. Henderson couldn't believe that the lieutenant would volunteer to stay in the field. He kept waiting for some other explanation, though he couldn't think of one.

Swift furrowed his brow. "Sir, I know I can speak for the platoon—we appreciate you sticking with us."

Henderson nodded. "Hell, we don't want to break in a new lieutenant—that's too much work. Thanks for staying with us."

When Henderson returned to the bunker, he sent word that they had a squad meeting in ten minutes. While waiting, he grabbed a canteen full of black cherry Kool-Aid and tipped it to his lips, downing half of it in an attempt to quench his thirst and soothe his dry throat. Sweat dripped from his face as humidity hung in the air, and the temperature climbed higher. *Shit, it must be one hundred degrees already.*

As the squad members gathered around Henderson, he took a long, deep breath. He still wasn't accustomed to giving the orders. "Listen up. We've got a new mission. The platoon goes to the Horseshoe to look for Charlie. I want each man to carry an extra belt of machine gun ammo. Take four grenades each too. Get what you need; we'll be in the bush for a while. If you need any additional equipment, let me know." Henderson paused and allowed himself a smile. "LT is staying as the platoon leader. He's not rotating out. Any questions?"

Porter raised his hand.

"Come on, Porter?"

"It ain't like that this time." Porter returned his hand to his lap. "I have a question. I'm not fucking with you."

"Okay, Porter, what?"

"Do I go with the squad or the command group?"

"You belong with the command group, so check with Lieutenant Brighton. See where he wants you."

"I'll check." Porter turned to shoulder his ruck.

"Ronnie, we'll miss you."

Porter grinned at his friend as he slid on the rucksack.

•

Henderson awoke early the next morning. He lifted his rucksack, along with his rifle and helmet, and strode into the fresh morning air. When Henderson reached the rear of the bunker, he dropped his heavy backpack, stuffed with four days of rations and six quarts of water, Kool-Aid, and the ammunition he needed. He placed his helmet on top of the bulging pack.

Once he had lit a cigarette, he looked around at the bunkers and buildings, reflecting on the first days the company built the firebase in the middle of these rice fields. It felt like days ago, instead of two months.

As he stared at the bunker, his mind replayed the night the VC killed Mitch. A tear rolled along his cheek. He wiped it away and threw the cigarette on the ground, smashing it with his foot.

From behind him, Professor approached. "Are you ready for breakfast?"

"Always. Leave Laurel to guard the position." Henderson smiled. "How many days left?"

Professor's eyes widened, then his heart sank. "One hundred and thirty-five to go."

"I think we've been here longer. You sure it's right?"

"Yeah, I'm sure. We got *boo-coo* days to go." The words sounded wrong coming from Professor, but they'd all heard them so many times, it was no wonder that Professor knew precisely what to say.

While the three soldiers ate breakfast, they talked of the platoon and how they might perform, going back to the bush after being on the hill for two months.

Henderson swallowed. "Losing the edge gets you killed. I don't want that for any of us."

"Amen." Rocky looked toward the heavens. "We've been on this hill for two months. That's a long time not being in the bush."

Professor cleared his throat. "I'm not sure any location will matter all that much. We've seen a lot of shit on this hill—that will have helped keep us sharp, the same as if we had been out in the bush. Danger is danger. No matter how you size it up—it keeps you on point. Still, it's not the same as being out there."

"The squad will do fine." Henderson's command tone returned. "I'm happy we're leaving the firebase; we'll have more freedom. And, it doesn't sound bad to be leaving the place where Mitch died—you know, leave those memories buried here."

Silence surrounded the table as they finished eating. Once done with the last real hot dinner they would have for weeks, the three friends walked, taking their time. They followed the worn, hard-packed trail their boots had created from the many trips walking to and from the helipad, mess hall, showers, and shitters during the last two months.

The friends looked forward to a good night of sleep. Rested soldiers are safer soldiers.

•

The following morning, after breakfast and a short nap, Henderson slid on his rucksack and faced the others. "Saddle up. Move out!"

The Second Squad walked along the trail to the top of the hill, their rucksacks slowing them. They didn't stop until they reached the helipad. Swift signaled for the men to assemble to the right side of the waiting helicopters, along with the First Squad.

As they waited to board, Henderson saw a line of tired, dirty soldiers walking at a slow pace along the road toward the bunkers the platoon had vacated. *Must be Bravo Company, taking over the hill.*

Once loaded, the three helicopters lifted, one after another, accelerating northwest toward the Horseshoe. The men of the Second Squad watched the unfriendly terrain zoom by as the chopper streaked low along the rice fields.

I hope I'm as a good leader as Sergeant Stahl. Henderson sighed.

With the engines slowing, Henderson pulled the charging handle of his M-16 to the rear and released it, slamming a bullet into the chamber. He hit the forward assist with the palm of his right hand to make sure the round seated, then his right thumb slid over the selector switch, making sure the weapon was on safe. Henderson's actions signaled to the rest of the squad to lock and load their weapons.

With his body tense, Henderson prepared to jump as soon as the Huey landed or the enemy opened fire on them—whichever happened first. As soon as the chopper skids thudded on the ground, the Second Squad jumped off and ran toward a hedgerow to their front to secure the landing zone. Then, seeking cover, the First Platoon waited for the rest of the company to arrive.

•

As Brighton moved along the hedgerow to position the platoon, he caught up to Henderson and Nash. "Sergeant Henderson, move a team to cover the north and one to cover the east. Sergeant Nash, move a team to cover the south, with one to cover the west."

Brighton reached over his shoulder, taking the handset from Ledger. "Tango six, this is Tango one-six. Over."

"Go ahead, Tango one-six. Over," Lyons said.

"Tango six, we are in position. Over."

"Roger. The rest of the element is on the way. Out."

Whop! Whop! Whop!

Henderson looked to the south and spotted nine or more helicopters flying in their direction. "Get ready! The company is coming in!"

The choppers landed, one after another, and the men of the Second Platoon and Third Platoon jumped to the ground and ran for cover, forming a larger perimeter.

Henderson lay near Brighton and heard the communication from the broadcast.

"Tango two-six and three-six, Tango six. Over," Lyons said.

"Roger, this is Tango two-six. Over," the Second Platoon leader transmitted.

"Tango six, this is Tango three-six. Over," the Third Platoon leader transmitted.

"Tango two-six and three-six, move out on the main trail. Over."

"This is Tango two-six; wilco. Out."

"Tango three-six; wilco. Out."

The company strode toward the jungle vegetation in columns of two. With a slow pace, they merged into a single file, disappearing into the thick canopy of the jungle as they ascended the mountain. As the last man disappeared from view, Henderson took a glance.

It's so peaceful.

He knew better than to become lulled into a false sense of security. He knew the VC was watching their movements.

Brighton quickened his step. "Sergeant Henderson, take us west into the Horseshoe."

"Okay, LT."

Henderson faced the Second Squad. "Laurel, you have my back. Stay thirty feet behind me. Your job is to protect me. I want you to observe what I do, because soon walking point is your job. Got it?"

"Yes, Sarge."

Henderson gave Professor a knowing glance. "Keep an eye on Laurel."

"You got it, Sarge." Professor winked at Henderson.

Henderson increased the length in his stride. "Now, let's move."

He turned away from the squad and faced the west side of the Horseshoe. He walked with slow, wary steps.

Within fifteen minutes, his worries of returning to the field had vanished. He knew he hadn't lost his edge. The point position in the bush became as natural to him as waking in the morning. His adrenaline pumped, and it felt as if he were high.

Henderson walked several klicks through the elephant grass, attempting to bypass hedgerows as he made his way to the night logger position. Once stopped, he checked the area. After establishing it safe, he waved the platoon forward.

Nash walked to Henderson's position and stood next to him, surveying the jungle.

Brighton walked over to Henderson. "Sergeant Henderson, you have four positions, running west to south. Don't forget claymores and flares."

"No problem, LT."

"You have four positions running east to north," Brighton said to Sergeant Nash as he looked to his right. "Don't forget claymores and flares."

"Got it, sir."

•

After they set claymores and trip flares, the men of the Second Squad sat around their positions and prepared dinner. P-38s twirled, punching their way around lids and opening cans of C-rations, while C-4 burned in the makeshift stoves, heating the entrée as the soldiers bullshitted with the buddies sitting next to them. The conversation became invariably the same—what food they missed from back home.

Henderson removed a can of chicken noodles from his rucksack. "I can't say I missed this stuff."

"I know what you mean. Mess hall food spoiled us all," Professor said as he opened a can of turkey loaf.

Henderson swallowed a spoonful of chicken noodles. "What food do you miss most from the world?"

"I love McDonald's—a Big Mac, and especially French fries. Oh yeah, a strawberry milkshake too. My favorite meal." Laurel poked at the strange-looking pork slices.

Rocky lifted his chin. "I miss the elk and deer. I can get steaks, jerky, hamburger, and sausage, to name a few. It's not unusual to get a couple of hundred pounds of meat. You can fix it a ton of different ways."

"What about you, Professor? Where did you go to eat?" Henderson took another bite, as if his meal were from a five-star restaurant.

"I went to the Caffè Mediterranean, known as the Caffè Med—you can find it on Telegraph Avenue, in Berkeley. It was mainly a coffee shop, but sandwiches always taste better with stimulating conversation. I met a lot of interesting people there. What about you, Eddie? What food do you miss the most?"

"I miss my mom's pot roast, with mashed potatoes. She always served lemon pound cake for dessert." Henderson realized he would never have that again. Maybe Mitch's mom made a good pot roast.

Once they had eaten, the team relaxed as Henderson gave the guard rotation for his position. He would be first, then Rocky, Laurel, and Professor last—each soldier had two shifts of one hour and thirty minutes.

Henderson stowed his cooking equipment. While in the rucksack, he removed his poncho liner and spread it, for his sleeping area. He rubbed DEET on the exposed parts of his body—he hadn't missed that smell.

After lighting a cigarette, he sat, enjoying the quiet evening. As he watched the sun slide behind the mountains to his front, Henderson thought of Mitch, and how he missed him. He remembered the promise he had made to him, and a now-familiar sinking feeling filled him, even though he was now back amongst people who might understand.

I wonder what Professor would think about all of this.

Henderson took a long, last drag from his cigarette.

When I get home, will I kill Billy?

He felt a little guilty, because he hadn't told his buddies that he had called Sandra too.

His rage resurfaced at the thought of it. *Maybe I will kill Billy!*

He closed his eyes and reflected on that horrible phone call.

"Sandra, this is Eddie Henderson."

"Oh, Eddie, are you okay? I so miss Mitch." She sounded upset, which made the words burn worse in his ears.

"You lying bitch! How can you miss Mitch? You broke his heart."

Sandra gave a little sob. "I didn't mean to hurt him. I loved him."

"What do you mean? You wrote a damn 'Dear John' letter to him."

"I know, bu—"

"Bullshit, Sandra!"

"But, I couldn't help it. Being in love with someone who isn't there… it's not easy. Life doesn't stop. I fell in love with Billy. I know it was wrong. I know."

"You don't have to worry about being in love with Billy. I'll be home soon."

"Eddie, what do you mean?"

"Soon, Sandra."

He slammed the handset into the cradle.

Henderson felt ashamed, because he knew that if he kept this anger, he would kill Billy. *Hell, I won't even think twice about doing it.*

•

The platoon woke from an uneventful night. The Second Squad undertook the day like any other in the bush: smoke a cigarette, cook, eat breakfast, smoke another cigarette, pack gear away, and wait for the command to move. The squad then humped for eight to ten hours a day, knowing that they were bait to draw the enemy into the open—a typical day in Vietnam.

Henderson caught Professor's attention. "What is today?"

"Monday. You know, the one that follows Sunday."

"Shit, it's that time! Everyone take your malaria pills—the orange one too." Again, Henderson skipped the weekly big orange pill.

Brighton stood, glaring at the platoon. "Get ready to move out!"

Henderson attempted to stand, but the weight of his rucksack kept him from rising.

"Come on, little fella." Professor grinned as he grabbed Henderson's hand, pulling him to his feet.

Once he stood and regained his balance, Henderson balanced the weight on his back. "You call me *Sergeant* Little Fella."

Laughing, the men of the Second Squad followed Henderson as he strode along the overgrown trail, toward the valley on the other side of the hill. After the platoon had humped for six hours, Henderson climbed a fifty-foot mound, which wasn't tricky, but the wait-a-minute vines and the heat slowed the pace. He had to stop to unwrap or cut vines, which clung to his legs.

Once he reached the top, Henderson held his right hand up, fingers extended, for the men behind him to stop. He suddenly dropped his hand as he sought concealment behind the high elephant grass.

"Pass it along for LT to come here." Henderson nodded to Laurel.

The men passed the word from soldier to soldier, until the message reached Brighton. He moved along the line of waiting men, bent near to the ground, and crawled the last twenty-five feet, stopping next to Henderson. "What's the problem, Sergeant?"

"Three hundred meters slightly to the south, inside the hedgerow. Looks like a group of NVA sitting near a cage of some type, but I don't know what it is."

After he lifted the binoculars, Brighton zoomed in on the enemy soldiers, tracking the field glasses to see what it was they were sitting around.

"What the fuck?!" Brighton looked through the binoculars for several more minutes.

Henderson's eyebrows furrowed. "What do you see, sir?"

Brighton handed the binoculars to Henderson. He waited as Henderson adjusted for his vision and tracked the object.

"I'll be damned." Henderson couldn't stop peering through the binoculars.

Brighton tightened his jaw. "It looks like they have a POW. He's an American."

"Oh, fuck! It can't be!" Henderson zoomed the lens for a better look.

"What do you see?"

"It's the crew chief from the Hook. Charlie has him in a damn bamboo cage, like an animal! He looks like shit. And he's hurt."

Brighton shot Henderson a questioning look. "You sure it's him?"

"I'm sure, LT. I watched him when we were flying on the Hook; I remember what he looks like."

Brighton turned to pass a message to Ledger. "Tell Ledger—"

"I'm right here, LT," Ledger said, passing the handset.

Brighton transmitted, "Tango six, this is Tango one-six. Over."

"Roger, Tango one-six. Over," Lyons said.

"Tango six, we found the crew chief from the Hook. POW. Over."

"Say again Tango one-six. Over."

"I repeat. Found the crew chief from the Hook. We're going to get him. Over."

"Tango one-six, Roger. Need any support? Over."

"Need gunship, with dustoff in the air at my location on standby. Over."

"Wilco, Tango one-six. On the way, and good luck. Out."

Brighton took a deep breath and observed the terrain for a moment. "Ledger, call the platoon sergeant. Have him and Sergeant Nash come here."

"Tango one-six-Papa, come to the front. Bring the First Squad leader. Over."

"Wilco. Out," Brown transmitted.

Swift crawled to the right of the lieutenant. To the left of Henderson lay Nash. They passed the binoculars around for Swift and Nash to see the prisoner. They verified the number of NVA, but other than confirming what they saw—the men said nothing. The sight spoke for itself.

Finally, in a tight voice, Brighton said, "Charlie has a POW."

Swift continued to peer through the binoculars. "I count six of them."

Brighton stared at the cage. "That's our count too."

"What's the plan?" Nash asked.

After a moment of hesitation, Brighton took a deep breath. "Leave Michaels with Reeves, Rocky, and Ames for supporting fire. Sergeant Swift and Brown, stay with the gunners."

"Where do you want Second Squad?" Henderson glanced down the line.

Brighton pointed at a hedgerow. "Sergeant Henderson, move your squad behind the hedgerow running east to west, into the hedgerow where the crew chief is held."

"And First Squad?" Nash clenched his fist.

"I'll go with Sergeant Nash from the opposite side, coming in behind the NVA position." Brighton looked at the two squad leaders to make sure they understood. "I'll open fire, as the signal to attack. Henderson, move your squad into the enemy from the flank. I'll do the same from the rear."

"Any support, LT?" Swift asked.

"There's a gunship and dustoff already in the air. I'll direct the gunship if needed. I want to get the crew chief alive. He's suffered enough. Sergeant Nash and McKinney, your only job is to get the crew chief from the cage. You will carry him to this hill. Everyone, drop your rucksacks here. Take weapons and ammo only." Taking a deep breath, Brighton tried to remain calm. "Any questions?"

The others remained silent.

Brighton took the handset from Ledger. "Shark two-three, this is Tango one-six. Over."

"Go ahead, Tango one-six. Over."

"Shark two-three, these are the coordinates to fire on my command; Bravo Sierra five-three-four-five-seven-eight-six-two. Over."

"Wilco, Bravo Sierra five-three-four-five-seven-eight-six-two is the target. Wait for your command. Out."

Brighton handed the handset to Ledger. "Okay, let's move. Be quiet and be careful."

After hearing the order to move, Henderson slid from his rucksack, leaving it, as did the rest of the squad. He used the concealment of the tall elephant grass, walking low and bent over as he circled to the backside of the hedgerow, with the rest of Second Squad following.

Brighton and the First Squad dropped their rucksacks and followed a narrow trail in the tall grass to approach the enemy from the rear.

With the heat, humidity, and fear—now that he and his men were closer to the enemy—breathing became difficult for Henderson as he followed the trail on the edge of the hedgerow. Walking with slow steps, he looked at the ground, took a step, then looked for the next step. Henderson knew he needed to walk at a slow pace to save the crew chief. Nervous energy burned like electrical currents, running from the ground to the top of his head as he followed the path.

After thirty minutes, Henderson arrived at his designated position. He peered through the vegetation and observed the crew chief, who sat in the cage while the NVA ate their meal.

Henderson signaled for Professor and Laurel to pass him, to his left. They crawled twenty-five feet for a better line of sight to the cage. Henderson had two soldiers to his left, and Madison, Ransom, and Hays to his right.

At this point, we wait for the lieutenant. For Henderson, waiting had never been harder.

When they were within seventy-five feet to the rear of the enemy, Brighton signaled the patrol to disperse to the right, so they would be on the other side of the cage. This way, he made sure that they didn't receive any M-60 machine gun fire from the hilltop. He maneuvered Sergeant Nash and McKinney to be in a direct line to the cage.

Once the patrol moved into position to the rear of the enemy, he motioned for his men to crawl forward through the elephant grass, into the hedgerow. As they inched their way closer and closer, Brighton saw the crew chief—a skinny man, with eyes sunken, he was unshaven, dirty, and the uniform he wore was in rags. He looked like death warmed up.

Within fifty feet, Brighton saw the NVA sitting around a fire pit, eating and talking in low voices. He confirmed that the six soldiers were together. He raised his M-16 and, with his right thumb, he slid the selector switch to semi-automatic, aimed, and squeezed the trigger. As the round ripped through the enemy's head, the soldier jerked, falling to his right side.

Brighton transmitted, "Shark two-three, fire. Over."

"This is Shark two-three. You got it, Tango one-six. Out."

As soon as he heard the M-16 fire, Henderson ordered his squad to their feet, and they rushed toward the NVA.

When the NVA saw the advancing American soldiers, they ran to the other side of the cage to put the POW between them.

From the hilltop, the two M-60 gunners opened fire, killing two of the captors as they stood in the open.

High in the sky, the Shark fired thousands of red tracers, penetrating the hedgerow where the enemy stood. Tree branches snapped off, with the ground turning over every couple of feet, killing any enemy in the path of the incoming rounds.

While they moved forward, Second Squad fired at the enemy as they retreated. Henderson charged, shouting, "Move forward. Don't shoot at the cage!"

Lieutenant Brighton darted his eyes toward the cage. "McKinney and Nash, get the crew chief."

When the two squads merged around the cage, they provided cover fire for McKinney and Nash.

Caught by surprise in the crossfire, the NVA got off a handful of wild shots, but didn't stop the advancing platoon.

As the two platoon members rushed forward, McKinney pulled his survival knife from its sheath to cut the rope which secured the gate of the bamboo cage. After cutting the cord, he opened the gate as Nash reached into the cage to help the crew chief leave his prison.

Confused, the prisoner crawled to the far corner, not wanting to go. He didn't seem to see or know his rescue team at all.

McKinney extended his hand. "We're Americans. We're going to take you home. Can you walk?"

Nash took a step into the cage. "You're safe. You need to come with us. We need to hurry."

Within seconds, the crew chief recognized that the Americans wanted to rescue him. He shivered, tried to stand, but was too weak, so allowed the rescuers to lift him. While grabbing onto their shirts, the crew chief held on as if his life depended on it. "Thank you, thank you, thank you," the crew chief mumbled while McKinney and Nash carried him.

Brighton observed his men carrying the crew chief. "Shark two-three, ceasefire. Over."

"Wilco, Tango one-six. Out."

Once the gunship received the command to ceasefire, the pilot stopped shooting. He flew the helicopter higher, circling the platoon as they scrambled to return to the hill, remaining to protect them.

Both squads ran to the hedgerow Henderson had followed to get the crew chief, from where they retraced the route to the hilltop.

After he reached the platoon position, Brighton took the handset. "Delta four-five, safe to land; smoke red. Over."

"Affirmative, red smoke. Out," the pilot transmitted.

Red smoke drifted skyward, and Henderson guided the dustoff to the LZ. Nash and McKinney trotted toward the medevac, carrying the crew chief. At the open doorway, they slid him onto the deck of the helicopter, but he wouldn't let go of them.

"Don't leave me."

"We're not leaving you; you're going home." McKinney released his grasp on the former POW.

The crew chief forced a smile. "Thank you." He let go of his hold on McKinney and Nash.

With engines gaining power, the blades rotated faster. Then, the helicopter lifted, speeding toward Chu Lai. The men of the First Platoon stood, eyes skyward, watching as the dustoff disappeared over the horizon.

Henderson removed his helmet and wiped the sweat on his forehead. "I can't imagine what he went through."

"Hell, it's been more than two months." Professor watched the dustoff fly away.

Rocky said, "At least he's alive."

Brighton talked loudly enough for the platoon to hear. "Great job, First Platoon! You saved a life today—a hell of a lot more important than taking a life. Good work."

After lighting a cigarette, Henderson handed it to Professor, lit another—handing it to Rocky—then lit his own. The three soldiers stood side by side, taking drags of their cigarettes without saying a word, while looking at the valley below, where the NVA had held the crew chief captive.

A BATH AT THE SONG TRA KHUC RIVER

The long night ended, and Laurel was thankful for the sunlight peeking over the horizon. "Wake up, Sergeant Henderson."

"What's going on?" Henderson's eyes flew open. He didn't hear gunfire.

Laurel stood over Henderson, smiling. "Sun's up. Time to have breakfast."

"Go wake the others." Henderson stood, stretching.

Laurel moved around the squad positions, prodding the sleeping men until they stood. Henderson observed soldiers lighting cigarettes as soon as they woke. Next, the makeshift stove glowed from the burning C-4, heating water for coffee or hot chocolate, and the morning entrée. Preparing for the day had become automatic; the soldiers didn't have to think about what they were doing—they simply did it.

Professor walked over to Henderson. "We've been in this Horseshoe area for over a week now, with little contact. I'm not complaining, but where are the VC? This peace has me feeling edgy."

"I don't know, but I know what you mean. Why is the damn VC leaving us alone?"

Porter overheard the conversation. "It's because they know I'm with you guys."

Men within hearing distance of the conversation burst into laughter.

After lighting a cigarette, Henderson took a drag. "Bet you're right, Porter."

"Look at the mountain, Sergeant Henderson." Madison pointed south, toward a ridge running along the side of a mountain. The squad turned their attention to it.

Rocky shielded his eyes as he stared. "It looks like a trail of animals, or people."

Brighton walked to Henderson's position, carrying his binoculars. "It's around a hundred villagers, carrying food and supplies to the NVA base camps hidden in the mountains."

"Can't we call in artillery or gunships on them, sir?" Madison shifted his weight.

"No, they're civilians."

"Well, it sucks, LT."

Brighton grabbed the handset and readied himself for the conversation. "Tango six, this is Tango one-six. Over,"

"Go ahead, Tango one-six. Over."

"Tango six, around one hundred civilians climbing the north side of the mountain—grid Bravo Sierra four-seven-three-seven-four-seven—carrying supplies. Over."

"Roger, Bravo Sierra four-seven-three-seven-four-seven. We'll check it. Out."

Before he turned to walk to his position, Brighton eyed the squad. "We'll move in an hour. Henderson, we'll be heading north, toward the river. Once you get to the riverbank, stop. We'll stay there to have chow."

"Okay, LT." Henderson flipped his cigarette to the ground as the lieutenant walked away. Then he looked at his squad members, knowing they had heard the orders. "Okay, guys, you heard the man. Bring in the claymores and flares. Eat, pack, and get ready to move in an hour."

After he ate breakfast, Henderson lit a cigarette and took a long drag, blowing the smoke into the air and watching it float away with the light breeze. He drank the last of his hot chocolate, and once he had cleaned the metal canteen cup, he placed it into his rucksack. Next, he rolled his poncho liner, stuffing it into the pack too—ready for a new day. He looked at Professor. "How many days left?"

"One hundred and seventeen to go." Professor packed his gear.

Brighton stood, lifting his right arm skyward. "Let's get ready to move."

"Saddle up! Move out!" Henderson stood, with the weight of the pack holding him back. Professor and Porter grabbed his hands, pulling him to his feet.

Henderson smiled. "Thanks, guys."

With long strides, Henderson moved through the platoon area, heading north toward the river, with the Second Squad following. He followed the trail downhill, through the six-foot-high elephant grass, where they made their way to the rice paddies and flat land.

After four hours, Henderson halted in a hedgerow. The platoon stopped behind him.

Henderson wanted to ensure it was safe before the platoon moved to the river to stop for chow, but he sensed that the area didn't look right. He looked at Laurel. "Pass it to Brighton—I'm taking a patrol to the riverbank, to check it."

The message worked its way through the men.

"Laurel, Professor, come with me," Henderson said, inching forward.

With slow, watchful steps, the three men approached the riverbank, looking for any sign that the VC were there. From the shore of the fifty-foot-wide river, they concluded that Charlie was nowhere in sight. Henderson moved to an area which provided cover for the platoon, and where he had a good view of the river to their front, with the rice fields to their rear.

Henderson turned toward Laurel. "Go to the platoon and lead them here."

Professor slumped in relief, ready for a rest.

Laurel beamed with pride. "Yes, Sarge, I'll get them." He turned away and ran toward the waiting platoon.

Professor gave Henderson a knowing glance. "He'll lose his enthusiasm for this work soon enough."

While waiting, Henderson and Professor lit cigarettes. They sat enjoying the smoke and watching the slow current push the dark water along its banks. Henderson spotted polished stones, lying along the shore. He thought of his youth, when he had gone rafting at a river near his home.

Even in the shade, the heat became unbearable. The two soldiers wiped sweat from their faces and pulled at their uniforms as they stuck to their sweat-soaked bodies. Henderson took his helmet off to let the breeze cool his head. "Fuck, it's hot!"

He heard a noise to their rear, and turned to see the platoon walking toward them. Laurel, leading the way, had a massive smile on his face.

Maybe it's time to let him walk point. Henderson twisted his lips. "You think he's ready?"

Professor smiled. "Although no time is ever perfect … yes, it's time."

Deep down, Henderson didn't want to stop walking point. He enjoyed the rush, the control, protecting the platoon and being the first. But he knew that the time had come for him to assign point to another platoon member. Being the squad leader, he should follow the point man, giving instructions to the squad when needed—he knew he couldn't maneuver the unit while walking point. It was time for Laurel to take over.

"Yeah, you're right." Henderson finally acknowledged that it was time to pass the responsibility to someone else. And who better than Laurel?

Once the platoon had walked into the thicket of bamboo and trees covering the riverbank, Brighton assigned squad positions. The Second Squad would protect the north side, near the river, with First Squad watching the south side, facing the rice fields. After placing Rocky and his M-60 in a position to provide covering fire for the platoon's front and across the river, Henderson placed the rest of the squad.

The men dropped their rucksacks—then they settled into their positions.

Henderson removed paper and pen from his backpack, then leaned against his pack to begin a letter. Before he could write a word, Porter walked over and stood next to him.

Henderson looked up at his friend. "What, Porter?"

"Can we jump in the river and bathe, like we did in the South China Sea?"

At first, Henderson hesitated, thinking of his men's safety. "Yes, but I want guards posted. They need to stay alert. One team at a time and only for ten minutes. You understand, Porter?"

"Come on, I know."

"Yeah." Henderson glanced out into the trees. Every deep shadow could potentially hide an enemy—that was the world in which they lived. "This isn't like at the sea." *Be alert.*

As Porter walked away, he yelled, "Second Squad, time to bathe!"

Once Alpha Team stripped off their uniforms, Henderson watched the naked men run toward the river and jump from the embankment, doing cannonballs. Loud splashes and laughter echoed across the valley.

He picked up his pen and paper, deciding to write to Mitch's parents.

> *"Dear Mrs. and Mr. Drexler,*
> *I'm sorry I haven't written, but we've been busy.*
> *I had a great time in Hawaii. I met a girl, and her name is Cheryl. I'm back in 'Nam now, with my buddies. We sure do miss Mitch. It's not the same without him…"*

When he finished writing, Henderson folded the two sheets of paper and slipped them into an envelope.

As laughter resonated across the platoon area, he saw Alpha Team leave the river. The men put on dirty uniforms over their wet bodies, as Bravo Team stripped and ran for the water. Again, splashing and laughter erupted across the rice fields, while Alpha Team provided security. He noticed a team from First Squad in the water too.

Henderson strolled over to Professor. "When they finish playing—I mean, *bathing*—have them eat lunch."

"Roger that," Professor said, toweling himself dry.

No sooner had Professor spoken those words the ground vibrated. An explosion shot a fountain of water up into the air. *Bam!*

The grunts hit the ground, while the men in the river scrambled for the shoreline.

Professor yelled, "Grenade!"

As he jumped to his feet, Henderson saw a naked soldier lying with his face in the mud, his legs in the water, and the rest of his exposed body on the riverbank.

Crack! Crack! Crack! Gunfire exploded from the other side of the river.

When Henderson fell to the ground, he detected the muzzle flashes in the location where the VC hid. Rounds zinged about the Second Squad as AK-47s fired, ripping through the trees, snapping branches and tearing bamboo stalks.

Henderson screamed, "Open fire!"

Rocky fired the M-60 into the overgrowth on the opposite side of the river, spraying rounds from left to right, as Ames fed the belts of ammo into the gun.

Professor sent one grenade after another. As he watched the explosions, he adjusted his aim. Adding more firepower, the rest of the team shot at the VC.

Porter realized that the wounded soldier hadn't moved. "I'm getting Flores!"

"I'm going with you!" Madison screamed over the sounds of the firefight.

Henderson ordered, "Give Porter and Madison covering fire."

As they ran along the bank toward Flores, still lying in the mud, Porter and Madison heard the enemy bullets whizzing by their heads, or thud into the earth. Once they reached Flores, they dragged him to the top of the embankment, toward the overgrowth.

AK-47 rounds followed them, throwing up loose dirt as they climbed the riverbank, heaving Flores over the crest of the bank.

Another soldier ran toward the struggling soldiers and grabbed Flores to assist, helping to pull him over the top of the bank. They dragged Flores, while crawling twenty-five feet for cover. Although Flores was a small man, it still took all of their strength to move him. Henderson caught a glimpse of Flores's naked body, dripping water, as the three team members moved his limp body to safety.

Once they reached the squad position, Madison rolled him over so Porter could check his wounds. Within seconds, he discovered that two large chunks of shrapnel had penetrated Flores's heart.

Porter looked around. "Damn! Not a thing I can do. He's dead."

"Fucking gooks!" Madison screamed angrily.

While Porter and Madison stared at the opposite bank, they aimed at the suspected enemy positions, unloading magazine after magazine. With their anger controlling their actions, they expended ammunition faster than they routinely would.

Whoosh!

As an RPG left the launcher and headed in their direction, Porter pushed Madison further into the soft ground, taking cover. After hearing a loud thud at the riverbank to their front, they waited.

After a moment, surprised, Porter removed his hand from Madison, looking toward the river and waiting for the explosion. Madison crawled forward, with his head exposed over the bank. He saw the RPG round, buried halfway into the side of the embankment.

"It's a dud!" Madison yelled over the sounds of weapons shooting.

As he laughed, Madison crawled toward Porter.

Whoosh! Another RPG took flight toward their position.

Wham!

The round hit in the center of the hedgerow, throwing bamboo stalks, dirt, and shrapnel across the platoon perimeter. Porter got to his knees, waiting on the call for help. Then, he looked at Madison. "Nobody hit."

Brighton called for support. "Tango six, this is Tango one-six. Over."

"Roger, Tango one-six. Over," Lyons said.

"Tango six, need fire-mission, Bravo Sierra four-seven-two-seven-seven-six. Over."

After several minutes of static, the radio squawked. "Tango one-six, the grid isn't in our AO. Fire-mission declined. Over."

"Tango six, you've got to be kidding! Over."

"Tango one-six, no mission. Out."

Earlier, the platoon had received a briefing that the area across the river belonged to the 198th Infantry Brigade—a unit needed permission to fire artillery or air strikes into another unit's Area of Operation.

Brighton stared across the river. "But this has to be a goddamn exception! It's the enemy, not American forces."

Without hesitation, Henderson decided to ignore the order. "Fire LAWs!"

Laurel and Ransom each grabbed a LAW from their rucksack. At the same time, they removed the pull pin, extending the launchers. They checked to their rear to make sure no platoon member was behind them, then, with the sights up, they aimed at the enemy positions.

Both LAWs fired. *Bam! Bam!* A flash of flame erupted from the rear of the launchers.

Within a second, two explosions vibrated along the river. *Wham! Wham!* Dirt and trees flew up into the air.

Only silence followed.

Henderson watched the other side of the river for movement. The VC were either dead, watching them, or had fled, following the explosions.

After hearing the call for a medic, Brighton knew he needed a dustoff. "Tango six, this is Tango one-six. Over,"

Lyons said, "Go ahead, Tango one-six. Over."

"Need dustoff at my location. One KIA. Over."

"Wilco, Tango one-six. In route. Sorry to hear. Out."

Brighton handed the handset to Ledger and muttered, "Yeah, sure you are."

•

Nash popped green smoke and readied to guide the chopper, when he heard the blades hitting the air. As the sound of the helicopter grew louder, he prepared to bring it safely to the LZ. As the dustoff approached, he raised his M-16 over his head with both hands, guiding the Huey into the landing zone, as the platoon watched for the enemy.

Each gripping a corner of the poncho holding Flores, a group of soldiers carried their brother to the waiting medevac. After they placed Flores onto the litter, the crew chief covered him with a blanket.

The four soldiers stood at the open doorway, saying their final goodbye as the chopper lifted, heading to Bronco.

Brighton scanned along the riverbank until he noticed Henderson and Nash. "Squad leaders, on me."

The two squad leaders met halfway and walked together toward the lieutenant's position. Henderson put his arm around Nash to comfort him. "Sorry about Flores. Seemed like a good guy."

"Thanks." Nash rubbed his lips together. After a thoughtful moment, he sighed. "It don't mean nothin'."

Henderson squeezed his shoulder, then walked with him. Once the two squad leaders arrived at the lieutenant's position, they removed their helmets and sat on them, facing Brighton and Swift.

Brighton shook his head. "We're staying near here tonight— east, two hundred meters. Have your men ready to go in twenty mikes. After we reach our logger position, we'll stop. The First Squad has the south side, with Second Squad on the north side. No swimming! Any questions?"

"I'm going to let Laurel walk point, if it's okay, LT." Henderson huffed. The decision didn't seem as big or weighty now.

"It's your call, Sergeant."

Once Henderson returned to his position, he walked over to Laurel and another soldier. "Make sure you destroy the two LAW tubes. We don't want the enemy to use them for another weapon."

Both soldiers said, "Sure, Sarge."

"Saddle up! Move out! Laurel, you're on point."

"You mean me on point?" Not waiting for a response, Laurel slid into his rucksack, stood, and walked with long strides to the front of the platoon, with Henderson following him. "Yes, Sarge."

As Laurel took careful steps, he watched for the VC and booby traps, as Henderson had taught him. Henderson could tell that Laurel was extra vigilant to prove that he could walk point.

In a short time, the platoon arrived at their destination and stopped for the night. After they placed claymores and trip flares to the front of their positions, the men relaxed and ate their dinner meal.

As he ate, Henderson looked over at Laurel. "Good job, Ray."

Laurel sat, beaming. He gulped the can of fruit cocktail and wiped his mouth with the back of his hand. "Thanks, Sarge."

Henderson closed his eyes, thinking of the woman he had met in Hawaii, with the freckles and the contagious laugh. The thought of her made him smile.

He retrieved his pen and paper, and scribed a letter.

> *"Cheryl,*
>
> *I'm with my buddies. I'm sorry I haven't written sooner. We left the firebase I told you about, and things have been great. We walk around most of the day. Today, we stopped at the river, swam, bathed, and relaxed.*
>
> *I think of you often, and miss our conversations and..."*

Once he had finished the three-page letter, Henderson folded it with neat, straight lines. He inserted it into a new, crisp envelope, with her address written on it. Cheryl had given Henderson thirty self-addressed envelopes before he left Hawaii.

As the sun slid behind the mountains, Henderson walked the perimeter, checking on the squad. He made sure they had what they needed, and that their positions were as safe as they could be, in the terrain they chose.

I'm ready for some sleep.

Henderson positioned himself against a tree. It took him no time at all to drift off.

•

"Rise and shine." Professor kicked Henderson's foot.

"Morning, already?"

"Yeah, and that makes it your favorite time of day—time to eat."

The men of Second Squad woke and carried out the morning ritual—use C-4 to heat a canteen cup of water, for coffee or hot chocolate; eat fruit and cake. Next, they put their gear into their rucksacks. They accomplished the morning ritual without anyone saying a word. Once they had cleaned their weapons, the chattering amongst the men increased.

While the men loosened up a bit, Ledger brought Brighton the handset.

"Tango one-six, this is Tango six. Over," Lyons was saying.

Brighton picked up the handset. "Roger, Tango six. Over."

"Tango one-six, we go to stand-down in two days. Over."

"Great news! I'll give the grid in two days for pickup. Over."

"Roger, Tango one six. Out."

Loud enough to be heard across the perimeter, Brighton yelled, "Squad leaders, on me!"

Once the three leaders sat, Brighton rubbed his ear and spoke. "Good news. We're going to Chu Lai for stand-down in two days. We'll continue to patrol along the river until we leave. Let's stay alert, so we can get a couple of days rest."

"Yes, sir," the three responded in unison.

•

The platoon stopped for the night. Once claymores and trip flares were placed around the perimeter, the men of the First Platoon prepared their dinner meal.

As the soldiers sat bullshitting, Henderson looked at his squad members, sensing their excitement. On this night, the only stories told were of what they would do on stand-down while in Chu Lai—go to the PX, swim in the South China Sea, eat steak, get drunk, take a shower, and sleep in bunks with pillows and sheets—those were the topics of discussion. Laughter erupted as they talked; simple pleasures in life made them happy.

Laurel approached Sergeant Henderson and sat next to his squad leader and mentor. "What's a stand-down?"

Henderson's mind drifted to somewhere else as a broad smile crossed his lips. "In two- to three-month intervals, a company in the battalion goes to Chu Lai, the division firebase. They leave the field to get away from the war and enjoy some of the luxuries of home—the soldiers get three days of rest. Think of it as going to a place where you are safe, have good food, and you can sleep as much as you want for three days. Hell, they even have a band play each night, with women singers and dancers. And you get to drink as much beer as you want for free."

With eyes wide, Laurel smiled. "Sounds great, Sarge."

TAKING A BREAK DURING WAR

Two days later, the platoon woke early. The men ate breakfast and packed their rucksacks in anticipation of the chopper ride to Chu Lai.

As he looked around, it amazed Henderson how the smallest things could become so significant to a man in the bush, fighting the Viet Cong. He thought of the thousands of men his age who had no idea what it felt like to be in Vietnam; they took their lives for granted. *Hell, we appreciate every breath we take over here.*

Swift popped smoke to signal the helicopters to land in a prepared area on the hilltop. Snapped from his daydream, Henderson gazed upward.

Whop! Whop! Whop!

The Huey blades slapped at the air as the three choppers flew toward them and lowered to the ground to land. The door gunners swiveled the mounted M-60 machine guns as they watched for the enemy. If any were to surface, they would die.

The First Platoon ran toward the three helicopters and boarded in the usual order. As the last man, Swift climbed onto the deck of the first Huey.

The three choppers lifted. They flew north toward Chu Lai.

Henderson and Professor sat on the deck, side by side, with their feet dangling over the skids as the helicopter zoomed high over the river and the rice fields. It reached Chu Lai in a very brief time.

While they circled the landing pad, waiting for permission to land, Henderson noticed the white-capped waves rolling toward the beach and the clear, blue-green water. Next, Henderson caught sight of the buildings, showers, shitters, and the smoke rising from the grills. He began to get excited.

After landing on the asphalt helipad, the men jumped from the helicopters and ran to the edge of the pad. Once they had gathered in a group, Brighton said, "Follow me for a briefing with the first sergeant."

The platoon walked in a group, though differently to how they were accustomed, following the lieutenant. The other two platoons were already waiting. They stopped and stood outside a large, green, one-story building, boarded halfway up, with screening the rest of the way to the roof.

Hall said, "Welcome, Alpha Company."

After a brief cheer, the men quietened to wait for Top to finish. He fondly looked across the sea of faces staring at him. "For the next three days, we'll grill steaks twenty-four hours a day. A band will play each night, starting at twenty-hundred hours. We'll have free cold beer and soda. However, you need to take care of each other. Don't get into trouble; don't leave the compound drunk; don't get into trouble off the compound; hell, don't get into trouble, period! Enjoy yourself. Your platoon sergeants have your building assignments. Your next step is to turn in your weapons— then, have fun!"

While in line, by platoon, the men approached the Conex; an eight-by-twenty-foot metal shipping container which the engineers had converted to store weapons. They turned in their rifles, grenades, mines, and C-4 for the next three days, while they stayed at the stand-down area.

As Henderson waited, he turned to Professor. "Shit, I hate leaving my weapon. I already feel itchy. What if we get attacked?"

"We need to count on the REMFs to protect us." Professor's mouth barely suppressed a grin.

While laughing, Porter, Rocky, and Ames said in unison, "Yeah, right."

Though he hated to call attention to his newness, Laurel fidgeted. "Sarge, what's a REMF?"

"'Rear Echelon Mother Fucker,'" Porter said with a laugh. Anyone within hearing distance snickered.

Henderson put his arm around the shoulder of his protégé. "Grunts don't have much respect for the men who stay in the rear for their three hundred and sixty-five days, but we can't survive a day without their support; we need them. It's a love-hate relationship. To make fun of them feels right."

After turning over their rifles, Henderson and the rest of the Second Squad strolled toward the building which would house them for the next three days. As they walked into the barracks, the men found it the same as any other army barracks—metal bunks, stacked two high, each with a mattress, and lockers lining the wall.

Porter threw a pillow at Professor, hitting him in the face. "Hey, we have a bunk, a pillow, two sheets, and a blanket. That's better than a poncho liner on the ground."

The men laughed as they claimed bunks, while storing their rucksacks and steel pots in the wall lockers without even thinking of securing them. Their brothers wouldn't steal from them, and anyone found in the barracks who didn't belong there would get their ass kicked.

In no time, Henderson and Alpha Team went to the showers. There, they received clean uniforms. After dressing in the clean clothes, they left the filthy garments they had worn for several weeks in a pile—the fatigues and underclothes would later be cleaned and issued to another soldier. Then, it was back to the barracks.

"Hey, guys, you ready for a steak?" Henderson asked.

His brothers jumped to their feet at the same time, heading to the door without answering. As they walked along the path, the squad members looked at each other, their pace quickening with each step. They broke into a sprint to ensure they got the best steak first. Laurel won.

Once at the mess hall, the men of the Second Squad loaded their trays with rib eye and all the trimmings. Porter found a vacant table and signaled to them to join him.

Henderson smiled. "Okay, guys, you know the rules. You can come and go as you please, but don't be stupid. No guard. No Charlie. No worries. And don't get into trouble. The MPs here love putting grunts into the stockade. When you get ready for bed, be quiet; respect your buddies. Keep an eye on each other, got it?"

Porter raised his hand.

Henderson rolled his eyes. "What, Ronnie?"

"Who's getting the Jim Beam?" Porter's blue eyes twinkled.

"Finally, a good question from you."

The men at the table chuckled.

"I asked Smitty, the supply clerk, to get us four bottles—should be enough. You guys let him have some too."

"Wow, Sarge, you think ahead. Maybe LT made a good choice, making you the squad leader." Rocky stroked his mustache.

With renewed energy, the men gathered inside the largest building, where soldiers opened the most popular bottles: bourbon, rum, vodka, or tequila. They shuffled cards, ready for a game. Over half of the company settled in for a three-day card game, only taking breaks to eat steak, shower, and listen to a band.

Henderson found Smitty standing in a corner, holding a large paper bag. He headed over toward him.

Smitty handed Henderson the paper bag. "Here's what you asked me to get. I threw in another bottle."

"Thanks, Smitty; means a lot. Join us." Henderson set the bag on the table and removed one of the bottles of Jim Beam.

"Sure, Sarge. Thanks," Smitty stammered with a gigantic smile.

Henderson mixed the Jim Beam with Coke, until each person had a full glass.

Madison raised his glass. "To the fallen."

The squad raised their glasses as one. "To the fallen."

Porter raised his glass. "It don't mean nothin'."

Henderson clinked his glass against Professor's as the men of the Second Squad repeated, "It don't mean nothin'."

The drinking, eating, and partying commenced.

The bond of brotherhood was evident over the next three days—no different to being in the bush together. The men had spent twenty-four hours a day together, day after day, for months. Now, during the stand-down, where it was safe, they wouldn't separate from one another.

Professor checked the time. "Time to go watch the band."

"Go on ahead. I'll put the booze away and catch up with you." Henderson took another sip.

After they left the building, the Second Squad turned left and headed for the stage, where the band played. As the men got seated, the musicians tuned their instruments, while three scantily dressed Filipino women checked the sound equipment. Before the band played, Henderson slid onto the bench between Porter and Professor.

It turned into a long night—it seemed that the entertainment went on forever. Their imitation of most songs wasn't even close to the original artists, but they gave it a shot. The three women vocalists mispronounced words and were off-key at times, but the skimpy outfits made up for their lack of talent.

Porter yelled to Henderson, over the music, "Look at the lead singer! How can she get such small tits to sway with the music like that?"

"No bra." Henderson smiled at his friend.

When looking at the stage, Porter's eyes moved from left to right, and right to left, watching the singer sway with the music.

After the last song played—"We Gotta Get out of This Place"—the soldiers stood, applauding and hooting at the three girls on stage. One of the girls then removed her top, shaking her body so her breasts swung in circles.

The applause and encouragement grew louder for the woman to take off more clothing. Within minutes, the girls and the band disappeared behind the curtain.

The soldiers laughed and talked as they stood to leave. After leaving the stage area, the men went to the poker games, or back to the barracks for some sleep. Most of the Second Squad walked silently to the barracks.

Henderson fell asleep before 2300 hours.

•

The next morning, after they slept late, Henderson, Porter, Rocky, and Professor dressed. They walked along the sandy path to the mess hall for breakfast. Steak and eggs were on the menu.

Once through the line, the three soldiers found a vacant seat. They slid their trays onto the table and sat on the hard, wooden bench.

Henderson said, "Shit, I forgot my hot chocolate." He returned to the serving area.

Rocky nudged Professor in the side. "How do you think he's doing?"

"I think he's performing more than adequately, so far. I don't think his losses have interfered with his decision-making. Give him time."

Rocky nodded. "Me neither."

Once seated, Henderson took a long swallow of the hot chocolate and set the mug next to his tray. "It's a lot better than the packaged stuff from C-rations that we have in the field."

They ate in silence. It was easy for all of them to slip into thoughts of home in such a peaceful environment, and Henderson began to wonder what he would do with himself.

First, of course, he had his promise to keep. This time he would plan it better.

As Henderson finished his meal, he looked at Rocky. "Thinking of hunting when I get home. What's the best rifle and scope to hunt mule deer?"

"Well, let me think." Rocky sipped his coffee for a moment. "I would go with the Winchester Model Seventy, with a Weaver scope. Hell, the Marine Corps snipers are using the same rifle, right here in 'Nam. I have the same model, but I don't use a scope. I like to get in close."

"I'll remember. One more question. Will one shot in the head put a mule deer down?"

"You bet it'll put him down—with no problem."

Professor leaned in with keen interest. "I wasn't aware that you hunted, Eddie."

"Thinking about it. Nothing else, just thinking."

"For mule deer?" Professor's eyes narrowed.

Henderson glanced toward the mess hall door. "Yeah, mule deer."

•

For the next two days, Second Squad swam in the South China Sea, played poker, ate hot meals, listened to the bands, and relaxed. A shower each morning was the highlight of their stay. Henderson made several trips to the Post Exchange, and on one trip bought a Seiko watch, which illuminated at night. The men emptied the bottles of bourbon.

At noon of the third day, the men of the First Platoon got in line to retrieve their weapons. With a rifle in hand, they walked back to the barracks. Henderson put on his steel pot and slid the rucksack straps over his shoulders, standing as the weight tugged him backward.

Before they left the building, Porter said, "Get ready to lose the three most important things in your life."

"What are those?" Laurel frowned.

Porter poked Laurel in the ribs. "Security, rest, and food."

Laurel pushed Porter away from him. "I like that." Both soldiers laughed.

Once they had their gear, the soldiers walked through the doorway into the bright sunlight and headed to the helipad. With blades rotating, three Hueys sat patiently, waiting for the grunts to board.

Henderson noticed the door gunners checking their machine guns. He smiled, thankful for such attentive soldiers protecting them while they were in the air.

As he waited for the platoon to gather, Henderson looked at Professor. "How many days left?"

"Ninety-eight to go."

"You sure it's right?" The number felt smaller this time.

"Yeah, I'm sure."

Swift signaled, and the platoon boarded the three choppers.

With legs dangling, Henderson watched the stand-down compound become smaller as the Huey lifted and flew south.

CHAPTER 24

THE PARTY IS OVER

The Hueys landed near a village. Henderson didn't look at any of the mountains. For the moment, his attention was focused on the villagers, and getting to safety. The platoon dismounted, running for cover. As the sound of the helicopters flying back to Bronco echoed across the field, there were no shots fired.

It seemed like a good day so far.

Henderson stood to survey the area. "Alpha Team to my right and Bravo Team to my left."

He found the air humid and hot, with an overcast sky. Henderson mopped the sweat from his face, looked around, and noticed most of the men doing the same.

While the platoon hid behind dikes in the center of a rice field, waiting for the company, a slow drizzle fell, soaking the soldiers.

At first, Henderson appreciated the rain, cooling his body from the heat and humidity, but in a short time, he shivered.

There was no such thing as comfort out here.

Whop! Whop! Whop! Huey blades hit the air. Henderson looked skyward, spotting eight to ten Hueys flying toward him.

"Heads up," Brighton said. "The company is landing."

As he watched the front, Henderson looked for any movement or suspicious activity from villagers, who might shoot at the incoming choppers. When each helicopter landed on the wet ground, the men of Alpha Company jumped off and ran for cover. Once a helicopter emptied, it lifted, rotated, and accelerated toward Bronco, while the door gunners watched the ground below them.

"Tango one-six; two-six; three-six, on me. Over," Lyons transmitted.

Once the three platoon leaders arrived at the company commander's location near the center of the paddy, they knelt on one knee, not wanting to sit on the wet ground.

Lyons looked at his platoon leaders and said, "Okay, the party is over. We have a change in our mission. We'll be searching several of the valleys first. I expect you to clear the valleys you're assigned in two weeks." He pointed west, toward the mountains. "Then, we'll move into the mountains. Once you're patrolling the mountains, the mission is to destroy NVA or VC base camps. Battalion S-two reported there could be several large bases, with company-size units. Any questions?"

"Do we destroy the weapons and food captured?" Brighton said, wiping mud from his pants. "No way can we hump stuff from there."

Lyons folded the map. "Yes, destroy it. If you don't think you have enough C-4, call it in with your resupply while you patrol the valley."

"Do we expect problems with resupply, because of the weather, or being in the mountains?" Rangel asked.

Lyon's nodded. "I recommend you get extra rations, water, and ammo when in the valley—the last resupply before you start climbing the mountain. I know the extra weight will be a bitch, but that's better than not eating, or not having enough water and ammo."

The Third Platoon leader, Smyth, got to his feet. "Where are our primary locations, once on the mountain?"

"Damn, Smyth, I forgot, didn't I? First Platoon, Bravo Sierra four-nine-one-seven-two-eight; Second Platoon, Bravo Sierra four-nine-two-seven-one-nine; Third Platoon, Bravo Sierra five-one-six-seven-one-one. The mountaintop locations have enough room for the resupply chopper, or a dustoff if needed. Any other questions?" Lyons looked at each platoon leader.

"Good luck. I'll be with the Third Platoon. Move out."

As the three lieutenants stood, they said in unison, "Yes, sir." They turned and walked back to their platoons.

After Brighton briefed the platoon NCOs, he didn't ask for questions or wait for a reaction. Instead, he cut off responses. "Second Squad takes point. Move out."

Henderson looked at Laurel. "Move out, point man."

•

As they walked through the deep paddy water, the Second Squad formed into a single file, with Laurel leading—Henderson followed, then Professor. The rest of the Alpha Team came after them, with Bravo Team behind.

After the platoon had walked more than two klicks, they entered the valley and were no longer worried about villagers or livestock. Henderson knew that if anything moved in the valley, it wasn't friendly—and the layout of the hills ahead didn't look friendly.

Henderson took longer steps to catch up with Laurel. Once he reached him, Henderson tapped him on the shoulder. Laurel stopped and looked at his squad leader.

Henderson pointed to the surrounding area. "Look around. This valley is an easy ambush site. You have the high ground on three sides. Look to your rear. The entrance to the valley is narrow. The enemy can easily seal it, preventing us from escaping. Not aiming to scare you, but use all your senses."

"You got it, Sarge." Laurel's throat pinched. He turned to face the front, took short, calculated steps, and headed toward the center of the valley.

As Professor reached Henderson, he said, "Think he'll do okay?"

"I do." Henderson shifted the weight of his rucksack. If he didn't think that, then they were all in a lot of trouble. "Sure hope so."

The platoon followed Laurel, moving forward, dispersing so that no soldier walked directly behind another. They kept at least fifteen feet between each other. Henderson found the pace agonizingly slow, but he understood why they moved as slowly as they did through the elephant grass which covered most of the valley. At some places, Henderson saw Laurel moving through six-foot-tall elephant grass, which prevented him from seeing to his front. Henderson knew that Laurel was scared, but was impressed as he kept pushing the grass away, moving forward.

Behind him, to his right, Henderson heard an anguished howl.

The platoon hit the wet ground, waiting for the enemy to open fire. After several moments, Henderson heard a soldier cry, "Medic!"

"What the hell?" Henderson mumbled as he ran in the direction of the scream.

He spotted Porter, standing in the grass. He didn't look injured—merely frozen. Henderson ran toward him, and once he reached the spot, he looked to see what Porter was staring at on the ground.

Henderson focused his eyes. "Oh, my God!"

Nash lay in a large hole, face down, impaled by two punji sticks. One went through his upper chest—the other pierced his stomach. As he walked over the concealed cover of the punji pit, which held eight sharpened stakes, pointed upward, he hadn't stood a chance. He had fallen five feet to his death, without warning.

Henderson took a deep breath, wanting to shout and release his frustration, and his fear of death. As he looked at Nash, he once again realized the cruelty that one man could inflict on another. But under no terms could he learn to live with it. He wanted to vent—to let it all out—but he didn't have the words. Any words which would help were out of his reach.

What he wanted was to stand over the VC who had set the trap and say, "He's not dead until he's dead."

Porter shivered. "What do I do?"

Brighton ran to where the two soldiers stood. "What the hell is going on over here? Why aren't we moving, Henderson?"

Brighton then followed Henderson's gaze. "What the…"

"It's Nash, L.T." Henderson sighed.

Brighton clenched his fist. "Okay, move away. Establish a perimeter. Henderson, I want you to get Sergeant Nash out of there."

"Will do, sir."

Henderson looked behind him, to his friends and brothers. "Porter, Ames, Rocky—you're with me; into the pit. Everyone else stays at the rim, to lift him."

As the four soldiers slid along the dirt wall, into the pit, Henderson felt his hatred rise. "Be careful. Don't touch the tip of the stakes; they could have shit or poison on them."

As they got underneath Nash, the four men pushed him skyward. Once free, they hoisted him over the side of the pit. The waiting soldiers pulled him over the top and gently placed him on the ground.

McKinney walked over to the pit and looked at his dead squad leader—his friend. "I hate the little bastards!"

"Tango six, this is Tango one-six. Over," Brighton transmitted. His voice was unemotional, but his eyes showed some of the desperation which leaked from everyone in the squad.

"Go ahead, Tango one-six. Over," Lyons said.

"Tango six, one KIA; need dustoff. Over."

"Wilco, Tango one-six. Didn't hear firing. What happened? Over."

"Punji pit, Tango six. Out."

After the radio call, Brighton looked at Swift. "Medevac coming. Get ready to guide it."

"Yes, sir." Swift popped red smoke in the clearing.

Whop! Whop! Whop!

As the men of the First Platoon looked skyward, they saw a single Huey approaching. Swift raised his M-16 over his head and brought it in for a landing. Once on the ground, Henderson, Professor, Rocky, and Porter carried Nash to the dustoff, where they slid his lifeless body onto the deck. Within a minute, the chopper lifted, flying to Bronco.

Within seconds, another man was gone—swallowed by the land.

Before anyone could say a word, the sky opened with rain so hard that they couldn't see more than several feet to the front. Most of the platoon dropped their rucksacks and yanked out their ponchos, though they were already wet. The grunts slid their rucksacks on first and, while helping each other, they pulled the poncho over their body and backpack, keeping both a little drier.

Henderson walked over to McKinney and put his arm around the big guy. "Sorry. I liked Nash too."

McKinney wiped the rain from his face. "It don't mean nothin'."

After they finished talking, Brighton said, "McKinney, you're the First Squad leader. Consider yourself a sergeant. I'll let Top know."

"Okay, LT."

"Sergeant Henderson, get ready to move. Head northwest. We'll logger at the base of the mountain, roughly five hundred meters from here. We'll leave at zero-eight-hundred hours tomorrow morning, to patrol along the base of the mountain, heading south. Any questions?"

The two squad leaders remained silent, so Brighton said, "Let's go."

"Saddle up! Move out!" Henderson ordered when he reached the Second Squad. He was glad that his voice came out firm.

Laurel stood and adjusted his poncho. He walked in the direction Henderson told him to head.

As he took long strides, Laurel felt guilty for what had happened to Nash. It had been his job to keep the men behind him safe. He'd failed them, he thought. Irrational or not, the guilt ate at his gut.

Once the platoon reached the base of the mountain, Brighton assigned positions to each squad. The men went on with their evening chores, including placing claymores and trip flares. With the rain stopping, but the sky dark, they prepared their evening meal. The squad ate, deep in thought, pondering the horrible death that Nash had experienced.

Henderson noticed Laurel, and suspected that he thought Nash's death his fault. "Laurel, it wasn't your fault. You had no idea the VC had buried a punji pit fifty feet to your right. Hell, you had no idea what was going on within *five* feet around you. You can't prevent your brothers from getting injured or dying—you can only do your best. Nash dying could have happened any day, anywhere."

Laurel looked at Henderson as he brushed a tear from his eye.

Porter noticed how bad Laurel felt too. He changed the subject. "Did you hear the news?"

"What news?" Henderson asked.

"Nixon gave a speech and announced some Vietnamization Program a couple of weeks ago." Porter looked around at his brothers.

Henderson threw an empty can of peaches to the ground. "Shit, that can't be good. That means we'll probably have to stay longer."

"No. In fact, it's the opposite." Professor rose to a sitting position. "I read about it in the *Stars and Stripes*. They're starting to withdraw troops, reoutfit, and train the south. They're even expanding the government to rural areas. Maybe the war will end soon, but don't count on it affecting you."

"It's about time," Henderson said.

Count on it or not, knowing that there might be an end lifted a weight he didn't even know he'd been carrying.

•

Each day in the valley was the same—get up in the morning, eat and hump around the base of the mountain. Then, stop for lunch and hump more. Then, stop for the night, have dinner, and get some sleep. Henderson suspected that all the men carried their ghosts with them on this daily repetition, as he did.

After they had patrolled for two weeks, the men of the First Platoon were tired, wet, and wanted to be somewhere else. The only good thing was that the enemy had left them alone, and nobody else had hit a booby trap. No new dead was something to celebrate.

Laurel stopped at the assigned destination and signaled for Henderson to move forward.

As Henderson walked toward Laurel, he looked around, deciding where to establish the perimeter. He used his instincts to inspect the area; it seemed safe. Henderson signaled the platoon to move into the logger position. Within twenty minutes, the platoon had each position ready for the night.

The grunts hid under their ponchos, struggling to stay as dry as possible. It appeared to be a losing battle. Heavy rains fell, slowed to a drizzle, then poured again. The rain pattern allowed the water to run through their area, creating small streams. Fortunately, the rain stopped right at mealtime.

Henderson walked over to Laurel as he cooked his turkey loaf over the can holding the burning C-4. "Good work today."

"Thanks." Laurel lifted the simmering can of turkey loaf. "Sarge, how long will it rain like this?"

Professor interrupted. "From today until late-December. It's the monsoon season; it'll rain continually. Be ready to stay wet. By the end of it, your skin will feel waterlogged."

"Professor is right." Henderson shrugged. "This is our first monsoon season too, so our experience is limited, but when we first arrived, the old-timers warned us. We need to do the best we can. One thing I'll warn you about is crossing streams. You need to be careful, because the water moves fast—sometimes it can come from nowhere, like a freight train. When you hit a stream, wait for me to come to the front."

Laurel set the can back on the stove. "Sure, Sarge, I'll wait. Anything else?"

"Keep your feet dry and change your socks often," Rocky said. "When you put on a dry pair, wring out the wet pair and put them against your skin. Your body heat will dry them. You'll have them ready for the next night. It's an old mountain trick I learned. Use foot powder daily; it will help some."

"Shit. The rain is starting." Raindrops hit Henderson's poncho hood, which covered his head. "Let's post guards and get whatever sleep we can. You know the rotation."

Stopping by Professor's position, Henderson asked, "How many days left?"

"Seventy-eight to go."

"I think we've been here longer. You sure it's right?"

"Yeah, I'm sure. But we're getting short."

The men of the Second Squad settled in for the night under their ponchos. Each soldier had his hood pulled low over his face, leaving enough space for him to see. This was how they slept.

Underneath his poncho, Henderson lit his last cigarette of the day. He lowered his head inside the poncho, took a drag, and exhaled through the small opening. Rain pelted him during the night, with small streams of water running underneath where he sat.

This is miserable shit!

•

When the sun appeared over the rice paddies, the soldiers woke. Removing the poncho and shaking it became the first order of the day. The men were soaked, even after hiding under their ponchos. There was no escaping the rain.

Henderson stood, pulling out a cigarette. After several attempts, he got it lit. While enjoying his first smoke, he observed the mud and puddles the rain had created.

Swift walked to the center of the perimeter and threw a smoke grenade to his front. As the green smoke rose to the sky, the supply chopper came into view. After Swift had guided the Huey in for a landing, Henderson sent Ames, Hayes, and Ransom to help unload the supplies. He made sure the outgoing mail got on the chopper too.

After the helicopter landed, Henderson caught sight of a soldier jumping off of the chopper, the weight of his rucksack causing him to sink into the wet, soft paddy. He appeared familiar, but Henderson couldn't confirm for sure. The soldier talked with Swift, then walked over to the First Squad position.

As the soldier approached, McKinney stood, staring at him. "I'll be damned! It's Livingston."

"No way, Sarge!" Michaels's stared in amazement.

Livingston walked into the circle of First Squad members. "I didn't go home."

Each soldier hugged Livingston, telling him how sorry they were that he'd had to return to the platoon, the bush, and the VC.

Livingston shook McKinney's hand. "So, you're a sergeant, McKinney? What happened to Sergeant Nash?"

McKinney lowered his head. "Yep, I am. Nash got killed a couple of weeks ago. Fell into a punji pit."

Livingston's gaze fell to the ground. "It don't mean nothin'."

"Take a load off." McKinney forced a smile. "Tell us what happened after you left on the dustoff."

After he dropped his rucksack, Livingston lit a cigarette and looked around at his brothers. "Not much to tell. Once I got to the hospital in Chu Lai, they took me right away for surgery. The bullet didn't hit arteries and, lucky for me, didn't destroy muscle tissue either. They cleaned the wound, sewed me up, and gave me time to heal, with some rehab. Then they sent me to you guys."

"Sorry you didn't get to go home." McKinney sighed. "It should've been your ticket out of here."

"Yeah, me too." Livingston looked around the platoon. "Where's Doc? I want to thank him."

McKinney followed his gaze. "The VC killed him on the firebase over a month ago."

Livingston's face contorted to the point that he wasn't recognizable. "Shit! I owe him my life."

Crack! A single shot fired.

Livingston stopped talking, and his head jerked. He took a deep breath, collapsing to the ground. Blood flowed from the gaping hole in the side of his head.

The grunts fell to the ground, taking cover. McKinney hit the ground next to Livingston, staring into his lifeless eyes.

Heads rose off of the ground as the platoon searched for the sniper.

After several minutes, Brighton yelled, "All clear!"

Porter ran to Livingston to check if he had survived. Within seconds, he stood. "He's dead."

"Bullshit!" McKinney threw his M-16 to the ground.

Henderson walked to McKinney and put an arm around his shoulder. "What shitty luck."

McKinney stood silent for a moment. "It don't mean nothin'."

Brighton walked to where Livingston lay. "Tango six, this is Tango one-six. Over."

"Roger, Tango one-six. Over," Lyons said.

"Tango six, need dustoff. One KIA. Over."

"Tango one-six, in fifteen mikes. Out."

After the dustoff took off, McKinney looked at the First Squad. "Off your asses. Let's get the supplies."

Both squads distributed the supplies, packing the rations, water, and ammunition into their rucksacks. Their packs must have weighed fifteen additional pounds with the extra supplies.

Brighton walked over to Henderson. "Have Laurel move out. Use the trail to the left to start climbing the mountain."

"Saddle up! Move out!" Henderson ground his teeth as he pointed at the trail. "Laurel, follow the trail along the mountain. Be careful."

CLIMBING THE TROUNG SON MOUNTAINS

Henderson ascended the muddy, winding trail, which ran no wider than the length of his rifle. He slipped on the muddy path as he followed Laurel, making sure he kept no more than five feet behind him. As they climbed higher, the jungle growth thickened, shielding the ground from the sun with its tall canopy of trees. Henderson watched the sun disappear as he looked skyward.

The stillness became eerie. Henderson didn't hear birds or animals, only the rustle of branches, with the occasional rattle of gear as the line of men behind him climbed the mountain west of Firebase Hill 100.

The skies opened, dropping buckets of water. The rain dripped through the canopy, soaking the soldiers as they struggled along the waterlogged path. Laurel stopped to slide his poncho on, as did the rest of the platoon, then continued along the overgrown trail.

After walking for four hours, Henderson stopped next to Laurel. "We'll stop here to have a bite. No fires. You need to move fifty feet up the trail for early warning. I'll join you in a few."

Laurel slipped off.

Henderson looked to his rear, to Professor. "Pass the word. We're stopping to eat. Laurel and I are moving along the trail to check it—we'll eat there."

Professor nodded. "Got it." He turned to face the rear, to tell Rocky, and the message went along the line of waiting soldiers.

After Laurel hiked the trail another fifty feet, he dropped his rucksack on the path and removed a can of fruit cocktail and crackers for his meal, using his P-38 to open both cans. While eating the fruit, he watched the front.

Within minutes, Henderson approached and dropped his rucksack—not on the path, as Laurel had, but off to the side, by a tree. He looked at Laurel through the slit in his poncho. "Move off the trail to eat. Sit with some cover."

Laurel moved his rucksack next to Henderson. "Thanks, Sarge. I have a lot to learn."

Henderson opened a can of apple sauce. "No shit. But don't worry about it. We had to learn the same things as you."

When he finished his meal, Henderson removed a Marlboro from his damp cigarette pack. After the third attempt, he lit it, took a deep drag, held it in, and exhaled, enjoying his first smoke in hours. Laurel, imitating his squad leader, lit a cigarette and took a long drag.

While they sat, Henderson heard the water splatter onto the trees' leaves, before the drops fell onto his head. The dripping sound echoed throughout the jungle.

After the chow break, the platoon moved forward.

As Laurel crested the top of the mountain, he saw the sizeable open field, covered in elephant grass, to his front. The clearing had a dense jungle surrounding it.

Henderson walked toward Laurel. "Well, we made it. Good job. I'm having the platoon wait until we check it. Ready?"

"Yes, Sarge."

The two soldiers slid into the elephant grass, walking along an old trail to the center of the field. Henderson needed to establish if the enemy waited for the platoon, or they could move through the area to the jungle on the north side—an ambush was the last thing he wanted.

First, Henderson made his assessment, then asked, "Laurel, what do you think? Is it safe?"

"Yes, Sarge, I believe it is."

"Call the platoon forward."

Brighton had already approached them. Laurel moved the elephant grass to see down the trail. "All clear, LT."

Brighton gave Laurel a nod, acknowledging him before turning to Henderson. "Sergeant Henderson, we'll establish our perimeter on the north corner in the jungle, at the highest point, for protection. Move your squad in first; I'll have the First Squad follow."

"Got it. Will do."

Brighton looked at Laurel. "Good job today."

"Thanks, sir," Laurel stammered, embarrassed by the compliment.

Exhausted from the hard eight-hour climb and being wet, the men dropped their rucksacks, which thudded hard when they hit the soggy ground. What the soldiers wanted at this moment was to fall asleep. They knew it wasn't possible, having much work to do to build their camp. The grunts knew that they were going to use this area as a base camp.

They searched for the best place to string their ponchos as tents. Two soldiers would share one poncho for the shelter, with the second poncho as a floor. The men used tree branches in the center to lift the poncho like a roof, and sturdy twigs for stakes, to hold the poncho onto the ground. When pulling guard, they would sit in front of their tent, attempting to stay dry.

Next, they chose where to set up the claymores and trip flares. Because of the terrain, and this being a base camp, they placed more than usual, and spaced them farther from the platoon perimeter too.

The night was long, but uneventful.

•

As he woke to the sounds of rain hitting the tent, Henderson restrained a groan. "This is going to be another long, dreary day."

Professor rolled over, stiff from sleeping on the hard ground. "Don't tell me it's raining."

Before leaving his tent, Henderson removed his damp poncho liner. He stepped into the drizzle and walked from shelter to shelter, telling his men to get moving.

After breakfast, Henderson called the squad together. "For the next few months, we're going to patrol around the mountain, looking for NVA base camps. One team stays here, while the other goes on patrol—we'll alternate each day. First Squad does the same. Lieutenant and Ledger will go with us; Swift and Brown go with First Squad. Stay alert. We don't want to hit an NVA force larger than us. Any questions?"

Porter raised his hand.

Henderson frowned. "I'm gonna be sorry, but what do you want to know, Porter?"

"Sergeant Henderson, you hurt my feelings." Porter grinned devilishly. "I wanted to know who I go with."

"Well shit, Porter, a *good* question. I guess you'll stay here each day, but you should check with LT."

That was the start of the monsoon season for them.

•

After more than a month of walking the trails through the jungle, leeches were the only enemy contact Henderson had. The men found the leeches hungry, the creatures waiting for a soldier to brush past so they could latch on for a meal.

Henderson spent many evenings removing leeches with a lit cigarette. He'd watch them until they burned and fell to their deaths. Pouring salt on leeches became a form of entertainment, as the squad gathered around to watch them wither and fall to the ground. The men then cheered, as if they had beaten the NVA in a firefight.

Despite being the only enemy, leeches weren't the only problem. Henderson had lost weight, and the jungle rot on his arms and legs worsened. One evening, Henderson stopped by Porter's position to have him check the sores.

"Hurts like hell. What can you do, Porter?"

Porter pushed Henderson's right sleeve up his arm. Henderson jerked it away. "Crap, that hurts! What kind of doc are you?"

"The infantry kind. Stop being a baby." He didn't need to point out that he wasn't a medic at all. "I need to look at the sores."

After he examined the bloody, pus-filled sores, Porter twisted his lips. "Let me clean these up, but you gotta leave the bandages on to keep them clean and dry."

"How do you expect me to keep it dry? It's been raining for a month." Keeping clean was a joke; he didn't even feel the need to mention it. He hadn't been clean since stand-down.

"At least check with me every couple of days, so I can apply new bandages. Now, drop your pants."

"Do what?"

"Gotta check your legs too. Quit being a sissy."

Once Henderson's jungle rot was cleaned and bandaged, he headed back to his shelter for some rest—not that he ever really felt fully rested.

•

Early morning, a week later, Henderson followed Laurel, with the rest of the Alpha Team behind him. They took short steps, struggling through the thick jungle growth along an unfamiliar trail, swinging a machete. Laurel worked hard to widen the path as they moved. Henderson concluded no one had used the trail in years, but he knew it led to the ridgeline of the hills, next to their base camp.

Brighton assigned the squad a mission—to patrol north of their camp to a hilltop. Since arriving in the mountains, this would be the first time the fire team had traveled this far north.

The dim light under the canopy appeared more like the sun was setting behind the horizon, instead of being in the early morning position in the sky. The ground and vegetation remained wet, even though it hadn't rained for several days. The smell of wet, rotting vegetation on the jungle floor overpowered Henderson's sense of smell.

As Henderson passed individual trees, bushes, and plants, he detected a sweet smell amongst the generally bitter odors. He breathed hard and found that the hot, muggy air he sucked into his lungs had a stale taste. Although the canopy blocked the sunlight, the heat and humidity became unbearable, draining his energy.

When he broke through the overgrowth, Henderson walked into Laurel, who stood still, staring at the sight to his front. Henderson's heart rate spiked, expecting something ghastly.

Then, he was surprised at the beauty he witnessed.

Nearly seventy-five-feet high, a waterfall poured clear water into a pond, flowing roughly twenty-five meters from them. The spray of the water, as it spilled over the rocks, hit him with a fine mist, cooling his hot, sweaty body. Henderson found the air fresh as he took slow, even breaths.

The sun shone brightly without the canopy blocking its light, reflecting off of the barren rock cliffs; the water and the sunlight gave the area a surreal glow. Blue, red, and white lotus flowers, with low-lying, lush-green vegetation, surrounded the pool. A sweet, tropical scent drifted from the edges of the pond. What he witnessed was far different to the interior of the jungle.

Professor stopped twenty feet behind Henderson. "Why are we stopping?"

"You need to see it. Bring the team."

"Okay, we're coming."

The team strode to Henderson's vantage point.

"Well, look at that." Professor surveyed the waterfall, in awe. "I'll be damned if I ever expected to locate something so grand here. This is beautiful."

"It is." Henderson drew in a deep breath. "Peaceful, too."

Rocky started unbuttoning his shirt. "Let's strip—we can bathe. It's the cleanest, clearest water I've ever seen in 'Nam. Reminds me of home."

As he looked at the jungle growth around the waterfall, Henderson searched for any signs of danger. He saw nothing, but a second opinion couldn't hurt. He didn't want to see anyone dead today. "Laurel, what do you think?"

"Looks good to me, Sarge."

"Okay, you guys, go ahead. Ames, stay with me. We'll guard the area. Then, switch."

Before Henderson could finish his sentence, Rocky jumped into the pond, naked. Within seconds, Laurel dived into the pool, then Professor.

As Henderson sat guard over his brothers, he watched and listened to them being twenty-year-olds, playing. The roar of the water tumbling over the smooth rocks, with the cool breeze following, strived to lull Henderson to sleep.

Professor sat next to Henderson, allowing the sun to dry his wet body. "Your turn to go in."

"I don't know if I can move. I haven't felt this peaceful since Mitch…"

"I know. Me too."

On the return trip, the men of Alpha Team were clean, relaxed, and full of life for the first time in months. The monsoon rains, mountains, and the evasive enemy had nearly sucked the life out of them.

To be young again.

Henderson frowned.

•

Several weeks later, while eating breakfast, Brighton gave an order. "Ledger, go tell Swift, Henderson, and McKinney that there is a meeting in thirty minutes."

"Yes, sir." Ledger slushed along the muddy trail to the NCO positions to deliver the message.

They waited in a group, while Brighton gulped the last of his coffee.

"We're moving to the hilltop to the north—the same one Henderson didn't make it to a couple of weeks ago. According to the CO, Intel reports that the NVA has a company-size base camp, with a training center, located there. We'll move out at zero-nine-hundred hours. We should reach the suspected base camp by thirteen-hundred hours." Brighton paused for a moment. "Ledger, stand over here. I need to use your back."

Ledger did as asked. Brighton pulled out a map and held it against Ledger's back while tracing the plan with his finger. Silence settled around them as they waited for what Brighton would say next.

"Each squad leaves two men to guard our base. Staff Sergeant Swift stays here. Travel light. The platoon uses the same trail Henderson used, but once we get to the hill, we'll split into squads. First Squad remains on the south side of the hill, while Second Squad moves to the east side. I'll be with the First Squad; Brown with the Second Squad. Henderson, I'll radio the order to move in on the camp. Any questions?"

"How likely is it we'll find the base camp?" Henderson lifted his brow.

"The battalion S-two claimed aerial surveillance spotted the camp as early as yesterday. Odds are they're there."

"Any helicopter or air support?" McKinney asked.

Brighton shrugged slightly. "We'll have Spooky flying overhead, if the weather holds. If it turns bad, we won't have any support. We'll be out of range for artillery support from Firebase Hill One Hundred. Okay, let's get ready to move out."

Henderson returned to his squad and briefed them on the new mission.

The men stowed their rucksacks in the tents, keeping two bandoliers of ammo, two grenades, a canteen, first-aid pouch, and a couple of cans of food to take with them on the mission.

"Check your weapons—make sure they're dry. Clean and oil each part, so it moves smoothly." Henderson walked away from the squad.

Brown carried the PRC-25 radio on his back to Henderson's shelter. "Ready to go, Sergeant Henderson."

"Glad you're with us. Stay behind me and in front of Professor."

At the designated starting time, Laurel walked along the familiar trail toward the hill to his north.

As Henderson followed Laurel, he wished they were heading for the waterfall instead of an enemy base camp. The platoon humped the morning away, arriving at the ambush spot thirty minutes earlier than the lieutenant had anticipated.

Brighton knelt, looking at his map. "Henderson, come here."

Henderson squatted next to the lieutenant, following his finger as he traced the route. "Move your squad to the east, following the trail, and get as close as you can to the camp. Radio me to let me know you're in place. Spooky opens fire first, then I'll give the order to move into the camp. We'll sweep from the south, as you sweep from the east. There should be ten huts in this one-hundred-meter area. Any questions?"

"No questions. Got it."

Henderson returned to the squad. "Laurel, I'm taking point from here. Don't take it badly—it's easier for me to lead than trying to explain." After brief instructions, Henderson took point.

The Second Squad followed Henderson, taking short, guarded steps as they maneuvered through the jungle growth. Within thirty minutes, Henderson had the two teams online, crawling through the wet, jungle floor toward the edge of the clearing.

To his amazement, he saw many NVA and VC soldiers. The smells drifting from the enemy base camp were the same village odors he had grown accustomed to during his time in 'Nam.

"Tango one-six, this is Tango one-six-Papa-Romeo," Henderson whispered into the handset. "Element in position. Over."

Brighton said, "Tango one-six-Papa-Romeo, standby for Spooky. Out."

Henderson then listened to the call over the radio.

"Sierra two-three-one, fire-mission Bravo Sierra four-nine-nine-eight-seven-three-eight-one. Over," Brighton said.

"Tango one-six, confirm fire-mission Bravo Sierra four-nine-nine-eight-seven-three-eight-one. Wilco. Out," the pilot replied.

With this conversation complete, Henderson turned his full attention to the enemy camp. His jaw dropped when he saw that there were women there—woman soldiers. In amazement, Henderson watched the female soldiers in the enemy camp interacting with their male counterparts. One cleaned an AK-47, while another cooked rice in a large pot. Two others carried an RPG with three rounds of ammunition. He heard others, talking and laughing. The male soldiers appeared to treat them as equals.

He determined that the NVA carrying the RPG should die first. As he aimed at her chest, Henderson wondered if he could kill a woman. Hell, he was taught never to *hit* a girl. But he understood that this woman was an enemy soldier who would kill him, given the opportunity.

His right index finger uncurled from the trigger, curled and uncurled, as he decided. Sweat dripped from his brow, splashing on the plastic stock of his rifle. As his index finger curled around the trigger again, he squeezed. The round exploded down the barrel of the rifle, and he felt the light recoil of the butt of the M-16 into his shoulder.

The female soldier's legs buckled as the round ripped through the center of her chest and exploded out of her back, between the shoulder blades—the bullet left an exit hole three times larger than the hole in her chest. She lay on the ground, staring at the sky, dead, with the RPG still in her hands.

The miniguns fired into the village, hitting every two meters with the 7.62 rounds, each fifth round a tracer. Henderson observed the red rain falling from the overcast sky. He watched the NVA, including another female soldier, fall to the ground, their bodies torn apart from being hit multiple times. The straw from the huts flew off of the sides and roof, exposing the interior to the squad.

"Open fire!" Henderson yelled to the Second Squad.

Enemy soldiers ran toward the squad's hiding place, attempting to run from Spooky. Rocky fired round after calculated round toward the enemy soldiers, killing one after another, before they realized that the direction in which they traveled wasn't an escape route. Turning to run south, the NVA then ran into a hail of machine gun fire from Michaels, where Brighton had the First Squad concealed at the edge of the camp, ready to pounce. Firing on the American platoon became the only choice the NVA had; they couldn't escape.

Henderson spotted an NVA soldier rise out of a spider hole and aim at the machine gun to the south side of the camp. He squeezed off several unhurried rounds from his AK-47 before Henderson could react. Henderson saw the assistant gunner, Reeves, fall to the ground.

An M-79 grenade then exploded on the enemy position.

Henderson turned, noticing Professor staring with his weird smile. "Great shot, Professor."

"Medic! Medic! Medic!" boomed along the line of the First Squad.

Porter stood, choosing the best route to run toward the injured man.

Crack!

After his third step, an AK-47 round struck Porter square in the chest, knocking him backward.

Brighton directed the machine gun with the riflemen of the First Squad, as did Henderson with the Second Squad. The crossfire from the infantry platoon, along with the death of steel from above, had the enemy running.

After five more minutes of continuous shooting, Brighton ordered the platoon and Spooky to ceasefire.

Henderson leapt to his feet and ran to Porter. He found him sprawled on the jungle floor, with blood flowing from the large hole in his chest. Porter lay smiling, with his right arm extended, as if he were attempting to ask one of his entertaining questions as he died.

Henderson looked around, confused, hurt, and pissed that he had lost another brother. He didn't cry, because there were no tears left to shed.

Professor rushed over, stopped, and looked at Porter. Tears rolled down his cheeks. Henderson dropped to his knees and grasped Porter's hand, shaking his head in disbelief. He felt as if his world was collapsing, pain coming and going like waves, hitting him in the face. He called out to Porter, but knew the connection was gone—their time together had ended. Sadness traveled through his body, affecting every cell.

Professor placed an arm over Henderson's shoulder. "It don't mean nothin'."

Henderson couldn't say it.

"So much death. I don't have the strength—not anymore."

BACK TO THE WORLD

At last, a dry, sunny day on the mountaintop.

Henderson and the squad sat around their tent area, drying out their clothing. After he lit a cigarette, Henderson relaxed and enjoyed a morning with no missions. Nothing became his goal for the day. Next to him sat Professor and Rocky, the last two remaining brothers he had started his tour with to survive this hellhole.

A shadow fell over him as he sat, staring at the field of elephant grass. He raised his head and saw the lieutenant looking at him.

"Henderson, Professor, Rocky, you'll be on the supply chopper this afternoon, returning to Bronco."

"What for, LT?" Henderson's eyes squinted as he looked up into the sun.

"You three received a one-week drop. You're going home early."

Rocky stared, open-mouthed.

Professor seemed to draw back, considering what he had heard.

"What?!" Henderson's forgotten cigarette dangled from his lips. "No shit, sir? You can't fuck with us, even if you are a lieutenant!"

"This is no joke. You're going back to the world. Pack your stuff. Be ready to go."

Then, Brighton turned and walked away, headed to his tent.

"I'm packing up my stuff!" Professor beamed a smile broader than Texas. "This is a gift horse whose mouth I am not looking into this time. Get ready, before someone changes their mind."

Rocky stood and grabbed his rucksack. "I'm with you!"

The three soldiers got underway, packing their gear and giving away ammunition. They handed out the food they no longer needed. They went about the task under a haze of unreality. Henderson kept expecting to wake up and realize that this was some fantasy, as he lay dying in the elephant grass. His mind reeled, even as his body hurried to accept the opportunity.

When his things were packed, Henderson approached Laurel. "You can have my two-quart canteen of black cherry Kool-Aid. Here are seven packets of cocoa and five cans of chicken noodles, and this is a new pair of socks I've been saving."

"Thanks, Sarge. I appreciate it." Laurel stuffed the treasure into his rucksack before Henderson could change his mind.

"You'll do fine. Keep your head down; remember to stay alert." Henderson hoped Laurel would make it—so many hadn't. It would be a waste to lose Laurel too.

Once the three short-timers had tightened their rucksack straps, they lined the rucksacks along the edge of the clearing to be ready for the supply chopper.

Henderson turned to face the tents. "Hey! Second Squad! All of you, get over here."

The squad assembled around Henderson.

"Professor, Rocky, and I got a one-week drop from our three hundred and sixty-five days. We're going to the world."

The men were silent, because they knew these three had been with the platoon the longest. There would now be a change—the sameness in their lives would be interrupted.

Ransom looked toward Brighton. "Who's going to take over the squad?"

Brighton approached the group of men. "Good question." He turned to the remaining team leader. "Madison, front and center."

"Yes, LT." Madison approached the lieutenant.

"You're promoted to Acting Sergeant, effective immediately. I've already told Top."

Brighton and Henderson pinned Madison's stripes to his collar.

"I'll be the fourth squad leader in less than a year! I hope it's not bad luck."

"You'll do fine." Henderson straightened Madison's collar.

"Ames, you got the machine gun." Madison swallowed, giving his first command.

"By the way, Henderson, Top told me your orders came through last month, permanently promoting you to Sergeant. Congratulations." Brighton extended his hand to shake Henderson's.

"Thanks, sir."

Whop! Whop! Whop!

The sound of the supply chopper echoed through the jungle. Swift stood in the landing zone, throwing a yellow smoke grenade into the center of the cut elephant grass. As the helicopter descended, he guided it to the landing zone until the skids touched the wet field.

Henderson watched in wonder, as if it were his first time seeing the chopper. He noticed every mark, every gleaming bit of metal—he even noticed the pilot's expression. This Huey was his ticket home.

Once the Huey settled on the ground, three replacements jumped off into the soggy field.

Henderson looked at Professor and Rocky. "Hell, those replacements can't even be nineteen—only kids."

Swift studied the fresh, young faces. He shook his head and pointed them in the direction of Brighton. "Head to the LT; I'll be there in a minute."

Henderson, Rocky, and Professor ran to the Huey as the crew chief kicked out cases of C-rations and ammunition. They helped the crew chief get the last item off of the deck—a bundle of clean uniforms and socks.

"The clean clothes will make the guys happy!" Henderson yelled over the roaring turbine engine.

Before they boarded, Swift shook each of the three soldier's hands without a word, then turned to walk back to the camp.

Once they were seated on the deck, the Huey lifted.

The three men looked down, for the last time, at their platoon brothers. They raised their weapons, signaling a farewell. The men on the ground let out a cheer, raising their rifles for their three platoon brothers as the chopper rotated to the right and sped south, toward Bronco.

The men didn't speak during the flight, as if to do so would somehow break the spell. They looked at each other and smiled.

The helicopter landed on the helipad at Bronco. The dirty, wet soldiers jumped to the ground and ran to the opposite side of the pad. Carrying their light rucksacks, they strolled to the company headquarters to see Top.

After they entered the first sergeant's office, Rocky allowed the screen door to slam shut.

Hall sat at his desk, puffing on his pipe. Hearing the door slam, he yelled, "Damn it, quit slamming the door!"

Taking another puff from his pipe, Hall then said, "Welcome home. Turn in your weapons and gear, get showered, and please put on a clean uniform. You even get new boots. Return here to see me when you finish."

"Will do, Top." Henderson turned and reached for the screen door.

While heading to supply, it registered with Henderson that he was returning home. He wasn't sure where home would be, but the thought of leaving Vietnam made him smile. Looking at Professor and Rocky, he sensed that they felt the same—except that they knew where home was.

An hour later, the three walked back into the office. Rocky didn't let the screen door slam this time.

Hall smiled. "You three clean up nice. Before we get to saying goodbyes, I got a couple of administrative items to go over with you.

"Rocky, Professor, you're promoted to Sergeant." Hall handed them sergeant stripes and their orders. "These are your orders to return to the States. The three of you will catch a flight to Cam Ranh Bay, on a C-one-thirty, this afternoon, and fly to the States tomorrow. At Fort Lewis, you'll receive your discharge paperwork."

After handshakes and slaps on the back, they left the office.

The three soldiers walked with long strides toward the airfield. Henderson looked at the buildings, mess hall, helicopter pad, and the soldiers bustling around the base, which supported the grunts who killed the enemy.

"Good luck."

•

Once they arrived in Cam Ranh Bay, the processing went smoothly.

The next morning, Henderson watched the rising sun cast warm tones, with vibrant hues of color, onto the landscape. *Another beautiful sunrise,* he thought as he sensed the tension and fear escaping his body and mind.

Henderson understood that the sudden surge of happiness was because the war had ended for him, but he wondered if it would last. And what demons were hitching a ride back with him.

The three combat brothers waited to board their "freedom bird" back to the world.

•

As Professor looked out of the plane's window, he watched the clouds zoom past. He nudged Henderson. "You want to have another drink?"

"Make it a double."

"Rocky, do you want one?"

Professor smiled and nodded, as if to answer for him.

"Give me what you're having."

Henderson smiled and stopped the stewardess. "We'll have three double Jim Beam and Cokes."

The stewardess smiled as she poured the drinks, handing a full glass to each soldier.

Rocky knew, when they left Alaska, that they were on the last leg of the flight. "How much longer until we land?"

She looked at her watch. "We should be landing in less than two hours."

The stewardess then moved to the row behind Henderson, asking if anyone wanted a drink.

Henderson looked at his friends and raised his glass. "To the fallen."

"To the fallen."

The men were silent, deep in their thoughts.

Not long after finishing their drinks, Henderson and Professor nodded off to sleep, with Professor's head on Rocky's shoulder.

"Please fasten your seatbelt; we'll be landing in ten minutes."

The passengers snapped out of their sleep, clicked on their seatbelts, and made sure their seats were in the full upright position. Henderson could sense the excitement building as they came in for the final approach. Once the wheels squealed on the concrete runway, the men erupted with screams of joy. Henderson figured many of the men on the plane had had thoughts like his over the past year— that this might be the one experience they wouldn't live to see.

As Henderson walked down the steps to the tarmac, he felt sensations of happiness at returning to the "world," but also a sense of sadness for his brothers who didn't come home with him.

Professor put his hand on Henderson's shoulder. "Welcome home, brother."

"You too, Professor. Welcome home."

The three soldiers walked to the waiting bus, boarded, and within minutes, the door swung closed. The driver, a soldier, pushed the gearshift into first, drove along the airstrip, changed gears, and headed for the gate.

Henderson looked out of the window as they drove through the gate. There, he saw hundreds of young men and women, holding signs denouncing the war. Some of the protesters spat at the bus as it drove by them. Their chant echoed throughout the bus, *"Hell, no, we won't go!"*

With the bus moving at a slow pace, the protesters followed, yelling, "Baby killers!" They spat at the men, who watched from the windows as the driver turned onto the highway and accelerated toward Fort Lewis.

Rocky shook his head. "Now, that's a welcome home."

"I taught them well, didn't I?" Professor squirmed in his seat. "Hate seems to communicate easier than love. The war is wrong, but to treat soldiers like this is wrong too."

"You didn't know, Professor." Henderson pursed his lips. "We only did what they asked of us."

Protesters welcomed the busload of soldiers as it drove through the front gate of Fort Lewis. "Baby killers! We don't want your kind here!" they screamed while giving the middle finger. They spat at the soldiers, who sat behind the windows, staring in disbelief.

Henderson huffed, "Why in the hell are they so angry at us? We're the ones in 'Nam, fighting the NVA and VC. Fuck them!"

The driver drove into a parking area and stopped. "Okay, this is your stop. I'm sorry about the protesters. Not everyone is going to act like assholes."

•

Out-processing from the army took longer than expected. The three soldiers received new dress uniforms, haircuts, and a steak meal. After dinner, the friends—brothers—sat on their bunks, talking about the protesters and going home.

I don't have a home.

Henderson thought of returning to Drexler's parents, but going back to them without their son seemed harder, now that it was possible.

The next morning, while waiting for Rocky, Henderson gazed at Professor. "I'm not going to chow right away. I need to talk to the clerk, because my orders are incorrect."

"Not a problem. We'll meet back here afterward."

"See you later."

Henderson left the barracks, strolled to the Detachment Commander's office, and approached the clerk. "Can I see the commander?"

"Wait a minute, Sergeant. Let me check." The clerk left for the commander's office. After a couple of minutes, the clerk reappeared. "Go on in; he's waiting for you."

Henderson entered the commander's office and saluted. "Good morning, sir…"

•

Later in the morning, the three friends waited to update their administrative records and receive discharge documentation. One by one, they filed by a desk manned by a clerk who explained their orders. They verified the information on the DD Form 214—the Certificate of Release or Discharge from Active Duty.

When Henderson had completed the processing, he walked outside toward the parking area to join his two friends.

Professor held his discharge high in the air. "The most important document you'll ever receive."

"Me too." Rocky held his certificate for all to see. "I'm a civilian."

They boarded the military bus for the Seattle International Airport to catch their flights home.

As the bus dropped the fifty soldiers off at the airport entrance for departures and Henderson walked down the steps onto the curb, he felt confused. *Where will I go?*

Rocky hurriedly walked around him. "Let's go, Henderson."

Professor bought a ticket to Oakland, and Rocky's ticket was for Denver.

"Next," the ticket agent said. "Hello. Next."

Henderson woke from his daydream, approached the counter, and said, "Sorry. A one-way ticket to the Oakland International Airport, please."

Henderson paid and walked to the aisle, joining Professor and Rocky.

Henderson hugged Rocky. "Stay in touch. You have Cheryl's address and phone number. If you need anything, call me. Remember, your mountains are cold, not like in 'Nam."

"You got it, Eddie. I will."

Professor broke between the two brothers and hugged Rocky. Looking him in the eye, he said, "Rocky, I wouldn't be here if it wasn't for you. You have all my information. If you need me, I'll be there for you."

"I know you will. Tell the kids not to spit or say mean things this time."

"I will; I promise."

The three laughed.

Rocky walked toward his gate, looking over his shoulder at his friends for the last time as he smiled and waved goodbye.

After Rocky turned the corner, Henderson and Professor went to the bar to wait the two hours for their flight to Oakland. Once seated, Professor ordered two Jim Beam and Cokes. The waitress reappeared with the drinks and set them on the table.

Henderson lifted his glass. "To the fallen."

"To the fallen."

"Just think, two days ago we were in the jungles of 'Nam"— Henderson set his glass down—"and now here we sit, in the States, drinking."

"It's insane, isn't it?" Professor took a sip of his drink.

As Henderson looked around the bar area, he noticed many of the customers appeared familiar. "Professor, aren't those guys the soldiers we returned with on our flight?"

"Damn. You're right. Look at them, dressed in civilian clothes."

"I guess they don't want anyone knowing they've been to 'Nam."

After they finished the drink, Professor signaled the waitress and ordered two more bourbons.

Henderson twirled the ice cubes in his glass. "What are you going to do when you get to Berkeley?"

"I'll use my GI bill to get my doctorate. Then I'll teach. I'm going to protest the war while going to school."

"Your protesting will mean more, being a veteran."

"I know. Damn politicians! Look how many brothers we lost." Professor took a long drink. "You going to see Cheryl?"

Henderson smiled at the thought of her. "Yeah, I wrote to her earlier. She said I could stay with her for a couple of weeks, until I decide what I'm going to do."

"What *are* you going to do?" Professor stared into Henderson's eyes. "I didn't see you buy a ticket for Indianapolis."

"No, I'm flying with you to Oakland. I'll call Cheryl shortly to ask her to pick me up at the airport."

Henderson shifted his weight in his seat and looked around. "You remember this morning, when I didn't go to breakfast with you guys?"

"Yeah, go on." Professor leaned forward, taking a large sip of his drink.

"Well, I re-enlisted."

Professor choked on his drink. "What?! Why did you do that?"

"I can't leave the guys in the bush. I need to go back. Besides, there's nothing to keep me here, with Mitch gone."

"I wish you would've talked to me!"

"It's a decision I needed to make."

Professor leaned in closer. "What about Billy? You know what I'm talking about—don't pretend you don't. I don't buy that shit about shooting a mule deer."

Henderson stared at the passing passengers as he gulped his drink. "I plan to fly to Indianapolis a couple of days after I get to Oakland. I'll visit Mitch's parents while I'm there. I don't want to stay with them, because it will make them miss Mitch more."

Professor leaned in further. "Okay, what about Billy?"

"I don't know if I can keep my promise to Mitch." Tears rolled down Henderson's cheek. "Can I commit murder?"

Professor patted Henderson on the shoulder. "It's okay, Eddie."

"What am I supposed to do? He's my brother. He saved my life many times. Look at the hardships and the good times we shared. Any one of us would do what another asked of us. Hell, we're like brothers because of 'Nam."

Henderson stopped talking and stared at his drink for a moment. "I don't think of myself as a killer. Have I killed? Sure. But I killed people who were trying to kill my brothers and me. But can I kill for Mitch?" He took a long, slow sip of the bourbon. "It's the last thing he asked of me."

The announcement to board the flight to Oakland interrupted the two friends. They stood to walk to the gate.

As the two soldiers, looking sharp in their dress uniform, walked along the corridor, families moved to the opposite side of the walkway to avoid them. One young woman looked at them and yelled, "Baby killers!"

WELCOME HOME

Henderson and Professor walked up the stairway to board the waiting aircraft for the flight to Oakland. As Henderson took the last step, he heard someone to his rear comment, "Those two should've stayed over there." Laughter from other passengers followed the hateful statement.

Red-faced, with his heart pumping, Henderson turned to face the loudmouth, but Professor grabbed his arm. "Let it go, Eddie. He's not worth the trouble."

"But… Yeah, you're right. I'm tired of fighting."

The two veterans stepped into the cabin, while a good-looking stewardess greeted them with a genuine smile. She checked their tickets and pointed them in the direction of their seats. As Henderson passed by, she whispered, "Welcome home."

Those two words brought a smile to Henderson's lips. *I bet she's been on flights to Vietnam and back, and suspects what we went through.*

Professor grabbed the window seat, while Henderson sat in the aisle seat. Both removed their jackets, which displayed their combat ribbons and awards. As Henderson stood and stowed them in the overhead bin, he sensed eyes staring at him. His mind shot back to Vietnam, those stares creating the same feeling he had when the NVA were waiting for him to walk into an ambush. He shook off the unseen glares. After sitting, he buckled his seatbelt.

"I'm ready for a drink. How about you?"

Professor clicked his seatbelt and tugged it to tighten the strap. "You know me; always ready to taste some bourbon."

Once the aircraft leveled its flight path, Henderson stopped the stewardess who had greeted them. "Can we have two bourbon and Cokes? And make them doubles, please."

Her eyes twinkled in the poorly lit cabin, and her smile made Henderson's blood rush to his face. "You got it. I'll be right back."

"You need to quit flirting. Cheryl is waiting for you." Professor grinned as he squirmed in his seat to get comfortable.

Henderson poked Professor lightly in the ribs. "Hey, trying to be nice, that's all." Henderson settled into his seat. "How many days left?"

Professor watched the clouds zoom by through the cabin window. "Well, Eddie, it's the twenty-fifth of February, nineteen-seventy. So, no days left."

The two soldiers smiled at the exchange.

As an afterthought, Professor sighed. "Did you tell Cheryl you re-enlisted?"

Henderson sat silent for a moment, sipping his drink. "No, I haven't. I'm not sure when I'm going to tell her. But I will."

Professor leaned forward. "Good luck with that." He patted Henderson on the knee.

Both soldiers finished their drink and drifted off to sleep, Henderson's head on Professor's left shoulder. On occasion, Professor would let out a whimper. "Help. Gooks everywhere." Henderson stirred, as if answering his plea.

The speakers crackled. "Please fasten your seatbelts; we will be landing at the Oakland International Airport in ten minutes."

As the plane descended, Henderson sat upright and watched the concrete airstrip getting closer and closer. The bump jarred him as the wheels touched hard. The two combat veterans' gazes met, and each smiled—a smile of deep sadness, knowing that the end of their journey was close.

Once the plane stopped at the terminal, both soldiers stood, and Henderson grabbed their jackets from the overhead bin. After sliding their coats on, they waited to depart. Neither said a word.

They stepped into the aisle and followed the passengers as they streamed out of the exit door. Henderson didn't hear the talking, laughing, and bustle of the other passengers. His mind had wandered back to Vietnam, thinking of the brothers he had lost during the past year. Especially Mitch. Coming home without Mitch tore at his gut. It hurt.

Professor put his hand on Henderson's shoulder and whispered into his ear, "It'll be okay. You'll do fine."

Henderson snapped back to reality, wondering how Professor always knew his thoughts. "Thanks, man."

Passengers moved slowly down the narrow aisle.

Finally, Henderson walked into the bright sunlight glistening through the open door. He descended the steep stairway into the cool February air, with Professor following. Once Henderson's foot touched the concrete, a shiver ran along his spine, causing goose pimples to spread across his body.

Tears welled in Henderson's eyes. "Welcome home, Calvin."

Professor placed his hands on Henderson's shoulders and gazed into his eyes. "Welcome home, Eddie."

Passengers glared and walked around the two soldiers. Several of the passengers snickered at the two men as they affirmed that they were home and safe. A young man with long hair and a scruffy beard, wearing a dirty, tie-dyed T-shirt and blue jeans, stopped in front of the two soldiers. "Hey, man. I'm four-F and not fighting your fucking war."

Henderson, with his fist clenched, could only stare at the boy.

Professor instinctively moved between Henderson and the agitator, placing his arm around Henderson's shoulders as they walked into the terminal.

As soon as Henderson entered, he searched for Cheryl. He spotted a young woman running toward him with flowing, red hair, and immediately knew it was her.

She jumped into his arms, almost knocking him down, but he held her tight and twirled her round and round. He gently let her slide to the floor and gazed into the depth of her green eyes. "I missed you and thought of you every day."

Cheryl met his gaze. "I missed you so much. Welcome home." She stood on her tiptoes, planting a long kiss.

An elderly woman approached Professor and tugged on his coat sleeve. He looked down and a huge smile appeared on his face. "Mom! I told you that you didn't need to meet me."

She reached up and hugged Professor as tightly as she could. "Calvin, of course I'll meet you. I'm your mother."

After the introductions, the four walked toward the exit. Once outside, Professor and Henderson stood face-to-face, staring at each other. Without a word, the two brothers hugged.

Then, Professor stepped away from Henderson, took his mom's hand, and walked toward the parking garage. Henderson watched his brother until he had disappeared behind the parked cars.

Cheryl grabbed Henderson's hand into hers and pulled lightly. "Come on, let's go."

"Yeah, let's do it."

Hand in hand, the two young lovers walked toward Cheryl's car. She stopped at a honey gold-colored sixty-six Mustang. "Get in. Are you hungry? Do you want to stop anywhere?"

Henderson threw his duffel bag into the back seat, then lowered himself into the passenger seat. As he sat, he moved the seatbelt out of the way. "Can we go to your place?" He turned to stare at Cheryl as she started the car. "I want to be alone with you—nothing else."

She pulled out of the parking lot and shot him a mischievous smile. "Me too."

As the car roared along the highway, he rolled down the window. The cold air rushed over his face and blew his hair in every direction. His body hadn't been this cold in a year, but it felt refreshing to him. Cheryl's red hair blew with the wind too.

Henderson took in her features—round, emerald-green eyes, perfectly spaced, with a small, upturned nose and full lips. When she smiled, dimples appeared. Next, he followed her smooth neck to her breasts, visible through the thin material of her blouse. He could see her hard nipples. He smiled. "You're not wearing a bra, are you?" *Was it me or the cold air that stimulated her?*

She sat straight in her seat and took a firm grasp of the steering wheel. "No, I'm not."

"Well, I'm not complaining, but why?"

Cheryl brushed strands of hair from her face and glanced at Henderson. "Not wearing a bra is a political protest. It symbolizes freedom and the rejection of the traditional views of femininity."

"I guess a lot has changed in the last year. There are war protests, civil rights protests, women's rights protests… It looks like we're messed up here in the US."

Henderson reached for the handle and cranked the window closed. The car became quiet without the rush of the wind. He sat without saying a word, watching the buildings fly by, while thinking of his brothers in Vietnam.

The car came to an abrupt stop. "We're here. That's my apartment building to your front."

After he flung the door open, Henderson stepped onto the sidewalk. "Looks like a nice apartment building. Are you happy here?"

"I'm so much happier now!" Cheryl walked around to where Henderson stood and put her arms around his neck. "So much happier."

"Go back, baby killer!" two youths shouted as they drove by.

He followed the car with a hard stare until Cheryl placed her hand on his cheek and moved his face toward hers. "Eddie, it's okay. Don't let the little fuckers get you down."

Out of nowhere, a loud belly laugh echoed off of the buildings. Henderson realized it had come from him. "I've never heard you cuss before. I guess you *are* a liberated woman."

She punched him lightly on the arm. "Let's go upstairs."

Once inside, Henderson surveyed the apartment. He found it clean, neat, and, with all the feminine touches, he knew that a woman lived here. "I like your place. It must cost a fortune to live here."

Cheryl hung Eddie's jacket in the hall closet. "My dad and mom help. I also have scholarships and grants."

"How is your dad doing? Is he back home?"

"He's home and retired. Mom said he's doing okay, but I think he's having problems adjusting." She took his hand into hers and walked toward the bedroom. "Let's talk about us."

After he undressed, he sat at the end of the bed. His heart raced faster as he watched Cheryl undress. *She is so beautiful and sexy.*

Naked, she sat on his lap and placed her arms around his neck while looking into his eyes. "I've missed you so much."

Holding her, he fell backward onto the bed.

•

From a deep sleep, Henderson bolted upright in bed. "Mitch, I'm coming. Hold on." He flipped to his side, falling to the floor. "Where's my rifle? I can't find my rifle!"

Cheryl slid out of bed and sat on the floor in front of him. "Eddie, it's okay. You'll be okay."

He jerked away. "Help Mitch!"

She took his hands into hers. "Eddie, you're home. You're safe."

He sat upright and looked around the room, with sweat dripping down his face. His pounding heart pushed blood through his veins until he thought his heart would explode. Then he realized.

"Shit. I'm sorry, Cheryl."

She cradled him in her arms as he wept. "It's okay. It's okay." She rocked him softly.

•

As the sun peeked through the bedroom curtains, Henderson rolled over and stared at Cheryl. He brushed her hair aside and thought that she was as beautiful asleep as she was awake. Not wanting to wake her, he slid out of bed. Once he pulled on his pants, he walked into the kitchen. As he looked for the coffee pot, a voice startled him.

"Looking for something?"

He turned as Cheryl walked into his arms. He stared at her. "Good morning, beautiful."

"Okay, I guess that'll get you a cup of coffee. Now, out of my way and I'll get it started."

They sat at the table, sipping coffee. Cheryl glanced over the newspaper, while he stared out of the window.

Henderson set his cup down. "Do you have class today?"

"I do. Late morning and this afternoon."

"Okay, I'll use that time to buy some civilian clothes. I can't walk around in a uniform all day. Maybe people will quit yelling at me if I'm not wearing it."

Cheryl looked up with a smile. "You'll look handsome either way."

She jumped up, running toward the bedroom, laughing. "Got to shower and get to school."

He sat at the table, staring out of the window at the strange landscape of buildings and antennae blocking his view of the blue sky. Not a single tree, rice paddy, or jungle growth, as far as he could see. He sensed a presence—then a hand rested on his shoulder.

"Mitch?"

"No, it's me." She leaned down and kissed him. "I'm off to school. I left you a key, by the coffee pot. I'll be home by three."

Henderson pushed his chair back, stood, and embraced her. "I'll be here."

As she pretended to push him away, she smiled and ran for the door. Cheryl waved and closed the door.

Once he had cleaned up, he dug out a pair of slacks and a sport shirt, which he had worn on R and R. After he dressed, he looked in the full-length mirror, observing a skinny young man staring back with haunted eyes, hair cut shorter than the norm, and wearing black army dress shoes. *What a dork!*

Next, he went into the living room and sat in a chair next to the table which held the telephone and telephone book. He flipped

open the book to the yellow pages, then to "Department Stores"—
he found a JC Penney's a block away.

Now, for the real task.

Flipping through the pages, he stopped at "Gun Stores" and
slid his finger down the row of gun stores. He stopped as he located
one not far from Penney's.

Two more tasks to do.

He flipped back to "Airlines" and dialed the number.

"Good morning. I want to make a reservation to Indianapolis
on Sunday, returning Monday afternoon."

The agent confirmed the dates. "You can pick the tickets up at
the airport counter."

Henderson tapped his foot. "Thank you."

Next, he dialed Mrs. Drexler.

"Good morning, Mrs. Drexler."

"Oh, Eddie, you're home!"

"Yes, I am. I wanted to let you know that I'll be visiting Sunday
evening, if that's okay."

"You can visit anytime. Mr. Drexler and I are excited." He could
feel her warmth through the phone. "Will you stay for dinner?"

"Yes, that would be great. I remember what a great cook you
are."

The conversation lasted less than five minutes before Henderson
hung the phone in the cradle.

After Henderson locked the apartment door, he walked down
several flights of steps and out onto the streets of Berkeley.

The hustle-bustle and noise of this small city startled him. His
heart pounded while his eyes darted everywhere, searching for the
enemy.

Calm down, calm down! Nothing out there to hurt you.

Once he determined the correct direction to JC Penney, he
strolled along the sidewalk, taking in the scenery. Within twenty
minutes, he reached the store.

It took a short time for him to select several pairs of slacks and
sport shirts. He took his time looking at shoes, deciding on a pair of

penny loafers. He paid the salesclerk, asking, "Can I change into my new clothes?"

She slid the bag toward him. "Sure, go ahead, young man."

He picked up the bag and walked into the dressing room. Once he had changed into the new clothes, he looked in the full-length mirror. *Not a dork now.*

Someone entered the stall next to his, slamming the door shut, and Henderson watched his reflection duck behind the chair. *Guess I'm still a dork!*

Once he had left the department store, Henderson strolled a block north to the gun shop. He entered, hesitated, then walked toward the counter. Being his first time in a gun store, he had no idea how to buy a gun. He stopped and looked at the rifles hanging on the wall behind the salesclerk.

"What can I help you with, son?"

Henderson eyed what he thought was a Winchester. "I'm looking for a Winchester Model Seventy."

The clerk smiled and turned to the back wall. "You have a good eye. This is what you want." He handed the rifle to Henderson.

Henderson held the rifle and felt its weight, thinking it was heavier than the M-16 he carried. "It feels good. Do you have a Weaver scope too?" He remembered what Rocky had told him about the gun and scope.

The clerk reached under the counter and placed the scope on the counter. Henderson laid the rifle down next to it. "I need a box of ammo, a bag, and I'd like to use your range to get the sight right."

"Let's settle up, and you can use the range." The clerk took the cash and rang up the sale.

After he zeroed the rifle, Henderson disassembled it and wiped it clean. Next, he wrapped the parts in a clean towel the clerk had given him. Along with the ammunition, he placed the rifle into the bag, laying his new clothes on top of the gun.

"Thanks." Henderson waved and walked toward the door.

When he returned to the apartment, he slid the bag under the bed on the side he slept. He didn't want Cheryl finding it and asking a bunch of questions. He sat on the end of the bed with his head in his hands.

Can I kill for Mitch?

I promised!

A TRIP TO INDIANAPOLIS

The honey-gold Mustang pulled into the parking spot outside the departure terminals. Cheryl jumped out and ran to the passenger side.

Eddie already had his bag in hand, ready to check in for his flight. She slid her arm through his and turned toward the entrance.

He took a step and stopped. "You don't have to walk me to the gate. I don't want you to miss class."

"Don't be silly. I want to be with you when you leave." She tugged on his arm to get him moving.

Once checked in, they walked to the departure gate for the flight to Indianapolis. They sat, with Henderson's arm around her shoulders. He stared at the airplanes landing and taking off. When the speaker made a loud *pop* sound, Henderson started to dive for the floor, but caught himself in time—he still had the reflexes of a combat soldier. He sat, tapping his foot to a beat no one else heard.

Cheryl sensed Eddie's nervousness. "Eddie, don't worry. You'll do fine with Mitch's parents."

"I don't know. I hope the Drexler's don't ask for details." Henderson's foot tapped faster

A ticket agent picked up the microphone. "Flight five-five-five to Indianapolis is ready for boarding." The words echoed throughout the waiting area.

The young couple stood and embraced. Henderson looked into Cheryl's eyes and kissed her. He released her from his grasp. "I hope you'll always be proud of me."

"Don't be silly. I'm proud of you."

Henderson walked out of the terminal door and up the stairway to board the waiting aircraft for the flight to Indianapolis. As he took the last step, he turned and saw Cheryl, waving from inside the terminal. With a determined look on his face, he moved down the aisle to his seat.

He decided to use the five hours in the air rehearsing what he would say to Mr. and Mrs. Drexler. First and foremost, he didn't want to talk about any details. His face flushed with guilt. He couldn't tell them that he hadn't blown the claymores—and if he had, Mitch might be alive. *It's my fault Mitch is dead.*

He shook the thought off and moved on to his second purpose for the visit.

As he looked up at the overhead bin, Henderson thought of the bag that held the rifle and ammunition, which lay underneath his clothes. He had found Billy Matheson's address by calling information before he left, and it would only be a matter of time before he kept his promise.

•

The wheels touched the ground, jarring Henderson from his dreamlike state. Once the plane rolled into the terminal area, the passengers disembarked, walking into the terminal. Henderson carried his bag with a firm grip as he walked outside the airport doors.

When a cab pulled to the curb, he opened the rear door and slid onto the back seat. "Take me to nine-one-nine Rosewood Drive, please."

The driver turned in his seat. "You got it." He started the meter and drove off.

As soon as he closed the door, Henderson lit a cigarette, inhaled deeply, held the smoke for a moment, then exhaled. The nicotine fix made him feel sharper and not as restless. He knew that quitting would be ideal—Cheryl didn't like his smoking. *Maybe someday soon.*

When the driver exited the highway, Henderson noticed the tree-lined homes, with white picket fences in front of each. The yards were manicured and well kept. It reminded him of his old home in North Carolina, and he sensed his mother and father's presence. *Why did they have to die?*

The driver approached a four-way stop, pressing the brakes. "We'll be there in about five minutes."

Henderson shifted in his seat. "Thanks."

The apprehension of talking to Mitch's parents ate away at his insides. As he watched the houses slowly fade, he thought of the night Mitch died.

An explosion lifted the bunker roof, forcing Professor and me to take cover. As the enemy rushed our position, Professor and I fired as many rounds as we could.

I jumped from the roof and ran into the bunker, where Doc lay dead, without legs; there was blood everywhere.

I heard Mitch cry out, "I'm here. Over here!"

When I got to Mitch, I knew it was too late. There was a hole in his gut the size of a baseball.

We talked. At the end, I promised Mitch.

Squeaking brakes woke Henderson from his daydream. "We're here."

Henderson read the house number, nine-one-nine. "Thank you." He paid and opened the car door.

As he walked toward the front door, he attempted a quick rehearsal. However, his thoughts became jumbled and left him confused. After he stepped onto the front porch, he stood in the cold air, unable to move, his finger inches away from the doorbell.

The door swung open.

There stood Mrs. Drexler with a surprised look on her face. "My God, it's Eddie!" She wiped her hands on her apron. "John, Eddie is here." She wiped her hands again and embraced Henderson, dragging him into the house.

Henderson dropped his bag to the floor while hugging Mrs. Drexler back.

He felt like he had returned home. The aroma of food cooking and the woman he hugged both reminded him of his mother. When he noticed Mr. Drexler standing behind his wife, it could have been his father standing there.

Am I home?

Mr. Drexler extended his right hand. "Okay, let go of him, Martha." She smiled and dropped her arms. The two men grasped each other's hand, shaking firmly. "Welcome home, Eddie."

Without warning, Mr. Drexler pulled Henderson into his arms, giving him a big bear hug. He quickly released him. "You're looking good."

"Thanks, Mr. and Mrs. Drexler."

Mr. Drexler put his arm around his wife's waist. "Eddie, as far as we are concerned, this is your home too."

Henderson wiped at the tears which ran down his cheeks. "I appreciate that. Mitch and I were brothers."

Once she had patted at the tears streaming down her face and blew her nose, Mrs. Henderson walked into the living area. "Eddie, John, come in here. I'll get some coffee."

Mr. Drexler sat in his favorite recliner, while Henderson sat at the end of the sofa, facing him. With the silence building, the two men looked around the room. Henderson's foot began tapping, faster and faster.

"Here's the coffee." She set a mug next to Mr. Drexler and a cup next to Henderson. "I'll be right back with mine." She returned, sitting at the other end of the sofa. "Eddie, how have you been doing? Are you staying with that girl? I can't remember her name."

"Her name is Cheryl. I really like her. I've been back a couple of days. Doing okay, I guess."

Mr. Drexler took a sip of coffee. "Are you going to stay in Oakland?"

"I am for a while..." He hesitated. "I re-enlisted—I'm going back to 'Nam."

"What the hell?" Mr. Drexler spat his coffee back into the cup. He set the cup down. "Why would you do that? Why didn't you talk to me first?"

Henderson's eyes darted around the room. "I didn't think to talk to you. I didn't want to bother you, because of Mitch." His foot tapped faster. "I need to go back and be with my brothers."

Mrs. Drexler looked at Henderson like a mother would. "Eddie, it's okay; we'll support any decision you make." She shot a look at her husband. "Right, John?"

"Yes, dear." Mr. Drexler stood and looked down at Eddie. "I'm sorry. I don't want you to get hurt, that's all."

Eddie stood, and the two men shook hands.

Mrs. Drexler stood up. "I have a pot roast, mashed potatoes and lemon pound cake for dinner."

"That's my favorite meal. I missed that in the jungle."

"I know. Mitch told me." The room went quiet for a moment. "Let's go to the kitchen, so we can eat and talk."

Once they were seated at the table, Mrs. Drexler heaped the food onto a plate and passed it to Henderson, then to Mr. Drexler. Next, she made her plate. They ate in silence.

Henderson wolfed down the last of the pot roast on his plate. "Mrs. Drexler, this meal is as good as my mom's. Thank you."

She smiled. "You want some more?"

"No thanks, I'm full."

"How about some lemon pound cake and coffee?"

"Well, I'm not *that* full. Thank you." Henderson smiled, handing her his plate as she stood.

Mr. Drexler took a bite of cake and stared into his coffee mug. "Eddie, tell us about your time with Mitch during the war."

"Yes, do tell us," Mrs. Drexler said as she wiped at a tear.

Henderson's foot tapped faster as he looked around the room. He desperately wanted a cigarette. "We had a lot of good times together. It wasn't all bad over there." He shifted in his chair. "I remember when we sat around a well, talking while filling canteens, and the time we had to run as hard as we could, because a typhoon was coming. We laughed at each other, because we were wet and muddy."

They smiled as he kept talking. "One day, we fell into an animal pen and got buffalo shit—sorry, I mean dung—all over our uniforms. An elderly village woman cleaned them for us while we stood there, naked, holding a palm leaf to hide our manhood."

Mr. and Mrs. Drexler laughed.

He stopped talking and took a bite of cake. "He was sad the day he got the Dear John letter from Sandra—it broke his heart."

I shouldn't have said that.

Mrs. Henderson rolled her eyes and looked away.

"Go ahead, Eddie."

He sat forward in his chair. "We grew closer when we were building the firebase."

"Is that when he died?" Mr. Drexler gulped.

Mrs. Drexler sat up straight. "Oh no, John. Don't ask."

Both feet were tapping. "Yes, it was." Henderson poked at the small piece of cake on his plate. "I held Mitch and talked to him until he died. He said he loved you both."

Tears streamed down Mrs. Drexler's face. "Did he feel any pain?" Her hands trembled as she picked up the mug, spilling coffee onto the table.

Henderson wiped at a tear. "No, he didn't feel any pain. He died peacefully, talking about you two."

Mr. Drexler reached across the table and put his hand on Henderson's. "Thank you, son."

"Yes, Eddie—thank you for being Mitch's friend." Mrs. Henderson stood, leaned down, and kissed him on the cheek. She began clearing the table.

He needed to get away for a moment. "I'm going out front to have a cigarette."

As he stood on the front porch, he took out his Zippo, turned the wheel, and lit a Marlboro. He took a long drag and exhaled. He thought about the conversation with Mitch's parents, and hoped it was going okay. After taking another drag, he shivered, as he sensed Mitch standing next to him. Henderson wondered how many times

Mitch had stood on this porch, looking into the street, as he was doing now. *I'm sorry, Mitch.*

Once he had finished the cigarette, he walked into the house. The Drexler's were sitting in the living room. Mr. Drexler held a glass of bourbon. "Eddie, let's toast to Mitch." Pouring Eddie a glass, he handed it to him. Then, Mr. Drexler raised his glass. "To Mitch."

Henderson tapped his glass against Mr. Drexler's. "To Mitch."

They sat, finishing the glass of bourbon.

"It's time for me to go." Henderson fidgeted with his shirt collar as his foot started tapping again.

Mrs. Drexler stood. "Not so soon. You can sleep in Mitch's room."

"No, ma'am, I can't do that. I have a room for tonight and a flight back to Oakland tomorrow afternoon." He stood and extended his hand to Mr. Drexler, "Thanks for everything, sir." They shook hands like father and son.

Henderson walked into Mrs. Drexler's arms and hugged her tightly. "Thanks for the care packages. Professor and Rocky say hello."

She let go, wiping at the tears streaming down her face. "We love you, Eddie."

"I know, and I'll be back. Mitch was my brother; you two are like my mom and dad now."

Henderson then walked outside and strolled along the sidewalk toward the hotel, carrying his bag. He turned and waved at the Drexler's as they stood on the porch.

As he walked in the cold, night air, he thought about how the evening went. He wasn't surprised by their reactions to his stories, or when he told them about Mitch dying. It was a little surprising the way Mrs. Drexler had reacted when he had mentioned the Dear John letter, although it shouldn't be. Henderson thought she liked Sandra, whom she had known since she was a little girl.

Once he reached the motel, Henderson approached the front desk. "I need a room for tonight."

"Got one on the first floor—room one hundred and twenty-one." The clerk pushed the book toward Henderson for him to register.

"Room one hundred and twenty-one—that sounds familiar." Henderson smiled as he signed the registration book. He then remembered that it was his room number in Hawaii.

The clerk handed him the key to his room. Henderson nodded thanks and walked along the hallway until he reached the room. After he entered the room, he turned on the lights and stowed his bag under the bed.

Only one thing left to do.

•

As he left the room, he turned the lights off. He walked out into the night air, turning down the sidewalk toward the apartment building, which sat three blocks from the motel.

Once he reached the corner, he stopped and stared at the house where Billy Matheson lived. A wry smile crossed Henderson's face.

Across the street from Billy's house sat a small, three-story apartment building. Henderson figured that if he could get to the roof, he would have a clean shot. He would arrive there before the sun came up and wait. Billy would need to leave the house sometime in the morning to go to work.

He walked to the rear of the apartment building and climbed the fire escape to the roof. As he walked across the rooftop, he surveyed the ambush site—no different to how he had done many times before.

When he reached the wall facing Billy's house, he knelt. He moved ten feet to his right, which put him in line with the front door and driveway. The house was dark, but the street and driveway were well lit. He assumed Billy and Sandra were asleep. After he had laid a piece of white cloth on the ground, he stood.

A perfect spot for an ambush.

He retraced his steps back to the hotel. Once in the room, he picked up the phone. "This is room one hundred and twenty-one. Can you give me a wake-up call at five, please?"

"Yes, sir. Wake-up call at five a.m."

"Thank you." Henderson placed the phone in the cradle, disconnecting the call.

Next, he removed the rifle from his luggage and started to assemble the Winchester. Once done, he slid it into a larger cloth bag he had and then slipped it under the bed.

He stretched out on the bed and fell asleep watching *The Andy Griffith Show*.

•

Ring! Ring! Ring! The sound startled Henderson as he fumbled to get out of bed. He soon realized it was the telephone. "Yes?"

The clerk coughed. "It's five a.m., sir."

"Thanks." Henderson placed the phone in the cradle.

After he walked into the bathroom, he splashed water on his face. When he looked in the mirror, he saw a young Eddie, with a determined look on his face. He splashed more water on his face.

This time, his reflection stared back—a scared Eddie, looking at him with haunted eyes. With resolve, he turned away from the mirror and walked into the bedroom to retrieve his bag. As he left the hotel, Henderson didn't look back.

The walk took minutes, while the cold air bit at his hands. He rubbed them together for warmth. Henderson used the time to go over his plan one last time.

Once he had reached the fire escape, he climbed to the rooftop, where he spotted the white cloth and moved toward it. Behind the wall, he remained hidden.

As he unzipped the cloth bag, his hands trembled—he grabbed the rifle. From a kneeling position, Henderson used the wall for support and aimed at the front door. He had a clear shot—all he had to do was wait for Billy to walk out of the door. Then, *bam!*

Thirty minutes later, the front door opened, and Billy walked from the porch to the driveway.

Henderson put the crosshairs of the scope on Billy's forehead, his finger gently resting on the trigger.

One more step.

Sandra stepped out. "Billy, wait."

Henderson watched Sandra run toward Billy, handing him a lunch pail. They embraced and kissed. Henderson put the scope on Sandra—then, he lowered the rifle.

Goddammit! She's pregnant.

With his back to the wall, he took deep breaths.

Tears welled in his eyes.

Mitch, I can't do it. I can't.

He looked back at the house as Billy held and kissed Sandra. He didn't move a muscle as Billy walked to his car. He heard the car start, then the roar of the engine echoing along the street as he watched it drive away. The sound of the engine disappeared into the early morning.

Henderson sobbed like a child.

But he knew in his heart that he had done the right thing. He wasn't a killer.

•

On the plane ride back to Oakland, Henderson stared at the seat to his front. He didn't converse with anyone or drink his favorite drink, Jim Beam and Coke.

The sense of failure, along with guilt, overwhelmed him. He had never thought he would let Mitch down. He had made a promise to a dying brother.

But he had also chosen not to kill a man who wasn't trying to kill him. That had to be worth something to Mitch.

•

As they rolled along the roadway from the airport, Henderson sat quietly, staring out of the passenger window, watching the cars flash by. Cheryl drove. Intermittently, she glanced in his direction, and he sensed that she was worried about him.

"I'm okay. Just tired."

She shot him a glance, smiled, but didn't reply.

Henderson turned the knob and smiled as he recognized the song the radio blared out.

"Where Have All the Flowers Gone…?"

EPILOGUE

From a deep sleep, Eddie Henderson bolted upright in bed. "Mitch, I'm coming, hold on!" He flipped to his side, falling to the floor. "Where's my rifle?! I can't find my rifle!"

Cheryl slid out of bed and sat on the floor in front of him, as she had done many times over the years. "Eddie, it's okay. You will be okay."

He jerked away. "Help Mitch!"

She took his hands into hers. "Eddie, you're home. You're safe. It's me, Cheryl."

He sat upright and looked around the room, with sweat dripping down his face. His pounding heart pushed blood through his veins, until he thought it would explode. Then, he realized. "Shit. I'm sorry, Cheryl."

She cradled him in her arms. "It's okay. It's okay." She rocked him softly.

After ten minutes, they crawled into bed and tried to sleep.

Eddie's eyes wouldn't close as he stared at the sunlight filtering through the window. He rolled over and stared at Cheryl. He brushed her hair aside and thought that she was as beautiful today as when they had first met, thirty-five years earlier.

•

Early in the afternoon, Eddie walked along the hallway with short, unsteady steps, heading to his favorite chair in the living room. Once seated in the overstuffed burgundy recliner, he held the power button, lifting his legs while lowering the back to a comfortable position. He started reading.

The front door creaked as it opened.

His three sons, Mitch, Ronnie, and Ed, walked into the spacious living room. As they approached, he observed the three young men of average height with muscular builds, sporting short, auburn hair—all were wearing army combat uniforms. His three sons appeared as battle-hardened men—no longer the boys who had left home a year earlier.

As Eddie struggled to get out of the chair, he held the power button, raising the recliner to an upright position. It moved painfully slowly. Wearing rumpled cotton exercise clothes which hung loosely on his thin frame, Eddie stood to greet his sons as quickly as he could manage.

They had enlisted in the army in 2004, three years after 9/11. While they were in Iraq for a year, in 2005, they served in different units—Mitch with the 101st Airborne Division; Ronnie with the 82nd Airborne Division; and Ed with the Third Infantry Division. When they returned home from Iraq several weeks before, the three brothers wanted to see their mother and father.

Once on his feet, Eddie grabbed Mitch first, hugging him hard. "Welcome home, son."

"Thanks, Dad. It's great to be back."

"Come here, Ronnie; let me hug you." After a long hug, he released his son. "Welcome home."

"Love you, Dad."

Next, he focused on Ed. "Now it's your turn, little fella."

"I told you not to call me that, Dad." With a mischievous smile spreading across his round face, he embraced his father.

Beaming, the father wiped at a tear as it rolled down his hollow cheek. "Welcome home, son." He wrapped his arm around Ed's shoulders.

"Cheryl, the boys are here!"

Cheryl ran from the bedroom, turning the corner into the arms of her three sons. She couldn't stop hugging and kissing them.

"I missed you! I missed you! I love you!"

Eddie watched the family reunion with a smile plastered on his face. As the love of his life, Cheryl, kissed their boys, he noticed that she still had the trim figure of a twenty-year-old, as strands of gray hair mixed with the red. Her green eyes glowed with happiness. He hadn't witnessed her smile in the way she did now for a year.

His smile faded, because he understood what his three sons had endured in the past year. Being in war changed a man, and he hoped that they hadn't experienced all of the horrors that war offers. Eddie realized that he wished for too much.

Finally, Cheryl let go of her sons. "Let me finish dinner. You three must be starving."

Mitch rubbed his stomach. "We are. We haven't eaten since this morning."

Ed hugged his mom. "Are we having my favorite meal? I love the pot roast with mashed potatoes you make."

"Yeah, Mom. Can't find it anywhere that tastes like yours." Ronnie licked his lips. "It's a Henderson original."

"Of course I made your favorite. I have lemon pound cake for dessert for you boys too."

Eddie looked at Cheryl with a twinkle in his eyes. "How about me? I like pound cake."

Cheryl gave Eddie a loving glance before she left to check the oven.

Eddie shuffled toward the kitchen, bent over. "Let's go sit in the kitchen while your mother finishes dinner."

The three sons followed their father into the kitchen and sat at the table. Cheryl pulled a bottle of Jim Beam from the cabinet and a two-liter Coke from the refrigerator, placing the bottles on the kitchen table. Mitch set five glasses next to the bourbon.

Ronnie picked up the bottle of bourbon and looked at his father. "Looks like you've lost more weight, Dad. How are you feeling these days?"

"I've been better. The cancer is about the same—that's what the doctor said at my last visit a couple of weeks ago."

Two years ago, Eddie had made an appointment at a Veterans' Administration hospital. After days of testing, the doctors discovered that he had prostate cancer related to the use of Agent Orange in the war. The bad news was that the cancer had spread. The doctor had diagnosed it at stage four.

Cancer wasn't his only health issue. During his interview with a psychiatrist, it was determined that Eddie suffered from post-traumatic stress disorder, commonly referred to as PTSD.

Mitch squeezed his father's shoulder. "Goddamn Agent Orange."

"Mitch, don't use that language." Cheryl's face turned red, concealing her freckles for a moment.

"I'm sorry, Mom, but it's true. Look at Dad—he's only fifty-five." He squeezed his father's shoulder again, more gently this time. "Sorry, Dad; no offense meant."

Eddie held his oldest son's arm with a weak grasp. "It's okay. I understand. I'm not happy about my cancer, but at least the Veterans' Administration is better now because of you guys coming back from Iraq and Afghanistan."

Eddie didn't want to talk about his cancer. *Nothing you can do about it*, he thought. "Ronnie, pour us a drink. Pour one for your mother too."

Everyone picked up their full glasses. Eddie held his glass out for a toast. "Sons, welcome home."

The family clicked their glasses and said, "Welcome home."

"You know, your mom and I didn't greet you at your unit airfield because we weren't going to choose which one of you we would meet. But I've read and watched on TV the welcome home that you boys get—I think it's great."

Mitch looked over the rim of his glass. "I guess a lot better than you got, Dad."

"Yeah, the American people weren't kind to the returning Vietnam soldiers—called us names and spat at us."

"Hopefully, the Vietnam vets will get the recognition they deserve." Ed raised his glass to his father.

"Maybe we will now, because of guys like you three."

After dinner, they remained at the table, having the second drink of the evening.

Cheryl shot Eddie a loving look. "You know the doctor said you're not to drink."

"I know, but this is a special occasion. Our sons are home from war."

As Eddie looked at his sons, he experienced a sense of pride in them for serving their country. But he understood what they had lived through the past year. As he watched his boys with a keen eye, he recognized a trembling hand, the lack of eye contact, jumping at a small noise, and the occasional blank stare, or not paying attention to the conversation. Even a sudden burst of anger at one another didn't go unnoticed by Eddie. It saddened him that his sons might carry the brutality of war for the rest of their lives. He didn't want them to suffer.

Eddie knew that talking to Cheryl had helped him through the years. Professor often visited, but they seldom talked about Vietnam, or the hardships they endured there. He recognized, however, that attending group sessions at the VA appeared to help him deal with his demons.

Maybe if my boys spoke about their time in war, they won't go through what I went through, he thought.

"I know everyone has a different experience from war. How about you share your time with me?" Eddie looked around the table at his three sons. "We'll start with the oldest. Mitch, you're up first."

"Well, Dad, if we're starting with the oldest, that would be you. You share the story of your time in Vietnam, and I'll share my story about my time in Iraq. How about that?"

Taking a sip of his drink, Eddie pondered whether sharing his story with his sons would be a good idea. When he wrote about his first time in Vietnam, many years ago, he had never intended to share it with anyone. He hid it away in a drawer, underneath his socks.

Staring at the drink he held, Eddie swirled the ice, watering down the bourbon in his glass. No one said a word.

"Cheryl, would you get my memoir and bring it here, please?"

She stood and walked into the bedroom, returning after a couple of minutes with a stack of typewritten paper, bound together. She handed it to Eddie.

"Thanks, honey. I guess it's a good thing we have a full bottle of bourbon."

She displayed a flirtatious smile, but her eyes shot Eddie a disapproving look. "You're not supposed to drink."

He flipped through the manuscript, reading a sentence or two on a couple of pages while lost in his thoughts. After several minutes, he looked around the table, noticing his family watching him.

"When did you serve in 'Nam, Dad?" Ed asked.

"I arrived early-March of sixty-nine, and left late-February of seventy."

Ronnie reached across the table and touched his father's hand. "So, you've been back about thirty-five years now?"

"Doesn't seem like it. But, yes, thirty-five years.

"Here you go, Mitch. It's my story. There are some things you'll learn that I'm not proud of, but that's war. Please, read to us."

Ronnie and Ed leaned over, close to Mitch, attempting to read the words on the first page. Ronnie's eyes widened. "Why that title?"

"Listen to the story and you'll find out."

"Okay, Dad, I'll read it. The title of Dad's book is *It Don't Mean Nothin'*."

Mitch turned to the first page of his father's book and began reading.

•

As the early morning sun climbed over the horizon, light filtered through the kitchen window. The family sat, looking intently at Mitch, listening to every word he read. The table had dirty plates and glasses stacked in one corner.

Mitch looked up from the manuscript. "*'The end.'*"

Ronnie poured the last of the Jim Beam into his glass, while staring at his father.

Cheryl gave him a mother's look. "Ronnie, don't you think you've had enough?"

"About as many as you had, Mom."

The family laughed, knowing that their mother hardly ever drank. With a smile, Cheryl stood to clear the table.

Mitch slid the manuscript toward his father. "Dad, your book answered a lot of questions. But you've never mentioned going back to Vietnam, or re-enlisting in the army. What happened?"

"While I was with your mother in Berkeley, I came down with malaria—I guess I should have taken the orange pill every week! I don't know why I didn't listen to Sergeant Stahl."

Ed leaned forward in his chair. "Did you go back to Vietnam?"

"Yes, I did. But that's another story."

Mitch leaned in closer to his father. "What about Billy Matheson?"

Eddie lifted his glass, taking a sip of bourbon. He sat, staring out of the kitchen window. After taking a long drink, he stared at the ice cubes floating in the glass.

"Dad, what about Billy Matheson?"

"I never kept up with Sandra." Eddie took another sip of his drink. "I still go to Indianapolis to visit your Grandma and Grandpa Drexler."

"We haven't seen them in a couple of years." Ronnie took a long drink. "When did you see them last?"

"Your mom and I went with Professor and Rocky to see them in the assisted-living home while you were gone. We spent three days there."

Mitch sat up in his chair. "We'll visit them while we're on leave."

Eddie looked around the table at his three sons. "They asked about you boys— you're their only grandchildren. I don't expect them to live much longer."

Ed glanced over the laptop's computer screen. "Dad, I looked up 'It don't mean nothin'' on the Urban Dictionary website and found a description."

"What does it say?" Ronnie asked.

"I'll read it." Ed positioned the screen and began reading.

"*Coined by GIs in Vietnam. A reverse coping expression, indicating that it means everything and I'm about to lose it. Usually used to dismiss witnessing or experiencing something so horrific that it can't be comprehended by the psyche. Alternatively used as an expression of relief that one has avoided being killed, even if they are injured or maimed. Witnessing one's close friend being killed, turning away, and saying with a stone face, "It don't mean nothin',"'*

Eddie took a long drink as he looked out of the window. He recalled the night that Mitch died, and Professor telling him to say it, *"It don't mean nothin'."*

"That pretty much explains it."

Looking at his father, Mitch then raised his glass. "Welcome home."

With tears in his eyes, Eddie toasted with his family. "Welcome home, boys."

ABOUT THE AUTHOR

Glyn Haynie enlisted in the United States Army at the age of eighteen. His military career spanned twenty years, during which he served his country until his retirement in March of 1989. Glyn Haynie turned nineteen soon after arriving in Vietnam, where he found himself fighting with the  American (23rd) Infantry Division. Before retiring, Haynie served as a drill instructor, a first sergeant and, finally, as an instructor for the US Army Sergeants Major Academy (USASMA).

After retiring from the army, Haynie earned an AAS degree in Management, a BS degree in Computer Information Systems, and an MA degree in Computer Resources and Information Systems. He worked as a software engineer/project manager for eight years, before teaching at Park University as a full-time instructor. Haynie continued as an adjunct instructor for thirteen more years.

Glyn Haynie and his wife of thirty-two years, Sherrie, currently reside in Texas. They have five children, fourteen grandchildren, and four great-grandchildren. Three of their sons have served combat tours in either Iraq or Afghanistan. This is a family in which service to their country is a tradition.

To learn more about Glyn Haynie and his work, please visit his website:
>	http://www.glynhaynie.net
>	E-mail: glyn@glynhaynie.com

I hope you enjoyed this book. If so, would you do me a favor?

Like all authors, I rely on online reviews, and your opinion is invaluable. Would you take a few moments now to share your assessment of my book on any book review website you prefer? Your opinion will help the book marketplace to become more transparent and useful to all.

Thank you very much!
Glyn.